Praise for Christine Wenger

"Christine Wenger makes a promising debut with this touching story, tugging skillfully at readers' hearts with her characters' vulnerabilities."

—*RT Book Reviews* on *The Cowboy Way*

"An enjoyable story with a sweet romance, some humorous moments and a cute ending sure to bring a smile."

—*RT Book Reviews* on *The Cowboy and the Cop*

"Wenger's couple is a treat to watch in this heartfelt and emotional romance. Their banter is as heated as their lovemaking."

—*RT Book Reviews* on *Lassoed into Marriage*

Praise for *New York Times* bestselling author Cathy McDavid

"McDavid's characters are wonderful, and her story really showcases the hardships and love it takes to blend families."

—*RT Book Reviews* on *Cowboy for Keeps*

"McDavid does a fine job portraying a complex heroine dealing with immense guilt and self-doubt. This romantic story has some beautifully crafted, tender moments."

—*RT Book Reviews* on *Come Home, Cowboy*, Top Pick

"The dynamics of the Beckett family saga intertwine with a second-chance romance offering an emotional look at love, loss and learning to forgive."

—*RT Book Reviews* on *Her Rodeo Man*

HOME ON THE RANCH:
ARIZONA REUNION

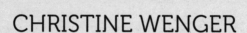

CHRISTINE WENGER

New York Times Bestselling Author
CATHY McDAVID

**Previously published as *How to Lasso a Cowboy*
and *Her Cowboy's Christmas Wish***

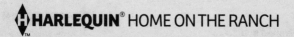

HARLEQUIN® HOME ON THE RANCH

ISBN-13: 978-1-335-50716-7

Home on the Ranch: Arizona Reunion
Copyright © 2018 by Harlequin Books S.A.

First published as How to Lasso a Cowboy by
Harlequin Books in 2011 and Her Cowboy's
Christmas Wish by Harlequin Books in 2011.

The publisher acknowledges the copyright
holders of the individual works as follows:

How to Lasso a Cowboy
Copyright © 2011 by Christine Wenger

Her Cowboy's Christmas Wish
Copyright © 2011 by Cathy McDavid

Recycling programs
for this product may
not exist in your area.

HARLEQUIN®
www.Harlequin.com

Printed in U.S.A.

CONTENTS

Christine Wenger has worked in the criminal justice field for more years than she cares to remember, but now spends her time reading, writing and seeing the sights in our beautiful world. A native Central New Yorker, she loves watching professional bull riding and rodeo with her favorite cowboy, her husband, Jim. You can reach Christine at PO Box 1823, Cicero, NY 13039, or through her website at christinewenger.com.

Books by Christine Wenger

Harlequin Western Romance

Gold Buckle Cowboys

The Cowboy and the Cop

Harlequin Special Edition

Gold Buckle Cowboys

The Rancher's Surprise Son
Lassoed into Marriage
How to Lasso a Cowboy
The Cowboy Code

The Hawkins Legacy

The Tycoon's Perfect Match
It's That Time of Year
Not Your Average Cowboy
The Cowboy and the CEO
The Cowboy Way

Visit the Author Profile page at Harlequin.com for more titles.

HOW TO LASSO
A COWBOY

CHRISTINE WENGER

To my St. Margaret's, Ludden and Powelson buddies, Janice Egloff DiFant and Patty Tomeny Holgado.

Time sure flies, but we're still having fun!

Prologue

Jenna Reed studied the new clothes that she'd bought for her long-awaited trip to Europe. They were organized by day, stacked in neat piles on the bed in her guest room and her matched set of tomato-red luggage was open and ready to be filled.

She reread the now dog-eared itinerary that she'd received from Happy Singles Travel, Inc. She knew it by heart, but she still loved looking at it. Their motto was printed in lime green on the top of their letterhead: "Travel with us, meet new friends and discover new places."

She would have rather traveled with her current friends, but they were all too tied up with their husbands and/or kids. Though she was disappointed, she understood. So, she was going with seventy-five other singles, mostly women, for three glorious weeks in Europe!

Finally, Jenna was going to live it up. She hadn't had a vacation since she'd started teaching fourth grade after college. When other teachers at Wilson Road Grammar School took the summer off, she worked summer school and tutored kids whenever she was asked. Among her peers, she was the teacher who never said no.

She loved teaching mostly because of the kids. She thought of them as *hers* and threw her whole being into her work. But they *weren't* her kids, and at age twenty-nine, she'd given up looking for Mr. Right. She just wanted Mr. Right *Now*. Someone special. Someone she could hang out with and who liked to do the same things that she did.

She'd once wanted to settle down and have children, but all that changed when she approached her thirtieth birthday. With no romantic prospects, she decided that she had too much living to do—and *now* was the time for her to enjoy life. So she cut her workload and began making plans to change her life from a humdrum, staid existence to one of excitement and adventure.

As part of her new life plan, Jenna decided to make a drastic career change and applied for a year-long position teaching English in China. Every time she thought of her application being accepted and making a move, excitement shot through her.

Even if she didn't get the position, she'd take a leave of absence and travel, visiting places that she'd only read about. And this European vacation would be the perfect start to her new plan.

Jenna sat on the edge of the bed, holding on to her

itinerary, and imagined meeting her knight in shining armor at a bistro in Paris or at the Parthenon in Greece. Maybe he'd strike up a conversation with her as she watched him maneuver his yacht through the glittering waters of Cannes or bump into him on the Rialto Bridge in Venice.

Wherever her mystery man was, she wanted him to know that she'd be landing at Heathrow Airport in London in exactly seven days, ten hours and thirty-two minutes.

The phone rang, startling her our of her daydream. She rushed to pick it up.

"Hey, sis."

"Tom! How are you?"

Calling her brother was on her list of things to do. She'd planned on letting him know when she was leaving on her trip. Then her excitement dissolved. Her brother only called her when he needed something or if it was bad news. She braced herself.

"I called about Andy—" he began.

She just adored her ten-year-old nephew. "Oh, Tom! Is he okay?"

"Relax, Jenna. He's fine. He just didn't do well on his final report card. He's failing reading and math. He's going to be held back in fourth grade unless he goes to summer school."

"That's too bad."

"Yup." There was a moment of silence. "And since he could use some extra help, I thought of you, since you teach fourth grade. I figure if you came down here to Tucson, you could tutor him and babysit at the same time. I've been helping him myself, but I'm not doing that great of a job. He's not getting it."

"I'm sure he's getting it, Tom. You're a very patient father."

Then something hit her—Tom had said *babysit*.

"Uh… Tom, why do you need me to babysit? Where are you going to be?"

"As long as you're going to be here at the Bar R, I figured that I could enter as many bronc-and-bull-riding events as I can during the summer. It'd be the perfect opportunity for me to win some extra money, pay for some repairs that I need to do around my ranch. Besides, Andy needs braces, his babysitters are costing me a fortune and Marla just filed for divorce. I need to retain a lawyer."

Jenna was silent. She knew that Tom was still reeling from his wife leaving him for another man. Marla said that traveling the bull-riding circuits kept him away from home too much.

"When do you need me?" Jenna asked.

"Next week."

"Tom—" Jenna's heart sank. Her brother never asked for anything, and she owed him so much. "I meant to call you, but time just got away from me. I'm supposed to leave for Europe on vacation this Tuesday. I'll be gone for three weeks, but—"

There were no buts. She'd do anything for Tom and Andy. After their mother and father died in a terrible auto accident when Tom was a senior and she was a freshman in high school, Tom assumed the role of parent even though they lived with their grandparents. It was Tom, the champion bull rider, who'd helped her with her college tuition. It was Tom who loaned her the money for a down payment on her house when she got her teaching job in Phoenix.

And Andy was the sweetest nephew an aunt could have, and Jenna knew that Tom needed the extra money. Besides, she didn't want Andy to have trouble in school.

She sighed. Her European vacation was spinning down the toilet, but her family needed her. Still, she held on tighter to her itinerary, not wanting to part with it.

"Sis, I understand. I can make other arrangements."

"Don't you dare," Jenna said adamantly. "I can postpone my trip." She'd waited this long to spread her wings, she could wait a little longer. "And I took out travel insurance, so there's really no problem."

She stared at the new clothes that she'd bought throughout the year, just for this trip. The clothes were totally inappropriate for the summer at Tom's ranch in Tucson. She'd need old shirts, old shorts and even older jeans. And her beat-up old cowboy boots. If Tom wasn't going to be around, she'd probably have to do some work around his ranch, too. And she sure as hell didn't need her new navy raincoat in the Arizona desert.

"A week from today, then," Jenna said. "I'll drive down in the morning, and get there around noon. Is that okay?" Instead of flying to Europe on that day, she'd be driving to Tom's ranch.

She could hear Tom let out a relieved breath. "I can't thank you enough. I really appreciate this."

"It'll be great to spend time with Andy," she said, meaning every word. "How long are you going to be gone, Tom?"

"As long as I can. And as long as Andy is okay with me being gone. He'll be thrilled that you're going to

come for a visit, so he won't miss me all that much.
I had a little talk with him and prepared him in case
you said yes, and he understood. He said that he was
going to root for me and Uncle Dustin on television."

"Uncle" Dustin Morgan wasn't Andy's real uncle.
He was an old friend of Tom's from high school. The
two had been traveling together from rodeo to rodeo
for years.

Every time she talked with Andy, most of the conversation centered on Dustin, a man she'd thought
about with steady frequency since she'd first laid eyes
on him in algebra class in freshman year at Catalina
High School in Tucson.

"Uh…um…" Tom began. "Speaking of Dustin, I
invited him to come and stay at the ranch when he's
released from the hospital. He needs to heal up a bit
from his accident."

Jenna knew from watching the Albuquerque event
on TV that Dustin seriously injured his ankle when a
bull stepped on him. She worried about his injury and
worried even more when the sports medicine doctor
for the bull riders stated that he was being taken to a
nearby hospital for emergency surgery.

But wait…was Tom expecting her to take care of
Dustin? He couldn't possibly think that she'd know
what to do. She was a teacher, not a nurse.

"Tom, you asked Dustin to stay at the ranch?" Her
heart began racing when she realized that Dustin Morgan would be living under the same roof with her.

"Yeah. He's going to stay here with you and Andy
and look after the ranch for me. He won't be any trouble for you."

What she remembered about Dustin from high

school was her intense crush on him, but she'd been too much of a geek to even relax around him. She'd longed to date him, but he was way too popular, and she was way too much of a bookworm for them to have anything in common.

The only thing they had in common was Tom, and Jenna couldn't wait until Tom brought Dustin over to their house.

Then she remembered the sadness she felt when he was offered a full ride—a complete, four-year scholarship to the University of Nevada at Las Vegas. Instead of accepting it, he'd hit the circuit to compete with the Professional Bull Riders. He never graduated with their senior class.

What a waste, she thought, although he made a small fortune riding bulls.

"Dustin can help you out with Andy, too," Tom added.

She was about to tell him that she didn't need any help with Andy, and that she'd feel uncomfortable practically living with Dustin Morgan, but it sounded like a done deal.

No trouble?

She doubted that.

"Thanks again, Jenna. You know I appreciate this, and so does Dustin. Andy will, too, when he passes to fifth grade."

"No problem, Tom," she lied. "See you next Monday."

They hung up, and Jenna just sat, reeling.

Looking down, she saw that she was still clutching her itinerary. Soon, she'd have to call and cancel her wonderful trip.

After a while, she lovingly placed the item into her brand-new tomato-red, twenty-nine-inch upright with the 360-degree wheels.

Maybe she had to cancel for now, but as soon as possible, she'd reschedule—just as soon as Tom figured out when he'd return. She was needed by her family, and that was okay.

But it seemed as though she was always needed, mostly by those she called the "four Ps": her pupils, their parents, the principal or her peers, and she always had to postpone her dreams of romance and adventure.

She sighed. Now, Dustin Morgan, fresh from the hospital, needed her.

Then she smiled as she began to pick up her clothes. She might still be a geek, and Dustin might be one of the most popular bull riders in the PBR, but maybe her stay at the Bar R would somehow give her a chance to spread her wings, just like she'd planned to do on her European trip.

And maybe…just maybe… Dustin would turn out to be the adventure of a lifetime.

Chapter One

Dustin Morgan struggled to get out of a taxi in front of Tom Reed's ranch house.

He tugged his crutches out of the vehicle and positioned them under his arms while the driver unloaded his duffel bag.

Unfortunately, in the short-go round in Albuquerque, a bucking, whirling, two-thousand-pound Brahma named Cowabunga bucked him off, then stomped on his ankle, crushing it. After surgery, Dustin sported a massive amount of hardware to keep his bones together, along with a heavy cast.

Damn it.

Thanks to Cowabunga, he'd have to skip the usually profitable summer circuit.

After a couple of years of always being a bridesmaid, he'd finally hit number one in the rankings, and now he couldn't ride. While he sat at home and watched the Professional Bull Riders on TV with his leg up, there'd be several young guns who would jump over him in the standings. But maybe, if everything went as planned, when he got back he could move up again in time for the PBR World Finals in Las Vegas in early November. Fingers crossed.

He paid the taxi driver, turned toward the house and took a hearty breath. He could smell the scent of animals on the air. Damn, how he loved that smell!

He was itching to do something where he could work up a sweat, but his surgeon had told him to take it easy. Dustin couldn't grasp that concept. There had never been a time when he'd taken it easy.

When he was younger, he entered junior rodeos and rode anything with fur. As a sophomore in high school, he played football and caught rodeos every chance he could. When he turned eighteen, he was able to qualify for the Professional Bull Riders circuit as well as the Professional Rodeo Cowboys Association. He rode bulls in the PBR. In the PRCA, he rode broncs.

And he'd managed to avoid serious injury—until now.

Dustin studied the long ranch house and the outbuildings of the Bar R Ranch. Someday, he'd have a spread like this.

He looked at his duffel bag lying on the Arizona dust. Dustin couldn't believe that he'd agreed to stay at Tom's place. The only thing that had convinced him to come here was the fact that Tom needed him—and to be honest, he owed Tom big time. Tom had saved his life two years ago by pushing him away from a rogue bull. His friend would always sport scars from being gored.

"I have a favor to ask of you," Tom had said when he'd visited Dustin in the hospital after his surgery.

Dustin had struggled to stay focused, still a little groggy from the painkillers he'd been given. "Hit me with it."

"Since you're going to be laid up for a while, how about heading to my ranch and overseeing the operation? I don't want you to work, just supervise the foreman and the hands. You're going to be recuperating anyway—how about doing it at the Bar R?"

"I—I don't—"

"My sister will be there taking care of Andy for me. And Andy would just love a visit from you. It's been a long time, Dustin."

"Jenna?" His eyelids drifted closed for a moment, but Jenna's image appeared in his mind. In high school lugging a load of books. Studying under the big tree by the school cafeteria while everyone else was having fun. Being elected class president every year for four years. Giving the valedictorian speech at graduation.

He'd always liked her energy, her sense of independence, her willingness to get involved and the fact that she was comfortable being alone and didn't follow the crowd, like he always had.

Back then, she'd had long blond hair that she usually wore in a ponytail tied with a piece of rawhide and usually pierced by at least one pen and one pencil. That was Jenna, always studying, always writing in a notebook. Her spring-green eyes were magnified by wire-rimmed glasses that rode low on her nose.

He'd spent many a high school class secretly watching her.

He'd wanted to talk to Jenna on numerous occasions—to ask her out—but he'd always thought that she wouldn't give him the time of day. It wasn't as if she was a snob—she was very friendly to everyone but him—so he figured that Tom had told her to stay away from him. Tom was very protective of Jenna after the death of his parents, and Dustin had to admit that he'd had many girlfriends. Jenna could see that for herself. But they were just friends—or they were buckle bunnies—and they weren't Jenna.

So, to get his Jenna fix, Dustin often went to Tom's house, not only to hang out with Tom, but to catch a glimpse of her, too.

"You're going to need someone to help you manage," Tom continued. "With your folks being in Alaska and your apartment on the third floor of a building without elevators, you don't have much of a choice. You help me, and Jenna will help you."

There was something wrong with his reasoning, but Dustin couldn't put his finger on it back at the hospital. If only Tom would leave so he could sleep.

Sleep…blessed sleep. The pain was exhausting him, and he didn't want to take too many pain pills if he could help himself.

"It's okay with Jenna," Tom said. "She's looking forward to seeing you again."

That struck Dustin as strange. He doubted if Jenna even remembered him from high school. He hadn't had a decent conversation with her in years. Matter of fact, the last time he'd talked to Jenna for any length of time was at Andy's christening ten years ago. He was Andy's godfather; Jenna was Andy's godmother.

Now, as he stood at the gate of Tom's ranch, he remembered the promise he'd made to Tom years ago—a promise he regretted to this day. He'd given his word to Tom that he'd stay away from Jenna. Therefore, his interaction with her was limited to fleeting glances and some short blips of conversation whenever she attended the PBR events.

He might as well be back in high school.

Dustin flung his duffel over his right shoulder and thought of Tom. When you traveled with a man to and from rodeos you got to know him really well. Tom was more than a good friend, he was like a brother, and he didn't want to betray Tom's trust.

Dustin had almost told Tom that he wasn't going to stay at his ranch to recuperate. He didn't want to be a burden on Jenna or on anyone. He could take care of himself—somehow, someway—but he hadn't been able to find his voice.

He remembered falling asleep, dreaming of spending the summer with pretty, smart Jenna Reed. In his dream, Jenna didn't think of him as the class clown, the class jock or as someone who didn't take advantage of a four-year scholarship to hit the road to ride bulls. She thought of him only as a man.

But this wasn't a dream. This was reality, and he was about to spend most of the summer with Jenna.

Then again, maybe it *was* a dream.

"Aunt Jenna?" Andy said sweetly. "Can I go outside now? I want to watch the guys break Maximus."

Jenna smiled and ran her fingers through her nephew's sandy hair. His blue eyes were wide with hope. How could math and reading compete with a bucking bronc?

"Do the first seven decimal problems and you can go. We'll do reading comprehension later."

She leaned over to Andy and pointed to the problems on page fifteen of his math book. She'd seen progress with Andy during the week that she'd been tutoring him, and she didn't want to lose the momentum.

She did the breakfast dishes as Andy labored over his workbook.

The doorbell rang. "I'll get it," Jenna said, walking into the living room to get the front door.

She looked through the peephole. Standing on the porch, propped up by a pair of crutches, was none other than Dustin Morgan.

His hair was darker than ever, and his eyes were as blue as the Arizona sky above. If possible, he looked better than he had in high school. Her cheeks heated just looking at him. TV didn't do him justice.

Jenna could never forget the guy who'd flirted with every girl in high school. That is, everyone but her.

He'd been a star quarterback and the best player on the basketball team in freshman and sophomore years as well as a rodeo champ. He had all the girls drooling over him, including her.

But he never paid her any attention. In fact, she was the only female he seemed to avoid.

And he'd turned down a full scholarship so he could ride with the PBR. Jenna had never been able to understand this.

She swung the door open, and he smiled widely. Her

gaze drifted to his crutches, his torn sweatpants and the cast that went from his foot to his knee.

"Hello, Dustin. It's been a while." She offered her hand. So far, so good.

He took her hand for several heartbeats and held it before he finally shook it. She could feel the calluses on his palms and fingers.

It was a simple thing, just a handshake, but at his touch, she felt like a giddy schoolgirl again instead of a levelheaded almost-thirty-year-old.

"It's good to see you again, Jenna."

He smiled warmly, and she could understand why a gaggle of buckle bunnies always vied for his attention.

"You, too. Although I see you on TV all the time at the bull riding events or…or…" She lost her train of thought for a moment. "But this arrangement is going to be…different."

Jenna could hear the quiver in her voice, and wondered why seeing Dustin up close and personal was unnerving her.

"I guess you're stuck with me," he said.

She pulled her hand away from his. Maybe then she'd relax. "I—I guess I am," she blurted anxiously. Then, realizing what she said, she tempered her statement. "But you need help, and Tom said that you're going to oversee the ranch, so that'll help out. Besides, Andy is over-the-top thrilled that you're going to be here."

"It'll be fun to spend time with the little cowboy," he said.

She avoided his eyes and stared down at his cast and crutches. "I am sorry that you hurt your ankle. Cowabunga walked all over you."

He pushed back his cowboy hat with his thumb. "Thanks. It wasn't my best dismount, but I got lucky. It could have been a lot worse."

Jenna shuddered. "You did get lucky."

He shrugged. "You know what they say about bull riding—it's not *when* you'll get hurt, but how bad and how often."

An awkward pause hung in the air between them. Were they doomed to make innocuous small talk the entire summer?

"Let's go inside so you can sit down," she said. "I'll get your duffel."

"I can get it," he said quickly, scooping it up from the ground and then trying to get his crutches over the threshold.

She moved closer. "What can I do to help you?"

"Nothing. I can do it myself." She heard the edge in his voice.

What was she supposed to do to assist him? He seemed put out that she even offered to help.

They'd better figure out a way to exist in harmony. Didn't he understand that, for the most part, they'd be living together? She'd have to watch out for him, cook for him, do his laundry and help him get around on those crutches.

Would she have to help him bathe, too?

Her face heated in embarrassment and her heart raced at the thought of seeing Dustin Morgan naked.

Well, she'd wanted adventure and excitement, didn't she?

The cast was so awkward! It felt like he was lugging around an extra thirty pounds of dead weight. To make things worse, his duffel slipped off his shoulder, slid down his arm and crutch, and hit the floor of the porch.

He struggled to pick up the damn thing.

Jenna offered to help, but there was no way he wanted to impose on her—a woman that he barely knew but had adored from afar since high school. No way.

And there was that damn promise he'd made to Tom niggling at the back of his mind. Was this Tom's idea of a joke, having Jenna and him live together for several weeks? Or didn't Tom remember their conversation in the ambulance when Tom had saved Dustin's life?

Dustin remembered it very clearly.

"Thanks for saving my life, partner. I didn't see that bull heading for me. I owe you big-time," Dustin said.

"Forget it. You'd do the same to me. And the only thing you owe me is your promise."

Dustin held his breath. He knew what was coming.

"My sister. I see you looking at her." Tom winced in pain. "She's...not as...experienced as you are. She's been protected her whole life, first by my parents, then by me. You're like a brother, but you love the women too much. You'll hurt her, you know. And you know, you'll never be around for her, riding the circuit. She deserves someone who'll be home all the time."

Dustin looked at Jenna waiting for him to enter the house. He'd rather cut off his riding arm than hurt her, but his friend was right about him never being there for her—not when he was still riding—and he figured he had several good years left in him yet.

So Dustin renewed his promise to stay away from Jenna. But, again, maybe Tom had forgotten about it, or why else would he have asked him to stay at the ranch knowing that Jenna would be there?

As if on cue, Jenna snatched the duffel from him, and held the door open, giving him a wide berth to maneuver inside the living room.

Damn. He hated feeling like an invalid.

He should have holed up in his apartment, done things for himself. But the surgeon who'd operated told him that if he took it easy, he'd heal quicker, and he'd return to the PBR quicker.

That was his goal. He was poised to win the PBR World Finals in Vegas, and that was just what he was going to do. With the money he'd win, he could hang up his spurs and finally settle down on a ranch of his own.

That's what he'd been saving for all these years on the road. His own spread.

But first, he had to heal, and Tom had convinced him that this was the best place for him. Maybe it was—but being with Jenna 24/7 was a bonus.

"Uncle Dustin! Uncle Dustin!"

Andy came running into the living room of the Santa Fe-style house and stopped two feet from where Dustin had collapsed into a side chair and stretched out his leg.

"Hey, partner! How've you been?" He held out his hand, and Andy shook it. "It's been a long time."

"I see you on TV all the time, you and my dad. Oh, and J.R., and Skeeter, and Cody and Robson and Adriano and—"

Dustin laughed as Andy named the entire roster of riders. The boy couldn't be cuter. His eyes were bright blue, his hair sandy and he was probably taller than other kids his age. But ever since his mother had left, the spark had faded a bit from the boy's eyes.

"I think you've gotten taller," Dustin said.

Andy grinned. "Really?"

"I wouldn't say it if I didn't mean it."

As Andy read what his father and some of the other riders had written on Dustin's cast, the cowboy eyed Jenna, who was sitting on the couch opposite him.

She was more beautiful than he remembered, all wholesome and not made up like the buckle bunnies he often met on the circuit. Her blond hair tickled her chin, and turquoise stones dangled from her ears.

He glanced at his duffel. It barely had enough clothes for two days. He'd only packed it for the Albuquerque bull riding, not for a stay in the hospital or for a long stay at Tom's ranch. Beside it lay his crutches.

"I need to go shopping. All my clothes are in my apartment in Tubac," he said mostly to himself.

"You live in Tubac? The artist colony?" Jenna asked wide-eyed.

"Yep. That Tubac." He lived two floors above a shop that sold various types of jewelry, pottery and paintings.

"I'd be glad to drive you to your apartment," Jenna said.

"I don't want to impose on you any more."

Tubac was an hour's drive from Tucson. Maybe he could pay one of the ranch hands to drive him there and get some of his stuff.

He didn't tell Jenna that he painted western scenes—riders on bucking bulls and broncs. Cowboys mending fence. The saguaros and mountains around Tubac and Tucson. It had been just for fun at first, but then he'd started selling his work through some of the local craft shops.

"Well, I'd better show you the guest room," Jenna said, moving to hand him his crutches.

"I can do it."

Her perfume drifted around him—something light and flowery. It suited her.

"You're probably hungry, too. How about if I make you a sandwich or something?" Jenna asked.

"I promised Tom that I'd ramrod his ranch while I'm laid up. I'll try and stay out of your way and not bother you."

She shook her head. "It's not a bother, Dustin. I'm happy to help."

He was sure that she was trying to be polite, but he didn't intend to be a burden on her, or anyone. That wasn't his style. He was just here to help Tom while he was on the road, and he could do that on crutches.

And he was going to enjoy Jenna's company while he was here.

In spite of his injury, one good thing could come of it—he would finally get to know her better. But no matter how much he was still attracted to her, nothing would come of their close proximity—he'd see to that. He'd made a promise to Tom. And Dustin Morgan was a man of his word.

Jenna's senses were reeling as if she were back in high school. She tried to play it cool, just as she had back then, but her cool probably seemed standoffish.

Later, as she made Andy and Dustin ham-and-cheese sandwiches, she thought of Dustin's blue eyes—his sexy gaze was more intense than ever. His lips seemed more sensuous and his black hair looked even softer.

But his smile and good nature were what always charmed the high school girls. When he turned on his smile, flashing those whiter-than-white teeth, no female was immune.

Jenna had attended several PBR events through the years, but to see him up-close and personal for the first time in ages made her heart race and her cheeks heat. She hoped that as they spent more time together, she'd get over her high school reaction. After all, her schoolgirl crush on him was over. Wasn't it?

She was too old for crushes, darn it. She was just admiring a handsome man. That's all.

At the table, Dustin and Andy were deep in conversation about bull riders and their statistics. Too bad that Andy didn't pay as much attention to his arithmetic as he did riding percentages.

Jenna smiled as she set the sandwiches down in front of them. "Anyone want anything to drink?"

"Please," Dustin said.

"Please," Andy said, and Jenna figured that if Dustin asked for a glass of fish oil, Andy would want the same. Just looking at Andy, she could see that the boy was under the spell of Dustin Morgan.

Well, Jenna Reed was going to fight her attraction. Her thirtieth birthday was right around the corner, for heaven's sake, and she wasn't going to fall for one guy. It was time for her to live, to explore and to take risks.

But how was she suppose to do that at Tom's ranch?

She set glasses of milk in front of Andy and Dustin. Dustin pulled out a chair for her from his sitting position as best he could. She smiled her thanks and sat down next to him, looked straight into his dark blue eyes and took a long breath.

"I prepared the guest room for you. It has its own bathroom and shower. I thought that would be more convenient." Jenna took a bite of her sandwich, but she was too nervous to eat any more, sitting so close to Dustin and inhaling his musky scent.

"Thank you. I'm dying to take a shower." He turned to Andy. "But I can't yet due to this dang cast. I can only take a bath, and I can't get it wet."

A picture of Dustin naked flashed into her mind, and her throat went dry. She gulped down some milk.

"Jenna, you haven't said much," Dustin said. "We've got some catching up to do. What are you doing these days—are you still based in Phoenix?"

He leaned over the table as if prepared to give her his complete attention. That was another trait of Dustin's that made the females swoon.

"I've been teaching fourth grade. In my spare time—which isn't much—I coach the district's spelling-bee team and debate team."

Dustin took a bite of his sandwich. "That sounds like a full load."

"It keeps me busy," she said.

"So you're teaching the same grade that Andy had trouble with. No wonder Tom asked you to help him out." Dustin ruffled the boy's hair. "So how are you doing with your math and reading, partner?"

Andy shrugged. "Okay, I guess."

"He's doing terrific," Jenna said, handing Andy his napkin so he'd wipe his mouth. "He's made a lot of progress already."

"It's bor-ring," Andy said, resting his cheek on his palm. "Totally bor-ring."

Dustin shrugged. "Well, maybe I could help,"

Andy nodded. "Cool, Uncle Dustin."

It was very nice of him to volunteer to help Andy, but Jenna was a little put out. She was a teacher, for goodness' sake—she could manage herself.

She tried to figure out something else to say. "How are your parents, Dustin? Tom told me that they like Alaska."

"They love it. My father has taken up hunting again, and Mom has a nice circle of friends that she met at church." He met her gaze. "I still miss your parents, Jenna. Your mom and dad were good to me."

Jenna closed her eyes. She could still see the accident, although the police and Tom hadn't let her approach the scene.

Damn that drunk driver.

She blinked back her tears. "There's not a day that goes by that I don't miss them, too."

Dustin cleared his throat. "Well, if you'll both excuse me, I think I need to rest a little. It's been a long trip."

"I'll show you to the guest room," Jenna said.

"I know where it is."

Of course he did. He visited the ranch often.

"Do you need any help?" she asked.

"No."

She frowned. "If you don't need help, then why are you here?"

He raised an eyebrow. "To supervise the ranch operation."

"You're also here to rest and heal."

Obviously, he wasn't the type to be waited on, but if he refused to let anyone help him, then what was she supposed to do?

Jenna followed Dustin into the hallway that led to his room, so Andy wouldn't overhear their discussion.

"Dustin?" she whispered.

He turned and raised an eyebrow.

"I can't understand why you are refusing my help."

"I'm not refusing. I just need to do things for myself."

She rolled her eyes. "But you can't do everything. Admit it."

"Maybe not, but I sure as hell am going to try."

"Why?"

"Because I always have, Jenna. I've always been self-sufficient. I don't know how to be anything else. I've been on my own since I was eighteen. I've had a lot of responsibility. I've seen a lot, done a lot and no one has ever held my hand through my injuries."

She felt a pang of sadness for him, although he didn't seem sorry for himself at all. He didn't have a home to return to in between bull riding events, not really. She knew his parents sold their ranch when Dustin graduated from high school and took off, and they continued to travel in a motor home. Dustin remained in the Tucson area. He didn't have family around. At least she had Tom.

In a way, Dustin had Tom, too.

But still, he needed help, and he was here. So was she.

"I know you want to remain self-sufficient, and I'll let you do that, as long as you don't hurt yourself doing so. How's that?"

He grinned and touched her arm. His hand callused from riding, was warm to the touch.

"It works for me."

"Good," Jenna said, nodding. "Have a good rest."

She returned to the kitchen, and while Andy finished his lunch, Jenna busied herself in the kitchen, thinking of her conversation with Dustin. She washed a handful of dishes and put everything away.

She sighed as remembered that she would have been in Brussels today.

Just as she closed the refrigerator, she heard a crash and a muffled curse.

"Stay here, Andy," Jenna ordered.

She ran to the guest room, where Dustin was on the floor facedown. Turning his head, he looked up at her, then winced in pain. He was wearing only a pair of white boxers.

"Are you okay?" Jenna knelt down on the floor next to him. She touched his shoulder and ran her hand over his arm. His skin was tanned and warm to her touch, his body tight and muscled. "Anything broken?"

"I'm fine," he said quickly. "Just feeling foolish. I tripped."

"Let me help you up, Dustin," Jenna said. "I don't see how you can do it alone."

Dustin shook his head. "Thanks, but there's no way you can lift me. I'm too heavy. Just get that chair over by the desk and hold it still. I'll use that as leverage."

She held the chair in place and watched as Dustin slowly raised himself up from the floor, dragging his cast. She couldn't help noticing the play of arm, shoulder and back muscles as he pivoted onto the bed, tired.

"Let me cover you up," she said.

"Thanks," he said, avoiding her gaze.

"Maybe you'll let me help you more, Dustin. You could have seriously injured yourself."

"I'm fine."

"Blockhead," she muttered under her breath.

"What's that?"

"*Blanket.* I'll get you a blanket."

She found a brightly striped serape and covered Dustin with it, averting her eyes from his too-perfect body and noticing the circles under his eyes instead.

"Are you willing to admit now that you need my help?" she asked.

He chuckled. "Nope."

She shook her head. "You stubborn…um…ah… *bull rider.*"

"Aww…such praise." His eyes were half-shuttered, but she could still see the twinkling blue hue. "You're the best, Jenna. I mean it."

She'd waited years to hear him say that.

"Close those blue eyes, cowboy. We'll talk later."

"Can't wait to catch up. I want to know what you've been doing. I want…to know…all about you."

He was out. Sleeping. And she was walking on sunshine.

Maybe Dustin wasn't Mr. Right. But he might be Mr. Right Now.

So what was she going to do about it?

Chapter Two

As Dustin slept, Jenna spent the afternoon helping Andy with his reading. He was making painfully slow progress, but it was progress just the same. They still had a lot of work to do yet.

"Sound out the word, Andy," she advised. "You'd know the word if you broke it down to smaller words or sounds."

"Cot...ton...wood," he said slowly.

"It's a tree," Dustin said from the doorway.

He was hanging over his crutches and looked more than a little rumpled.

"Hey, Uncle Dustin!" Andy said, his cute little face brimming with happiness. "Did you have a good sleep? Aunt Jenna said that it's important, that you'll get better faster."

"That's just what my doctor said, buckaroo." He

smiled at Andy, then turned to Jenna. "I didn't mean to disturb your lesson."

Andy answered instead. "You didn't." He slid his chair away from the kitchen table and looked hopefully at his aunt.

"Can I go now?"

"Finish the paragraph first," Jenna said.

He pulled his chair back and glanced at the page. "The cot-ton-wood tree is found in North America and can live many, many years."

Dustin cleared his throat. "The cottonwood tree is a good, sturdy tree, Andy. We had one on my father's ranch, and he found out that it's been around for four hundred years." He paused. "That's almost as old as your father."

Andy giggled until Jenna thought he was going to fall out of the chair. Then Dustin pointed to the reading workbook and Andy sobered.

"The cottonwood tree is found in North America and can live many, many years," Andy read once again, then turned to her. "Just like Uncle Dustin said."

"I think we can stop for today, Andy," she said with a sigh.

Dustin put a hand on the boy's shoulder. "I saw a basketball hoop hanging from the barn wall. What do you say we shoot some hoops?"

"Awesome!" Andy replied.

"You're going to have to spot me some points," Dustin said.

"Don't do it, Andy," advised Jenna. "Dustin was an awesome basketball player in high school, and an awesome quarterback, besides being a champion rodeo rider."

Dustin raised an eyebrow and looked at her strangely. "So, you remember that much about me from high school?"

"Well, you were Tom's best friend. He always talked about you. Besides, I went to the games. I saw you play." Absolutely she remembered him. Who wouldn't? He'd always been the perfect jock.

Dustin's eyes twinkled and a smile lit his face. He seemed...pleased by her answer.

Then he winked at Jenna, and her mouth went dry. Darn it. One wink from him in her freshman year of high school would have provided her with four years' worth of joy. But they weren't in high school anymore—and she'd have to remember that.

"I want ten points," Andy insisted.

"I'll spot you ten points only, and that's highway robbery," Dustin protested good-naturedly, continuing the banter.

Jenna knew that the big, lanky cowboy would give Andy anything that he wanted. She knew Dustin's generosity from talking to Tom, and it never failed to tweak her when it came to the boy's birthday, just a bit.

It seemed like Dustin always knew the perfect gifts for a growing boy—a dirt bike, a basketball, a bat and glove—whereas she saw to it that he had a supply of nice clothes for school and books befitting his age.

Of course, Andy's excitement and thankful hugs would be for the fun things, rather than the practical, so Jenna was grudgingly glad that Dustin's gifts made Andy happy. Sure, she could have given him toys and such, but he was growing so fast, and needed clothes. Besides, she always felt the need to be his stand-in mother in the place of the ever-unhappy and lethargic Marla who'd *think* about shopping for Andy when school was well underway.

As she put together a lasagna for dinner, she could hear the easy dialogue between Dustin and Andy through the open window.

"You shoot like a girl," Andy said.

"I'm on crutches, for Pete's sake."

"I want twenty points from you. Twenty. Even though you shoot like a girl, you still can shoot," Andy said.

"No way, kiddo. We settled for ten."

"Hey, we didn't shake on it."

And on and on it went. Jenna slipped the lasagna into the refrigerator and went outside to join them.

"Want to play, Jenna?" Dustin asked when he saw her approach.

"I was just going to watch."

"C'mon and play along with us. You can be on my team," Dustin said.

"That's not fair," Andy whined.

"What if I give you twenty points?" Dustin asked.

"Thirty."

"Done."

Dustin tossed Jenna the ball. She took a shot. Perfect!

"Beginner's luck," she said with a grin. And it *was* beginner's luck. She wasn't much of a jock.

Ironically, as she started making the occasional basket, Dustin began to miss shot after shot. Unless he was letting Andy win.

How sweet of him.

But, she thought wryly, she didn't have to *let* Andy

win. She wasn't that great a player, and most of her shots bounced off the rim.

Despite their good-natured fun, she was all-too aware when Dustin took off his shirt and she saw more proof of his strength.

Suddenly, she felt hot, breathless and shocked at her reaction to him. Mercifully, she'd thought to bring out three bottles of water. She grabbed one and took a long draw, desperate to cool herself and calm her racing pulse.

"Break," she yelled, pushing her bangs off her forehead. She handed both of them a bottle of water. "Dustin needs to rest for a while."

Dustin smiled his thanks, gingerly lowered himself onto a bench and took a long drink. Jenna could see his strong neck move as he swallowed.

She took another sip of water. Darn, it was getting hot out here…

Andy cupped his hands around his mouth. "Time's up!"

Dustin stood up with difficulty. When he got the ball, he passed it to Jenna. She aimed and made the basket.

They gave each other a high five, but then Dustin's fingers curled briefly around hers and an undeniable jolt shot through her body. It was nothing, she told herself.

She was overreacting.

Admittedly, she didn't have much experience with men. She'd been a wallflower in high school, and her current lifestyle didn't allow her much free time to meet anyone. That's why her trip to Europe had meant so much. She'd needed that vacation for more than one reason.

Not only was it going to be a well-deserved vacation, but it would give her the opportunity to meet men.

For someone about to turn thirty, she hadn't dated much at all. In fact, Jenna could count her dates on one hand—none of which resulted in a serious relationship.

As someone who wanted to get married and have a family, in that old-fashioned order, she hadn't exactly had the time or the opportunity to meet many men.

But now she and Dustin were living together, so to speak, and she had the perfect opportunity to find out if she liked him as much as she'd always thought—and heaven knew she'd thought about him a lot throughout the years.

And she certainly wasn't going to think twice about her brother's silly command to stay away from Dustin, issued after her parents died when she was in her teens. Now, she could truthfully say they were acquaintances who only spoke when Tom was there to chaperone, come to think of it.

Dustin's reputation and occupation spoke of experience with women. He'd always been a player, whereas she hadn't even been in the game.

But she could change that. She remembered a magazine that she'd bought and stuck in her suitcase. It had advertised a specific article about how to catch a man and keep him.

Now, where did she put that magazine?

Dustin pretended to drop the ball, letting Andy retrieve it.

But his mind wasn't on basketball. It was on Jenna

and the increasingly obvious attraction between them. She'd ignored him in high school, but surprisingly, she was being nice now. And she'd changed so much. She seemed more relaxed and less stressed. He'd never lacked for female companionship, but this one girl from his past still had a hold on him—and she was the only one he could never have.

He couldn't understand why he was noticing everything about her: the way her blond hair glinted in the desert sun. How her tank top lifted just an inch or so, showing a tanned, taut midriff whenever she threw the basketball. How her whole face lit up when she smiled.

Normally it might not be much of a challenge to use their close quarters as an opportunity to finally get her into bed, but she was Tom's baby sister—and she was definitely off-limits. Even though they were the same age, that didn't matter. She'd always be his best friend's younger sister.

But he'd made his promise long ago. Maybe Tom had forgotten his edict by now. He must have, or else why would Tom push him toward recovering at the Bar R when he knew that Jenna would be there?

Dustin remembered back in high school when he'd told Tom that he wanted to date Jenna. Tom had squashed the idea in a hurry.

"Forget it," Tom had said. "Jenna is something special—she's not just another cheerleader. Keep your hands off her. Promise me."

Dustin hoped that everything was cool with Tom. He knew that if he became involved with Jenna— even after all these years—it would be the end of his friendship with Tom.

He couldn't blame Tom—after all, aside from Andy, Jenna was his only family.

It wasn't worth risking Tom's displeasure by dating Jenna, especially when they weren't just friends, but business partners as well. They co-owned several rank bulls and broncs here on the Bar R.

He tried to concentrate on the game, but he missed his shot, and this time it wasn't on purpose. Jenna was just too distracting.

Just then, she tripped on one of his crutches and fell into him. They both toppled into a heap on the blacktop.

"Are you okay, Jenna?" he asked after they both caught their breaths. He slipped a hand under her head to protect it from the hard surface.

"I'm fine. Just feeling a little clumsy."

"These crutches…" he began. "It's my fault."

He continued to look into her eyes, her big, brilliant green eyes. It wouldn't take much to close the distance between them and taste her full lips.

Something nagged at him, but he pushed it to the back of his mind. All he wanted to savor right now was the unbelievable feeling of holding Jenna in his arms.

"I'm so sorry!" she gasped, leaping to her feet all too soon. "Oh, Dustin! Did I hurt you?"

Actually, it was a little bit of heaven. Her scent, her body close to his, her weight pressing on him. Nice. He didn't give a hoot about the pain that throbbed around his ankle. "I'll live."

"That's the second time you've been on the ground today. You must be—"

"I'm fine," he said. But he wasn't. He had parts

that were killing him, and he didn't mean the parts that were in the cast.

"Let me help you," she said, brow furrowed in concern.

"Just hold on to my crutches, and I'll use them to pull myself up."

He did, but it took him four tries.

"Nice job, Andy." He shook the boy's hand, then hobbled over to the porch, and slumped into one of the rocking chairs. Looking down at the jeans he'd cut up to pull over his cast, he decided to get his mind off Jenna and think of something else.

Like his lack of clothes.

"Jenna, I'm going to get a ranch hand to give me a ride to my apartment so I can pick up some clothes and things."

"I'd be glad to drive you to Tubac," she said, taking a sip of water. "I don't mind at all. Besides, Andy and I could both use a change of scenery. How about tomorrow morning?"

Dustin sighed. So much for trying to stay away from her. Still, there was no polite way to refuse. "I'm meeting with the ranch hands at the bunkhouse first thing in the morning. It shouldn't take long. I just want to have a better handle on the workings of Tom's ranch."

"We can go after your meeting," she said.

"That would be great. Thanks."

He was looking forward to the meeting, and as much as it killed him to impose, the ride with Jenna and Andy would give him something else to look forward to in the morning…

* * *

The desert morning dawned hot and bright. Dustin washed his hair in the sink and the rest of him as best he could, vowing to rig up something so he could take a shower or a bath. He could already hear Jenna and Andy in the kitchen. The smell of coffee and something cooking, pancakes maybe, drifted in the air, making his stomach growl.

He could get used to this.

It was all so…homey.

He thought of all the buckle bunnies who hung around the rodeos. They were usually heavily made up and wore low-cut and tight-fitting clothes. Jenna wasn't like them at all. With her no-frills beauty and modest clothes, Jenna was more attractive than any woman he'd met on the circuit.

He could get used to this, if he didn't have other, more immediate goals. He needed to get back to riding bulls and win the PBR Finals in Vegas. That was his plan. Not giving in to a flirtation that could only lead to trouble.

Dustin lumbered into the kitchen and took a big whiff. He hadn't had a good breakfast since…well, it had been a while.

"Morning."

"Good morning, Dustin! How did you sleep?" Jenna's smile brightened the room.

"Better than usual. Breakfast smells great."

"After your meeting with the hands, we'll head out to Tubac," Jenna said, placing a steaming mug of coffee and a plate of eggs and pancakes in front of him.

He'd died and gone to heaven.

Breakfast was fun. Jenna steered the conversation

in the direction of Theodore Roosevelt and his part in the making of the National Park System.

That must be the topic of Andy's next reading comprehension essay. Jenna impressed him as a great teacher. He wondered why she'd become one.

When he found himself thinking about her far too much, Dustin excused himself and made his way to the bunkhouse to meet the men. All of them were good guys and hard workers, and they obviously kept the ranch running smoothly. The meeting was over in record time.

When he went back up the path to the main house, he noticed that Jenna had moved her forest-green Chevy SUV closer to his route so he didn't have far to walk.

The ride went fast without a lot of traffic on either I-10 or I-19 South. They talked and laughed and, on a couple of occasions, he glanced at Jenna and noticed her looking back at him.

The three of them pulled up to his apartment building almost an hour later.

"Andy, will you hand me my crutches?" Dustin asked. "I'll give those stairs a try."

Jenna sighed loudly. "You're really going to try to climb three floors? Isn't that the reason you're staying at Tom's ranch, so you don't have to make that climb up and down? You can't go up there. It's too soon after surgery."

"I'm not asking you for more help," he replied.

"Just tell me what you need," she said with a hint of impatience in her voice. "And give me the key."

He shook his head. Damn that bull for doing this

to him. Scribbling a quick list, he told her where she could find everything.

"I'll owe you a nice night out when this cast is off." He looked deep into her spring-green eyes. "I mean it."

Jenna blushed and laughed. "Promises, promises. Don't worry. I'll remind you."

He heard the hesitation in her voice.

"You won't have to remind me. I won't forget."

And he wouldn't. His promise to Tom didn't mean that they couldn't go out and have a good time.

Right?

Jenna never expected that Dustin would live above a shop called Tubac Treasures. It was a charming shop, too, painted in bright primary colors, the window filled with all sorts of Western treasures.

"Here's the key to my apartment," Dustin said, handing her a silver key on a PBR key chain. "The entrance is out back."

She didn't mind going up to his apartment. What she did mind was rifling through his belongings. It would be like invading his privacy.

"Would you like to come with me, Andy?" Jenna asked.

"Nah. I'll stay here with Uncle Dustin. I want to hear about his ride on Black Pearl."

"Okay."

Noticing a small key on his key chain, she guessed that it would open his mailbox, so she decided to pick up Dustin's mail on her way upstairs. His box was packed full—junk mail, a couple of magazines and a huge manila envelope from the sports agent who also represented Tom. Jenna knew immediately what the overstuffed envelope meant—fan letters, most of which were probably from women.

Dustin always was a chick magnet.

She would like to think that she was immune to his charms. She could appreciate a good-looking guy as well as anyone, but Dustin Morgan wasn't for her. She didn't want to be another notch on his belt. Besides, they didn't have anything in common except that he rode bulls and she liked to watch bull riding. That was all.

When she slipped the key into his apartment door, it opened immediately. It was so stuffy inside that she searched for the thermostat in the living room and clicked it to Cool.

She looked around and was surprised to see that the apartment was nicely decorated. Could he have done this himself? Or was it the handiwork of a girlfriend?

She froze. Did Dustin have a special woman in his life?

Telling herself it didn't matter—she wasn't interested, remember?—she moved into the bedroom. She didn't know what to expect—mirrors?—but it was neat and clean and conservative. The king bed was covered by a brown plaid comforter. Two dressers made of thick dark wood and a couple of matching nightstands were the only other pieces in the room.

Western art adorned the walls—beautiful ink drawings painted in watercolors. There were pictures of cowboys riding bulls and broncs, old pueblo villages, saguaros, mountains. She was particularly drawn to a beautiful painting of the old San Xavier del Bac Mission, on the outskirts of Tucson. It was perfect in every detail.

The artist was talented—very talented. She squinted to make out the name, but could only see a capital *M.* She'd have to remember to ask Dustin who the artist was. He or she must be in residence in Tubac, and she'd love to invest in some of their work.

Checking her watch, she realized she'd already been in the apartment for ten minutes. Hurrying to his dresser, she pulled open a drawer and grabbed shirts, sweatpants and clean socks and—she tried not to look—underwear, along with a pair of sneakers from the closet. She packed everything inside a duffel bag she'd found on the closet shelf.

She paused to admire the San Xavier painting again, then set the thermostat back to Off and hurried downstairs before she lingered to explore the other bedroom.

She'd learned a lot about Dustin in this trip. He lived alone. He was an art collector. And someone—a girlfriend?—had probably decorated his apartment for him.

Back at the car, she put the duffel bag in the backseat next to Andy and settled back in the driver's seat.

"I can't thank you enough, Jenna," Dustin said.

"No problem." She waved his concern away. "You have a beautiful apartment. Who decorated it for you?"

"I did it myself," he said.

Strike one.

"And you live alone right now?" She knew it wasn't any of her business but she couldn't help herself.

He nodded. "I've always lived by myself."

Strike two.

"And the artist whose paintings you collect…well,

he or she is just fabulous. I particularly like the one of San Xavier Mission. It's magnificent."

"Thank you," he said.

She got into the driver's seat. "Could you tell me the name of the artist? I'd like to commission another one."

Dustin laughed. "I don't know if I can tell you the artist's name. He's very exclusive."

"I'd really like to know."

"Okay," he said. "Since you've been so good to me, I'll tell you his name." He winked. "His name is Dustin Morgan."

"What?" She was stunned. "You're the artist?"

"I am."

Strike three.

Dustin Morgan was an artist—an *exceptional* one. Who would have thought?

Chapter Three

Dustin was amazed that Jenna thought so much of his paintings. She was as excited as if she'd just discovered the next da Vinci.

Da Vinci he wasn't.

As far as Dustin was concerned, he didn't want to talk about his art. He wanted to eat. They'd stopped for lunch at a little hole in the wall that had the best Mexican food in all of Arizona.

"I paint for fun, Jenna," he said, hoping that would end the discussion.

She paused from eating her chicken chimichanga. "But you are so talented!"

"I sell my work at the store downstairs from my apartment."

"But you're bigger than Tubac Treasures. I mean, I

minored in contemporary art in college, and I can see how good you are."

How could he make her understand how he felt about his art?

"Jenna, my drawing and painting is just a hobby. It's not who I am. I'm a bull rider."

"You're so wrong, Dustin. You're an artist, too."

She didn't get it. Probably because she had always been driven about everything.

From what he'd heard about Jenna throughout the years via Tom, she hadn't changed much. She always thought big and jumped right in to make something happen, whereas he was content just doing what he did—bull riding and watercolors.

He squirted more jalapeño sauce on his tamale. "When it stops being fun and starts becoming work, then that's when I quit."

Andy wiped at his mouth with a handful of napkins. Andy looked like he had more taco on him than he was initially served. "School is work, Uncle Dustin. I want to quit."

Jenna shot Dustin an exasperated look.

"I didn't mean school, Andy. You need to go to school so you can learn as much as you can and eventually get a good job," Dustin said, hoping he could clarify things.

"I'm going to quit school as soon as I can and be a bull rider like you and Dad and win a lot of money."

Jenna opened her mouth to say something, then shot a pleading look in his direction.

Dustin leaned toward Andy. "I wanted to go to college after high school. I wanted to study business and how to manage animals. It's called animal husbandry.

Both of those things are really important when you want to run your own ranch, which I want to do someday."

Andy appeared to be listening, so he continued. "I couldn't go to college because my parents needed help on their ranch. So, I worked at the ranch during the day, rode bulls on the weekend, and went to night school three nights a week."

"When did you study?" Jenna asked.

"Every spare moment I could," Dustin replied. "It wasn't easy, but I wanted something to fall back on when I retired from the sport."

Jenna smiled at him and nodded. "You deserve a lot of credit, Dustin."

"Thanks." He basked in her smile for a while, they turned to Andy. "And your dad deserves a lot of credit, too, right Andy? I'm sure you know that he's taking classes online. True?"

Andy nodded solemnly. He knew when he was outnumbered.

"So, two bull riders in the top ten of the rankings, and your aunt, Jenna, who moved here to help you pass, can't be wrong."

"Oh, okay," Andy said grudgingly, getting up from the table. "Excuse me. I need to use the bathroom."

Jenna nodded. "You're excused."

After Andy left, Jenna shook her head. "Congratulations on getting your degree, Dustin. Now I know why you turned down that scholarship to UNLV. Your parents needed you."

She reached across the table and put her hand over his.

It was an impulsive gesture, but when she didn't

move it away, he stroked the top of her hand with his thumb. Her eyes grew as wide as the belt buckle he wore. All too soon, Andy returned from the restroom, and Dustin pulled his hand away.

He shrugged. "I just did what I had to do."

Sometimes he thought it was all for nothing, because all too soon his parents gave up, sold the place and moved on. That had hurt him. He'd loved that ranch and had worked hard alongside his parents so they could keep it in the family. He always thought that his dad had called it quits too soon.

Dustin had hoped to buy back the ranch after he started climbing in the PBR standings, but it had virtually disappeared. A developer subdivided it into housing and a golf course.

Andy joined them in the booth and reached for his soda.

Jenna cleared her throat. "Dustin, speaking of school, have you taken any art classes?"

He grunted. Jenna certainly had a one-track mind.

"No. I haven't, but I've studied Western art on my own."

"Studied on your own? That's really wonderful, Dustin."

Dustin bit back a grin. It figured that Jenna, the eternal bookworm, would be impressed by that.

"Everyone done?" he asked, changing the subject. Inside his cast, his ankle was throbbing and itching. He didn't know how much longer he could endure the damn thing.

Dustin peeled off some bills and dropped them on the table, including a hefty tip for the service. Jenna was digging in her purse for her wallet, but he waved her away. "I got it, Jenna."

She smiled her appreciation. "Next time we all go out, it'll be my treat."

A big hit of pleasure washed over him. He'd like nothing better than to go out with them again. Or even better on a bonafide date with Jenna.

Jenna stood at the kitchen sink peeling potatoes for dinner. Dustin was at the bunkhouse, talking to the ranch hands. Andy was shooting hoops in the yard.

The ride to Tubac had been a welcome change from two weeks of getting Andy up for summer school, tutoring him at night and doing the cooking and cleaning. Until today, she hadn't been off the ranch in a week.

Maybe this weekend, they could go to Old Tucson, visit the movie studio where they made westerns, or even go out for lunch or dinner.

Of course she'd invite Dustin. He had to be bored sitting around most of the day with his ankle up.

Dustin. She was always a little too jumpy with him and felt that she always had to be "on." He made her so nervous—her heart racing, her cheeks heating and her mouth bone dry—that she just couldn't relax and be herself.

She had to forget about him and concentrate on the task at hand—getting Andy up to speed on fourth-grade reading and math. He was making excellent progress, but he wasn't having fun. She'd have to change things up, try something besides his reading workbook. But what would pique his interest? Comic books?

Out of the window, she could see Dustin struggling to walk with his crutches up the narrow path from the bunkhouse on uneven terrain. She really should ask one of the hands to widen the path. It was overgrown with prickly pear cactus and other desert vegetation.

Wiping her hands on a towel, she hurried outside to help Dustin. She didn't want him to fall again. "Maybe we should get a wheelchair for you."

He answered her suggestion with a scowl. "I'm fine, Jenna."

"Well, be careful." His bare toes were inches away from the sharp needles of a prickly pear cactus.

He followed her gaze. "I know about cacti. I've lived in Arizona all my life."

"So have I," Jenna said firmly. "So don't get stuck."

"I don't need a nurse. I'm a bull rider, for heaven's sake. I can manage a pair of crutches."

"Fact one: I am not a nurse. And fact two: It was that sport that put you in that cast, cowboy. If you can't stand to be helped, then just stay in the guest room and starve to death." Her cheeks heated. "And stop your complaining. You know, I could have been in *Ireland* today, but instead I'm here."

Jenna couldn't believe she'd said that. Turning, she ran down the path, up the porch steps and into the house. Leaning against the back of the door, she caught her breath.

"Why did I say that?" she muttered.

"Say what, Aunt Jenna?" Andy asked from the doorway of the kitchen.

She jumped. The last she knew, Andy was playing basketball.

"It's nothing, sweetie. Go back to your game."

He shrugged and left. Obviously, the explanation wasn't that exciting.

Dustin. She could hear him struggling and grunting up the steep porch steps. The way he was acting, she should just let him fend for himself.

But she wanted him to get better, so she was going to help him if he liked it or not. Then Mr. *Tough* Cowboy could get back to the *tough* sport of bull riding and out of her hair.

Complaining? He wasn't *complaining*. If anything, he was just stating fact.

Dustin vowed to be more appreciative of Jenna's help. He just wasn't a good patient—he preferred to take care of himself.

But what did Jenna mean about Ireland?

As he struggled up the steps to the porch, he tried to remember what she'd said.

I could have been in Ireland today.

She wouldn't have given up a trip to Ireland to take care of him, would she? Nah. She really didn't even know him, and throughout the years, she'd barely spoken to him.

If she gave up a trip for anyone, it would have been for Andy.

He planned on getting Jenna alone and asking her to clarify what she'd meant.

Andy ran up the porch steps. "Uncle Dustin, what are you going to do now?"

"I think I'll talk to your Aunt Jenna for a while."

"Do you wanna shoot some hoops?" Andy asked.

"I'll play with you later tonight. Deal?"

Andy burst into a big grin, then it faded as his

shoulders slumped. "I forgot. I have to be tutored to-night."

"Maybe, if things go well with your tutoring, it won't take that long, and we can play. Cool?"

"Awesome."

They bumped knuckles, and Andy leaped off the stairs and was gone.

He'd love to be that young and agile again. Recently, he'd been thinking of hanging up his spurs and settling down—after he won the finals in Vegas, of course. He wanted a ranch like the Bar R and a wife to share it with. Maybe even a couple of kids.

Dustin sighed. Here he was only thirty, and he was thinking about his life like an old man. The best was yet to come, but it wouldn't—couldn't—be as a bull rider. Bull riders had short careers. There weren't many still riding over the age of thirty-five.

He caught a glimpse of Jenna through the front window, reading a magazine in the living room. He could almost picture walking through the door after a hard day's work and being welcomed home by her. They'd kiss and talk about their day. Their children would be totally loved, perfectly behaved and their report cards would contain all A's.

And later, at night, he and his wife would make love.

Jenna swung the front door open, pulling him out of his daydream. "Don't worry. I'm not opening the door for you, I just wanted to get some fresh air." She left the door open and went by him in a blur, leaping off the steps of the porch just like Andy had.

Must be a Reed trait.

Dustin would give anything to jump those stairs and follow her.

Instead, he walked into the empty house and wondered if his dreams of a gold buckle, marriage and a family would ever come true. Because regardless of his dreams, he couldn't have Jenna.

Jenna was in the kitchen helping Andy with decimals when she heard a loud thump along with the granddaddy of all curses. Dustin had fallen again.

Her first thought was to rush to help him, but knowing that her assistance wasn't welcome, she forced herself to concentrate on her nephew and his fourth-grade math.

"I think Uncle Dustin fell. Aren't we going to help him up, Aunt Jenna?"

"If Dustin needed our help, he'd give a yell."

"He did yell. He yelled fu—"

"Andrew Reed!"

"Oh, all right. I wasn't going to say it."

"And Dustin shouldn't have said it, either. I'm going to have a talk with him." As she got up stiffly from her chair, she knew that she sounded like the teacher that she was, and Dustin was about to experience her wrath—just like one of her students would.

She found him in the living room, sitting on the couch. When Dustin saw her standing there, he hurried to explain.

"I was trying to get the remote from on top of the TV," he said. "It was just out of my reach, and I lost my balance with this damn cast. I used the crutches for leverage to get to the couch."

"Dustin," she said firmly. "Your language—"

"Sorry. If I offended you, I apologize."

She nodded, noticing how pale he was from the exertion, and the awkward angle of his bad leg.

"I'd offer to try and make you more comfortable, but I know how much you want to do things on your own," she said, feeling that they'd had this discussion before.

He just sat there with his arms folded, looking... frustrated.

"I'm getting too weak, sitting all day. I need to lift weights or something," he said. "I'm not used to just sitting around, and I shouldn't take it out on you."

Jenna didn't move.

"So...thanks." Dustin looked up at her. "Why don't you get back to your lesson?"

Obviously, he was embarrassed. But his apology—for both his profanity and his rejection of her—was sincere. Maybe, finally, she could try to figure him out.

Jenna went to the door and called Andy in from the kitchen. "Andy, take a break. Shoot some hoops if you want. I'll give you a call when we're going to start again."

Andy hesitated. The sweet kid wanted to lend a hand. Jenna waved him away. "Go ahead."

Andy hurried out the door, and Jenna took a seat on the rocker.

"Okay, cowboy. Now that I have your undivided attention, please explain why it's so hard for you to accept any help from me."

Several seconds went by before he spoke. "I've always done things by myself. It's as simple as that. It's not you, Jenna, although I don't want to impose on you anymore than I already have. I truly appreciate everything you're doing for me."

Dustin leaned back into the sofa cushions. "Every time I've been injured, I've managed by myself. I live alone. I can't count on anyone being there every time. Besides, I'm a big, tough cowboy." He leaned toward her. "But getting to know you again is an extra bonus."

Jenna's heart soared. She looked at his sky-blue eyes, his smile that seemed sincere. "Thanks. I feel the same way about you, but—"

Dustin chuckled. "I knew there'd be a *but*."

"*But,* I think you're wrong about accepting help. I get where you're coming from, though."

He raised an eyebrow. "Anything else you'd like to know?"

"Are you involved with someone?" she blurted, then took a deep breath. Could she be any more obvious?

"No. I'm not."

She sat back in her chair, relieved. So, he was fair game.

"What about you, Jenna? Do you have a boyfriend lurking in the cacti? A passel of children somewhere?"

She grinned. "No children. No husband." Her smile faded a little. "My students are my children. I mean… I would have liked children of my own, but it didn't happen. Now, I'm moving on. I've cut down on my hours and I promised myself that I'm going to travel more. No moss will grow under these…flip-flops."

He was quiet for a while, studying her. Jenna felt that she'd disappointed him somehow. She decided to change the subject.

"You know, Dustin, I've been wanting to ask you something else."

"Shoot."

"Did you save your parents' ranch?"

Dustin nodded. "For a while. Then they got an offer they couldn't refuse and sold out and bought a place in Florida. Now they're in Alaska." He looked down at the carpeted floor. "They gave me some of the money from the sale, which I've invested in rough stock here at Tom's ranch." He lowered his voice, as if thinking out loud. "When I win the finals, I'll buy my own ranch. And someday, I'll have a bunch of children who I'll teach to rope and ride and…"

He stopped and looked deep into her eyes. "So, now you see, Jenna—" Dustin lifted the bad leg and stretched it out in front of him. "I had no choice but to turn down that scholarship."

"I admire you, Dustin. I do. And you even found time to get your bachelor's degree."

He smiled. "And don't forget my master's."

She stared at him, willing her brain to wrap around what he'd just said. Finally, it sank in. He had a master's degree, and he was riding bulls?

"Really?" Jenna stopped rocking and leaned forward. "What's your master's in?"

"Business. And my bachelor's degree is in animal husbandry." He grinned. "Tom and I will take the rodeo world by storm by breeding a new generation of bulls and broncs."

She couldn't help but be impressed. Dustin was certainly a self-made man, and she just knew that his dreams—including those of a ranch and children— would come to fruition.

While her dreams would have to wait. Again.

"Jenna, there's something I've been meaning to ask you, too."

"Shoot," she echoed.

"What did you mean when you said you could have been in Ireland today?"

She was quiet for a moment. "I canceled a three-week trip to Europe because Tom asked me to help Andy pass fourth grade." She sighed. "I would have been having dinner in Dublin tonight."

"Did Tom know about your trip?"

She nodded. "I shouldn't have told him. He would have made other plans, but I insisted on helping Andy."

"And then you got stuck with me, too."

She held up a warning finger. "I didn't *get stuck* with Andy or you. My trip will be rescheduled."

She remembered that her plan was to have a whirl-wind fling with a sexy European. But now Dustin, the man she'd always longed for from afar, was sitting across from her, making her pulse race.

"Andy needed me. Tom needed me. And you need me more than you know," she said.

"You're wrong, Jenna. I know exactly how much I need you." Leaning forward, he issued those two small sentences with great intensity and seriousness.

What he said, how he said it and the expression on his face took her breath away, and she doubted very much that they were talking about his ankle.

Now that she knew Dustin was interested and available, her new plan was to have a fling with a sexy American cowboy.

Chapter Four

The next day, Jenna tried to concentrate on the biography she was reading, but she couldn't. Instead she looked out the window and saw Dustin talking to Adriano, one of the ranch hands. Dustin and he were in an animated discussion, no doubt talking about their greatest bull rides.

She studied Dustin's profile—his square jaw, the hint of a beard, twinkling blue eyes, his perfect nose and lips.

His sensuous lips.

They made her think yet again of the crush she'd had on him in high school. How many times had she doodled their initials in a heart with an arrow through it?

She'd been to every football and basketball game and rodeo event that he'd played in their first two years of high school. She'd been desperate to try and get his attention, but it was nothing more than unrequited love.

She couldn't have been more socially awkward back then. Books were her salvation, and her curse. Her mother always remarked that she should get out more, go to dances and the like, but she hadn't wanted to see Dustin out with other girls.

But now she was too old for crushes. Even though she'd wanted to get married back then—to Dustin— that wasn't the case anymore. She'd decided a while ago that a fling was the way to go.

If she'd gone to Europe, would she have met several men by now? Indulged in some harmless flirting, and then continued on her trip?

But she didn't know how to flirt. Not really. She could recite the periodic tables and calculate pi to the nth degree, but she didn't know how to seduce a man.

Yet here in front of her was a very eligible, sexy man. Just being around him had heightened every nerve in her body. Trouble was, he was treating her more like a sister than a potential lover, except for a couple of flirtatious comments and absentminded touches.

Could she seduce Dustin?

Her heart beat wildly and her mouth went dry as a plan began to formulate in her mind.

Jenna once again thought of the magazine she'd bought back in Phoenix, just for the article entitled "Ten Ways to Seduce a Man."

She'd thought that the article would help her get a

jump start on her goal of seducing a man in Europe. Now, she had another plan.

She knew that she was knowledgeable when it came to academics, but she was totally lacking in whatever she needed to seduce a man—especially a man like Dustin. A man who was right here, right now.

The magazine was still in her suitcase, and she hurried to her bedroom to retrieve it. *Women's Universe* was glossy and slick, loaded with pictures of celebrities and self-improvement articles.

Sitting on the bed, she opened the magazine, turning to page thirty as indicated on the front cover.

She'd read the narrative later. For now, she'd just skim the highlights. The list of tips for catching a man's eye by dressing—and acting—sexy or confident seemed practical yet…daunting. Wearing lots of makeup, leaving her hair loose and wild had never been her style.

But who was she to argue with *Woman's Universe?*

Well, there was no time like the present to give it her best shot. She tossed the magazine aside and hurried to her closet.

She slipped off her T-shirt and put on the turquoise peasant blouse she'd bought for her vacation, arranging it so it would drape off her shoulder.

Bending over, she flipped her hair forward and brushed it out. Then she tossed her head back and shook it, giving her hair an instant wind-blown look. Then she touched up her makeup, adding lip gloss and blush.

Smoothing down her khaki shorts, she looked at herself in the mirror. Okay, it wasn't her usual style, but she looked pretty good. Confident that she'd done the best she could, she headed out to dazzle Dustin.

She couldn't wait to see his reaction to tips one, two and seven.

Dustin limped over to where Andy was playing basketball.

"How about some more one-on-one?" Dustin asked.

Andy's face lit up, then slowly dimmed. "I can't. I have to do homework."

"Aunt Jenna's working you hard, huh?"

He shrugged. "It's boring."

"Can I help? I'd be glad to."

"You'll help me?" Andy took off at a run. "Wait there. I'll be right back," he yelled over his shoulder.

Dustin sat down at the patio table. He didn't have to wait long before Andy came racing back, a backpack dangling from his hand.

"It's math homework. I have to do page fifteen and sixteen about decimals." Andy rolled his eyes. "What do I need decimals for?"

"To figure out your money, for one thing."

Andy pointed to the worksheet in the book. It was pretty dry, just rows and rows of addition and subtraction. The next page was multiplication and division.

"Let's look at the first problem. Imagine we're watching bull riding. I rode seven point two seconds. Your dad rode six point nine six seconds. How much time did we ride in total?"

Andy's pencil scribbled. "Fourteen point sixteen seconds," he said quickly.

"What was our average score?" Dustin asked.

"Hey, that's not in the book!"

Dustin chuckled. "Just tell me. I know you can do it."

"Seven point zero eight." Andy grinned.

"Easy, huh? Let's do another one."

And they did. One after another. They did the average NASCAR miles. The division of miles per hour of three racers. More bull riding. And football players gaining yardage.

Jenna appeared after another bull-riding problem. At least he thought it was Jenna. She looked…different. Her hair was loose and she was wearing a lot of makeup. He wondered if she was going out somewhere, and his heart sank as he speculated that she was going on a date. But she would have asked him to watch Andy, so that couldn't be it.

Dustin forced himself to concentrate on helping the boy. He seemed to be learning, so he was going to keep presenting various scenarios. "Three bull riders belonging to the Young Guns team rode a total of 366.75 points. Average their score because the announcer wants to let everyone know on the air," Dustin said, glancing at Jenna.

"Whoa!" Jenna had her hands on her hips. "You were supposed to do your homework on your own, young man."

"But Uncle Dustin is making it fun!" Andy said, looking up from writing his answer. His mouth gaped open as he pointed at Jenna. "Hey, Aunt Jenna, why are you so dressed up?"

Swallowing, she patted her hair and tucked in a bra strap "I—I—um…"

A light breeze carried the scent of her perfume toward Dustin. Roses.

"I'm sorry that I interfered, Jenna," he said sincerely. "I had asked Andy if he wanted to shoot hoops, but when he said he had homework, I thought I'd help. Blame me."

Jenna held up a finger, telling him to wait, and smiled woodenly at Andy, who still looked at her like she'd just dropped in from another planet. "Andrew Reed, please go into the house and finish your homework on your own. Okay?"

"Yeah."

When Andy was out of hearing range, Jenna turned to Dustin. "I'm not blaming you. And if Andy is learning by your method, then that's perfectly fine with me."

Actually, it sounded as if she were annoyed—and he decided to call her on it. "You don't sound perfectly fine. You sound mad."

She fussed with the hem of her blouse. "I'm mad at myself. I should have taught Andy using sports examples like you did. Math can be dull to a kid. You made it come alive. I just bored him to death with the standard textbook because I was so focused on catching him up with the rest of his class."

He studied her spring-green eyes, now surrounded by blue eye shadow. "Don't be too hard on yourself, Jenna. Not every problem on every test is going to have a story about bull riding or car racing on it."

She tugged on her blouse again. Her bra strap peeked out, and she impatiently tucked it back in. He'd never seen anyone fight with a bra and a blouse so much.

"Just wait until I use the amount of manure a bull can produce when Andy has to learn square feet and cubic feet," Dustin said, grinning.

Jenna laughed. He loved the sound of it, and wished that she'd do it more often. She was way too serious.

He tried not to look, but her hair was sticking out in several places. She nervously tucked it behind her ear. Better.

Dustin didn't know what her new hairstyle was all about, or what was up with her choice of blouse, but he'd figure it out sooner or later.

To be honest, he didn't know if he liked her new look. She was always fresh-faced, her hair tucked into a ponytail, with a dusting of freckles on her nose and a bright smile. Right now, she looked like some of the buckle bunnies that followed him and the other riders.

He had to admit that he liked the fact that the gauzy blouse revealed a little more skin. Hell, he'd always thought that she was an attractive woman, but now... well, she just didn't look like the Jenna he'd always known. The woman he'd always wanted.

His cell phone rang. He answered the call, making a gesture of apology to Jenna.

"Hey, Jeff," he said, greeting his agent. "I'm doing okay."

There was some idle chitchat about the weather before Jeff got around to the purpose of his call.

"Remember that commercial for Scents of the West—the one for the men's aftershave called Eight-Second Ride? Anyway, the film crew is coming out to Tom's ranch to shoot the commercial with you in it. They know you have a cast on your ankle, but they'll work around the thing."

Dustin didn't like this part of being on top of the standings, but he owed it to his sponsor to support their products.

"When?" he asked.

"Tomorrow, if you're up to it."

"I'm doing okay. What time?"

"First thing in the morning."

He had planned on hitching a ride with one of the hands to check on the progress of the fence mending on the border of the south pasture. Then he'd wanted to update himself on the breeding and birthing records of the rough stock.

All that would have to wait until after the commercial. He certainly couldn't turn down the cash.

"I'll be ready," Dustin said. He disconnected the call and went into the house to tell Jenna about the taping. He wasn't sure how she would feel about yet another disruption that would distract Andy.

Letting himself into the living room just as it started to rain, he found Jenna sitting on the sofa watching a game show on TV.

He hung his wet hat on the rack behind the door and sat down on a side chair.

"Uh… Jenna. I have something to tell you."

She raised an eyebrow. "Okay," she said cautiously.

"A film crew is coming here to shoot a commercial tomorrow morning. Early."

"Oh?"

"I'm in it. It's something my agent dreamed up for publicity. I hope you don't mind."

"I don't mind a bit. It sounds exciting," she said, wetting her lips.

It was an insignificant gesture, but it immediately got him thinking of hot, wet kisses and a soft, warm mattress…and Jenna.

He started to tweak his hat to her, but remembered he'd hung it by the door. "See you later."

He hurried to the kitchen. Noticing a magazine ruffling in the breeze from the open window, he thought he'd read it to take his mind off Jenna.

When he saw it was *Woman's Universe,* he tossed it back on the table.

Then his eyes caught the heading in blazing orange letters: TEN WAYS TO SEDUCE A MAN. Curious, he turned to the story. Skimming the article, he smiled, then sobered. Like the burn of cheap whiskey, a shot of jealousy ran through him. What guy was she thinking of seducing when she was doing her hair and putting on sexy clothes and perfume? Was he a neighboring rancher, or someone she taught school with?

He inhaled and closed his eyes to clear his head. It shouldn't matter what she did. She was off-limits. He shouldn't care.

But he did.

Breakfast with Jenna the next day was very awkward. It was just the two of them, as Andy had already left on the bus for summer school.

Jenna's hair looked like she'd just walked out of a wind tunnel, and she kept staring at him and asking him a million questions.

He still wanted to know who was the lucky object of the "Ten Ways to Seduce a Man" article—and why she thought she needed a magazine to teach her how to lure a man. Didn't she realized how attractive she was?

Right now, he felt like he was going through a police interrogation with all the questions she was asking him.

But when she got him to talk about bull riding, he was off and running.

"What bull do you like to ride the best?" she asked, leaning closer to him, her green eyes intent.

"Black Pearl," he replied, taking a sip of coffee. Once again, he was struck by how different she looked with full makeup—and by a longing for her more simple, straightforward look. The look of the girl he'd always wanted.

Then, as he leaned back in his chair, he spotted her legs—her tanned, crossed legs. On the tips of her ruby-red polished toes dangled a blue flip-flop. She was swaying it back and forth.

He'd never thought that a blue flip-flop was sexy, but now he watched, hypnotized by the movement of her calf muscles and her knee as she swayed the rubber sandal.

It hit the floor, and he was at the ready to retrieve it and slip it back on her foot as if she were Cinderella at the ball.

But she slipped her foot into the flip-flop again and returned it to the dangling position.

Damn that magazine article!

When he finally looked up, she met his gaze with a smile. She knew exactly what effect she was having on him.

"So what's it like to have a whole gaggle of buckle bunnies after you?" she asked.

"I don't have a gaggle," he said trying to concentrate on answering the question but dying to look at her legs again.

"I've seen them buzzing around you, just like the

girls, in high school. You've never lacked for female companionship, have you?" she asked.

He shrugged. How could he answer that without sounding conceited?

Sway...sway...

She raised an eyebrow. "You were always surrounded by cheerleaders and every cute girl within a fifty-five mile radius."

But it was you I wanted.

He chuckled. "I think you're exaggerating."

"Not by much, Dustin, and you know it. You were voted King of the senior prom. And you took the head cheerleader."

"Karen McArtle asked *me* to go with *her* to the prom."

He barely could remember Karen's face. In fact, he'd only accepted to see Jenna all dressed up. She didn't have an actual date. She just went with her friends from the debate club.

He took another sip of coffee so he didn't have to look at Jenna's green eyes

Can't look at her eyes. Can't look at her legs.

He'd wanted to ask her to the senior prom, but he hadn't dared. For one thing, Tom wouldn't have liked it, and Jenna showed absolutely no interest in him. Besides, he didn't think he could have handled a rejection from her, not with all the pressure he was under at the time to help his parents.

"Did you enjoy yourself at the prom?" he found himself asking.

She looked as shocked as he felt for asking such a dumb question after all these years.

"I can't remember," she said, brows furrowed. "It was so long ago."

"I wanted to ask you to dance," he blurted. But he hadn't. The darn promise he'd made to her brother stopped him cold.

Her eyes widened in surprise. "You did?"

"I did."

She tilted her head, and suddenly he couldn't take his eyes off her lush lips. "Then why didn't you?"

He shrugged. "You were busy with your friends."

"I would have danced with you, Dustin," she said softly.

His mouth went dry, and it was hard for him to form a response, but he tried to be casual. "Yeah?"

She blushed. "Sure."

Double damn. All that night he'd debated and warred with himself, only to discover years later he could have held Jenna in his arms. How many other opportunities had he missed out on? Was this summer his chance to finally let her know how he'd always felt about her?

I wanted to ask you to dance.

Jenna picked up the dishes and flip-flopped her way to the sink. She hated the darn things. She'd only brought them to wear around the pool.

But they'd worked well enough. She smiled as she loaded the dishwasher. Dustin couldn't take his eyes off her legs.

Clearly *Women's Universe* knew their stuff!

And she'd lied to him about the senior prom, she thought with a rush of guilt. She remembered that night vividly, but she couldn't admit that to him.

How she'd wanted to ask Dustin to take her! But what could she do? The day she worked up enough courage to ask *him*, Tom mentioned that Dustin was out of town with the rodeo. When her courage vanished, there he was, hanging out with her brother at their house.

As she put soap into the dishwasher, she flashed back to Dustin walking into the gym with Karen. She'd almost burst into tears. Dustin looked so handsome in his black tux, flashing a contented smile. She got through that evening by avoiding him.

Why the hell hadn't he asked her to dance?

Her face heated as she thought about dancing with Dustin. That would have made the evening special. Instead, she cried herself to sleep that night, feeling alone and unwanted.

It was hard being a geek in high school. All the boys wanted cheerleaders, or bubbly, social, popular girls. Smart, bookish girls usually went without dates.

She slammed the dishwasher shut and turned it on.

"Thanks for breakfast, Jenna. I appreciate it."

"You're welcome."

"Well," he sighed, "I'd better get ready to greet the film crew." He got his crutches and walked out of the kitchen.

She wiped off the table, tossed the cloth into the sink and sat back down.

She wanted him. More than ever.

She knew now that Dustin was not immune to the Ten Ways.

He obviously thought that big hair and a dangling flip-flop were turn-ons.

Well, that was nothing. She had a few tips left to try, and she was going to go all out.

Dustin was doing a slow burn. He was getting all worked up over a woman he'd sworn to stay away from.

The doorbell rang and Dustin was glad for something to take his mind off of Jenna. "I'll get it," he yelled in the direction of the kitchen. "It's probably the crew."

"Okay."

Shaking all their hands, he invited them in, and introductions were made—the director, the makeup artist, lighting director, assistant to the director and two interns.

"Can we see the pool area?" asked the director, Skip, a tall, thin man with a red cowboy hat that seemed too big for him. He sported a red bandanna around his neck.

"This way," Dustin said, motioning with his head.

On the way to the pool, he introduced them to Jenna, who was reading the paper in the kitchen.

"They'd like to see the pool," he explained to her.

She nodded. "Sure."

"Come with us," Dustin said. He wanted her to be there. After all, this was her brother's house, and it was her solitude they were all disturbing.

They walked through the sliding glass door and fanned out on the concrete patio of the rectangular pool.

"Looks perfect," Skip said, turning to Dustin. "But

we have a problem. Just as I pulled into your driveway I received a call that the actress that we were going to use had an allergic reaction to a bee sting. She's out. I'll have to call for another. Or we could just shoot you alone, but then we're going to have to come up with another script. So it might take longer then we thought. We might have to stay overnight—in a hotel, of course."

Dustin didn't relish dragging this out or being in the desert sun with a sweaty cast on for any length of time. Besides, there was a beautiful woman right here who could fill in perfectly.

"How about Jenna?" Dustin asked.

Chapter Five

Dustin watched as six pairs of eyes looked at him, then shifted right to Jenna. She looked shocked, then her cheeks heated into two pink stains.

"Oh, I couldn't," she protested softly.

The director rubbed his chin. "What do you think, Leslie?"

Leslie was the makeup artist. She walked over to Jenna and studied her face, touched her hair, made her turn around twice.

Jenna rolled her eyes. "I can't. I—"

"Her hair is a disaster right now," Leslie proclaimed. "But I can work with it."

"Jenna?" Dustin asked. He wasn't beneath pleading. He was uncomfortable doing this kind of thing and wanted to get it over with. Besides, doing the commercial with Jenna would be more fun. "Would you mind helping out?"

"I'm not an actress. I'm a fourth-grade teacher."

"You'll be perfect. And the sooner this shoot is finished, the sooner we can get back to normal around here," Dustin said. "Whatever *normal* is."

"Look, Jenna." Skip, the director, put his arm around her, and Dustin clenched his fists. "Dustin is the focus of this commercial. You just have to walk on and hug him. You don't have to do any lines. That's it."

Jenna looked apprehensive. Then her lips softened into a nervous smile. "I'll be glad to fill in."

Skip clapped his hands. "Terrific! Let's get to work, people."

Jenna sat on the edge of the tub in the master bathroom, watching as Leslie lugged in what looked like a canister vacuum cleaner. "Where can I spray-tan you, Jenna?"

"Spray-tan?" Jenna started to laugh but bit it back. She didn't want to hurt Leslie's feelings. "In the shower, I guess," she said, praying that it would wash off if it got on the tiles.

After Leslie got set up, she instructed Jenna to go into the shower with just her bra and panties on. "Wear something that you don't mind throwing away," she suggested.

She didn't mind throwing away any of the underwear she'd brought with her to the Bar R. It was just utilitarian, not the fancy stuff that she'd bought for her trip to Europe.

Leslie handed her a shower cap and a pair of goggles. "Ready?"

"As I'll ever be," Jenna replied.

The spray was cool at first; but then she got used to it. "Turn around slowly," Leslie said. She turned, feeling like a chicken on a rotisserie.

After that was over, Jenna's hair was washed, conditioned, blow-dried and baked with a curling iron. It had more product on it than the shelves of the corner drugstore carried. But Leslie truly created magic. It looked sleek and sexy, with a lot of bounce and it was the best-looking hairstyle of her life.

Her finger and toenails were cut, polished and buffed until they gleamed. Her makeup took forever—it felt as if every pore was filled with a different kind of cream or powder. But at last she was done, and turned to the mirror for a look.

Wow. She didn't even recognize herself.

She couldn't wait to see Dustin. Wouldn't he be surprised?

Leslie left the room but soon returned holding up two strips of colorful material.

"What's that?" Jenna asked.

"Your costume," Leslie replied.

Jenna swallowed hard. "What is it supposed to be?"

"A bikini."

"I see…a bikini for a men's aftershave commercial." Jenna sniffed. Actually, she didn't see, but she understood. "Bring it on." They both laughed.

Jenna took the bathing suit from Leslie and fingered the shiny material. "I hope it fits."

"We can alter it somewhat," Leslie added with a grin.

"Can you add a yard of material to it?" she said, slipping into the suit.

A knock on the door halted their laughter. "Are you about ready?" Skip yelled. "I don't want to lose the light."

Jenna looked at herself in the mirror and couldn't believe that the suit was actually flattering. Oh, she could stand to lose ten pounds or so, but she filled out the suit nicely.

"You're a magician, Leslie. I look…well, I don't look like myself."

Leslie put a hand on her shoulder. "You look gorgeous. I just enhanced what was already there."

She put on a bathrobe and nodded to Leslie, and they both left the bedroom.

A shot of excitement ran through her when she thought of Dustin's reaction to her look.

When Jenna returned, Dustin couldn't take his eyes off her. Her blond hair shimmered in the sun and curled softly around her face. Whatever makeup she had on brought out her green eyes.

She looked like the Jenna he'd always preferred—wholesome yet sexy at the same time. Her eyes twinkled either in amusement or in anticipation of acting in a commercial.

Then she slid off the bathrobe she was wearing, and his jaw dropped.

She wore a bikini with stripes of primary colors slashed across the strips of fabric. On her feet were her blue flip-flops, which matched the skimpy suit perfectly. Gold jewelry glistened around her neck and an ankle and dangled from her ears.

"Jenna?" he croaked. The fourth-grade teacher looked like a swimsuit model.

"Of course." She laughed and shifted on her feet. He noticed how long and shapely her legs were.

He couldn't swallow over the lump stuck in his throat.

"You look…wonderful," he finally said, thinking that Jenna didn't need "Ten Ways to Seduce a Man." She just had to show up dressed like this.

"Thanks."

But he'd liked her before, too—the Jenna who somehow twisted her blond hair and clipped it back with a barrette. The Jenna who wore cutoff jeans and a T-shirt to play hoops. The Jenna he'd see helping Andy with his reading or math, who was so patient and kind with the boy.

This Jenna was different. This Jenna crossed her long legs and dangled a blue flip-flop and aroused him more than any woman ever had.

She was hypnotic.

"Remember, we can only shoot Dustin from the thighs up," Skip announced. "I'm going to make it seem like he's sitting in a chair by the pool and taking in the sun and scenery. Jenna, you're the scenery."

She laughed. "I've never been called scenery before."

"Dustin, take your shirt off," ordered Skip. "You're lounging by the pool, not sitting in the chutes at a rodeo."

"Let's get this over with," Dustin mumbled.

Jenna smiled. "What would you like me to do, Skip?"

"I want you to walk toward Dustin and give him a secret smile, like you know something and he doesn't.

When you get to him, wrap your arms around his neck and put your cheek against his."

The camera crew helped Dustin into a chair and checked the lighting, and there he sat, waiting.

As Jenna moseyed toward him, Dustin's mouth went dry. Soon her arms slipped around his neck. He could smell her skin and feel the softness of her cheek against his. And felt his promise to Tom become that much harder to keep.

He pushed his hat back and raked his hair with his fingers.

Skip grinned. "That was perfect, Jenna. But Dustin, you looked uncomfortable." He shook his head. "I need you to be in the moment. Let's try it again. But this time, I'd like you both to get close so that your lips are almost touching, but not quite."

Dustin waited in anticipation of Jenna's arms going around him. He groaned when he realized that he'd thought that this would be fun. Instead it was pure torture.

What would Tom say about the commercial when it was released?

Maybe nothing. After all, it was just a little commercial. It didn't mean anything. He'd dreamed of being close to Jenna many times before, but just like then, this wasn't real. It was just acting.

Dustin looked into Jenna's eyes as if he were paralyzed. It seemed like it took hours for him to move close to her, to position his lips close to hers.

Dustin could hear the soft intake of Jenna's breath, and his heart beat faster. This was Jenna, the woman of his high school dreams, the woman who was always forbidden to him, the woman he admired from afar.

He got lost in the green depths of her eyes and then, in spite of Skip's direction to the contrary, his lips touched hers.

Dustin was kissing her!

Jenna tried not to react, to play it cool and act like his soft, sweet kiss didn't faze her in the least.

But her knees just wouldn't lock in place, and her heart was dancing wildly in her chest. Her face was so hot, she was sure that it would appear flaming red on film.

She slowly moved away from him surprised to see that he looked as shocked as she felt. Then he broke into a sly grin, the same grin that had charmed many a high school girl and scores of buckle bunnies. That Dustin Morgan grin was a killer, both boyishly charming and highly masculine at the same time.

He must be playing with her. Well, maybe the kiss didn't mean a thing to him, but it meant everything to her.

"Cut!" shouted Skip. "I like the kiss. It works. Dustin, put more passion into it. Everyone, let's take it from the top again and really give me passion."

Jenna tried to feel confident as she pasted on what she thought was a sexy smile. Her heart pounded as she slipped her arms around Dustin and ran her hands down the smoothness of his chest, then his arms. Jenna had always known that his arms would be thick with muscles and sinew, but she wasn't prepared for the rush of excitement that vibrated through her body at the feel of her skin against his.

She didn't know what had made her touch Dustin in such a way, but she figured that she might as well make the most of this opportunity. When the film crew left, it would be back to normal for them both—Jenna longing for Dustin, and Dustin treating her like a sister.

She watched as a smile teased his lips, but it wasn't his usual easygoing grin. Then Dustin's lips covered hers, lightly at first, then harder and more demanding.

Too soon, the kiss was over, and Jenna couldn't move, couldn't think. All she could do was remember that the camera was still on them. Excitement shot through her like a jolt of electricity, hot and shocking.

Dustin ran a finger down her cheek. They both leaned toward each other, touching foreheads, waiting for one of them to react. It was as if she couldn't believe what had just happened and neither could he.

"Cut!" yelled Skip. "That was terrific!" He turned toward the cameraman. "Tell me that we got that, kid."

"Got it, boss," said the cameraman.

"We'll add the voice-over in the studio," Skip said, checking his watch. "I can't believe how quick that was. Great acting! You should be a professional, Jenna. Any time you want a job, just call me."

I wasn't acting, Jenna thought.

She tried to reestablish eye contact with Dustin, but he was buttoning his shirt.

No matter what, Jenna knew that she'd never forget this day. The way he'd just kissed her…well, he was the one who should become an actor, because he'd almost had her fooled into thinking that he wanted her.

"I'll show you the way out, Skip," Dustin said, walking him toward the kitchen door.

As soon as they all left, Jenna eyed the pool. She wanted to go in—it had gotten pretty hot—but then her makeup would be gone along with her great hairdo. She wasn't ready to stop being Cinderella at the ball.

Then she sighed. Why should the hair and makeup matter when Dustin was just acting?

She walked to the diving board, hopped up, took four quick steps and did a perfect jackknife into the pool.

As she surfaced and began doing laps, she remembered how he'd bent his head toward hers and they touched foreheads. Was he as unaffected by the moment as she thought?

Hmm… She didn't have much experience in seduction, but even she could tell that he'd felt a spark, too.

Now she had to figure out how to turn it into an inferno.…

Dustin couldn't wait until Skip and his crew were gone.

He'd certainly made a mess of things with Jenna.

He could attribute the first kiss to the fact that a beautiful woman was only inches away from him, a woman that he'd longed for most of his adult life. And what a sweet kiss it had been, made all the sweeter because he'd waited *years* to kiss Jenna. And he wasn't disappointed.

Both kisses had rocked him to the soles of his feet and all the places in between. He'd wanted to wrap his arms around her and crush her body to his. He'd wanted to take her into his bed and make love to her.

He sighed. He'd just have to live with the memory of Jenna's kisses, but that galled him. After tasting her sweetness, he wanted more.

Looking out the window to the backyard, he

watched as she swam laps, the water sluicing over her shapely curves.

Jenna didn't need that silly magazine article. Nor did she need to be made up for a TV commercial ever again. Her natural beauty and personality were just fine. Perfect, in fact.

But obviously Jenna was trying to change herself for someone—someone who didn't appreciate her as she was. Just thinking about the ignorant fool who'd captured Jenna's attention made his blood boil.

What kind of an idiot was this guy?

Then it hit him. Could he dare hope that *he* was the one that Jenna was trying to seduce?

Nah.

But *could* he be the one?

If he was, he was one lucky cowboy—and there wasn't another with a thicker skull.

He watched as Jenna executed a perfect jackknife. Damn, he was hot and sweaty, and the cast was itchy. What he wouldn't give to join Jenna in the pool.

But maybe…

No.

Okay, so maybe Dustin did have a well-deserved reputation for being a ladies' man for a few years. And maybe that reputation had followed him into the present due to the inordinate amount of buckle bunnies who always hung around him.

Maybe he should have a talk with Tom and tell him that he'd like his permission—and blessing—to date his sister. But if Tom told him no, then what? Would he date Jenna anyway? Would that be the end of his friendship with Tom?

Or maybe he was completely mistaken that he was

the object of Jenna's attention, and he was hoping against hope.

But just the idea that he *was* the one sure made a cowboy feel good, even if it did pose a whole new set of problems that he'd have to deal with sooner or later.

After leaving the pool and managing to avoid Dustin, Jenna changed quickly into a pair of white twill pants and a royal-blue tank top. She slid back into her flip-flops and grabbed her keys. She was going to pick up Andy at school and talk to his summer school teacher, Mrs. Cummings. She wanted to know if there had been an improvement in Andy's reading and math work.

Besides, she had to get away from Dustin for a while and think.

As she drove, she thought about how his bare, muscled chest had felt beneath her hands. She'd known he was in good shape, but she hadn't been prepared for the heat that coursed through her body at the touch of his warm skin.

Jenna found a parking space in the front row of the parking lot and hurried into the school. The buses were lined up, and she wanted to catch Andy before he boarded.

St. Margaret's Grammar School was the school she and Tom had attended from kindergarten through eighth grade. The sisters were strict, yet caring, and they taught more than just the three R's.

She headed for the office and wasn't surprised to find Sister Elizabeth John still there. Her eighth-grade teacher was now the principal.

Sister was surprised to see Jenna. "What brings you here? It's lovely to see you."

"I came to talk to Mrs. Cummings and to give my nephew, Andy, a ride home."

"Go right ahead. Fifth classroom on the left by the cafeteria."

"Got it."

Jenna peeked through the class door and saw Andy sitting in the front row. Mrs. Cummings was going through a decimal problem on the blackboard, and called on Andy to answer.

He sat up straighter, then grinned as he figured out the answer.

"If my dad rides his bull for 2.3 seconds, Uncle Dustin rides for 7.35 seconds, and Adriano rides for 4 seconds, the total seconds are 13.65. The average of the three rides is 4.55 seconds. A little over half of what they need for a full eight-second ride."

"Excellent, Andy! Excellent." Mrs. Cummings clapped. "Of course, the problem is not about bull rides, but your answer is correct. Bravo!"

Bravo to Dustin, too, Jenna thought. It was Dustin who had figured out how to make learning fun for Andy, whereas Jenna had just bored her nephew senseless.

She remembered Dustin hunched over, intent on helping Andy with his math. It was quite the picture— a big cowboy helping a little boy. What a sweet man.

"Aunt Jenna...hi!"

As the classroom emptied out, Andy's voice penetrated her daydreams.

"Hi, honey. I heard your answer to that problem, and I'm so proud of you!"

Andy grinned. It warmed Jenna's heart to watch kids regain their confidence after a setback.

Mrs. Cummings walked toward them. She shook her head, smiling. "There's great improvement in Andy's math skills."

"How's his reading coming along, Mrs. Cummings?"

She saw a moment of hesitation from the teacher. "Andy's much improved in his reading, but we're going to continue to work on it."

"I'll work on it more with him at home, too. Thanks for everything," Jenna said.

As they walked on the gleaming floor with light green lockers on both sides, Jenna turned to Andy. "I think this great report merits some ice cream. Don't you think, Andy?"

"Sure!"

Jenna drove to an ice cream stand. They both ordered chocolate cones with sprinkles and ate them in the car, talking and laughing. When she pulled into the driveway of the Bar R, she saw Andy scanning the area. She was almost positive that Andy was looking for Dustin, just as she was.

Jenna forced herself to concentrate on parking the car, but then Andy let out a hoot when he spotted him.

"There's Uncle Dustin sitting on the porch," Andy said.

Jenna had seen him, too, and her stomach did a little flutter. She remembered how his lips had felt on hers—warm and tender—and she wanted more.

When she turned the vehicle off, she heard the click of Andy's seat belt. He grabbed his backpack and ran in the direction of the porch.

She saw the two of them speak, then Andy pulled a book out of his backpack and handed it to Dustin.

Jenna could hazard a guess by the color of the book's cover that it was Andy's reading book.

Was Dustin going to try to make the next reading lesson fun for Andy?

She hoped so.

Jenna felt a tug of jealousy. Here she was a professional teacher, and a cowboy without any teaching credentials was able to help Andy more than she.

As long as Andy was learning, what did it matter?

It didn't, she resolved, walking up the porch steps.

"Gentlemen, dinner will be ready in an hour, give or take." She was going to make burgers.

"Sounds good," Dustin said. "Can I help?"

She didn't know if she could be with him in the small confines of the kitchen. Didn't know if she was ready to inhale his masculine scent, or feel his wary gaze on her.

"No, you stay here and hang out with Andy. I have everything under control."

If only she did…

Chapter Six

Dustin rifled through Andy's reading book, but his mind was on Jenna. She was completely unaware of how beautiful she was.

"There's good stories in your book, Andy," Dustin said.

"Nah."

"Really. They look interesting," Dustin stated.

"Humpf," was Andy's reply.

Dustin figured that Andy would come around if he didn't push too hard. Sure enough, Andy soon got curious, and by the time Jenna announced that dinner was ready, Andy had read a story about saguaro cactus aloud to Dustin. They had a lively discussion about it at dinner.

But all the while, Dustin's mind was really on Jenna and the kisses that they shared. It was difficult being natural when all he wanted to do was to kiss her again. He tried to concentrate on Andy, but his gaze drifted to Jenna's lips.

It seemed that Jenna was focused on teaching Andy, but on several occasions, she turned to him and nodded, flashing him a big smile.

Damn. It made him happy when she smiled, made his day brighter.

As far as Jenna was concerned, if Dustin could get Andy interested in reading about saguaro cactus, then he could do anything.

As they were finishing dinner and Andy was excused to go play basketball, Dustin leaned over the table. "While you were visiting Andy at school, I found a magazine by the pool that I think might be yours. I put it on the coffee table in the living room."

"Magazine?" Her stomach churned. "Oh, yes. Thanks. I never finished reading it." She waved at the air, as if dismissing the importance of the magazine.

"Uh, Jenna?" he asked.

"Yes?"

"You looked great today. You know, during the taping of the commercial."

That was nice of him to say. She stopped in midbite. "I felt a little…odd, getting all fussed over, but it was interesting and a lot of fun. I can't wait until the commercial comes out."

"It was fun." He paused, as if working up enough courage to continue.

She waited, her stomach in knots.

"And Jenna?"

"Yes?"

"About that kiss…"

Her mouth went dry. "Yes."

"It was just part of the commercial. It didn't mean anything," Dustin said, his blue eyes locked on hers.

She shrugged and shot him an expression that conveyed it meant even less to her. "Of course. It didn't mean a thing. It was just acting."

She got up and started washing the pots and pans in the sink, scrubbing them within an inch of their lives.

Didn't mean anything? Wasn't he the one who kissed her first, when it wasn't in the script? Wasn't he the one who ran his finger down her cheek? That wasn't in the script, either.

That wasn't an act. He'd wanted to kiss her.

Jenna stole a glance at Dustin, but he caught her.

"What's wrong?" he asked quickly.

"Um… I just thought of something I forgot to do," she lied.

She tried to think over her wildly pounding heart.

Could Dustin possibly be lying to her, too? And why would he do that?

After the meal she'd just made, Jenna decided that she could use a little exercise. She missed doing her yoga routine. She hadn't done it since she'd arrived at the Bar R.

Changing into a pair of black yoga pants and a black sports bra, she grabbed her yoga mat and went outside to find a place where she could exercise without being disturbed.

She noticed Dustin talking to Andy and a couple of the ranch hands on the front porch. Jenna wondered if there were any issues about the ranch that she needed to address, but it seemed that Dustin was handling things. Good.

She noticed Andy walked toward the bunkhouse with the ranch hands, bouncing a basketball, probably hoping for a pickup game. Dustin settled into his favorite rocking chair on the porch.

Jenna decided that doing yoga by the pool would be the best place, so she cut through the wooden door that led to the backyard.

Facing the setting sun, she began her exercises with long, languid stretches—and then launched into several yoga positions.

She tried to concentrate on what she was doing, but she kept rehashing the commercial shoot.

Over by the lounge chair was where he first saw her in the colorful bikini. Over by the palm was where she first kissed Dustin. On the second shot, they'd kissed again.

She tried to clear her mind and concentrate on her stretching and breathing, but Dustin—the way he looked without his shirt on, the way he'd kissed her with contained passion, his smile, how he helped Andy—well, she just couldn't keep him from intruding on her thoughts.

She stood tall, starting the Salute to the Sun series, but out of the corner of her eye, she caught a flash of metal.

Crutches.

Dustin.

She turned to face him.

"I'm sorry," he said. "I didn't mean to disturb you. I just wanted to ask you something, but it can wait.

Please continue." He walked over to a lounge chair and slid into it.

He didn't look sorry at all. Matter of fact, he was grinning.

But how could she continue with him watching her? She couldn't.

Woman's Universe would advise her to take advantage of the situation, but that just wasn't...her.

Jenna rolled up her yoga mat and walked over to where Dustin was sitting.

"Believe it or not, I do some of those stretching exercises before every event. The PBR had a yoga instructor do a presentation with the thought that it might help us limber up, reduce injuries." He knocked on his cast. "Cowabunga had his mind set on running me over, so nothing could have helped me."

"You ran and dodged him as best you could, but he was like a freight train bearing down on you. And when he rolled you around on the dirt with his horns..." She shook her head, remembering how scared she'd been.

He raised an eyebrow. "It almost sounds like you care."

"Of course I care, Dustin," she snapped. Why couldn't he see that she'd always cared about him?

His eyebrows raised, just a little. "Well, thanks. And thanks for helping me out."

"What did you want to ask me?" she said.

"I'm so damn bored. I want to do something—anything."

"Like what?" she asked. "Like paint?"

"I wouldn't mind. It would keep me busy."

"I'd be happy to get your supplies from your apartment."

"Thanks, but—" He shrugged, then looked in the direction of the ranch hands.

"Are you afraid that they'll think you're not a real cowboy if you paint?"

"I just like being anonymous," he said quietly.

She shook her head. "Then paint in the kitchen. No one will know except Andy and me. Make me a list of what you'll need."

"Okay."

Jenna handed him a sheet of paper and a pen, and Dustin listed the supplies that he'd need, but his heart wasn't really in it. He could think of better things to do with Jenna than paint!

"Watch Andy for me. I'll be back in a while."

Dustin raised his eyebrows. "You're going *now?*"

"Sure."

Jenna felt his eyes on her as she headed into the house. She felt lighter, happier. This would give Dustin something to do, and she could watch him draw and paint. Fascinating.

A talent like his shouldn't be wasted, and she was going to do everything in her power to encourage him.

Dustin didn't want to paint. He wanted to hit the honky-tonks with Jenna.

He could picture her in his arms, moving to the music. Imagined kissing her again…imagined Tom breaking his other leg…

He looked down at his cast and swore under his breath just as Jenna came bounding out the front door and raced down the steps.

"Need anything else from your apartment?" she asked.

"I'm good. Just be careful driving."

"It almost seems as though you care," she said, echoing his prior words. Smiling, she got into her car and drove off.

I do care, Jenna. I've always cared.

He flipped open his cell and left another message for Tom. The sooner he talked to him, the better.

He'd told Jenna that their kisses didn't mean anything to him only because he couldn't let things go further until—unless—he got the green light from Tom. Because kissing her again would only lead to bed.

And that couldn't happen.

What a cozy scene, Jenna thought.

Andy was doing his homework at the kitchen table. Dustin was sketching on a big white pad and she was reading *Pride and Prejudice,* her favorite book, for about the hundredth time.

And she wondered, for about the two hundredth time, if Dustin was as clueless as Darcy.

I could get used to this, Jenna thought. If she closed her eyes, she could imagine a family of her own. The children studying, Dustin sketching or painting and she'd be reading.

Interesting how she'd put Dustin into her dream.

Soon, she noticed Andy's struggling to keep his eyes open.

"Andy, why don't you get ready for bed," she said.

He nodded. Standing slowly, he shook Dustin's hand and hugged Jenna around the neck. She patted his back.

Andy was old enough to take himself to bed, but she tagged along anyway.

"You like Uncle Dustin, don'cha?" Andy asked.

She nodded. "Sure. I like him," she said casually.

Andy tugged his T-shirt over his head. "He likes you."

"Oh, yeah?"

"Yeah. I see him looking at you."

She was about to pump the boy for more information, but restrained herself.

"Don't forget to brush your teeth, Andy," she instructed like a dutiful aunt.

She waited until Andy came back from the bathroom, then she tucked him into bed.

"I miss my mother," Andy said. "But I'm glad you're here, Aunt Jenna."

In all the time she'd been at the Bar R, Marla, Andy's mother, had never even called to talk to him.

"I know you miss her." Jenna hugged him and planted a noisy kiss on the boy's forehead that made him laugh. "I love you, Andy. Always remember that."

"I—I y-you…" There was no more forthcoming, Andy was sleeping.

She longed to give Marla a piece of her mind. How dare she ignore her son? Jenna just couldn't understand it. Her temper flared, but she tamped it back. She tucked the bed linens around Andy, gently kissed him on the forehead, then returned to the kitchen. She hurried over to the phone that was hanging on the wall, flipping through Tom's phone book.

"Everything okay?" Dustin asked.

"I'm just calling Marla. How dare she ignore her son!"

Marla didn't answer. Instead, a woman who identified herself as the housekeeper said that Miss Marla was in Cancún "with Mr. Josh."

"When are they expected back?"

"Two weeks."

"Do you have a number where they can be reached?"

The woman giggled. "They are on their honeymoon, but I have a number somewhere…"

"Never mind," Jenna said, hanging up the phone.

She leaned back against the wall, letting this new information sink in, wondering if Andy even knew that his mother had married again.

Jenna sighed. "I feel bad. He misses his mother."

"I overheard you on the phone. Marla's on her honeymoon?"

"With someone named Josh."

"Josh Eliott," Dustin replied. "I saw them together a couple of times at the Houston Livestock Show and Rodeo. He's a steer wrestler."

"Does Tom know?"

"Probably."

"I don't think he told Andy about Marla."

"Probably not. The last I knew he was waiting for a good time."

"I think the time is now," Jenna said. How could her brother not be around at a time like this? Or was Tom running away himself? She wondered if Tom still had feelings for Marla. Well, it was none of her business, but she'd make it her business if it concerned Andy.

She sat down at the table, but didn't pick up her book. Instead, she tapped her fingers on the table.

"I heard you with Andy on several occasions. You'd make a good mother," Dustin said.

She raised an eyebrow. "You think so?"

"I do."

"I think you'd make a good father. You're wonderful with Andy, too. You've helped him learn a lot."

"I'd love to be a father," he said quietly, then met Jenna's eyes. "Andy's going to pass to fifth grade."

She nodded. "We just have to make reading fun for him. Can you think of any books or magazines that would keep his interest?"

"The *Pro Bull Rider* magazine," Dustin said. "I have a copy in my duffel. It'd be perfect."

"Thanks, Dustin," she replied, then paused. "How many?"

He raised an eyebrow. "How many what?"

"How many kids would you like to have?"

He laughed. "Forty-five."

"I didn't ask you how many of the top bull riders would ride in Vegas." She chuckled.

"I'd like as many as I was blessed with." He looked deep into her eyes, and she felt her cheeks burn.

The thought of having children with Dustin made her feel warm all over. That's what she'd wanted before—children of her own—but since her "turning thirty" midlife crisis she'd mapped out a different course for her way-too-dull life.

"And, of course, I want a ranch," Dustin continued. "That's what I'm working for, Jenna. My own spread. I want to win the World Finals and retire."

"Good for you," she said. "That's a great goal."

"And what about you?"

"I want to travel, see the world, have adventures. I might teach in China for a year."

Dustin looked as if he'd just got head-butted by a raging bull.

"China? For a year? I didn't think that— I mean I thought that we'd—"

"We'd *what?*" she asked.

"Nothing. My mistake." He looked down at his hands that were intertwined together as if in prayer.

Jenna suddenly felt confused, weary. Dustin's plan of a home and children was appealing to her, but that was her old dream. Wasn't it? Besides, his plan didn't include *her.* She didn't know if it ever would.

"I'm tired," she said, sadness suddenly welling in her chest. She pushed herself from the chair, noticing the disappointment on Dustin's face.

Was it because she was leaving or was it something she'd said?

Chapter Seven

Dustin scratched his head.

They were having a good conversation. Why the sudden departure?

Dustin struggled to his feet and reached for his crutches. He was going to knock on her bedroom door and finish the conversation they'd started.

When Jenna answered the door, she greeted him with a thin smile, her green eyes misty.

Had she been crying?

He moved toward her, then stopped. What had he come here for?

Cursing under his breath, he pulled her toward him. His mouth slanted over hers, gentle at first, then demanding.

Then he broke away, raising his eyes to the sky.

"What am I doing?" he asked.

Jenna smiled. He took it as a sign that she wanted him to continue.

"We're making out." She chuckled.

"This isn't high school."

"No, it's not. It's better. Now, kiss me again, Dustin Morgan."

He did. He kissed her with every ounce of built-up passion that he'd had since high school.

"I want to take you to bed," he said.

This is it! Thank you Woman's Universe!

Dustin kissed her hand, and instead of being happy, a fog of sadness settled over her. Lately, she just wasn't herself—the big hair, the flirting, the bikini—all that was someone else.

Yet, Dustin wanted to kiss that someone else. He wanted to take that person to bed, not the real Jenna Reed.

What had she done?

She'd lost her mind.

"Jenna?" Dustin rubbed her back. "Did you hear what I said?"

"Yes. I—I did." She'd just wanted a fling, and now it seemed like the person who was about to have the fling wasn't even her.

"And?"

"Dustin, I just can't. It's not me you want." Regret welled in her chest. She walked to the bedroom door and motioned for him to leave. It was one of the hardest things she'd ever done in her life. "You'd better leave."

"Whatever you say." Dustin looked like she'd landed a sucker punch to his gut. In a way, she had.

"I'm so…sorry, Dustin. I'm really sorry."

* * *

It's not me you want.

What on earth did that mean?

Was she talking about that lame magazine article? He didn't fall for that stuff.

Oh, who was he kidding? He did fall for it. He fell for it all. And he wanted to think that Jenna had gone to all that trouble just for him, but he didn't know for sure.

She needn't have. Jenna was special just the way she was.

He didn't move. He just stood there like a lump—a broken-down lump of a bull rider who was still mooning over his best friend's very off-limits sister.

Even if he somehow conveniently forgot about his promise to Tom, how was he supposed to make love to Jenna with half his leg in a cast? Well, there were ways, but their first time together should be everything that he'd been dreaming of for all these many years.

He wondered if she was a virgin. Judging by her reliance on a magazine article, she wasn't all that experienced.

He should just come out and ask her if he was the one who she'd been trying to seduce.

There wasn't a bull he was scared to ride, but he was too chicken to hear Jenna's answer.

Later that night, Jenna sat in her room mulling over the past few days, and her experiments in the art of seduction.

Somewhere between the big hair and the makeup, she'd lost herself.

Yet in spite of everything, the Ten Ways had

worked! She should be thrilled. Dustin wanted to take her to bed. Wasn't that what she wanted?

After a restless night, Jenna got up early and made coffee. Sitting on a rocker on the front porch, she sipped the strong brew, still thinking of the events of the day before.

With any luck, Dustin wouldn't mention any of it.

The door sprang open, and Dustin hobbled out. "I smelled coffee."

Jenna got to her feet, searching his face and eyes for amusement, but there was none. "I'll get you a cup. Sit." She held the chair still for him. "You take it black, right?"

"Thanks," he said.

She roused Andy from his bed and instructed the sleepy boy to wash his face, comb his hair and get ready for school. Then she went into the kitchen to get Dustin a cup of coffee.

Back on the porch, she handed the coffee to Dustin. "It's so strong that a horseshoe could float on it."

"Perfect," he said.

"Dustin, about yesterday…and before…when I—I was trying to…"

He held up a hand to stop her. "Don't worry about it. I didn't mean what I said."

She raised an eyebrow. "About what?"

He looked at the door, then lowered his voice. "About us. About us sleeping together. It's a bad idea. I shouldn't have brought it up."

"Oh," she said, trying to swallow the lump in her throat. "I see."

"And I hope that the guy you like knows that he's one lucky stiff."

"I don't think he does."

Dustin grunted. "Then he's a fool."

Jenna bit back a smile. "No doubt about that."

Feeling restless, Jenna decided to go for a ride. So she saddled up a palomino by the name of Sparky. She always rode Sparky when visiting Tom and thought of the horse as her own.

Just as she was ready to mount, she felt someone watching her. Looking up, she saw Dustin silhouetted in the barn door.

"Hi," he said. "Wish I could join you. I'd love to go for a ride."

She shook her head. "Sorry."

He tapped the cast with the point of a crutch. "Just four more weeks with this thing," he said.

She felt an ache around her heart. He'd be leaving soon. Actually, so would she. Summer school ended in about three weeks, and Tom would be home.

She wouldn't be needed anymore.

Suddenly, she felt lonely.

But she'd be going back to school and she'd have a whole bunch of new kids to get to know. They'd keep her busy and keep her mind off Dustin.

"Need help?" he asked.

She laughed. "Did you forget that I was born on a ranch?"

"Not at all."

There was a long pause. Then he pushed his hat back.

"Damn. I forgot to tell you." He held up his cell phone. "Tom just called. He thought he'd catch Andy, but he missed him. He said he won the Memphis and the Billings events."

"Great!"

"He's leading the standings now," Dustin said.

"And now you're second."

"I expected that. I expect to be even lower as more time goes by. But the PBR's summer break will be coming up soon, so things will be at a standstill."

She took Sparky's reins and led her out of the barn. Dustin followed, then rubbed the horse's nose as she mounted.

"Where are you riding?" he asked.

"The ATV trails through the saguaros, then through the meadow. Just an easy ride; it's been a long time for me."

"Have a good time," he said, moving away from the horse.

Jenna walked Sparky behind the bunkhouse toward the start of the trail, and wondered if perhaps Dustin had wanted to talk to her.

She wondered what was on his mind.

He probably just wanted to reiterate that he didn't want to take her to bed.

Message already received.

She tried to erase the cardboard Jenna—the Jenna of the commercial and the Ten Ways—from her mind. She was going to go back to her regular self. She was a book freak, a suburban teacher, a mentor of two of her school district's most academic clubs, a rancher's daughter, a sister and an aunt.

She'd never give up her quest for adventure and love. But maybe she'd just go back to being herself and see what happened.

* * *

It was probably stupid of him to ride the ATV with his ankle in a cast, but he found that he could operate the hand controls quite easily.

With his crutches bungeed to the back, he took off down the path, following Jenna. He drove slowly so he wouldn't scare the palomino.

He paused at the trail where it opened up to the meadow, a kind of misnomer here in the desert. It was just a field with low scruffy vegetation. He and Tom rode ATVs and horses here all the time, but now Jenna was enjoying it.

As she trotted Sparky, her hair blew back in the breeze, its golden color shining even lighter in the afternoon sun.

Dustin could watch her all day. Her jeans were taut across her butt, and she wore a royal blue T-shirt and cowboy boots.

He liked this Jenna. He felt comfortable with her.

When he turned the handle with a little too much power, the ATV lunged forward. Jenna or Sparky must have heard it. Distracted, she turned sharply. Her horse stopped abruptly, and she fell from the saddle.

Dustin cranked up the ATV and hurried to where she'd fallen. He slid from the machine and hit the ground next to her.

"Are you okay?" he asked. "I'm sorry, Jenna. I didn't mean to scare you." His ankle throbbed, but he shook the feeling off. Instead, he pushed his body up with his hands to check her for injuries.

She stared up at him, her face flushed.

"Jenna, talk to me."

"You idiot," she yelled. "Don't you know better than to scare a horse?"

"I do know better."

She lifted up her head, and he slipped his hand under it as a cushion.

"I gave it too much juice. It just roared. I'm sorry."

She began to laugh. "I'm okay. Are you?"

He glanced down at the desert dirt all over his cast, hands and clothes.

"I'll live."

Dustin didn't make a move to get up. All he could think of was getting another taste of Jenna. He stared at her lips, and her smile faded. He looked into her eyes and twin emeralds looked back at him, a touch darker than usual.

He bent his head to kiss her and felt her hand around his neck, holding him close. With a slight groan, she met him halfway.

He tried to move, tried to feel the length of her body against his. It was impossible to position himself, but Jenna managed. Without taking her lips from his, she slipped under him. He felt her hands on his cheeks, down his neck, down the front of his shirt. He inhaled the sweetness of her, the smell of the sunshine on her clothes.

He moved as if in a dream, a dream that Jenna had starred in for so many years.

That reminded him of his promise to Tom.

Tom.

He'd forgotten to tell her that Tom wanted her to call him. That's why he'd followed her, he told himself. It was because of Tom.

He moved away, smiling down at her. She raised

an eyebrow as if to question why he'd broken the kiss. "I forgot to tell you that your brother wants you to call him."

She remained silent.

"It's nothing important. He just wants to talk to you about Andy's progress," Dustin explained.

"Okay," she said, scrambling to get up and dusting off her clothes. She didn't look at him.

Sparky was grazing nearby. Jenna gave a whistle, and the horse came walking to her.

He wished he could get up and not lie in the dirt like a snake, but his crutches were bungeed to the back of the ATV.

"Jenna, my crutches are…"

"On the ATV." Brushing off her clothes as she walked to the vehicle, she unhooked his crutches. Then she held them in place as he gripped them to boost himself up.

"Hold them tight."

"Dustin, I know the drill by now."

"Sorry," he said sheepishly.

With several grunts, he was able to stand up. She handed him the crutches and he slid them under his arms. Then he doubled over in pain.

"Dustin! Are you okay?"

"I'm all right. I just landed at the wrong angle."

"Maybe I should take you to the emergency room. Or at least to your doctor."

"I'll be okay."

"Don't be so damn stubborn!"

"Thanks, Jenna, but I'll be fine. I'll take it easy for a while." Sweat broke out on his forehead and upper lip. His ankle had bothered him before, but instead of changing its position, he'd kept kissing her. "It seems like I'm always thanking you."

"We've made progress, at least," she said. "Before, you wanted to do everything yourself. Remember?"

His eyes dropped to her lips. "There's some things that you just can't do yourself."

She smiled, knowing exactly what he meant, then climbed back on Sparky.

"I'll be back in a while," she said, then smiled even wider. "Then I'll make that important call to Tom, the one that you came all the way out here to tell me about."

She knew.

She knew that the forgotten phone call wasn't the only thing that had gotten him out here. He'd wanted to be with her.

The kisses were a bonus.

When he got back to the house, he hobbled up the porch, then collapsed into his usual rocking chair. He dialed Tom's number.

"Hello?"

"Hey, partner. I have a question for you. Remember way back in high school, freshman year, you made me promise to stay away from Jenna?"

"Yeah. I remember it clearly. Why?"

"I was just wondering if you're going to hold me to that promise." Dustin found himself holding his breath.

Tom was silent for a moment. "What the hell's been going on between you and my sister?"

"Nothing. Nothing. Just answer the question," Dustin said impatiently.

"Don't touch her, Dustin. This is my sister we're talking about. She's not one of your buckle bunnies."

"When was the last time you've seen me with a buckle bunny, Tom? Tell me."

Silence. "It's just that…well, Jenna's my sister. I don't want her to be another notch on your belt."

"Jenna's a grown woman with a mind of her own."

"I'm still holding you to that promise, cowboy. Jenna's something special."

"Damn it. I know that."

Tom clicked off the phone, and Dustin gritted his teeth until his jaw hurt.

What should he do now?

Should he go against his best friend's wishes and finally go after the girl of his dreams?

Jenna slowly paged through Dustin's sketch pad, not able to put it down. It wasn't as if she was invading his privacy, she told herself. She was just admiring his talent.

If he ever decided to stop riding bulls, there would certainly be a market for his paintings. His well-known name and legion of fans certainly wouldn't hurt, either.

He was also talented in other areas—the cowboy sure could kiss.

But why had he broken off their kisses so suddenly?

She knew his ankle was bothering him. She could understand that. He shouldn't have slid off the ATV to come to her assistance.

One thing she was sure of—now that she'd dumped the magazine and was back to herself, she didn't want to wait another sixteen years for Dustin to make another move.

The kitchen phone rang, and she picked it up.

"Hey."

"Tom! I was just about to call you. I hear you're winning event after event."

"I'm doing good. How's Andy doing?"

"Fabulous. I spoke with his teacher, and he's making progress. We have to work on his reading a little more."

"I can't thank you enough, Jenna."

"You'd better thank Dustin, too. He had a lot to do with teaching Andy."

"He did?"

"Absolutely."

There was silence, and Jenna wondered why. Her brother was never at a loss for words.

"Tom?"

"How is everything else going?"

"Everything's fine. Your ranch is running smoothly."

"Um… What about Dustin?"

Her cheeks heated. "What about him?"

"Everything okay?"

I want him, but he doesn't seem to want me.

She flushed if her brother could read her mind. "Oh, he's just impatient to get his cast off."

"Anything else I ought to know…uh…about Dustin?"

What was Tom fishing for?

"Not a thing."

"And you? Are you okay?"

"Tom, what are you trying *not* to ask?"

"Can't a brother just ask if you're okay?"

"I'm fine. We're all fine. If you're trying to ask me if you can stay on the road longer and hit more events, it's okay with me. Andy misses you, but I think he understands."

"Jenna, I'll be in Wickenburg for a bull riding on Saturday night. Do you think that Andy might want to attend? And Dustin, of course. Bring Dustin. I need to talk to him, get caught up."

"I'm sure they'd love to go."

"Great!" Tom said. "I'll call Andy about it later. And call me if you need me."

"I will."

"And Jenna?"

"Yeah?"

"Take care of yourself."

"I always do."

Jenna hung up the phone. Her brother was acting a bit strange. But for sure Andy would love to see his father and watch him ride, and Dustin was bored out of his mind.

Wickenburg was a little over three hours away, an easy drive, mostly on Interstate 10 West. Going to a bull-riding event was a win-win all the way around.

An extra bonus would be the fact that she'd be able to spend the day with Dustin.

Chapter Eight

Jenna drove the ranch's big red pickup down I-10 West.

Andy was so excited that he was ready to jump out of his jeans and boots. He'd been talking bull-riding stats nonstop, and about all the bull riders he would see. It would be the icing on the cake if his father won the event.

Dustin was mostly quiet, answering Andy with even more stats and riding percentages of the bulls.

Jenna had printed off the draw sheet and was aghast that Tom had drawn Dustin's nemesis, Cowabunga, in the long-go round.

"I hope my dad rides Cowabunga. He'll show that bull," Andy said.

"He sure will, partner. He sure will," Dustin said.

Even though Dustin carried on a lively conversation with Andy, he answered Jenna in short, terse sentences. It was as if he'd rather be anywhere else than in a tight truck cab with her.

Jenna pulled into a rest area for a bathroom break and for Dustin to stretch as much as he could. At the rest stop, Native Americans were selling jewelry and baskets, and Jenna paused to admire a green turquoise necklace that had caught her eye.

Soon Dustin was peeling off bills and handing them to the woman.

"What are you doing?" Jenna asked.

"I'm buying you a necklace," he said, waving off his change, and motioning to Jenna. "Turn around."

A rush of heat settled on her cheeks. "Dustin, you don't have to buy me—"

"It's my pleasure."

"But—"

"Jenna, it's nothing," he said tersely. "Turn around."

Tears pricked at her eyes. It had meant something to her. Dutifully, she turned around and lifted her hair up.

She heard him mumble, "This darn thing."

She turned and took it from his hands, unfastening the clasp for him. Handing it back, his hand closed around hers and lingered. Turning around, she tried to catch her breath.

She felt his knuckles skim the back of her neck.

"Lift your hair up again," he whispered, and she could feel the warmth of his breath.

The cool stones rested against her skin as he fumbled trying to fasten the necklace.

"Got it," he said.

She turned toward him. "What do you think?"

He gazed into her eyes. "Beautiful."

Her heart pounded wildly because he wasn't even looking at the necklace. He was looking at her.

Time didn't move. They didn't move. Until finally Dustin's eyes dropped to the green-blue stones.

He cleared his throat. "Beautiful," he said again, then turned and went to the truck, leaving her standing there. Suddenly, he stopped, and she waited for him to turn back. She wondered, hoped that he'd say something, anything.

But he didn't. He shook his head, then continued on.

"Thank you, Dustin," she whispered, fingering the necklace.

It didn't matter if it didn't mean anything to him—it meant everything to her.

Dustin longed to tell Jenna how he felt about her.

But he couldn't. Tom still stood between them.

It was getting harder and harder to keep his promise, though. So maybe it was time to move back to his apartment in Tubac.

But how could he leave Jenna?

In spite of his injury, this summer had been the best time of his life. He didn't want to cut his time short. After more than sixteen years of longing for Jenna, didn't he owe it to himself?

He swore under his breath. He was tired of psychoanalyzing everything from a dozen different angles.

He'd promised Tom that he'd oversee his ranch. But he'd also promised Tom that he'd stay away from Jenna.

Jenna walked toward the car with Andy, her blond hair shimmering in the sunlight. If it wasn't for Andy's chatter, there would have been complete silence on the rest of the ride, but the boy didn't seem to notice.

"There's a fair going on!" Andy explained as they caught sight of the rodeo grounds.

Dustin checked his watch. They had time to grab a bite to eat, let Andy hit some rides and visit Tom behind the chutes.

Dustin wasn't particularly looking forward to meeting up with Tom. He hoped that he and his friend could remain civil to one another.

"How about some barbecue?" Dustin asked, pointing with his crutch to a stand.

"Sounds great," Jenna said. "How about it, Andy?"

"Can I just have a cheeseburger?"

Dustin laid a hand on the little boy's shoulder. "Sure. They have those, too. And nachos with cheese sauce."

"Awesome."

They sat at a picnic table under the shade of a tent complete with ceiling fans.

"Will you go on some rides with me, Aunt Jenna?"

"How about the merry-go-round?" she asked, then chuckled.

"That's for sissies," Andy replied.

Jenna shrugged and made a sad face. "Then I'll have to go alone."

"I'll go with you," Dustin said quickly, shocking himself with the intensity of his statement. Jenna even looked at him strangely.

"I mean, that's about the biggest ride I can handle with this cast," he said, trying to look less eager.

They waited as Andy rode on every ride that plunged, pivoted and did a free fall to earth. While they were waiting, he noticed that Jenna sometimes touched the necklace he'd given her or fingered the silver chain. She seemed to be thinking.

He hoped that she was thinking about how pleased she was with the necklace.

Andy ran into a friend, Kyle, from school, and the boys went off with Kyle's parents to ride the roller coaster for the fifth time.

"How about that ride on the merry-go-round, Jenna?"

She looked at him and shook her head. "I'm sure you're just dying to go."

"I'm game," he said.

He handed the attendant two tickets and hopped up on the platform.

"I like the pink one with the flowing black mane," she said, mounting the intricately carved wooden horse.

Dustin mounted the horse next to her—a lime-green one with a light blue mane—with his good leg.

Please don't let any of the guys see me.

Thankfully, no one did…with the exception of the biggest mouth in the Professional Bull Riders, Cord Fetters.

"Well, Dustin Morgan," Fetters said, stopping at the fence that ran around the ride. "Be careful you don't fall off."

Fetters would have it all over the arena within five minutes that he was riding a green-and-blue horse on the merry-go-ground.

Dustin closed his eyes. The flack from the guys was going to be hell, but it would be worth it to see Jenna enjoying herself.

"Fetters, would it do me any good to ask you to keep your mouth shut about this?" Dustin asked.

"Not a chance. This is good stuff. This is what legends are made of."

Fetters scurried off as the organ music began.

"I'm sorry, Dustin," Jenna said. "I didn't mean to make you a laughingstock of the PBR."

"Don't give it another thought."

"But you're never going to live this down."

"Yes, I will," he said quietly. "I've lived down other things that were more serious."

"But—"

"Shush." He put a finger over her lips. "Don't worry about me, Jenna. I'm doing exactly what I want to do, and this is where I want to be—with you."

He could swear that her eyes looked moist.

What was he doing? He had to stop telling her what was on his mind and what was in his heart.

He was only leading her on, and he wasn't that much of a cad.

So from now on, he needed to keep his mouth and heart lassoed tightly and not let those lovesick comments escape.

That'd be about as easy as riding a short-go bull for a full minute.

Dustin stood close behind Jenna as she pitched plastic rings around milk bottles at one of the game stands.

She could feel the warmth of his every breath on her cheek, the low timbre of his voice hypnotizing her.

He gripped her wrist and moved it back and forth. "Aim for one on the end. Not in the middle. Take it nice and slow, nice and slow."

She missed. The ring bounced off the bottle and hit the floor.

"Three more tries," said the game worker.

"How many rings do I need to get to win that stuffed tiger?" Jenna asked.

"Two," he said.

"You can do it, Jenna. Easy now. Let it go when you're ready."

"I'm ready, Dustin." That little phrase had more than one meaning for her. She really didn't care about the orange-and-black tiger, she just enjoyed being this close to him.

Dustin continued to murmur encouraging words. She let the ring fly and got the bottle. Then another.

She clapped her hands and turned to Dustin. He hugged her to him, then quickly released her as if she carried the plague.

Taking her prize, she studied it. It was just a cheap carnival prize, but it would always remind her of today.

"I think you need some cotton candy," Dustin said, moving slowly on his crutches. "I see a stand straight ahead."

"I haven't had cotton candy in years." Jenna's mouth was already watering.

"Well, it's a mandatory item at a country fair, so let's go."

She picked out pink, and as Dustin was paying, she looked at the Ferris wheel. And suddenly, she had the urge to go on the ride with him.

"Ride the Ferris wheel with me, Dustin," she blurted.

"Sure." He pushed his hat back with his thumb. "Let's do it."

The wait in line was brief, and he gave his crutches to the ticket taker to hold. Hopping on one foot to the ride, he flopped into the seat. Steadying it, Jenna slipped in next to him and locked the safety bar in place.

She was going to ride on a Ferris wheel with Dustin.

Would he kiss her?

She rolled her eyes. She was acting like a high school girl!

She plucked at her cotton candy as the ride jerked them back to allow other passengers to board.

They went around, stopping and going, until finally they made complete circles. Then the Ferris wheel paused about three-quarters around.

Dustin leaned over and pointed to the corner of her lips. "You have cotton candy there."

"Would you hold this?" she asked, handing him what was left of the spun sugar so she could look for a tissue in her purse.

Instead of taking it from her, he stared at her, his blue eyes not blinking.

"Dustin?"

He wrapped his arm around her shoulder, pulling her closer to him, closer still.

Studying her face, he seemed to be thinking. Funny, she'd always thought Dustin was a man of action.

She waited, wondered. Should she make a move?

But she didn't have to wait long as his warm, full lips touched hers. His tongue teased the corner of her lip, and she opened her mouth for him.

Their tongues warred as he crushed her to him, breathing heavily, his lips never leaving hers.

Just as abruptly he let her go and stared down at the ground.

This was becoming a habit with him. "Dustin, what happened? What's wrong?"

But he didn't answer. He continued to stare at the ground. Then he swore under his breath.

She followed his gaze to the midway, where Tom stood, watching them.

She waved to her brother, but for some reason, Tom didn't wave back.

When they got off the ride, Tom hugged Jenna close, glaring at Dustin behind her back.

Dustin held out his hand and they shook, but Tom's grip was stronger than usual.

"Where's Andy?" Tom asked.

"With a friend of his," Jenna explained. "We're meeting him in the Agriculture Building by the butter sculpture at six. That'll allow a lot of time for you to take him behind the chutes so he can talk to the riders and look at the bulls."

"Here's three tickets, front row, center," Tom handed Jenna the tickets, then turned to Dustin, "Would you mind bringing Andy behind the chutes? Jenna, you could hold the seats."

Dustin wondered why she'd have to hold the seats since they had tickets. He could tell by Jenna's furrowed brow that she was thinking the same thing. Then he realized that Tom didn't want Jenna around when they talked.

"Uh…okay," Jenna said.

Dustin was dreading the moment that they'd have a confrontation. Today might mark the demise of their friendship and the end of their partnership, because he planned to tell Tom what he felt for Jenna. If that wasn't good enough for him, then so be it.

But they never had a chance to talk. Riders surrounded Dustin most of the time, making small talk and asking when he was going to return to competition.

"A couple more months, then beware," Dustin said. "I'm going to shake up the standings."

Andy was grinning from ear to ear, and he hadn't left Tom's side. Of course, he'd missed his father, and it was obvious that Tom had missed Andy.

From his position, Dustin could see Jenna sitting in the arena. She was studying the draw sheet, and suddenly she looked up and met his gaze. She waved, and he waved back.

A heartbeat later, Tom and Andy stood next to him.

"I'll see you after the bull riding, slugger," Tom said to Andy.

"Okay, Dad."

"Then I'm off to Idaho. I'll be back home in about a week and can stay for a while."

"Ride 'em all, Dad, especially that Cowabunga."

"You got it," Tom said. With a curt nod, he turned to Dustin.

"Andy, would you mind getting my bull rope over there?" he pointed to a lineup of ropes tied to a fence. "I want to show your Uncle Dustin something."

"Sure." Andy scurried off.

"I'm going to make this short and clear: stay away from Jenna. She's too good for you."

"I know that," Dustin whispered. "But I like her, Tom. I've *always* liked her. Always."

"You like every woman you've ever met," Tom said, meeting his gaze. "Look, Jenna isn't like the others you've been with."

"I know that."

"Jenna isn't…experienced. She hasn't dated much, and, well, let's face it, partner, you've been around. You have a reputation."

"I might have played the field, but with other women…well, it's just different. Jenna's special and I wouldn't do anything to hurt her. You have to believe me. I wouldn't lie to you."

"Okay. I guess you're right." Tom pushed his hat back and thought for a moment. "I still see Jenna as my little sister."

"She's not little anymore, dude. And you don't need to act as her father."

"I know, but…hey…" Andy appeared with Tom's bull rope, and that marked the end of their discussion. "Thanks, son," he said taking the rope from Andy. Then Tom turned to Dustin and nodded. "We'll talk more."

"I'm counting on that." Dustin tweaked his hat to his friend, and hoped that he would come around. Didn't Dustin deserve a chance at happiness? And he'd like to think that he could make Jenna happy, too. "Good luck tonight, partner. Call me."

Tom came in first in the long-go, and he rode Cowabunga for eight seconds without problems. He came in second in the overall standings.

After the event, there was a Team PBR autographing for the bull riders, and a line had already formed opposite Tom's place at one of the tables. There was no chance to continue the conversation with his friend.

Andy sat on a chair next to his father for a while, then began to tire.

"Time to hit the road," Jenna declared, motioning for Andy to join them.

After a traffic jam in the parking lot, they were back on I-10 heading to Tucson. It didn't take long for Andy to fall asleep between them. Right now, he was slumped on Dustin's left arm, and Dustin moved slowly to give the boy a more comfortable position.

"I had a wonderful time today," Jenna said, breaking the comfortable silence between them.

"Me, too."

He'd even ride the lime-green horse again if she asked.

He remembered their kiss on the Ferris wheel. Jenna tasted of candy and sugar, of carefree summer days and breezy summer nights.

They drove another five miles in silence until he spotted fireworks in the sky above one of the casinos off the interstate.

"I love fireworks," she said.

"Well, if you want to see them, get off at this exit," he said.

Clicking on her right turn signal to get off the highway, she came across a side street, where she pulled over to the side of the road where several other cars had stopped.

"Let's watch them from the tailgate," Jenna said getting out of the car. "But let's not wake Andy up. He's pooped."

Dustin hopped to the tailgate and released the latch, pulling it down. They both sat on it.

But he barely noticed the colorful explosions in the

sky; he only had eyes for Jenna. How her nose was perfect in silhouette. How her lips were made for kissing. How beautiful she looked in the moonlight.

Dustin took her hand, and he was rewarded with a smile. She squeezed his.

"This is so…awesome," she said, using one of Andy's favorite words.

"You're awesome," Dustin replied.

He put his arm around Jenna and pulled her closer to him. She was just too far away.

Jenna leaned back on her hands and looked up into the sky, brilliant with fireworks and smiled. He could watch her all day.

"This is just a magical night, Dustin. I haven't been out like this in…" She lowered her voice. "Well, I'm embarrassed to say."

"Don't be embarrassed, Jenna, not with me."

"I am."

He rubbed his forehead. "What about?"

"Well, I know you read that magazine article. I left it open by the pool by mistake."

"Yeah, you did."

He'd like to lie to her, tell her that he hadn't read it, but he couldn't do that. He smiled slightly.

"Tell me, Jenna. Who's the man? Who were you trying to seduce?"

She rolled her eyes. "You don't know?"

"No."

Jenna hesitated. "It was all for you, Dustin."

"I thought so. I'd hoped, but—" He tweaked the brim of his hat. "Why thank you, ma'am," he said, exaggerating a drawl.

She laughed. "I am so embarrassed."

"Don't be. It's the best thing anyone's ever done for me."

As the fireworks exploded overhead, Dustin kissed the woman of his dreams.

Then he made a decision.

Tom might never come around. He took his position as head of the family too seriously. Besides, it hurt him down to his bones that his friend really didn't think he was good enough for Jenna.

But he wasn't going to think of the past, not tonight.

Tonight would be the culmination of a perfect day.

Chapter Nine

Jenna helped a sleepy Andy find his bed. He collapsed into it, clothes and all. She unlaced his sneakers and covered him with a blanket, giving him a kiss on the forehead.

Closing the boy's bedroom door, she went to the living room and noticed Dustin standing by the front door propped up by his crutches. He'd barely entered the house.

"Come with me, Jenna," he said softly, holding out his hand.

She knew what he wanted, where this was leading. She found herself holding her breath as she took his hand.

Turning her hand, he kissed the back of it, and she melted.

"I want you," he said. "I've wanted you for a very long time."

His words washed over her like a velvet fog. She wanted to tell him that she'd wanted him since…forever. But the words wouldn't come.

"I wish I could carry you to my bed," he said, and her knees almost buckled.

Jenna laid her palm on the side of his face and smiled. "Follow me."

The walk to his bedroom had never seemed so long. When she saw the queen bed in the guest room, she chuckled.

This wasn't the place of her dreams. Whenever she thought of making love with Dustin, she thought of lush green meadows and misty waterfalls—not Tom's guest room.

But she wouldn't change a thing.

"Undress for me, Jenna."

With shaky fingers, she fumbled with the buttons of her blouse. Finally, the garment was free and she tossed it on a chair. This moment with Dustin was what she'd been saving herself for, for more years than she'd care to remember. She'd never wanted another man.

Dustin nodded for her to continue. She undid the clasp of her bra, and tossed it on top of her blouse. She stood in front of him, her breasts aching for his touch.

But he didn't touch her yet. "You're beautiful," he said, as heat rushed to her face.

"Your turn," she said, reaching for his shirt.

As she popped the snaps, her eyes never left his. When his shirt fell open, she ran her hands over the hard planes of his chest.

"You're beautiful, too," she said, then smiled.

He propped his crutches against the wall and shrugged out of his shirt, letting it fall to the ground. She helped him step out of his sweatpants and underwear.

Her eyes scanned his body. He was hard and strong, all of him.

"Kiss me, Dustin," she said softly.

"My pleasure."

As his lips slanted over hers, he crushed her to him, and she could see the evidence that he wanted her.

A tingling started low in her stomach, then gained intensity as it rippled out. This was Dustin Morgan, the man she'd fantasized about for years.

Dustin got comfortable on the bed, and she stretched out next to him. They lay together, kissing, smiling, touching and just happy to be in each other's company.

"Condom. My wallet," Dustin said, scanning the room. "Damn. It's in my pants."

"I'll get them," Jenna said, getting up. She picked up his pants from the floor and handed them to Dustin. Opening the wallet, he pulled out a foil packet.

In record time, he unrolled it over himself, and Jenna thought it was the sexiest thing she'd ever seen.

Her breathing came in short, deep pants, especially when Dustin pulled her on top of him.

She straddled him and, leaning over, kissed him as she guided him into her slowly. He filled her completely. She waited, not moving, just enjoying the sensations washing over her, wave after wave.

His hands were on her breasts, his fingers teasing her nipples, touching the green turquoise necklace that he'd said matched her eyes. It was the only thing that she hadn't taken off.

Her nipples were already hard, and now they ached. She wanted more. She began to move, feeling herself pulse around his hardness.

"Dustin," she moaned.

"I know," he said, breathlessly.

More waves washed over her, a forceful rush of physical and emotional release.

Then Dustin followed her over the edge.

Jenna had never experienced anything like this before. Granted, her experience was limited, but being with Dustin was everything she'd dreamed it would be.

Was it fate?

Dustin drifted back to earth, back to reality.

After making love twice more, Jenna was curled up next to him, sleeping. But he was wide awake, thinking.

Making love with Jenna was special. It was everything he'd dreamed it would be and more. She was a loving, giving partner.

What the hell did I do?

He'd broken his word to Tom.

Guilt rained over him like an Arizona monsoon. He could have gone to his room alone, but he hadn't wanted to. He'd wanted Jenna, and he'd wanted her tonight.

He'd been happy these few weeks at Tom's ranch with Jenna and Andy. For the first time in years, he'd felt like part of a family. It was only play-acting, he told himself, but now he knew that what he'd wanted all along—a loving wife, a good spread and children—would be perfect for him.

But he didn't want to come between Jenna and her brother, her family. And so he had to leave.

He slipped into his clothes, being careful not to wake Jenna. Grabbing his cell phone, he went out to the kitchen so he wouldn't disturb anyone and called a taxi.

"Yeah, I know that Tubac is quite a distance, but I'll make it worth his time," he told the dispatcher. "And I'll double the fee if you're here in ten minutes."

Going back to his room, he threw some clothes into his gear bag along with some of his paints, brushes and pens. He'd ask Tom to pack up the rest of his belongings and get it all to him.

He toyed with the idea of leaving a note for Jenna, but what would he say? I'm sorry?

It would be better if she hated him than for her to have to choose between him and Tom.

Then he waited on the front porch for the taxi to arrive to take him to his lonely apartment over an eclectic art gallery and gift shop.

Jenna reached over to Dustin, but all she found were crumpled sheets.

She didn't hear the telltale squeak of his crutches or sense his presence nearby.

Getting up from the bed, she slipped into her T-shirt and jeans.

She heard the sound of a motor coming from the front of the house, and she looked out the living room window. It was a taxi, and Dustin was getting into the backseat.

She yanked open the front door and stepped onto the cold floor of the porch. "Dustin? Where are you going?"

But he couldn't hear her because the taxi pulled away.

During the seven weeks since he'd left Jenna, Dustin hadn't had his head or his heart in bull riding. The San Antonio Invitational was his first event after recovering from his injury, and he had to ride two bulls and hope that he'd qualify for the short-go round to ride another. If he wanted to be a top contender in Vegas, he needed the points.

He couldn't wait to retire and have his own ranch. But he almost didn't care anymore. If he couldn't have Jenna, what was the sense?

Behind the chutes, he ran into Tom. They hadn't exchanged more than a couple of words since the Wickenburg event. Tom must have sensed him because he looked up from his conversation and nodded toward Dustin, then meandered over to where he was leaning on the chute gate. "What's up, partner?"

"Not much."

"How's the ankle?"

"It's okay."

Tom pushed his hat back with his index finger. "Keep your back straighter. You leaned over his head too much."

"Is that right?" Dustin felt the heat rush to his face. He wanted to punch Tom's grinning face.

"Yeah, that's right. I know you didn't ask for my advice, but that's never stopped me," Tom joked.

Dustin's hands ached from squeezing them into

fists. "You stick your nose into a lot of things where it doesn't belong."

"What's that suppose to mean?" Tom asked.

"It means that I love your sister. Now what are you going to do about it?"

"You *what?*"

"You heard me. And I swear, Tom, if you make some smart remark about me chasing buckle bunnies, I'll deck you right here. You know that I'm not like that."

Tom opened his mouth to speak, but Dustin held a hand up.

"I've loved Jenna since I started hanging around with you. And sure, I had some growing up to do, but no woman could ever take her place in my heart. That's why it looked like I was a womanizer. I kept looking for someone to replace her, damn it."

Tom whistled. "I knew you liked her, but—"

"I've always liked her. Now I *love* her," Dustin said strongly, then realized what Tom had just said. "You knew? You knew and you wouldn't let me date her?"

Tom put his hand on Dustin shoulder, but Dustin shrugged it off. "What would you have done in my position, Dustin? My parents had just died. I had to protect Jenna."

"From me?"

"From you! Put yourself in my place. You'd been around, cowboy. Jenna was naive. She couldn't have handled you. Not in high school, not in college. Probably not now."

Dustin wanted to put his fist through something, anything, but nothing was nearby—only Tom's jaw.

"Damn it, Tom. Jenna's going to be thirty years old. When will you think she can *handle* me?"

"Now."

"What?"

"You told me you love her. You won't hurt her now."

Dustin felt a sick feeling in the pit of his stomach. "You're so wrong, Tom. I've already hurt her."

Jenna accepted another flower arrangement from the delivery person and set it on the table to the right side of the door. She'd drop it off at the nearby nursing home on her way to work, just like she'd dropped off all the others.

This was the sixth arrangement in just as many days.

She opened the card and read it. "Please forgive me. Let me explain. Dustin." She tossed it on the pile with the others. Each card said just about the same thing.

It had been two months since they'd made love, since he'd walked out on her. Then suddenly the flowers started arriving. Well, she didn't want to talk, didn't want his excuses. She didn't want to ever see him again.

She'd wasted too many years of her life on Dustin Morgan.

Her face flamed when she thought of how she'd tried to seduce him.

In the end, what had worked? Her old jeans and a T-shirt, a wonderful time at a country fair and some fireworks.

And then they'd had fireworks of their own.

Jenna sighed. She'd thought that Dustin cared for

her—cared enough not to leave without saying good-bye or without some kind of explanation.

Had she done or said something that he didn't like?

She was tired of thinking about it, tired of wondering. And now, weeks later, he decided to apologize by showering her with flowers?

"No way," she said, fingering the yellow roses. "No darn way."

Walking into the living room, she turned on the television to watch the Columbus, Ohio, event. It was just her luck that a close-up of Dustin was the first thing she saw. Her breath caught in her chest.

He was being interviewed about his ankle and his rehabilitation. "I'm fine now. I had a nice recovery at Tom Reed's ranch, and the physical therapy worked. I'm as good as new."

The interviewer congratulated him on his climb back up the rankings to the number two position behind Tom.

"Thanks. Thanks a lot."

His smile lit up the screen, and Jenna could almost believe that he was there with her.

A commercial came on, and Jenna was just about to get some veggie sticks to snack on when she heard Dustin's voice again.

"Oh! It's our commercial," she said, aiming the remote at the TV to make it louder.

There she was in the bikini, walking toward Dustin, and she looked…fabulous.

And then they kissed.

Jenna remembered that it was Dustin who strayed from the script. It was Dustin whose warm, sensuous lips did amazing things to her insides. If she closed her eyes right now, she could relive every detail.

The commercial ended, and she smiled sadly. Even though she didn't go to Europe, she'd had a wonderful summer.

The doorbell rang again. If this was another flower arrangement, she'd scream.

But instead, it was a package delivery service. The delivery person handed her a box wrapped in brown paper. She knew it was from Dustin from the return address. She debated whether or not she should open it or just take it to the nursing home. After debating, she opened it.

It was the painting of the San Xavier del Bac Mission that Dustin had hanging on the wall of his bedroom.

She sat down on the couch, admiring it, thinking and blinking back tears that were stinging her eyes.

The ringing of her phone brought her back to reality. It was Tom.

"I saw that commercial," he said abruptly, without even a hello.

"Wasn't it terrific?" Jenna braced herself for Tom's response. For some reason, she didn't think he'd called to congratulate her.

"What on earth possessed you to do that?"

"The real actress was sick. I was there, so I did it."

"I see," Tom said, then there was silence. Jenna waited to hear what else was on his mind. "You looked good, I have to admit, and it looked as if that kiss was pretty real, and not acting."

Maybe it wasn't acting back then, but she didn't want to talk about it.

"Do you like him, Jenna?"

She took a deep breath. "Why are you asking me that, Tom?"

"Because if you do like him, I think I ruined things for you."

"How?"

"Dustin came to me, talking about a promise that he'd made to me way back in high school."

Her stomach roiled. "What promise was that?" she managed to ask.

"To stay away from you."

"Oh, Tom. How could you?"

"You were only a freshman in high school. Even through Dustin was your age, he was way ahead of you in experience. You were so naive back then. You still are."

"I'm almost thirty years old!" That explained a lot of things, like why Dustin pretty much ignored her. Then again, she was ignoring him. She'd made the same promise to Tom. "I can take care of myself. Don't you get that?"

"But Jenna—"

She cut him off. "But that was a long time ago."

"He'd asked me again about dating you. I told him no again."

Dustin had an attack of guilt, Jenna thought. That's why he'd left her that night. He'd thought he'd broken his promise to her brother.

"Well, you can just tell him that you changed your mind. This is my business, brother dear, not yours."

"I know that now, and I apologize. I had no business interfering. Like you said, you can take care of yourself, and it's about time I realized that."

She sighed. This was such a big mess.

"Do you like him, Jenna?"

"I think I love him."

There was silence on the other end.

"I'm really sorry, Jenna. I'll make things right. I promise," Tom said.

They said their goodbyes and although she knew where her brother was coming from, she was still miffed.

Dustin was constantly on her mind—their kisses, making love with him and the way he left without a word. He could send her all the paintings and all the flower arrangements in the world, and it wouldn't alleviate the hurt that she'd felt when he'd gone off in that taxi.

Tom pulled Dustin to a quiet corner of the cowboy's locker room in the Connecticut arena. "I'm sorry, Dustin…about Jenna. I really blew it with her…and you."

"You're apologizing?"

"I am." Tom nodded. "But you hurt her by leaving without telling her."

"I was thinking of you and your damn edict. Instead, I should have been thinking of Jenna." Dustin held up his hands in surrender. "I love her, Tom, and I think she feels something for me. Now give us your blessing and butt out."

"You have my blessing, but have you talked to Jenna lately?"

"No. She does not want to talk to me. I've tried. I've sent flowers…paintings… I just don't know what else I can do."

"Have you gone to see her in person?"

"No."

"What are you waiting for?"

Tom grinned, then held out his hand, and they shook. With Tom's blessing, Dustin felt like the weight of a Brahma bull had disappeared from his shoulders.

Tom raised an eyebrow. "I know how stubborn my sister can be if she's been wronged. It's going to be an uphill battle for her forgiveness."

Dustin nodded. "But it's a battle that I'm going to win."

It was open house at Wilson Reed Grammar School, and Jenna looked around her classroom and grinned. Parents and grandparents milled around the room. Everywhere were test papers with gold stars. On each child's desk was a folder with his or her work—math, spelling, essays, other tests and artwork. She always thought that art was a wonderful creative outlet for the kids. They seemed to love it, too.

Thinking about art reminded Jenna of Dustin. Actually, everything reminded her of Dustin, and she wondered what he was doing right now.

She was sure he'd moved on. She was just a one-night stand. But wasn't that what she'd been looking for, too? Just a simple seduction?

Now she wanted more. Or perhaps she expected more from Dustin.

Just as the open house was about to end, a man in faded jeans, a chambray shirt and a hat pulled low over his face walked in. He looked at the papers that she'd tacked to the front wall.

She'd know that butt anywhere. Dustin.

Jenna walked the last parent out. She and Dustin were the only ones left. Her heart slammed against her chest, and her mouth suddenly went dry. She cleared her throat.

"Dustin?" she asked.

He turned to her, and every nerve ending in her body started to tingle.

"Is there someplace we could go to talk?" he asked.

She was about to tell him that right here, right now, was fine, but the school would be closing soon. Then she debated as to telling him where he could really go, but she had to give him some points from driving from Tubac to Phoenix to talk to her.

"Are you looking for coffee or beer?" she asked, still not sure if she wanted to talk to him. As far as she was concerned, he'd done the unthinkable by leaving, and there was no excuse.

"Whatever you'd like," he said.

Suddenly she had the urge to go to the honky-tonk on Route 12. She could always watch everyone dance, if Dustin didn't say what she wanted to hear.

"That would be a beer," she said. "Follow my car." She wanted to drive herself in case she wanted to make an escape.

Fifteen minutes later, she pulled into the Cowboy Up Bar and Grill. It was the longest fifteen minutes of her life.

While driving, many things went through her head, including the fact that Dustin was here in Phoenix, and obviously he was going to try and apologize.

So where had he been for the past two months?

They walked into the Cowboy Up, and a wave of recognition for Dustin rippled through the noisy bar.

Fingers pointed, hats were pushed back for a better look, and there were several female squeals of delight.

Good grief.

She looked around, knowing immediately that she'd made a mistake by coming here. Cowboy attire was the dress code, and she stuck out like a sore thumb with her open-house teacher's attire—navy blue suit, a white crepe blouse, a pink paisley scarf, panty hose and sensible shoes.

The hostess was happy to give them a quiet booth in the back, but first he had to sign a menu for her. She held up a felt-tipped pen.

"I'd be happy to," he said good-naturedly, taking the pen. Her hand wrapped around his a little too long, and Jenna raised an eyebrow. The woman didn't care.

He signed his name, gave it back to her and was rewarded with an ear-piercing squeal.

She felt Dustin's hand on the small of her back as he escorted her to their booth. She steeled herself not to fall for his touch—she wasn't one of his buckle bunnies.

They could just be friends, that's all. Dustin was Tom's friend, and he could be hers, too.

Yes, friends. That'd be her goal.

"Would you like something to eat, Jenna?"

Suddenly she was ravenous. "Wings. Mild." And she was thirsty. "And let's order a pitcher of beer."

He gave their order to the waitress with the midriff-baring top and tight, faded jeans that were torn in just the right places.

"Oh-kay," she drawled. "I'll bring your order just as soon as I can, Dus-tin."

Coming here was a mistake. She could barely hear

him above the din of the place. She didn't want everyone knowing their business.

She wanted to leave. Right now. But they had just ordered.

Several people had gathered around their table for his autograph, and he was obliging. He talked to them, laughed with them and had his picture taken with them.

Jenna poured herself a beer, then took a sip. Then she started on the chicken wings without waiting for Dustin. When she finished eating, he was still signing autographs and talking to his fans.

Jenna slid out of the booth, grabbed her purse and left the Cowboy Up.

Chapter Ten

Jenna's phone was ringing when she got home, and she knew it was Dustin. She debated with herself whether or not to have her voice mail pick it up, then finally answered the call.

"Hello?"

"Why did you leave?" Dustin asked.

"Shouldn't I be the one asking you that?" she asked, referring to the night that they'd made love and he'd disappeared into a taxi.

"You're right. I'm sorry. I got caught up signing autographs, but I truly didn't mean to ignore you, Jenna. I didn't. I was almost finished when I saw you walking out the door. Forgive me?"

"Yeah." How could she remain mad at him? He'd gotten her point.

"Can I come over and talk?" he asked.

She'd like to talk to him and would like to see him—longer than she had at the Cowboy Up. "It's late, Dustin, and I have work in the morning," she said instead.

"I won't be long."

Relenting, she gave him directions and paced her living room trying to burn off her nervous energy. About fifteen minutes later, she saw his headlights flash through her front window as he pulled into her driveway.

Now it was time for Dustin to quit stalling and cowboy up. He had some apologizing to do.

Jenna waited until he rang her doorbell. Looking through the peephole, she waited for a few seconds so she wouldn't seem too anxious to see him.

He looked around as he entered the room. "Nice place."

"Thanks. I'm pretty proud of it." She motioned for Dustin to sit on the sofa, and she sat on a wing chair. Smoothing down her skirt, she crossed her legs and waited for him to speak.

"I want to explain about that night…and why I left." Dustin leaned forward, resting his arms on his legs. He clasped his hands, as if he were one of her students.

She found herself holding her breath.

"I left you that night because I felt guilty about breaking a promise to Tom."

"I know. I talked to Tom and told him that my life is my business and not his." She sighed. "But I don't know why I'm surprised. Tom has taken it upon himself to run my life since our parents died. That's why I moved to Phoenix, but it's still not far enough away from him."

They sat in silence for a few minutes, then Dustin gave a slight smile. "Look, don't be mad at Tom. He just wanted to protect you from me."

"Did he have a reason to?"

Dustin nodded. "I was young and reckless back in high school. And I probably would have hurt you."

She raised an eyebrow.

"Okay. I did hurt you." His sky blue eyes looked down, then met hers.

Jenna shook her head. "I guess I can understand your promise to my brother, but I'm going to be thirty years old in a couple of weeks, for heaven's sake. I'm not Tom's responsibility—I never was. I know he's always found it necessary to protect me, but for you to keep a promise that old…is just plain wrong."

"A promise is a promise. Besides, Tom is damn stubborn. He always was."

"It amazes me that you two have stayed good friends."

"I'm surprised that he suggested that I stay at the Bar R, especially when you were going to be there. The only reason I can think of is that he was doing me a big favor, and he expected me to keep my word."

"Still, you could have said goodbye to me, Dustin."

"I couldn't. You would have pushed for a reason, and I didn't want to come between you and your brother."

"And now?"

"We had it out. He gave me permission to date you."

"That was big of him."

"I—I told him that I loved you."

Jenna was speechless.

"You…love me?"

"Since as far back as I can remember."

Tears pooled in her eyes and threatened to fall. "Oh, Dustin... I love you, too."

His smile lit up his face. "Marry me, Jenna."

"Marry you?" Her voice cracked. She'd been waiting to hear those words for...forever. She didn't know why she didn't scream out "Yes!" but she didn't...she couldn't.

She tried to form the word, but it wouldn't pass her lips. Marriage to anyone wasn't in her plans right now. She'd promised herself adventure and lots of traveling. And there was the possibility of a teaching position in China.

"Dustin, this is all so sudden," she finally said. She had a lot of things to sort out.

"I don't want to waste another second without you."

"I need time to think," she said.

"What's there to think about?"

Jenna suddenly needed to be alone. She needed to figure out if the real Dustin was on a par with her fantasy Dustin. She had to separate fact from fiction.

She stood up. "I need time."

His smiling face melted into seriousness. "How much time?"

She shrugged. "How about the World Finals? I'll give you an answer then."

"That's six weeks away."

"I know."

Jenna snapped her fingers. She had a scathingly brilliant idea. "I think we should date."

"Date?"

She nodded. "I think we should get to know each other more."

"Know each other? I know everything about you."

"You don't know the *real* me."

Dustin sat back, looking serious. "Maybe you're right. Let's date." He stood but seemed reluctant to leave. "I'll give you a call tomorrow and ask you out, how's that?"

She smiled. "I'll accept, so don't be nervous about that."

He held out a hand to her, and she took it. His warmth enveloped her whole being. It felt right being with Dustin, but she wanted to be sure she knew him, not just her idealized vision of him.

But he said he loved me!

And I've always loved him…or was it lust? Or just a crush?

Dustin pulled her toward him, his hands spanning her waist. Her heart beat so wildly in her chest, she thought he could hear it. He kissed her so softly, so tenderly that she thought her heart was going to break.

She didn't want him to leave.

"Stay with me, Dustin. Stay tonight."

"Isn't this awfully soon for a first date?" he asked, eyes twinkling.

She took his hand and led him to her bedroom. Just inside, they dispensed with their clothes in a flurry of snaps, buttons and zippers.

They kissed and held the kiss until they fell onto her bed, tangled in the sheets and comforter.

"I do love you, Jenna."

Tears stung her eyes at the pure honesty of his statement, and she felt content and very much loved.

It seemed to take him forever to deal with the condom, but when he entered her, she felt happy, almost giddy. This strong, artistic, kind cowboy had asked her to marry him.

But was it too late for them? She'd made a life-changing decision to spread her wings, not settle down. But this was Dustin. Dustin!

She gave herself to him completely, yet she held back a little piece of her heart.

The next day, Jenna was called into the principal, Doug Patterson's, office.

"Hi, Doug," she said, slipping into the straight-backed chair in front of his desk. "What's up?"

"I got a call from the superintendent's office. Your application to teach English in China has been accepted. If you're still interested, you'll leave in a month." He shuffled through some papers. "It's a year's position. That's a long time." He looked at her seriously over gold-rimmed half-glasses. "Is this what you still want?"

Jenna's heart started pounding an excited rhythm in her chest. She'd applied for the position months ago.

"This is so exciting, Doug! I'm thrilled to have been chosen." She took a deep breath and thought of all the things she'd have to do to leave. "But I have to leave in a month? It's so soon. And what about my classes?"

"I'll have to get a replacement for you, of course."

A substitute teacher would be with her kids? Jenna's excitement dissipated. Of course they'd need another fourth-grade teacher.

And Dustin! What was she going to tell Dustin?

Her stomach churned. This was her dream job, and she had applied for it before she and Dustin became so close. Before…everything.

She took a couple of deep breaths. What had happened to the excitement she'd first felt? Now she felt sick.

"Jenna?" Doug asked, standing. "Are you okay?"

"I don't know, Doug. I have to think…"

"Think about it, and let me know by the end of the week." He smiled. "If you change your mind, that's no problem. The super can give the job to someone else."

"If I accept, will you hold my job here?" she asked.

"I'd take you back in a minute, but it might be out of my hands." He nodded. "I'll see what I can do, but I can't promise anything."

Jenna stood. "Fair enough." She held out her hand and they shook. "I'll let you know when I make up my mind."

Jenna's friends took her to the Cowboy Up for her thirtieth birthday. She two-stepped the night away with them and got asked to dance several times by various men.

But none of them were Dustin.

Due to his touring with the PBR, she hadn't seen him much of him since they'd made love, but the phone calls, texts, emails and gifts kept coming. She couldn't wait to watch him on TV, cheering for him until she was hoarse.

Her cheers for Tom were a little more reserved. She was still mad at him for interfering in her life. She'd called him and they talked for over an hour. It would take a while before Jenna would be able to forgive her brother, but it bothered her more that Tom didn't think enough of Dustin to trust him.

When Dustin called to wish her a happy birthday,

she'd told him about their gathering. He said he'd be there, but she doubted that he could spare the time to make a pit stop in Phoenix since he had to drive to Laughlin, Nevada, for the next event.

She shook off her problem with her brother and eyed the door like she'd been doing all night, hoping to see Dustin soon. With all the traveling he'd been doing, she'd definitely missed him. Her birthday would be complete if he could join her.

True to his word, he walked in a few hours later. He paused to sign a few autographs, scanned the bar, and spotted her waving to him. His grin lit up his face, then he made his way to where she was sitting with her friends.

After introductions were made, he tweaked his hat at her. "Happy birthday, Jenna."

She smiled, then got up and kissed him. Her heart fluttered when he whispered in her ear, "I love you."

Her stomach did a little flip. "Isn't that a little soon after our first date?" she joked.

He flashed his trademark smile and chuckled. "I guess you're right."

How could she leave Dustin? She just loved being in his company.

"Dance with me?" he asked.

She took his hand and they walked to the dance floor. It was a Texas two-step, and they fell into line. Dustin was a terrific dancer, and Jenna couldn't stop laughing as she bungled some of the steps.

They danced to a slow song, and her heart melted. Yet she knew she'd have to tell him about her possible job in China soon. Maybe later...

Jenna reminded herself that China would be the

adventure that she'd always wanted. It would be an incredible experience.

But as they swayed to the music, she wondered if she could leave Dustin, the man she'd always longed for. Now he'd asked her to marry him. Why wasn't she the happiest woman on earth?

Dustin pulled her even closer to him, as if he never wanted to let her go. His hand tangled in her hair, then he rubbed her neck. She closed her eyes and enjoyed the sensations coursing through her, capturing the memory. She might not see him again for a year.

The song ended and another began. She wanted to dance with him again and postpone what she had to tell him about China. An old Elvis Presley ballad came on the jukebox. The song spoke to her, bringing tears to her eyes.

Jenna moved back and met his gaze. "Let's go find a table. I have something to tell you."

Without waiting for his reply, she began walking toward a free table as Dustin waved off more autograph seekers.

"I'm sorry, everyone," he said. "I'm with a lady, and it's her birthday. I'd be happy to sign later."

They nodded good-naturedly and the crowd dispersed.

"Why did you do that? You enjoy your fans."

"I'll catch them later. Right now, I want to be with you before I have to leave for Laughlin tonight."

She felt elated that he wanted to spend what little time he had with her. She knew how important his fans were to him, and it made her happy that he felt she was more important.

They sat for a while at the table, listening to the rest

of "Love Me Tender." Tears threatened to fall as the song spoke to her and her situation. She didn't know how to begin, how to tell him that she'd be gone for a year.

Would he wait for her?

Dustin took her hand. "You got very quiet. What's going on?"

"I have something to tell you. It's important."

His smile faded. "Everything okay?"

"I was asked to teach in China for a year."

Somehow she managed to sound more enthusiastic than she actually felt.

He froze. "When…when did all this come about?"

"Actually, I applied for the job a few months ago, before summer."

"What about your job here? I thought you loved it."

"They said that they'd try to save it for me. If not, I'll just have to find another school somewhere."

Dustin shook his head slowly. "I thought we had something going, Jenna. I asked you to marry me."

"We do, Dustin, but we want different things," she said softly, hoping not to hurt him. "I still have a lot of living to do. I want fun. I want adventure. That's what I promised myself."

"So you're turning me down?" he said slowly, as if he didn't want an answer.

Jenna looked into his turquoise blue eyes. "No. Not exactly." She sighed. "I need more time."

He nodded, but she could tell by the expression on his face that she'd hurt him.

She was hurting, too.

"I see." Dustin looked past her to the dance floor. "When are you leaving?"

"Mid-November."

She could see the disappointment in the slump of his shoulders, the thinning of his lips—those perfect lips—and she wished she could turn back the clock to that perfect day in Wickenburg.

"I'm going to miss the finals. I'm sorry. I won't be there to see you or Tom ride. But I really hope you win."

"I'll win it. I'll win it all. And then I'll retire, find a ranch to buy and…"

She knew what he was about to say. He wanted a stay-at-home wife and a passel of kids. She hoped that he'd get his dream.

At one time, long ago, she'd dreamed the same dream as Dustin—a ranch full of kids and filled to the brim with love.

Now she was going to China—alone.

She couldn't ask him to wait for her. He should be free to pursue his future with someone who would make him happy.

She was going to China, to teach and travel and explore new places…just what she'd longed to do.

Then why did she feel so empty?

Chapter Eleven

Jenna was going to turn him down.

Dustin tipped his hat to her, gave her a quick kiss, mumbled goodbye and walked away.

As he walked to his truck, his mind was racing. Jenna was going to China? China was a million miles away from everything that he'd hoped for, dreamed of.

This was the worst kind of pain—the kind where his heart splintered into a million different pieces and no doctor could put it back together.

Dustin turned his car and headed north, to pick up Tom at a parking lot by I-10. Then they'd head for Laughlin, driving nonstop.

She wanted to travel, and he was tired of it. All he did was rush from event to event every weekend. He'd been doing that most of his life. After he won the finals in Vegas, he was quitting. He was going to settle down, either with or without Jenna…and it looked like it was going to be without her.

No. He'd wait for her. No matter how long it had to be.

In the glare of his headlights, he saw Tom leaning against his car sipping something out of a foam cup. Knowing his friend, it was coffee, strong and thick.

Tom had barely entered Dustin's truck before Dustin blurted, "What's with your sister going to China?"

"China? That's the first I've heard of that. What's she going to do there?"

"Teach English…for a year."

"Oh." Tom took a sip of his coffee, as Dustin turned his truck toward the interstate. "Where did you see my sister?"

"At a honky-tonk. It's her thirtieth birthday today."

"Oops. I forgot. And I forgot to give her Andy's present—it's a perfect paper in math and one in reading."

"She'll like that."

"Did you get her anything?" Tom asked.

Dustin felt the small box in his jacket pocket that contained a diamond engagement ring. "I bought her something, but then I changed my mind."

Tom dozed while Dustin rolled things around in his mind.

He'd known that she wanted to travel, that she was scheduled to take a trip to Europe and she gave it up to babysit and tutor Andy and take care of him. If she wanted to take *that* trip, he could understand that. He'd even go with her.

But to live in China for a year?

That just wasn't him.

He wanted to turn his truck around and go back and talk to her. He'd bring Tom. Maybe he could talk some sense into her.

Damn. What was he thinking? Tom had interfered enough in their lives.

Dustin had to be the one to talk to Jenna.

Could they work something out?

He was so shocked when she turned him down, he couldn't even think. There must be a solution.

He mulled things around his brain. Then it came to him. They could look for a ranch together—one that was already established—or look at land and build their own. With Jenna actively involved in picking out a ranch with him, she'd be invested in their future together. Then again, maybe she wouldn't want to do this.

"Where are we?" Tom said, half-asleep.

"About seventy-five miles away from Laughlin."

"You want me to drive?" Tom asked.

"I'm fine. Go back to sleep. I'll let you know when I want you to take over."

He doubted that Tom heard him. He was already snoring.

His friend had been on the road for a long time. Even though he'd gotten the money to make some improvements on the ranch, purchase more breeding stock and make the payroll, it had cost him dearly in time away from Andy.

Dustin had gone to Tom's ranch to ride some practice bulls, and he'd noticed how Andy was understandably clinging to his father. It was a tough life for a young boy—a mother who didn't care and was several states away and a father who was always on the road.

That's why he was retiring.

But if the woman of his dreams wanted to travel and he didn't, how could they ever compromise?

Jenna had fussed with her hair and spent an exorbitant amount of time on her makeup for her next date with Dustin. He was going to drive up from Tubac and she was going to drive down from Phoenix, meeting in the middle at Tom's ranch.

Dustin and Tom were shooting hoops with Andy when she arrived. They all stopped when she parked.

When she got out of the car, she heard Dustin whistle long and low. Butterflies settled in her stomach. He thought she was beautiful, made up or not.

"Aunt Jenna!" Andy yelled.

"How are you, sweetie?" she asked.

"I got an A in math and an A in reading."

"Good for you!"

She nodded at Tom. She'd talk to him sometime when Andy wasn't around. Surprisingly, he stepped toward her, pulling her into a hug.

Tom took Andy inside to make him lunch, and Jenna and Dustin were alone.

She moved in front of him and leaned forward to give him a kiss. He enveloped her in his arms.

"I've missed you."

"I've missed you, too." She felt warm in his embrace.

"So, where are we going? You wouldn't tell me on the phone."

"I thought you could help me check out a ranch that's for sale near the Catalina foothills off River Road."

"You want me to look at a ranch, Dustin?" She furrowed her brow, realizing the significance.

"Yeah." He put a hand on her shoulder. "I'm a cowboy, Jenna. I've been looking at ranches. A pal told me about this one, and I want your opinion. Then we'll go out to eat."

She knew the area they were going to visit. It was beautiful country, and several ranches remained in spite of the condos, apartments and single-family houses springing up around them.

Dustin said that he wanted her opinion, but Jenna knew it was more than that. He wanted her to help him pick out *their* future home.

"Dustin, I don't— I can't—" She took a deep breath and let it out, trying to relax.

"I understand. Your message was loud and clear. But I still want you go to with me."

"But why don't you take Tom with you? He's the rancher, not me."

"I know, but he's not you."

She sighed. "Okay. I'll go."

He smiled. "Thanks."

She closed her eyes, remembering their last conversation about marriage she'd turned him down and said that she needed more time. But the clock was ticking. She needed to let Principal Patterson know if she'd be taking the job in China—or not.

"You're in a good position to win the finals, Dustin. Is that why you're looking at ranches?"

He nodded. "Keep your fingers crossed. Our...er... *my* future depends on that win."

He'd really meant *our* future.

Jenna swallowed the lump in her throat. She hadn't wanted to fall in love with Dustin, but she had.

Hadn't she just want to seduce him? Well, she'd certainly done a great job.

They turned left onto River Road, and Jenna noticed several llamas on one ranch, their heads on long necks observing the vehicles that passed.

They passed by more ranches. Finally, Dustin slowed and made a left turn.

A burgundy-colored ranch house came into view— a sprawling Santa Fe structure with large windows overlooking a corral of horses. Sprawling prickly pear cactus and stately saguaros with their arms reaching to the sky were part of the natural landscaping around the house.

A porch ran the length of the front, and inviting white rocking chairs were positioned at even intervals.

"I love it already," Jenna said. "It's gorgeous and so homey. I can't wait to see inside."

"I hope you like it."

She could just picture herself rocking on the porch next to Dustin and looking at the beautiful scenery. She could get a teaching job in Tucson if she lived here.

Jenna didn't know what to do. She'd wanted Dustin as far back as she could remember. Now, when her dream was about to come true, she was hesitating.

She loved Dustin with her whole heart, but marriage would be the ultimate in settling down.

She owed him a decision.

What on earth was she going to do?

Dustin parked in the driveway next to the ranch house, and a man in jeans and a red Arizona Wildcats sweatshirt waved to them.

"Then you liked the house?"

"I did. I do. It's perfect," she said.

"I have a couple more places to look at. Do you want to go with me?"

"Dustin, I don't think that any other place would top this one."

"I agree, but I think I'll look anyway."

She nodded and spoke softly, "Whether or not we get married, I hope you buy the ranch of your dreams."

Dustin stared straight ahead, but his knuckles gripping the steering wheel were white. Jenna could sense the tension emanating from him.

"You know, Dustin, I've been asleep for thirty years. You might say that I've just woken up."

"You've been busy with your career," he said. "And I know, I know, you want adventure. But did you ever think that marriage could be an adventure?"

She'd never thought of it that way, but it would be a whole new life—and she'd be living it with the man she'd always loved.

"Do you know the name of the ranch?" Dustin finally said, his grip on the steering wheel not lessening.

"No."

"The Rocking JD."

"Dustin, those are our initials!"

"I know."

It was meant to be.

Married life could be an adventure.

The mantras kept rolling around in her head.

"We can't take all the credit." Dustin chuckled. "The ranch was named after the first settler of this area, J. D. Fordham."

She didn't care about the first settler. All she cared

about was trying to figure out if she should accept Dustin's proposal or not.

Still, the Rocking JD weighed heavy on her mind. She'd be happy there with Dustin.

Wouldn't she?

Dustin relaxed his grip on the steering wheel and took a couple of deep breaths. He'd thought that seeing the Rocking JD would nudge Jenna to accept his proposal.

Damn it. He'd thought she'd fall into his arms screaming "yes!"

He was pretty sure that it wasn't him. Settling down wasn't in her plans.

"Jenna, I've traveled a lot since I turned sixteen. That's fourteen years. I've given up most every weekend. If I ride in extra events, I'm traveling during the week, too. I want to stay put."

"You know, Dustin…when you go to a PBR event, you're in and out. You don't have time to get a feel for the area. You don't have time to go to museums or the historical society. You don't have time to try the local restaurants or have nice talks with the people."

Her face glowed with excitement, and her eyes sparkled just talking about traveling.

"That's true," he said.

"Wouldn't you like to do all that?" she asked.

"It sounds good." Or maybe it was Jenna's enthusiasm that made it sound good.

Dustin thought for a moment. "If I don't win the PBR Finals, maybe I'll stick around for another year and keep riding the circuit. You could travel with me. We could explore each city that I'm going to ride in."

"Travel with you for a year?" She tilted her head. "That would be wonderful. Besides, I could keep the buckle bunnies away from you."

He grinned. "If I win the finals, we could still travel, Jenna, to wherever you want. And if you want to go to China, well, could we just visit instead of staying there for a year?"

"Yes." She studied him. "You'd do that for me?"

"I would. But whether I win or lose, I'm buying the Rocking JD. I don't want someone else to buy it out from under me…us."

"I don't want you to lose it, either. I really love that ranch, Dustin."

"I can't picture anyone else living there but us, Jenna. I don't want to live there alone."

He waited for the big "yes" from her, but it didn't happen. What more could he do?

They drove in silence until they arrived at the steakhouse that Dustin wanted to try.

Getting out of the car, they held hands for a while, admiring the desert landscaping around the restaurant. It was similar to the landscaping around the Rocking JD.

Damn, Dustin thought, stealing another glance at Jenna. He was still waiting for her to be excited about his proposal, but it seemed that she was making her decision a tedious chore. Then again, she was deciding her entire future.

He pulled her into his arms and held her. He kissed her gently, then he broke the kiss and studied her face.

This was his Jenna, and he was all hers.

He hugged her and she rested her head on his shoulder. He heard a contented sigh. Didn't she know how right this felt—the two of them together like this? Together they could weather any storm, tackle any problems, run a ranch...

"You'll always come first with me, Jenna. Not the ranch, so don't worry about that," he said with confidence. "I can think of a dozen guys who could ramrod our ranch when we're not there."

"Our ranch," she whispered, and he could tell she liked the idea. "I could always teach here in Tucson."

His heart soared. Her response was a positive sign.

Jenna wrapped her arms around his neck and kissed him. It rattled him to the core. Couldn't she feel that they were meant for each other? If it weren't for her brother, they would have been together long ago. For sure, they'd even have a house full of kids by now.

"Jenna, I don't want to push you into giving me an answer. It's just that we've both been waiting for each other for...forever. I'm just hoping that you make the right decision, because I don't want to wait much longer."

"You'll have my answer at the finals, Dustin. I promise."

Epilogue

Jenna took her seat at the Thomas and Mack Center on the grounds of the University of Nevada at Las Vegas and settled down to watch the last day of bull riding.

The points were close, and she was already caught up in the excitement that seemed to fill the arena.

Her brother was first in the standings, but Dustin was a close second. The bull rider in third place, Ronnie Bugnacki, could win the event, too.

But they all had to ride their two bulls. One in the long-go, and one in the short-go.

The arena announcer was talking about how close the race was as the huge screens in the middle of the ceiling showed the top rides of the year by the top three riders.

Today would decide the winner.

Jenna sat on her hands so she wouldn't bite her nails.

Dustin could almost buy the Rocking JD Ranch with the money he'd win. Her brother could pay off the mortgage on his ranch and have enough left over for improvements.

Who would it be?

Jenna fingered the two signs on her lap. One of them was for Tom, the other for Dustin.

Today was the day that she'd promised Dustin that she'd give him her answer. She was content, knowing that she'd made the right decision. It was right for both of them.

As the event began, two "bulls" at each side of the bucking chutes spewed fire from their mouths.

"This is not a rodeo," said the announcer. "This is the PBR!"

The arena dirt suddenly came alive with the letters PBR outlined in fire.

The people in the stands shouted and clapped. It was almost time for the first ride.

Jenna looked at the arena clock behind the bucking chutes. The digital numbers ticking away reminded her that her life was going to change that fast.

The big screen in the middle of the arena showed Dustin tying his bull rope around Red Wine. Dustin gave a quick grin to the camera, flashing his brilliant smile. The men cheered as many of the women in the arena screamed in excitement. Jenna's heart pounded wildly in her chest.

"C'mon, Dustin. Reach for your dream," she said quietly.

Dustin rode Red Wine for eight seconds and made

a good get-off. The arena exploded. His score was ninety. The confetti guns popped as colorful streamers and bits of paper rained over everyone.

She saw Dustin looking around for her. When their eyes met, she waved, and he tipped his hat to her. The heat rushed to Jenna's face as dozens of people looked to see who Dustin Morgan was singling out. Jenna couldn't stop the stupid grin from appearing on her face.

She loved him. She didn't care who knew it. And she'd always love him, no matter what.

She touched the sign that she'd made for Dustin. He had one more bull to ride in the short-go. And the short-go bulls were the toughest yet.

Tom did just as well on Hard Luck and Jenna screamed. She held up a yellow sign with red letters that said, "Go Tom!" He received an eighty-eight.

Dustin had to beat Tom's total score by two points. Then he'd win the finals. He would win the aggregate for the year, too. Two little points.

Jenna sat through eight riders in the short-go. Now it was Tom's turn. He barely stayed on his bull and was hanging off the side of it at the time the buzzer sounded. He wouldn't get very many points due to his style, but he'd get a score. He got an eighty-four.

All Dustin had to do was get a score of eighty-six. It was high, but not impossible on the short-go bulls. He drew a bull named Eliminator, and Jenna hoped that wasn't a sign of things to come.

She held her breath when Dustin nodded his head. Eliminator exploded out of the chute and immediately turned right, into Dustin's hand. A good sign. The bull did four fast rotations, then switched sides and did four more. Dustin stayed on, clinging to the bull like a piece of lint. Finally, the buzzer sounded, and Dustin made a clean get-off, landing on his feet, but then he fell onto the dirt. Eliminator charged, and Jenna screamed, but Dustin was saved by the bullfighters who distracted the bull and got Eliminator to leave the arena.

Quiet settled over the crowd like a thick blanket as Dustin's scores came in. The third judge seemed like he was taking his sweet old time, and Jenna was running out of breath.

Ninety-two! Dustin got his two points and more for good measure. The arena went wild. More confetti spewed out of the guns. Dustin was hoisted up on the shoulders of several other riders. Someone gave him the American flag and he held it high.

Jenna's heart pounded in her chest, and excitement ran through her like an electric shock.

She was happy for Dustin. All his dreams were falling into place.

It was then that she held up her sign. She'd painted it in big black letters on yellow poster board. It said, "I'd love to marry you!"

He saw her and the sign, and a grin split his face. He motioned to his friends to let him down, and he ran toward her.

Climbing into the stands, he gripped her hand. "Are you sure?" he said.

"I'm positive," she said. "I love you, Dustin."

"I love you, Jenna."

He kissed her, and they both smiled.

Jenna put her index finger over his lips. "Let's buy that ranch and fill it with children."

"Agreed!" Dustin exclaimed, then sobered. "I do

have a present for you." He pulled out a beat-up envelope from the pocket of his jeans and handed it to her.

With shaky hands she opened it and pulled out its contents. Two tickets to Europe. A cruise! Tears flooded her eyes. "I've always wanted to go on a cruise."

A fan thrust a pen and a program at Dustin for him to sign. Dustin pushed it back. "Hang on. I'm proposing here." He knelt on one knee. "Marry me?"

She held up the sign again. "I'd love to marry you, cowboy."

"Good." Dustin laughed. "It's about time."

Jenna grinned as she pulled him to his feet and into her arms for a big kiss.

Applause erupted around them in the stands, and Jenna realized that the camera was on them. They were on the big screen.

Jenna didn't know what the world had in store, but she knew, just like Dustin said, and as sure as her heart was beating, that their marriage would be an adventure.

* * * * *

Since 2006, *New York Times* bestselling author
Cathy McDavid has been happily penning
contemporary Westerns for Harlequin. Every day,
she gets to write about handsome cowboys riding
the range or busting a bronc. It a tough job, but
she's willing to make the sacrifice. Cathy shares
her Arizona home with her own real-life sweetheart
and a trio of odd pets. Her grown twins have left to
embark on lives of their own, and she couldn't be
prouder of their accomplishments.

Books by Cathy McDavid

Harlequin Western Romance

Mustang Valley

Last Chance Cowboy
Her Cowboy's Christmas Wish
Baby's First Homecoming
Cowboy for Keeps
Her Holiday Rancher
Come Home, Cowboy
Having the Rancher's Baby
Rescuing the Cowboy
A Baby for the Deputy
The Cowboy's Twin Surprise

Harlequin American Romance

Reckless, Arizona

More Than a Cowboy
Her Rodeo Man
The Bull Rider's Son

Visit the Author Profile page at
Harlequin.com for more titles.

HER COWBOY'S
CHRISTMAS WISH

CATHY McDAVID

To my own darling Caitlin. You were truly the most beautiful baby ever born. I'm not exactly sure when you grew up into this incredible, lovely and supersmart young woman, but it happened. And I couldn't be any prouder. Love you forever, Mom.

Chapter 1

The big buckskin reared—at least he tried to rear. His thick, rangy body was too confined by the narrow chute, so he achieved little height. Frustrated, he pawed the ground, then backed up and banged into the panel with such force the reverberation carried down the metal railing like an electrical current.

"He's an ornery one," the cowboy sitting astride the fence said. "And smarter than he looks."

Ethan Powell considered the man's assessment of the horse he was about to ride, and decided he agreed. The buckskin was ornery and smart, and would enjoy nothing better than stomping Ethan into the ground.

Exactly the kind of saddle bronc he preferred. The kind he'd hoped to draw when he'd competed professionally. Nowadays his rodeo riding was restricted to this small, local arena and for "personal enjoyment" only. No sanctioned rodeo, or unsanctioned rodeo for that matter, would allow him to enter.

He understood. He just didn't like it, and was determined to change the Duvall Rodeo Arena's policies, if not the entire Professional Rodeo Cowboys Association. Before he could do that, however, he had to prove he still had what it took to go up against men who were, for the most part, younger than him and, without exception, physically whole.

"You gonna stand there all night, Powell?" the cowboy asked.

In the chute beside Ethan, the buckskin lifted his head and stared straight ahead, every muscle in his body bunched tight with anticipation.

Just like Ethan.

"Yeah, I'm ready."

Shielding his eyes from the bright floodlights that lit the arena, he climbed the fence and straddled it alongside the wrangler. Then he took another few seconds to study the bronc up close.

"Good luck," the cowboy said.

Ethan would need more than luck if he expected to ride this bad boy for eight seconds.

He'd been on plenty of unbroken and green broke horses in the last year. There was, however, a world of difference between those animals and one bred and trained to give a man the ride of his life.

Drawing a deep breath, he braced a hand on either side of the chute and lowered himself onto the buckskin's back inch by inch. Twice he paused, waiting for the big horse to settle. Once in the saddle, he took hold of the reins and slipped his feet into the stirrups, careful to keep his toes pointed forward.

The buckskin, eager to give his rider a preview of what was to come, twisted sideways. Ethan's left ankle was momentarily pinned between the horse's broad body and the chute. It might have hurt if he had any feeling in his lower leg.

He didn't and probably never would, unless medical science developed a prosthetic device with artificial nerve endings that could transmit sensation to the wearer.

When his ankle was freed and the buckskin was once again in position, Ethan slid the reins back and forth through his gloved hands until the grip felt right.

The moment the horse committed, he nodded to the wrangler manning the gate and said, "Go," hoping like heck he wasn't making a huge mistake.

With a loud metallic whoosh the gate slid open. Ethan tried to straighten his legs and set his spurs. He didn't quite make it. The prosthesis he wore failed to respond as quickly as his real leg did.

The buckskin lunged out of the chute and into the arena. Only his front feet touched the ground. His hind ones were raised high above his head as he tried to kick the moon out of the sky.

Ethan didn't have time to mark his horse, much less find his rhythm. With his weight unevenly distributed, the buckskin easily unseated him and sent him sailing through the air. Ethan barely glimpsed the ground as it came rushing up to meet him.

His shoulder absorbed the brunt of the impact, which he supposed was better than his face or prosthetic leg. That was until he moved. Pain, razor sharp and searing hot, ripped through him. He decided it was better to just lie there for a second or two longer.

Shouting, which seemed to come from far away, told him the buckskin had been safely rounded up and was probably gloating.

"Need help?"

Ethan glanced up, then away. What he'd dreaded the most had just happened.

"Nope, I'm fine," he told the pickup man looming above him. At least the guy hadn't gotten off his horse before offering his assistance. That would have been even more humiliating.

Ethan pushed up on one elbow, the one not throbbing, then climbed to his knees. Getting his good leg under him was a little tricky, especially given the way the world was spinning. He could feel the eyes of the crowd on him, with everyone likely wondering if he was going to rise under his own power and take on another bronc.

The answer was *damn straight*.

In a minute, after he could move his shoulder and arm without having flashes of color pulsate before his eyes.

"The first time's the hardest," the pickup man commented.

"So they say."

Except this wasn't Ethan's first time bronc riding. It was his first time since losing his leg fifteen months ago, while serving in the Middle East. He'd loved the marines almost as much as he loved rodeoing. Now both were lost to him.

Maybe not rodeoing, he corrected himself.

Standing upright, he brushed off his jeans and readjusted his hat, which had miraculously stayed on during the fall. Then he walked to the gate, doing his best not to limp. It wasn't easy. Another cowboy held the gate open for him and clapped him on the back as he passed. The resulting pain almost drove Ethan to his knees, but he didn't so much as blink.

Outside the arena, he paused to catch his breath. This wasn't going exactly as planned.

"Hey, Ethan!"

He lifted his head to see his childhood friend Clay Duvall approaching, his gait brisk as usual. Ethan and Clay had been close up until their early twenties, when Ethan's mother had died from complications following a heart transplant, and Clay's father had sold Ethan's family's land out from under them. Ethan had joined the marines and for almost eight years neither saw nor spoke to his former friend. His anger at the Duvalls had been too great.

It was Clay, however, who gave him the opportunity to realize his ambition of bronc riding again, along with a job breaking and training his rodeo stock. After a chance meeting with Clay three months ago, Ethan had realized he couldn't hold a twenty-one-year-old kid responsible for his father's actions, and the two had reconciled.

It had taken Ethan's brother, Gavin, longer to get over his animosity toward Clay. But now the two were partners in a mustang stud and breeding business, with Clay owning the wild mustang stallion and Gavin the mares.

Sometimes, when the three men were together, it felt as if all those years they'd been at odds with each other had never happened.

Ethan pushed off the railing, doing his best not

to wince as invisible knife blades sliced through his shoulder. "How you doing?"

"I was going to ask you the same question." Clay grinned good-naturedly. "That was quite a fall you took."

"I'll survive." Ethan rolled his shoulders. Big mistake. He sucked in air through his teeth and waited for the spasm to pass.

"What say we have the new nurse check you out?"

"Nurse?"

Clay hitched his chin in the direction of the empty announcer's stand. "She's here setting up the first-aid station for the jackpot."

"I thought you were bringing in an EMT and an ambulance."

"Too expensive. Found out I could hire a nurse for a lot less money and still meet the insurance company's requirement for providing on-site emergency care."

Ethan resisted. "I'm fine." He didn't want to be checked out. And he sure didn't want the other cowboys seeing him head for the first-aid station.

"Come on." Clay took a step in that direction. "We have a deal."

They did. Clay had agreed to let Ethan practice bronc riding as long as several conditions were met, one being that he have any injury examined by a medical professional. Ethan knew what a liability he was, that his chances of hurting himself were far greater than the next cowboy's. Clay was taking a sizable risk despite the waiver Ethan had signed.

If he didn't comply with his friend's conditions, there was no way on earth he'd be allowed to compete in the upcoming jackpot, much less practice for it.

Grumbling, he fell into step beside Clay, and the two of them headed toward the announcer's stand.

"You going to be ready in time?"

"Count on it." Ethan had until the Saturday after Thanksgiving, less than two weeks away, to last a full eight seconds on one of Clay's broncs. That was another of the conditions Ethan had to meet in order to enter the jackpot. "I'll be here every evening if I have to."

The door to the small room beneath the announcer's stand stood ajar. A minivan was backed up to it, the rear hatch open. As they neared, Ethan glimpsed plastic containers and cardboard boxes stacked inside the van and a handicap placard dangling from the rearview mirror.

Clay stopped suddenly and scratched the back of his neck, the movement tipping his cowboy hat forward over his furrowed brow.

"Something the matter?" Ethan asked.

"I was going to surprise you. Now I'm thinking that's not such a good idea."

"Surprise me with what?"

"My new nurse. You know her." He smiled ruefully. "That is, you used to know her. Pretty well, in fact."

Ethan had only a second to prepare before a young woman appeared in the doorway. She paused at the sight of him, recognition lighting her features.

Caitlin Carmichael.

She looked the same. Okay, maybe not the same, he decided on second thought. Nine years was a long time, after all. But she was as pretty as ever.

Her former long blond hair had darkened to a honey-brown and was cut in one of those no-nonsense short styles. Her clothing was equally functional—loose-fitting sweats beneath a down-filled vest. It was her green eyes, he noticed, that had changed the most. Once alive with mischief and merriment, they were now somber and guarded.

Something had happened to her during the years since they'd dated.

Was she thinking the same thing about him?

He waited for her glance to travel to his left leg. It didn't. Either she was very good at hiding her reactions or she hadn't heard about his injury.

"Hello, Ethan," she said, her voice slightly unsteady. "It's good to see you." She came forward, her hand extended. "Clay told me you were back in Mustang Valley and training horses for him."

"For a while now." He took her hand in his, remembering when their greetings and farewells had included a hug and a kiss. Often a long kiss.

An awkward silence followed, and he finally released her hand. "So, you're a nurse?"

She smiled. "I suppose that's hard to believe."

"A little." The mere sight of blood used to make her queasy. "I guess people change."

"They do." Her gaze went to his leg, answering Ethan's earlier question. She quickly looked away.

"I work mornings at the middle school and afternoons at the new urgent-care clinic in Mustang Village," she continued. "Have since the school year started."

"And now for Clay, too."

Her cheeks colored.

Why? Ethan wondered. It was on the tip of his tongue to ask how her husband or boyfriend felt about her busy schedule. Then it occurred to him maybe she and Clay were seeing each other. That would explain the embarrassment.

Ethan couldn't blame his friend. And it wasn't as if he had any kind of claim on Caitlin himself. Not after leaving her high and dry when he'd enlisted, following his mother's death.

"Speaking of which," Clay interjected, "Ethan's your first patient."

Her eyebrows rose. "You are?"

"It's nothing," Ethan insisted, sending his friend— soon to be *ex*-friend once again if he kept this up—a warning look.

He'd hardly gotten over the shock of seeing Caitlin. No way was he ready to be examined by her.

Any choice he had in the matter was taken from him when Clay all but shoved him through the door and into the dimly lit room.

The next instant, his friend was gone, leaving Ethan alone with the woman whose heart he'd broken, and who still owned a very large piece of his.

Caitlin pulled a flimsy metal folding chair into the center of the space and indicated Ethan should sit.

Gripping the back of the chair, he tested its strength. The legs wobbled. "You sure?"

She shrugged apologetically. "I'm still setting up." When he hesitated, she added, "There's always the cot."

He promptly sat, his long legs stretched out in front of him, his big frame dwarfing the chair. Ethan had always been tall, some had said too tall for a bronc or bull rider. What he'd done since they last saw each other was fill out. No longer lean and lanky, he'd grown into a wall of solid muscle. She supposed his two—or was it three?—overseas tours were responsible.

The extra weight looked good on him.

Who was she kidding? He just plain looked good.

Dark eyes, jet-black hair and a five o'clock shadow that should have looked scruffy but somehow managed to be sexy. And that smile of his. It had dazzled her at age seventeen, and never stopped during the four years they'd dated.

Wait. On second thought, he hadn't smiled yet.

He'd been pleasant and polite, but that devil-may-care charm was noticeably absent.

"I'm guessing you injured yourself?"

"My left shoulder," he said.

"Strained it?"

"Or something."

She stood in front of him and gently placed her hand on the afflicted area. He jerked at her touch.

"Does that hurt?"

"Some."

She suspected her proximity was responsible for his reaction more than anything else. There was a lot of history between them, after all, much of it unresolved.

"What happened?" She gently probed his shoulder.

"A horse decided he didn't much like me riding him."

It was on the tip of her tongue to ask how he managed that with a prosthetic leg, but she refrained. Clay had warned her that Ethan didn't appreciate reminders of his handicap, and refused to let it hold him back. Well, he'd always been competitive. First high school sports, then professional rodeo after graduation.

"Did you at least land on soft ground?"

"The arena."

"Thank goodness." She lifted his arm. "Tell me when it starts to hurt."

He said nothing, even when she raised it clear over his head. The clenching of his jaw told another story. She lowered his arm, then raised it again, this time to the side.

He squeezed his eyes shut, but remained stubbornly silent.

Bending his arm at the elbow, she pressed his hand into the small of his back. "What about now?"

"Okay." He released a long breath and shook off her grasp. "You win. It hurts."

So he wasn't invincible.

"You should see your doctor as soon as possible and get an X-ray," she told him, lightly massaging his shoulder. "You might have torn a ligament or your rotator cuff."

"I'll be better by morning."

He was back to being the tough guy.

"No, you're going to be worse. Trust me."

"I'll take some ibuprofen."

"Three a day, extra strength. Up to six if your stomach can tolerate it. Ice the shoulder for at least an hour tonight before you go to bed, and again in the morning. When you can't stand the pain anymore and decide I'm right, see your doctor."

He chuckled, and the smile she'd been missing earlier appeared, if only a shadow of the one she remembered.

"You have nothing to prove, Ethan." She laid her palm on his good shoulder. "See a doctor."

"You're wrong." He rose from the chair, either her touch or her words galvanizing him. "I do have something to prove."

One step on his part and they were standing toe to toe.

Unable to help herself, Caitlin looked up into his face. As his gaze raked over her, lingered on her mouth, the atmosphere surrounding them went from calm to highly charged.

So much for believing the attraction had died.

She retreated on unsteady legs. All these years apart, and he still had the ability to unsettle her.

"How's your family?" she asked. Breathing came easier with some distance between them. "Clay mentioned your brother's getting married."

"This spring. I suppose Clay also mentioned the two of them are partners in a stud and breeding business."

"No." By unspoken agreement, she and Ethan made their way to the door. "We really haven't talked much other than about setting up the first-aid station."

"Huh. I thought maybe you and he…"

"He and I what?"

"Had kept in touch." Ethan stepped aside, allowing her to precede him outside.

"We did up until he got married and moved away. I had no idea he was divorced and back in town."

"Then how did you wind up working for him?"

"He showed up at the school last Wednesday and asked me to run the first-aid station."

"Have you been at the school long?" They stopped beside her minivan.

"You really don't know?"

"Should I?"

"I thought maybe someone told you."

Mustang Village was a horse-friendly residential community, built in and named after Mustang Valley, the land Ethan's family had once owned, and where they had raised cattle for four generations. Their ranch, what was left of it, lay nestled in the foothills of the McDowell Mountains, and looked down on the village. Caitlin didn't think much happened that the Powells didn't know about.

She'd certainly heard about Ethan's injury, medical discharge and return home.

"I've worked at the school since August," she told him.

"That long?" he said, more to himself than her.

"Clay told me you're breaking horses for him."

"Trying to." Another half smile appeared. "Some of them aren't embracing the process."

"If anyone can change their minds, you can." Again she wondered how he managed such a physically demanding job. "Is your sister still living in San Francisco?"

"For five years now."

"But she visits, right?"

"Used to. Not much the last couple years."

"That's too bad."

"Sierra being gone so much is hard on Dad. He misses her. Misses Mom, too. Though he's doing a lot better lately since Cassie came to live with us. He's crazy about her."

Caitlin had met Ethan's twelve-year-old niece at the school. "I don't imagine recovering from the death of a loved one is ever easy."

"It's not."

The mention of his late mother put a damper on their conversation. It was right after Louise Powell died that Ethan had abruptly enlisted, leaving Caitlin to suffer the loss of not only a dear friend, but the love of her life.

A painful pressure built inside her chest.

Heartache.

It had been a long time since the memory of those unhappy days had caused such a profound physical reaction.

"How's your brother?" Ethan asked. "Gavin told me about the accident."

More pressure.

Discussing Justin was always hard for Caitlin. No matter how many obstacles he overcame and how many challenges he conquered, she could never forget that she was responsible for him being a paraplegic and having to spend the rest of his life in a wheelchair.

"He's graduating from Arizona State in December," she said, focusing on the positive. "With a master's in education."

"Good for him."

"We're all very proud. Now if he can just land a job."

"It's a tough economy."

"That, too."

Great strides had been made in the last few decades when it came to equal rights for handicapped employees, but Caitlin still worried about her brother's chances at finding decent employment.

Ethan distracted her by reaching into the back of her minivan and removing a carton of supplies.

"Hey, what are you doing?" She tried to take the box from him.

He swung it out of her reach. "Helping you unload."

"Ethan!" She sighed with exasperation. "You're hurt."

"My shoulder. Not my hands." He squeezed past her and carried his load inside.

She hurried after him.

"Where do you want this?"

Because she knew arguing with him was useless, she pointed to the folding table along the wall. "There. And don't even think about carrying anything else in."

He not only thought about it, he did it. She gave up and pitched in. Together, they quickly emptied the van.

"You're going to regret this tomorrow," she told him when they were done.

"You were never such a worrier before."

"It comes from being a nurse. So does being bossy." She leveled a finger at him. "Now get yourself home and take care of that shoulder."

"Yes, ma'am." One corner of his mouth lifted in an amused and very compelling grin.

Caitlin's heart fluttered. No doubt about it, the attraction hadn't died.

With the van unloaded, there was no reason for him to remain.

"Will I see you later?" she asked.

"Tomorrow, if you're here."

The thought shouldn't have appealed to her as much as it did. Ethan had hurt her. Terribly. She'd be wise to take care where he was concerned.

Even so, a sweet rush of anticipation cascaded through her.

"I'm sure Clay can do without you training his horses for a couple of days."

"Probably." Ethan buttoned his denim jacket. "I'm the one who can't do without the practicing."

"Practicing for what?"

"The jackpot."

She stared at him blankly. "You're not competing."

"I am. Or I will be if I can last a full eight seconds at least once before then. Clay won't let me enter otherwise."

"Is that how you fell tonight? Bull riding?"

"No, saddle bronc."

"Are you crazy?"

"A little, I suppose," he said jokingly.

"More than a little." She started to remind him that he had only one good leg, then stopped herself. "Bronc riding is dangerous. I really wish you'd reconsider."

"Not a chance." He turned to go, then paused. "I'm glad you're home, Caitlin."

A few minutes ago, such a statement would have elicited a breathy sigh from her, foolish though it may have been.

Not now.

He was saddle bronc riding again. With a prosthetic leg! Why didn't he just jump off a three-story building? The results would be the same.

Caitlin had cheered Ethan on from the sidelines all those years ago. She'd also encouraged him the same way she'd encouraged her brother. Winning competitions required a certain amount of risk, after all.

She'd learned too late that taking risks came with a steep price. In her case, her brother, Justin, was the one to pay.

It would be no different for Ethan, and she refused to be there when he injured himself.

Except, as the on-site emergency medical personnel for the Duvall Rodeo Arena, she most likely would be the one to treat him.

Chapter 2

Ethan hated to admit it, but Caitlin was right. His shoulder hurt like a son of a bitch. It had all night, affecting his sleep, his ability to dress himself and his mood.

What if he really had torn something? Then he wouldn't be able to enter the jackpot, that was for sure.

The idea of going to the doctor and getting an X-ray wasn't quite as distasteful to him as it had been the night before. Maybe he could go to the urgent-care clinic. If he was lucky, he might run into Caitlin again.

He no sooner had the thought than he dismissed it. More likely than not she was married or in a committed relationship. Of course, finding out wouldn't be all that hard.

And if she was single, then what?

He doubted she'd go out with him, not after the way

he'd dumped her with hardly a word. Then there was the matter of his leg—or lack of it. Beautiful, desirable women like Caitlin Carmichael didn't date men with missing limbs.

Gritting his teeth, he shoved his arms through the sleeves of his undershirt and tried to pull it over his head. He didn't get far. The pain immobilized him.

The next instant a knock sounded.

"What?" he hollered, his breathing labored.

The front door opened and his brother came in. "Good morning to you, too." He stopped midstep and eyed Ethan curiously. "Having a problem?"

Ethan muttered to himself, not pleased at having an audience.

"What did you say?"

"I hurt my shoulder last night."

"Breaking one of Clay's horses?"

"A bronc trying to break me."

"Ah." Gavin wandered toward the newly remodeled kitchen. "Any coffee?"

"There's instant in the cupboard."

"Instant?" He grimaced.

"Beggars can't be choosers."

Ethan didn't particularly like instant, either. But he'd discovered since living alone the last few weeks that brewing a pot of coffee was a waste when he drank only one cup.

He and Gavin and their dad had resided comfortably in the main house for over a year. When Gavin's daughter, Cassie, moved in with them this past summer, they'd continued to get along. Soon, however, Gavin's fiancée, Sage, and her young daughter, Isa, would be joining the family permanently, and that was a little too much closeness for Ethan.

The old bunkhouse had seemed a good solution. Converting it into an apartment was taking time, though, and living amid the chaos of construction did get tedious. But Ethan didn't mind.

After a lifetime of cohabitating with others, including a barracks full of marines, he quite liked his solitude. No snoring, music or loud TV disturbing his sleep. No having to wait for someone to finish in the bathroom. No arguing about whose turn it was to wash the dishes or vacuum.

No one watching him put on his prosthetic leg, then turning away when he caught him staring.

"Want some?" Undeterred by the prospect of instant coffee, Gavin removed a mug from the cupboard.

"Naw. I already had my quota today." Readying himself, Ethan raised his arms, only to hesitate.

What was wrong with him? He'd endured far worse discomfort than this. The months following his accident—a nice, gentle euphemism for losing the bottom half of his leg in an explosion—had been a daily practice in pushing the boundaries of his endurance.

It hadn't stopped there. The first thing Ethan had done when he returned home was reveal his intentions to start training horses again, his job before enlisting. His family had tried to dissuade him, but eventually came to understand his reasons and the need that drove him.

Since no respectable cowboy wore athletic shoes when he rode, Ethan had used some of the money he'd saved during his enlistment to purchase two pairs of custom-made boots that fit his prosthesis. Within a few weeks, he was riding, and suffering a whole new kind of torturous pain. With determination, practice and continual exercise, he found the pain eventually lessened, though he still had his days.

He didn't start breaking horses until a chance meeting with Clay Duvall. Over beers at the local bar, his old friend had listened while Ethan outlined his ambitions. Then he'd offered him a job. In addition to the arena, Clay owned and operated a rodeo stock business that specialized in bucking horses.

The idea of competing again hadn't occurred to Ethan until he'd watched the cowboys practicing at Clay's arena. What started as a vague longing quickly grew into a burning desire. Ethan was tired of people looking at him differently. Tired of their sympathetic smiles.

Once he started competing again, all that would change.

Ignoring the pain, he pulled on his undershirt, then walked through the partially framed living room to the freshly painted bathroom, where he removed a bottle of ibuprofen from the medicine cabinet.

"You need a day off to rest up?" Gavin hollered from the kitchen.

"Hell, no."

Both Ethan and his father worked alongside Gavin. With only thirty of the family's original six hundred acres remaining in their possession, they'd turned their ranch into a public riding stable. Many Mustang Village residents boarded their horses, took riding lessons or went on guided trail rides at Powell Ranch.

In addition, they'd started the stud and breeding

business last month, after capturing Prince, a wild mustang roaming the McDowell Mountains.

"Maybe you should take it easy today," Gavin suggested, when Ethan returned to the kitchen.

"Don't worry about me." He glowered at his brother. "What are you doing here, anyway?"

"Prince is off his feed. I'd like you to take a look at him before I call the vet."

"I will. Later."

"I was hoping you could do it first thing."

Ethan thought his brother babied the wild mustang too much. Then again, the future of their family business relied heavily on Prince and his ability to breed. While he'd successfully mated with several mares since his capture last month, it was still far too early to determine if any pregnancies had taken, much less what kind of foals he would produce.

Gavin studied him as Ethan downed the painkiller with a glass of water. "Have you considered seeing a doctor?"

"Caitlin told me the same thing."

That got his brother's attention. Instead of leaving, which was Ethan's hope, Gavin pulled out a chair at the dining table, removed his hat and made himself at home.

Great.

"You saw her?" he asked.

"Last night. She's working for Clay, running his first-aid station."

"Interesting."

Gavin's expression reminded Ethan of their father and, he supposed, himself. The Powell men all looked enough alike that most people immediately recognized them as family.

"That's what I thought, too," Ethan said, recalling the shock he'd felt when he first saw Caitlin. "She also works mornings at the middle school and afternoons at the urgent-care clinic."

"Uh-huh."

His brother was sure taking the news in stride. Then it hit him. "You knew she was back, didn't you?"

"We met when Cassie sprained her ankle in gym class, and the school called me to come pick her up."

"That was weeks ago. And you're only now telling me?"

"Figured it wasn't my place."

Another thought occurred to Ethan. "Caitlin ask you not to tell me?"

"No. Nothing like that."

"Did my name even come up?"

"We really didn't have time to talk. She was busy, and Cassie was complaining about her ankle."

Ethan started pacing the kitchen. Caitlin had known he'd returned to Mustang Valley and hadn't bothered to look him up.

Did he really expect her to, after the way he'd treated her?

Probably not. Change that to hell, no.

"Look," Gavin continued, "it just slipped my mind. I had a lot going on at the time. Capturing Prince. Starting the stud and breeding business. Sage and I getting engaged."

"Right," Ethan answered testily. He'd bet the entire contents of his wallet that running into Caitlin hadn't slipped his brother's mind. "I'm a big boy, bro. You don't have to watch out for me."

"Sorry. Old habits are hard to break."

Not exactly an admission, but close.

"Answer me this," Gavin said. "What would you have done if I told you she was back in town?"

"Apologize, for one." Which, now that he thought about it, wasn't something he'd done last night. "And make amends…if possible." He owed her that much.

"You going to ask her out?"

"Are you kidding?"

"Why not?"

"Even if I did, she'd turn me down flat. Besides, she's probably married by now."

"She isn't."

Ethan stopped pacing. "How do you know?"

"The subject came up."

"I thought you said you didn't have much time to talk to her."

"Doesn't take long to say, 'Hey, you ever get married?'"

Ethan groaned.

"What are you so mad about, anyway?"

Before he could reply, another knock sounded at the door.

"What now?" He stormed over and yanked the door open.

Clay stood on the other side. "You're in a fine mood." Without waiting for an invitation, he stepped inside. "I just came from Prince's paddock. He hasn't touched his food."

"We're heading there now," Ethan grumbled,

snatching his jacket off the back of the couch where he'd left it.

"Any more of that coffee left?"

"It's instant," Gavin complained from his seat at the table.

Clay drew back in surprise. "Don't you have a coffeemaker?"

Ethan glared at him. "Don't you?"

Clay glared back. "What's bugging you?"

"He's mad that I didn't tell him Caitlin was working at the school." Gavin rose from the table.

"Can we not discuss this?" Ethan headed for the door.

"You going to invite her out?"

He ignored Clay's question.

"I already asked him that." Gavin went to the sink and deposited his mug. "He says no."

Annoyed, Ethan shoved an arm into the sleeve of his jacket, then swore loudly when his entire left side seized with fresh pain.

"How's the shoulder?" Clay asked.

"Fine." Ethan opened the door and stepped out onto the porch.

Clay came up behind him. "You don't act like it's fine."

"I'll be all right."

"What did Caitlin say last night?"

"Ice the shoulder and take ibuprofen. I've done both."

"Did she tell you to see a doctor?"

"I don't need to see a doctor."

"Don't believe him." Gavin joined them on the porch, shutting the door behind him. "He's hurting."

Ethan anchored his hat to his head as a strong gust of wind swept past them on its way down the mountain to the valley.

"See a doctor," Clay ordered. "Until you do, and until you're cleared, no bronc riding."

Ethan swung around. "Dammit, Clay!"

"Sorry. That's the rule. Same for you as everyone else."

"The jackpot is a week and a half away. I need to practice."

"Then I guess you'd better haul your butt to the doctor today."

At the bottom of the long driveway leading from Powell Ranch to the main road, Ethan turned left. Three minutes later he reached the entrance to Mustang Village, with its large monument sign flanked by a life-size bronze statue of a rearing horse.

As he drove at a reduced speed through the equine-friendly community, he tried to remember what it had been like when there were no houses or buildings or people, only wide-open spaces and Powell cattle roaming them. He'd missed out on the construction of the community, having been in the service at the time. How hard it must have been for his father and brother to watch their family's hundred-year-old history disappear acre by acre, replaced with roads, houses, condos and commercial buildings.

He generally avoided Mustang Village. The reminder of all they had lost was too hard on his heart.

If not for his mother's failing health, they wouldn't have borrowed the money from Clay's father and used their land as collateral. If Clay's dad had honored the agreement and not sold the land out from under them, Mustang Village would never have been built. If not for the residents of Mustang Village, Ethan's family would be raising cattle rather than operating a riding stable.

A lot of ifs, and that wasn't even counting the most recent one—if he hadn't been standing where he was at the exact moment the car bomb exploded, he wouldn't have lost his leg.

Ethan turned his thoughts away from the past when Mustang Village's one and only retail strip center came into view.

It always struck him as odd to see hitching rails and bridle paths in a residential community. On any given weekend, there were almost as many equestrians riding about as there were pedestrians walking. Not so much during the week. Mustang Village resembled most other communities then, with school buses making runs, mothers pushing strollers, cyclists zipping along and dog lovers walking their pets.

Today, a work crew was busy stringing Christmas lights along the storefronts and hanging wreaths on lampposts. Already? Thanksgiving was still more than a week away.

A buzzer announced Ethan's arrival at the urgent-care clinic. This was his first visit. He always drove to the VA hospital in Phoenix for his few medical needs.

Inside the crowded clinic, a receptionist greeted him with a friendly "May I help you?" and handed him a clipboard. When he was done filling out the forms, she processed his co-pay and said, "Have a seat."

Ethan considered inquiring if Caitlin was working. But then the phone rang, followed immediately by a second line ringing. He left the receptionist to answer her calls, and sat in a chair next to a mother and her sniffling child.

He couldn't help thinking that if the bronc hadn't thrown him last night, he wouldn't be here now, anxiously waiting to see his former girlfriend again. Yet another if in a long, long list of them.

Except Ethan really wouldn't describe Caitlin as a girlfriend. She'd been much more than that to him, and he to her. Had his mother not died and he not enlisted, chances were good they'd have gotten married.

He really had to stop thinking about what might have been, or else he'd drive himself crazy.

"Ethan?"

His head snapped up when Caitlin called his name. "Yeah."

"Right this way."

He followed her down the corridor. Once he was weighed and his height taken, she escorted him to an examination room, where he sat on the table and she at the computer terminal.

"Why are you here today?"

Seriously? She knew darn well why. "I fell from a horse last night and hurt my shoulder," he answered, playing along.

"What part of your shoulder?"

"You examined me."

She gave him a very professional smile. "It's procedure."

He cupped his shoulder with his palm.

More questions followed, and she typed the answers into the computer. During the entire process, Caitlin treated him like any other patient, concerned, interested and like they hardly knew each other.

What did he expect? She was at work.

What did he want?

The answer was easy. To see that light in her eyes.

"The doctor will be right in to see you." Before closing the door, she smiled and said, "I'm glad you came in today."

He was tempted to jump to the wrong conclusion and reminded himself that her remark was medically motivated. Hadn't she urged him last night to have his shoulder looked at?

After a brief consultation with the doctor, Ethan waited again, this time for the X-ray technician. Returning from the imaging room, he waited a third time.

The doctor's news was good. Nothing was torn, only soft-tissue damage.

"Can I start riding again right away?" he asked.

"I recommend you take a few days off." The man studied him over a pair of reading glasses. "A week would be better."

"But there's no reason I can't ride."

"You could sustain further injury."

"Okay." Ethan nodded. He had every intention of getting on a bronc tonight, and he was pretty sure the doctor knew it.

"I'm going to prescribe an anti-inflammatory and a muscle relaxant. If you aren't better in two weeks, call for a follow-up exam or see your regular doctor."

"Thanks."

"You know—" the man removed his reading glasses "—if you're really that determined to ride, you might consider physical therapy to speed your recovery."

"Appreciate the advice, Doc."

"The nurse will be in shortly with your prescriptions."

Another wait, this one not long. Caitlin returned with three slips of paper in her hand. Ethan had to admit the sight of her in pale green scrubs was as surreal as seeing her in sweats. In college, she'd majored in journalism, with ambitions of being a TV reporter, and always dressed fashionably.

Admittedly, the scrubs looked cute on her, the loose material not quite hiding her very nice curves.

"Here you go." She handed him the prescriptions. "The doctor wrote one for physical therapy as well, in case you need something for the VA."

"I'll probably skip PT."

"Why? It will help."

He stood, folded the prescriptions and placed them in his wallet. "The nearby facilities don't take VA insurance. And I can't afford the time off work to drive into Phoenix."

"What if…what if I provided your physical therapy?"

"You?"

"I have some basic training. I'm not licensed, but I've taken several classes. For Justin. During his rehab, he'd strain his upper body muscles. And now that he's involved in wheelchair athletics, he's always overdoing it."

"I can relate."

"You two are alike when it comes to that." Her expression softened, and suddenly she was the seventeen-year-old transfer student who'd been assigned to sit next to him in calculus class.

Ethan was caught off guard and needed a moment to collect himself. "I don't think the VA will pay for a private physical therapist."

"I won't charge you."

He shook his head. "I can't ask you to do it for free."

"Who said anything about free?" She smiled then, *really* smiled, and he caught another glimpse of the confident, carefree girl he'd fallen in love with. "I was hoping we could negotiate a trade."

She had his attention now. "I'm listening."

She motioned him into the hall.

"I'm on the Holly Days Festival committee," she said.

The residents of Mustang Village had put on a big community-wide event the previous Christmas. None of the Powells had attended, but they'd heard about it. From everyone.

"The committee, huh?"

"You know me."

He did. She'd been an involved student in both high school and college. Cocaptain of the cheerleading squad, student council, National Honor Society.

"I thought the festival was strictly for residents."

"I'm a resident," she said brightly as they entered the reception area.

"Really?"

"I'm renting a condo. In the complex right across the street." She nodded toward the window. "I get to walk to work every day. Well, not to the middle school. But here."

Working *and* living in Mustang Village. Was that another bit of interesting information Gavin had conveniently forgotten to tell Ethan?

"The committee is hoping to try something different this year," Caitlin went on. "The parade was fun, but more people participated than watched."

"You saw it?"

"I did. I almost drove to the ranch, too."

Just how often *had* they narrowly missed crossing paths since his return home?

"Anyway, I remembered that old farm wagon of yours and was wondering if we could decorate it and have you drive people around the park."

"No one's used that wagon in years."

Her hopeful smile fell. "Well, it was just an idea."

Ethan had no desire to participate in the Holly Days Festival. Nothing involving Mustang Village appealed to him—with the exception of Caitlin. And she appealed to him far too much for his own good.

But hadn't he just told Gavin this morning that he wished he could make amends with Caitlin? Wagon rides at the festival wouldn't exactly clean the slate. But it was a start, and obviously important to her.

"We could pull the wagon out of storage," he said. "See what kind of shape it's in."

"Great!" Her green eyes lit up.

This was the moment Ethan had been waiting for, only her excitement was over an old wagon. Not him.

"Why don't you come out to the ranch?"

"When?"

Ethan massaged his left shoulder. "As soon as possible. I still haven't qualified for the jackpot next weekend."

"What about tomorrow, say around noon? I have a two-hour break between the school and the clinic. If the wagon is usable, we'll set up a schedule for your PT sessions."

"Sounds good."

"Hey, Caitlin." The receptionist held up a manila folder.

"I have to go," she said hurriedly. "Thank you, Ethan."

She collected the folder and called the next person's name.

Once again, Ethan was just another patient—and it didn't set well with him.

Chapter 3

In days gone by, Caitlin would have driven directly to the main house at Powell Ranch and parked there. Instead, she followed the signs and went around behind the cattle barn to the designated parking area.

"It's weird," her brother said from beside her in the passenger seat. "The place is totally different, but not different."

"Yeah, weird." She opened her door and stepped out.

Memories that had hovered the last few days promptly assailed her. Most were good, gently stroking emotional chords. One wasn't so good, and it quickly overpowered the rest.

"When was the last time you were here?" Justin asked, already maneuvering his legs into position.

"Oh, about nine years ago."

Nine years, four months and…she mentally calculated…eighteen days. Not that she was keeping track.

She'd arrived that last evening intending to join the Powells for dinner, something she often did in the past. Even before the meal was served, Ethan took her out to the front courtyard and sprang the news on her. He'd enlisted. Signed up a week after his mother's funeral. A rather important decision he hadn't even bothered discussing with Caitlin.

A fresh wave of hurt and anger unbalanced her now, and she paused, holding on to the van door for support.

Guess she hadn't moved past her and Ethan's bitter breakup, after all.

It must be seeing the ranch again. Or seeing *him* again—for the third day in a row.

Enough is enough, she told herself. She could manage working with Ethan, seeing him at the clinic, administering his physical therapy. He was nothing more than her patient.

With actions honed from much practice, she removed her brother's wheelchair from the rear of the minivan and carried it to the passenger side, where he waited.

She'd have set the wheelchair up for him, except he insisted on performing the task himself. Rather than argue, she gave in. Being independent was important to Justin, and she respected his wishes even though her instinct was to do everything for him.

After hoisting himself into the wheelchair, he and Caitlin made their way to the stables. She figured the office was as good a place as any to start looking for Ethan.

"Sure are a lot of people here," Justin commented, rolling his wheelchair along beside her.

A half-dozen riders were gathered in the open area near the stables. Several more were in the arena, riding alone or in pairs. One enthusiastic mother clapped while her preschooler trotted a shaggy pony in circles.

"I hear it's even busier when school lets out for the day." Caitlin remembered when the only people on the ranch were the Powells and the cowboys who worked for them.

"I'll wait here," Justin said when they reached the small porch outside the office.

He could easily maneuver the three steps leading onto it, but he probably wanted to give Caitlin and Ethan some privacy.

Easing open the door, she stepped tentatively inside the office. The sight of Ethan sitting with his back to her at an old metal desk gave her a start.

Not again, she chided herself. No more going weak in the knees every time she saw him.

Clearing her throat, she said, "Hello," then "Oh!" when the ancient chair swiveled around with a squeak.

The man wasn't Ethan.

"Hey." Gavin greeted her with a wide grin. "What brings you here?"

Caitlin vacillated between enormous relief and equally enormous disappointment. "I'm meeting Ethan."

"You are?"

Obviously he hadn't informed his family of her visit.

She didn't know what to make of that.

"If he's not around—"

"He's here. Shoeing one of the horses."

"Is it all right if I interrupt him?"

"I'm thinking he won't mind."

Caitlin wavered, then blurted, "Can I ask a favor of you?"

"Sure."

"My brother's outside. Would you check on him for me? Without making it look like you're checking on him?"

"How's he doing?"

"Good. And he's perfectly capable of handling himself in new situations."

"But you worry."

"Constantly."

"Not a problem." Gavin's cell phone rang. "Let me take this call first."

"Thanks." Caitlin hurried across the office and out the door leading to the stables.

It was like stepping back in time.

The rich, familiar scents of horses and alfalfa filled her nostrils the moment she crossed the threshold. Daylight, pouring in from the large doorways on both ends of the long aisle, illuminated the interior better than any electric-powered lights could. Soft earth gave beneath her feet with each step she took. A barn cat dashed behind a barrel, then stuck its head out to peer warily at her.

Caitlin glanced around, her breath catching at the sight of Ethan not thirty feet away. He was bent over at the waist, the horse's rear hoof braced between his knees as he used a file to trim it.

How did he do that with a prosthetic leg?

How did he do that with a bad shoulder?

Fine, he was resilient. She appreciated that quality in an individual. Admired it. But shoeing a horse while injured was just plain stupid. So was bronc riding.

She started to say something, only to close her mouth when Ethan released the horse's hoof and straightened.

He stood tall, his blue work shirt rolled up at the sleeves and stretched taut across his muscled back. The leather chaps he wore sat low on his hips, emphasizing his athletic frame. She couldn't remember him ever looking better. Or sexier.

When they were in high school, Caitlin had liked him best in his football uniform. Next best in the tux he'd worn to their senior prom. She'd been the envy of every girl on the cheerleading squad, and had relished the attention.

What an idiot she'd been. Shallow and silly—placing too much importance on things that didn't matter.

Ethan turned, and she wished suddenly she was wearing nice clothes. Not an oversize hooded sweatshirt and scrubs.

"You made it."

"I did."

He set the file he'd been using down on a box of tools. Next, he removed his chaps and draped them over the box. "Ready to take a look at the wagon?"

"Is that Chico?" Caitlin advanced a step, then two. "Can I pet him?"

"Of course."

"I remember him. I can't believe he's still around." She stroked the old horse's soft nose, and he snorted contentedly.

"That's right. You and Chico are already acquainted."

Caitlin was never much of a horse enthusiast, though she'd tried her best to share that interest with Ethan. When they did go on a ride, Chico was her mount of choice.

"He's Isa's horse now."

"Isa?"

"Sage's daughter. Gavin's soon-to-be stepdaughter. She's six and in love with this old guy."

"I'm glad." Glad the horse Caitlin remembered with such fondness was adored by a little girl and that some things around Powell Ranch hadn't changed.

"Do you still ride?"

"No, not since Chico." She didn't want to admit to Ethan how much riding—or any physical activity that held risk—scared her. She hadn't been like that before Justin's accident. Quite the opposite.

"I'll take you sometime." Ethan moved closer.

Caitlin's guard instantly went up. She continued stroking Chico's nose in an attempt to disguise her nervousness—at Ethan's proximity and the prospect of getting on a horse again. "We should probably take a look at the wagon. I have to get to the clinic soon."

They left the stables. Chico, Ethan assured Caitlin, would be just fine tied to the hitching rail, and was probably already napping.

As they rounded the corner of the cattle barn, she noticed lumber stacked nearby, along with a table saw, ladder and toolboxes.

"What are you building?"

"We're converting the old barn into a mare motel

for the stud and breeding business. Clay and his men are helping us."

Ethan took her elbow and guided her around more piles of construction material. She started to object and insist she was fine, then changed her mind. Like the other night when he'd insisted on unloading her medical supplies, it would be like arguing with a brick wall.

He led her to a corner of the barn where, behind a tower of wooden crates and beneath a canvas tarp, the wagon stood.

"Not sure we can get much closer," he said, stepping over a roll of rusted chicken wire.

Caitlin squeezed in behind him, acutely aware of his tall, broad frame mere inches from her.

He leaned over and lifted the tarp, revealing a wagon wheel. Without thinking, she reached out and touched the worn wood.

A memory of Ethan driving her around the ranch in the wagon suddenly surfaced, of her bouncing in the seat beside him and both of them laughing. How carefree they'd been back then.

She suddenly missed those days with a longing she hadn't felt in years.

Stop it!

Dwelling on that period of her life would do more damage than good. She and Ethan might have renewed their acquaintance, but that was all it was, an acquaintance. All it could be. Even if she finally got past the hurt he'd caused her, he rode saddle broncs for pleasure and broke green horses for a living. Caitlin wasn't capable of caring for someone who courted danger on a daily basis. Not after what had happened to her brother. She couldn't live with the constant worry and fear.

"Going to need a few repairs." Ethan wiggled a loose spoke.

Caitlin was relieved to get back on track. "And lots of cleaning."

"Hope you have enough volunteers."

She studied the wagon with a critical eye. "I might need more."

"I've been thinking. Would it be all right if we asked for a small donation? Completely voluntary, of course. Sage, my future sister-in-law, is starting a wild-mustang sanctuary here on the ranch, and she's having trouble obtaining funding."

"What a good idea. I can't imagine the festival committee having any objections."

"That'll make her happy."

Caitlin brushed dirt off the wheel. "When can we get started?"

"Saturday soon enough?"

"We'll have to be here early. I'm due at Clay's arena after lunch."

"Me, too."

"You're not riding!"

"Planning on it."

"Your shoulder!"

"I can't afford to miss any practices."

"Isn't it dangerous to ride with an injury? I'd think your reaction time would be slowed."

"I'll wrap it."

As if that would fix everything. His attitude was exactly the reason they would never date again, no matter how attractive she found him. Riding broncs was bad enough. Riding broncs with an injury was idiotic.

"I'll have a couple of the guys help me pull the wagon out," he said.

"I recommend you *supervise* a couple of the guys." She leveled a finger at him. "If you're going to ride on Saturday, you need to rest that shoulder and let it heal."

"Right."

He was impossible.

"I need to get going." She stepped over the roll of rusted chicken wire. "I don't want to leave Justin alone too long."

"You brought him with you?"

"He doesn't have class on Fridays and sometimes comes by for a visit."

"Justin drives?"

"A Honda Civic. Modified, of course."

"And he lives with your parents?"

"No, he has an apartment near campus with a roommate."

"Not that it's any of my business," Ethan said, "but if the kid lives on his own and drives, don't you think he'll be okay alone for a few minutes?"

She sighed with exasperation...at herself. "I can't help worrying about him. Call it big-sister-itis."

"His accident wasn't your fault."

Caitlin went still, swallowed a gasp. No one other than Justin and her parents knew of her guilt and the reason for it.

How in the world had Ethan guessed?

Stupid question. He'd always been able to read her better than anyone.

She averted her face, hiding the sudden storm of emotions churning inside her. Him, this place, the memories of happier times—it was all too much.

Ethan took her elbow again, helping her navigate the narrow path through the construction material. His fingers were warm and strong and far too familiar. Any hope Caitlin had for control flew out the window.

"You weren't at the river that day," he said, his voice gentle with understanding. "You couldn't possibly have been involved."

His compassion and sympathy were her undoing.

"I encouraged him to go," she admitted, her throat burning. "If he had stayed home, he wouldn't have landed on that rock and damaged his spinal cord."

"Come on. Name one senior at our school who didn't tube down the river and jump from the cliffs the week after graduation. It was a rite of passage."

"Justin didn't normally disobey our parents." As she had, she thought. "I told him he was eighteen and it was time he stopped acting like such a geek. I drove him to his friend's house, then lied to our folks about where he was going."

"Teenagers disobey their parents. It's what they do."

"Being popular was so important to me in high school. Justin was such a nerd back then. Shy and scrawny and brainy. He was practically invisible. I thought if he went tubing, he'd break out of his shell. Because of me, his life is ruined."

They came to a stop at the entrance to the barn. Ethan released her elbow, only to drape an arm around her shoulders.

"Trust me, you weren't the only one pressuring him to go tubing. His buddies were, too."

It would have been nice to lay her head on Ethan's chest as she'd done so often in the past, and let him comfort her.

She might have, if she wasn't convinced she'd be sending him the wrong message.

Wiping her eyes, she tried to ease away from his embrace.

He'd have none of it.

"When someone's seriously injured, like Justin, it's pretty common for family members and friends to blame themselves. My dad and brother were the same way. Kept thinking if they'd been there for me when Mom was sick, and after she died, I wouldn't have enlisted and been caught in that explosion. Eventually, they came to accept it was my decision to join the marines, and rotten luck I was standing where I was that day. Same with Justin."

Caitlin looked up at Ethan. "You don't think I was there for you when your mom died?"

At the time, she'd been so embroiled in her own misery over his abrupt departure, she hadn't considered the reason he left was because of her. How incredibly selfish.

"What? Of course not. I was the one unable to cope with my grief, so was pushing people away." He inhaled deeply. "I'm sorry, Caitlin. For abandoning you like that."

"I appreciate the apology."

"I know it's not enough to make up for what I did to you."

"No, it isn't."

He drew back at her brutal, but honest, admission.

"You're not the only one who had to deal with traumatic events," she said. "I did, too. And believe me, there were plenty of times after Justin's accident when I wanted to run away and leave everything behind.

But I didn't. I stayed and dealt with my responsibilities regardless of how difficult it was. I just wish you had loved me enough to do the same."

Caitlin's remark hit Ethan like a blow. How could she think he hadn't loved her enough? The whole reason he'd left was because he had loved her *too* much. She deserved more than a man who was emotionally devastated, out of work and whose family was financially ruined, thanks to one man's insatiable greed.

Before he could explain, Justin came wheeling toward them. Ethan was pleased to see the young man, even if his timing stank.

"Hey, there you are." He pushed his wheelchair forward, meeting up with Ethan and Caitlin outside the cattle barn. "How are you doing?"

"I'm good." Ethan shook his hand, which was sheathed in a worn leather glove with cutouts for his fingers.

"I was just talking to Gavin. He filled me in on all the changes round here."

"Lots of them. Some good, some bad."

"You miss the old days?"

No one had ever asked Ethan that. He took a moment to consider before answering. "I do sometimes. I miss the people, especially. My mom and sister." He glanced briefly at Caitlin. If she was aware of his unspoken inclusion of her, she didn't show it. "But all things considered, I can't complain."

"Me, either," Justin said, without the slightest trace of bitterness.

Ethan's respect for him grew by leaps and bounds.

If Justin felt self-pity at losing the use of his legs, he certainly didn't wallow in it.

"You in a hurry to leave?" Justin maneuvered his wheelchair so that he faced Caitlin. "I was hoping Ethan could show us the mustang."

"I can't be late for work."

Justin checked his watch. "I thought you didn't have to be at the clinic until two."

"I like to arrive a little early."

She sounded eager to go.

Ethan wanted the chance to explain his real reason for enlisting and leaving her, and was determined to find the opportunity. "It won't take long. Prince's stall is just behind the barn."

Justin started wheeling in that direction. Ethan followed, as did Caitlin, her gait stiff and her steps slow.

If she so obviously didn't want to be with him, why had she come along?

"I have to warn you," he told Justin, "the way there's bumpy."

"Can't be any worse than hiking Squaw Peak."

"You've done that?"

"Five times. Four of them in my chair." Justin beamed, his geeky smile reminding Ethan of the undersize, asthmatic kid he'd known when he and Caitlin were dating.

The smile, however, was the only thing about him that was the same. Justin had acquired some serious muscle on his upper body.

"Why do you keep him so far from the other horses?" he asked, guiding his wheelchair down the rocky slope to Prince's pen like a pro.

"He's too wild and unpredictable." Ethan kept his

eyes trained on the ground, watching out for potholes and rocks. What would cause another person to merely stumble could send him sprawling. "And being near the mares tends to…excite him, shall we say. Better he's off by himself."

Where to house Prince had been an issue when they'd captured him last month. Clay solved the problem by erecting a temporary covered pen near the back pasture.

"I've been wanting to see Prince ever since I watched your brother on the news."

Ethan chuckled. "You caught that, huh?"

"Are you kidding? He was all over the TV."

The media had gotten wind of Prince's capture; a horse living wild in a ninety-thousand-acre urban preserve was big news. Several local stations had dispatched reporters to interview Gavin. The attention had resulted in a slew of new customers, giving the Powells' dire finances a much-needed boost.

"Watch yourself," Ethan cautioned as they drew near. "Prince is wary of strangers. He still doesn't like me and Gavin that much."

Justin showed no fear and wheeled close. Caitlin reached for his wheelchair as if she wanted to pull him back. After a second, she let her hand drop, though it remained clenched in a fist.

Was it only Justin's fall that had made her overprotective?

As they watched Prince, the stallion raised his head and stared at them. Then, tossing his jet-black mane, he trotted from one end of the pen to the other, commanding their attention.

And he got it. Ethan couldn't wait to see the colts this magnificent horse produced.

"He's bigger than he looked on TV."

Ethan kept a careful eye on Justin, ready to run interference if he ventured too close to the pen. Caitlin, on the other hand, seemed content to observe from a safe distance.

"Have you ridden him yet?" It was the first she'd spoken since Justin joined them outside the barn.

"No. He's only halter broke, and barely that."

"But you are going to break him?" Justin asked.

"Oh, yeah. My goal is by Christmas."

"That doesn't give you much time."

"You're right. He and I are going to have to come to a new agreement soon about who's boss."

Prince pawed the ground impatiently, as if daring Ethan to try.

Justin grinned sheepishly. "Don't suppose there's a horse in that stable of yours I could ride."

"Anytime you want, buddy." Ethan immediately thought of old Chico. If he was trustworthy enough for a six-year-old, he'd do fine for Justin. "Give me a call. I'll take you on a trail ride."

Beside him, Caitlin visibly stiffened. "Justin, are you sure about that? You've never had an interest in riding horses before."

"I never played sports before, either." He slapped the arm of his wheelchair. "Turns out I'm pretty good."

"What do you like?" Ethan asked.

"Basketball. Baseball. Swimming. I'm considering taking up track and field."

"I'm impressed."

"Well, I couldn't do any of it without Caitlin's help. She's amazing."

Did Caitlin pay for her brother's athletic expenses? Ethan wondered. That would explain the three jobs and why she worked fifty to sixty hours a week.

"You'll do fine at riding, then," he assured him.

Caitlin removed her cell phone from her sweatshirt pocket and checked the display. "It's getting late."

After a last look at Prince, the three of them returned to the stables, Justin chatting enthusiastically about riding and Caitlin stubbornly silent.

When they reached her minivan, Justin hoisted himself into the front passenger seat.

"I'll get that," Ethan offered, and carried the wheelchair to the rear of the minivan, where Caitlin had the hatch open.

She closed it the second he'd stowed the chair. "See you Saturday."

"What about physical therapy?" If he was keeping his end of the bargain, she needed to keep hers. "I'd like to start right away."

"I don't get off at the clinic until seven-thirty most nights."

"Eight's fine," he said, ignoring her attempts to postpone. "If it's not too late for you." He rose at the crack of dawn and assumed she did, too, what with her schedule.

"No, eight's okay." She peered nervously at her brother, who was busy with his MP3 player. "We can start tonight."

"Anything special I should have on hand?"

"I'll bring my portable table. We can set up just about anywhere."

"Okay. Drive straight to the bunkhouse and park there."

"The bunkhouse?"

"I live there now. Moved out of the main house so Sage and Isa can move in."

"O…kay."

"If you don't want to be alone with me—"

"It makes no difference," she answered tersely.

Somehow, Ethan thought it did. He just wasn't sure why.

Chapter 4

"Easy, boy." Ethan held on to Prince's lead rope, gripping it securely beneath the halter. "That's right, there you go." He ran his other hand down the horse's neck, over his withers and across his back, applying just the slightest amount of pressure. Prince stood, though not quietly. He bobbed his head and swished his tail nervously.

On the ground beside Ethan lay a saddle blanket, which he hoped Prince would allow to be placed on his back. The step was a small but important one toward breaking the horse. If Caitlin arrived on time, she'd be able to watch him.

He resisted pulling out his cell phone and viewing the display. It was 8:18. He knew this because he'd checked the time four minutes ago when it was 8:14, and every few minutes before that for the last half hour. He doubted she was going to keep their physical-therapy appointment, not after the disagreement they'd had this afternoon.

"Uncle Ethan!" Cassie yelled. "What are you doing?" She and Isa came bounding toward the round pen.

The horse's reaction to the girls' approach was immediate. Prancing sideways, Prince tried to jerk free of Ethan's hold…and almost succeeded.

"Relax, buddy," Ethan soothed, his grip on the lead rope like iron. Luckily, he was using his right hand. Thanks to the way his shoulder felt tonight, his left arm was pretty much useless.

The mustang, eyes wide, stared at Cassie and Isa, who peered at him and Ethan from between the rails of the pen.

"You girls stay back, you hear me? And keep ahold of that pup. I don't want him getting kicked."

They complied, sort of, by retreating maybe six inches. Cassie did scoop up her puppy, Blue, a five-month-old cattle dog mix that was out of her sight only when she was at school or a friend's house.

"Gonna ride him, Uncle Ethan?" Isa asked.

Though not officially a member of the family yet, Sage's daughter had already started calling Ethan "uncle." Probably because Cassie did. Isa copied the older girl's every move.

Ethan didn't mind. In fact, he rather enjoyed the moniker—and his role of the younger bachelor uncle who constantly set a bad example for his nieces by swearing in front of them and periodically losing his temper.

Months of counseling after the car bomb explosion

had taught Ethan how to deal with his sometimes volatile and erratic emotions. Normally, he did a good job. On occasion, like earlier today, he wondered if maybe he'd quit attending counseling too soon, and should call the VA hospital for a referral. His buttons lay close to the surface and were easily pushed.

"Not tonight," he said, answering Isa's question. "Prince isn't ready."

"When *will* you ride him?" Cassie asked.

"Soon."

"That's what you said yesterday."

"Don't you girls have any homework?"

"We did it already," Isa volunteered.

"A TV show you want to watch?"

"We're still grounded until tomorrow," Cassie answered glumly.

"You're lucky that's all the punishment you got. If I'd pulled a stunt like you two did when I was a kid, Grandpa Wayne would have had me cleaning stalls every day before school and mucking out the calf pens."

Come to think of it, those had always been his chores. Both he and Gavin had helped their father and grandfather with the cattle business from the time they were Isa's age.

"Yeah, but if not for us, you wouldn't have captured Prince."

Cassie was right, even if her assessment of the situation was a mite skewed.

Last month, in an act of rebellion, she and Isa had taken off on horseback into the mountains without telling anyone where they were going. After a frantic two-hour search, they were found in the box canyon, along with Sage's missing mare and Prince.

The wild mustang had proved difficult to capture, requiring all of Ethan's and Gavin's skills as cowboys. It had also been one of the most exciting moments of their lives.

"Maybe not that night, but we'd have captured him eventually." Ethan continued stroking Prince, running his hand over the horse's back and along his rump. The movement aggravated the pain in his shoulder, but he ignored it.

"Did you ride a bronc earlier at Mr. Duvall's?" Cassie asked.

"I did." Ethan had gotten back to the ranch at seven and taken a quick shower just in case Caitlin showed up. He'd decided to work with Prince, because he didn't want to appear as if he was waiting for her—which he was.

"Did you make it a whole eight seconds?"

"Not quite. Almost four." Which was double his last time.

"Did you get hurt again?"

Why did everyone assume he couldn't fall without injuring himself?

"No, I didn't." He had, however, eaten a whole bucketful of arena dirt when he'd hit the ground. He should have taken another turn on a different bronc, but he figured one wreck a night was about all his body could handle.

He slowly bent and reached for the saddle blanket near his feet.

"What are you doing now?" Cassie asked.

"Hopefully, getting Prince used to this."

His plan didn't work. Prince reacted to the blanket as if a swarm of hornets might fly out from behind it at any second.

Wherever Prince had come from, and it was still a mystery, he'd never known human touch. Gavin claimed the horse was a descendant of the wild mustangs that had roamed the valley till the 1940s. Ethan thought that was impossible, but had yet to come up with a better explanation.

"Why don't you try a carrot or an apple?" Isa suggested. "That's what Mama used to train her horse."

"Good idea. What say you girls run in the house and see what you can find in the refrigerator."

Isa lit up. "Okay!"

"Uncle Ethan." Cassie turned and craned her neck. "Someone's here."

He saw the headlights of an approaching vehicle seconds before he heard the sound of tires crunching on gravel.

Had Caitlin finally arrived?

Excitement coursed through him when he recognized the familiar outline of her minivan.

Taking his eyes off Prince proved to be a mistake. The horse—possibly out of affection, probably out of dislike—butted Ethan in the shoulder. His injured shoulder.

"Shit!"

"Uncle Ethan!" Isa slapped her hands over her mouth. "You're not supposed to swear in front of us."

Cassie, a little older and a little wiser than her soon-to-be stepsister, appeared unfazed by the use of a four-letter word. "They parked in front of the bunkhouse," she informed Ethan, her eyes glued to the vehicle.

He unclipped the lead rope from Prince. "It's okay. You girls can go inside now."

Cassie and Isa didn't budge. Not until the minivan door opened and Caitlin stepped out.

"It's Nurse Carmichael from school," Cassie said with a very adult interest. "What's she doing here?"

Ethan slipped through the round-pen gate, leaving Prince inside. "If you must know, she's helping me with my shoulder." He set the saddle blanket on an overturned bucket by the gate, well out of Prince's reach.

"How?"

"Giving me physical therapy."

"Now?" Cassie furrowed her brow in an impressive imitation of parental concern. "Isn't it kind of late?"

"Seriously, you two," Ethan chided. "Get inside."

Unfortunately, Caitlin spotted them across the open area and started in their direction.

"Come on." Cassie grabbed Isa's hand. "Let's go say hi to her."

Ethan had no choice but to let them run ahead. He did well riding horses and walking from place to place, but he hadn't quite mastered the fifty-yard dash in under ten seconds.

Just as well. The extra time allowed him to study Caitlin. She didn't look as upset as she had earlier today. That, or she was hiding behind her nurse facade.

A tactic, he began to suspect, she frequently employed to keep people—him specifically—at a distance.

No more, now that he was onto her.

Caitlin was suddenly surrounded on all sides. "Well, hello, there."

"Nurse Carmichael." Cassie smiled exuberantly, her arm slung around the younger girl. "This is my stepsister, Isa. Well, she's not my stepsister yet, but she will be soon. Her mom's marrying my dad."

"Hi." The little girl stuck out her hand, her enormous grin adorable despite two missing teeth.

"Nice to meet you, Isa." Caitlin shook Isa's hand while gently disengaging her pant leg from the puppy's fiercely clenched teeth. "I heard you've been riding my old horse."

"Chico?"

"Uh-huh. He and I were good pals a lot of years ago."

"My dad never told us that." Cassie appeared suitably impressed.

"He may not have remembered."

"I don't know. He's got a pretty good memory. He's always boring us with stories about when he was our age."

"Yeah," Isa agreed, imitating Cassie's tone. "Boring us."

"He's not the one who took me riding." Caitlin glanced up as Ethan joined them, a familiar fluttering in her middle. "Your uncle Ethan did."

"Oh," Cassie said, as if she suddenly understood everything. "I see."

"Isn't it time for you two to hit the sack?" Ethan came up behind the girls and patted them on the head.

"Do we have to?" Cassie complained.

"Do we have to?" Isa echoed, only whinier.

"Get yourselves inside. Whether or not you go to bed is up to your parents."

"Just when it was getting good," Cassie mumbled under her breath.

"What about Prince?" Isa asked.

"He's fine in the round pen. I'll put him away later."

"Uncle Ethan's breaking Prince," Cassie announced with pride.

"He told me." Caitlin sent him a silent reprimand. "Except he's not supposed to do anything that might hurt his shoulder."

"Like bronc riding? 'Cause he went to Mr. Duvall's earlier."

"Exactly like bronc riding."

Would he ever learn? Ever change?

And what if he did?

"Scoot," Ethan admonished the girls, his voice warm with affection. "You've gotten me in enough trouble for one night."

"I'm not sure you need any help," Caitlin admonished.

"Never did."

So true. And for much of that trouble, she'd been his cohort. How many times had they sneaked out together when they were supposed to be home in bed? Or skipped class to head to the river? Or risked being caught making love when her college roommate was due back any minute?

No sooner were the girls out of earshot, the puppy chasing gleefully after them, than Ethan said, "About this afternoon—"

"It's okay. Really." Caitlin didn't want to talk about it. Not tonight. Maybe not ever. "Water under the bridge."

"I did love you. More than anything."

Why did he have to say that? "If you don't mind, Ethan, I've had a long day."

That did the trick, and he shut up.

They walked the short distance to his bunkhouse. Caitlin wasn't sure what to expect, having never been inside before. It had always been occupied by two or three ranch hands when she and Ethan dated.

They stopped at her van for her duffel bag and the portable table, which Ethan insisted on carrying despite her protests.

"This is nice," she commented upon entering the modest stucco structure.

"There's still a lot of work to do."

She noticed the partially framed walls dividing the single large room into a living room, bedroom and hall, and the smell of fresh paint lingering in the air. "It's bigger than I thought it would be."

He leaned the portable table against the kitchen counter. "To be honest, I didn't think you'd come."

"Like you said before, we have an agreement. And I don't back out on agreements just because the other person says something I don't like or don't agree with."

"Me, either."

"Good." Caitlin lightened her tone. "Because the committee is really excited about the Holly Days wagon rides." She removed her jacket and reached into the duffel bag, more than ready to get down to business. "I usually start with some heat therapy."

"Shirt on or off?"

"A T-shirt's fine."

Without any hesitation, he stripped off his denim jacket and work shirt and tossed them onto the couch.

Oh, boy. Clearly, she should have better prepared

herself on the drive over. Whoever thought plain white T-shirts could be so sexy?

Tearing her gaze away required effort. She looked at his feet. "You might want to change out of those boots." Then she remembered his prosthesis. "But it isn't necessary."

"Be right back."

He stepped through the partially framed wall into the bedroom. Sitting with his back to her on the corner of the bed, he removed his boots. She thought she heard the sound of a zipper.

Rather than stare, she busied herself setting up the portable table and warming a hot pack in the microwave.

Ethan returned a few minutes later wearing a pair of athletic shoes.

"Have a seat." She indicated the kitchen chair she'd pulled out. "I brought these for tonight." She touched the pair of two-pound hand weights she'd set on the table. "Do you by chance have any of your own?"

"Not here. There might be some in the storeroom. It's been a while since I've worked out."

Caitlin remembered when Ethan had played football and basketball. While he'd lifted weights in the garage, she'd kept him company, talking and flirting and doing her best to distract him. Most of the time, it hadn't worked. But there were times it had....

Removing the hot pack from the microwave, she tested the temperature before laying it on his shoulder. Next, she busied herself readying the portable table. In truth, there wasn't much to do. She wiped it down twice with disinfectant spray just to avoid standing around. Ethan, she was sure, would attempt to fill the lull with conversation of a personal nature, and she was determined to keep their session completely professional.

"Is Justin the reason you became a nurse?"

Caitlin had been fluffing a small travel pillow. At Ethan's question, she set it down. Usually when people asked, she answered that she'd always wanted to be a nurse. Ethan, however, knew better.

"Yes." She smoothed the last remaining wrinkles from the pillowcase. "After the accident, I took an active role in his care. Found out I could actually stand the sight of blood. I'm a pretty good nurse. Who'd have guessed?"

"Me."

"Right." She gave a small laugh. "The last thing I was interested in when we were going together was taking care of other people."

"You're a softie. The first to jump in when someone needs assistance. Of any kind. I always figured you'd work in a people-oriented field."

What had Ethan seen in her all those years ago that she hadn't seen herself?

"Let's start on those exercises," she said briskly.

She spent the next twenty minutes showing him several simple exercises designed to loosen his muscles, build strength, decrease pain and restore mobility. Some of the exercises were done with weights, others without. Some standing, some sitting. When they were finished, Caitlin instructed him to lie on the table.

"Face up or down?" he asked.

"Up."

She thought she'd prepared herself for this part of the session. Once again, she was wrong.

Bending over Ethan, she wrapped her arms around his upper body, leaning in so that their faces were inches apart. Their positions, and the ones that followed, sorely tested her ability to remain detached. His dark eyes locked with hers. His chest rose and fell with each breath he took. His masculine scent filled her nostrils and triggered an onslaught of sensual memories.

The cheerfulness he'd exhibited earlier slowly vanished, and his features went from animated to stoic to strained. He, too, was being affected by their close proximity.

Levering a hand beneath his shoulder, she lifted his arm over his head, stretching it as far as his constricted muscles would allow. Unable to stop herself, she looked down at his face, bracing herself for the jolt of awareness that would race through her.

It didn't happen quite like she imagined.

Ethan tensed, his upper body involuntarily lifting several inches off the table. "Son of a bitch! That hurts."

"Sorry." Caitlin immediately relaxed her grip. "I didn't realize…. Justin usually lets me know right away when I'm pushing him too hard."

"That'll teach me to tough it out." Perspiration beaded his brow.

"Yes, it will." She kneaded his shoulder, noting when the tension ebbed away. "I really didn't mean to hurt you."

"You sure? I was thinking it was your way of getting back at me for all the misery I caused you."

"You *are* joking, right?" When he didn't reply, she said, "Ethan!"

"Yes. I'm joking."

His words didn't reassure her.

"Caitlin." He reached for her hand and clasped it in his.

She made a token effort to pull away, then gave up. Seeing him on the table, knowing he was in pain, tugged on that soft spot in her heart he'd talked about earlier.

All at once, he sat up and swung his legs over the side of the table.

"Wait," she protested. "We're not done."

"No, we're not."

It took her a second to realize he wasn't referring to their physical-therapy session.

"You misunderstood me." She tried to back away.

He gripped her hand, holding her firmly in place. "I want to see you again. And not just for more PT or when you and your crew are here working on the wagon."

"Ethan, we can't. I can't."

"Give us a chance."

"It's impossible."

"I know you haven't forgiven me yet."

"I'm working on it."

"Is it my leg?"

"God, no! That doesn't matter to me in the slightest." Despite her vehement objection, she could see by his expression he didn't believe her. "It's your bronc riding. And breaking horses for Clay. And the mustang. And telling Justin he can come here and ride anytime he wants."

"Why can't he?"

"It's too dangerous."

"Probably no more dangerous than basketball or baseball. Especially on old Chico."

"He could fall."

"He could have tipped his wheelchair on the way to see Prince."

"That's different, and you know it."

"I wouldn't put him on any horse that wasn't dead broke. And we have safety equipment if he wants. Helmets. A harness."

"It's not that. Justin gets enthusiastic. Tries to do more than he can."

"Don't you think he's the best judge of his limitations?"

She frowned. "I should have figured you wouldn't understand."

"You're wrong. I understand your brother very well. A whole lot better than you do, I'm guessing."

"That's not what I mean."

"A guy being disabled doesn't give other people the right to run someone's life or make decisions for him. Not even family. No matter how good their intentions are or how guilty they feel."

She flinched as if struck.

"Caitlin." Ethan released her and pushed off the table, landing on his feet. "I'm sorry. I get defensive sometimes. Shoot off my mouth."

"You take chances, Ethan." She squared her shoulders. "Big chances. Without the slightest fear. Justin does, too."

"There was a time you liked that about me."

Oh, she had. Very much. "But not anymore."

"Justin's accident wasn't your fault!"

"That's not true. He got hurt pulling a stupid stunt I

convinced him to do." Reaching for the hot pack, she began packing her duffel bag. "When I first became a nurse, I trained in a trauma center. I thought it would help me better understand Justin's needs. You can't imagine the injuries I saw."

"Actually, I can. I spent two months in a military rehab center."

"Then you have to understand where I'm coming from." She shoved item after item into the bag. "I lost count of how many people I treated who were victims of sport or recreational-related accidents. Skydiving, drag racing, skiing and, yes, horseback riding."

Ethan came up behind her. "People get hurt just walking across the street."

Damn. He was close. Too close. If he touched her, she'd give in or break down or otherwise embarrass herself.

No, not happening. She was strong and could resist him and these feelings whirling out of control inside her.

"Fewer people get hurt walking across a street than they do jumping off a cliff into the river or riding a wild bronc." She paused, steeling her resolve. "I can't handle someone I care about being hurt. Or worse. Not again." Her voice warbled on the last two words.

"Does that mean you care about me?"

Not the response she was expecting. She zipped the duffel bag closed. "Of course I do."

"Would you go out with me if I wasn't riding broncs or breaking horses?"

"I don't know. Maybe."

"Okay." He grabbed his shirt and put it on, not bothering to button it.

Okay?

"Are you saying you'd quit bronc riding and breaking horses for me?"

He replied without missing a beat. "No. I don't believe people have the right to demand someone to give up their passion as a condition of the relationship. That's unfair. I wouldn't ask you to give up nursing, just like I wouldn't ask my brother to give up what's left of this ranch."

This time he gave her the response she'd expected to hear.

It also confirmed what she knew to be true. There was no chance for her and Ethan. Not as long as he cared more about what he wanted than he did about her.

Chapter 5

Ethan didn't think he'd ever seen Clay's rodeo arena so busy. At least forty men had shown up to practice for the jackpot next weekend. The majority of them were bull riders, the rest bronc riders. Family members or girlfriends tagged along, bringing ice chests and folding chairs and lap blankets to ward off the chill. Those who didn't gather around the lowered tailgates of their trucks sat in the bleachers observing the practice rounds with interest. Even more stood by or straddled the fences, chatting up the cowboys.

"What's with folks in these parts?" Conner asked, settling into a vacant spot on the fence alongside Ethan. "Don't they have anything better to do on a Friday night?"

"I was just thinking the same thing."

Like Clay, Conner had been Ethan's friend since

grade school. Conner sometimes helped the Powells, leading trail rides and giving roping lessons. He'd also been with them on that night in the mountains when they'd captured Prince. Conner's regular job was systems analyst for a large manufacturing plant in Scottsdale, though no one would guess by his well-worn jeans, scuffed boots and weathered cowboy hat that he held two degrees, one in computer science and the other in business management.

"Your brother invited me for Thanksgiving dinner."

"You coming?"

"Can't, pal. Going to be at the folks'."

"Come over later for dessert if you want."

This Thanksgiving would mark the first holiday the Powells had celebrated since Ethan's mother died. Of course, Ethan hadn't been home for most of those Easters, Thanksgivings and Christmases. He was really looking forward to the dinner this year, brightened considerably by the addition of Cassie, Sage and Isa.

"Are you riding tonight?" Ethan asked as he watched the young man preparing to go next, studying his techniques and comparing them to his own. The kid was inexperienced but showed real potential. He might do well at the jackpot.

"Hell, no." Conner snorted. "I'm not about to risk scrambling my brain."

According to Caitlin, that was exactly what Ethan did on a regular basis.

"You used to like bronc riding. Bull riding, too."

"Yeah, before I grew up."

What did that say about Ethan?

His attention wandered to the makeshift first-aid station beneath the announcer's stand. Caitlin had arrived a half hour earlier, unloaded several boxes and grocery sacks, then disappeared inside. She had yet to emerge. He hoped she was simply busy and not avoiding him after their...what? Second disagreement?

He didn't much like the habit they'd fallen into of late.

"Something bothering you?" Conner asked.

"Just got a lot on my mind."

"Like qualifying for the jackpot?"

"Oh, I'm going to qualify. If not tonight, then tomorrow."

Ethan had put his name in about ten minutes before Conner arrived. He figured he had a little time before heading over to the chutes.

"Clay letting you practice with that bum shoulder?"

"It's better." And it was better. Marginally. He hadn't included that qualifier when he'd talked to Clay, however. "I have to go in for a follow-up exam before the jackpot."

Another chance to see Caitlin.

"Then what's with the scowl?" Conner asked.

Ethan decided he didn't care for old friends who knew him too well. "I did something stupid last night."

"What else is new?"

He drew back in mock offense. "That's a fine thing to say."

"And true." When Ethan remained silent, Conner burst into deep, rich laughter. "Come on. Fess up, buddy."

"I sort of asked Caitlin out."

"Sort of?" Conner's brows shot up.

"I might have suggested that she and I test the relationship waters."

"Relationship waters! Just how much Dr. Phil do you watch?"

"You're not helping."

"All right." He laughed again. "What did she say?"

"In a nutshell, no. Not so long as I'm riding broncs and breaking green horses."

"You going to quit?"

At that moment, Caitlin emerged from the first-aid station. Shielding her eyes from the bright flood-lights, she scanned the arena and nearby stands. Ethan guessed she was searching for Clay. Her gaze lit on him momentarily. No sooner did his pulse skyrocket than she nonchalantly looked elsewhere.

"No, I'm not going to quit," he told Conner.

"Why not?"

"Hell, I've barely started again."

"Why continue? We all know you can do it."

There it was again, the reference to him having something to prove.

"Except I *haven't* done it. Not for eight seconds."

"Is bronc riding really that important?"

"It's not the bronc riding."

"What then?"

"I just want to be Ethan Powell again. Not Ethan Powell who lost his leg while serving in the Middle East."

"That isn't how people think of you."

"Not you, maybe. But everybody else does."

"When did you become a mind reader?"

Ethan ignored Conner. People who were physically whole didn't understand. Didn't notice the stares. Ethan noticed. There were at least a dozen individuals casting discreet glances in his direction this very moment. And if he possessed superhearing, he was sure he'd catch his name being mentioned in every conversation at some point during the night.

Conner rested his forearms on the fence and shifted his weight from one foot to the other. "What makes you sure everyone walks around thinking there goes Ethan Powell, the peg-legged cowboy?"

Conner was lucky they were such good friends. If not, Ethan wouldn't let him get away with that last remark, teasing or not.

"I don't know," Conner mused out loud. "If it were me, and a gal as pretty as Caitlin Carmichael asked me to give up something for her, I'd be inclined to oblige."

Ethan's attention zeroed in on Caitlin. She stood beside the announcer's booth, pushing a breeze-blown lock of hair back from her face. He liked the shorter cut, once he'd gotten past the initial shock. The strands curled attractively around her face in a way they hadn't before. She wore jeans tonight and, unlike all the other loose garments he'd seen her in, they fit her to perfection.

Conner nudged Ethan in the ribs. "Why don't you go over and talk to her."

"We didn't exactly part on good terms last night."

After his declaration, she'd hurriedly packed her things. Refusing his help, she'd carted the portable table out to the van and hightailed it off the ranch without so much as a backward glance.

Ethan had spent another restless night, this one less from shoulder pain and more from mentally kicking himself for being such a fool.

"Ethan Powell!" The young woman Clay had recruited to help out checked off Ethan's name on the clipboard she was holding. "On deck."

He pushed away from the fence. "Guess I'm up."

"You sure about this?" All trace of joking was gone from Conner's voice.

Ethan shot Caitlin another glance. No question this time, she was staring straight at him. Even at this distance, he could discern the worry on her face. Or was that pleading?

If he wanted to, he could turn around, walk away from the chutes and toward her. Show her he was willing to compromise in order to test those relationship waters he'd mentioned earlier.

But when he took that first step, it was in the direction of the chutes. He sensed her tracking him the entire way. He also sensed her disappointment.

It wasn't enough to make him change his mind. Not with the dozens of spectators also tracking him and waiting for him to fail, thinking maybe he'd lost a part of his mind in that explosion along with his leg.

As the big brute he was about to ride greeted him with bared teeth and flattened ears, Ethan began wondering the same thing.

Caitlin watched Ethan amble over to the chutes, her agitation mounting with each step he took. She so wished he'd give up this stupid—make that insane—idea of riding broncs. What was the matter with him? With all men? They had some kind of ridiculous ambition to risk life and limb just to prove they were tough.

Without consciously planning it, she moved trance-like toward the arena fence. Ethan had disappeared behind the chutes, preparing for his turn. Just as she reached the railing, he reappeared. Scaling the fence, he straddled the top and waited, conversing with the cowboy beside him.

Caitlin's initial thought was how lucky that the first-aid station was fully stocked and operational. Her second one—she hoped to heck he didn't need it.

"Think he'll go a full eight seconds this time?"

"Don't know. I still can't believe he's trying. If anything goes wrong...jeez, he's already lost one leg."

The people next to Caitlin were discussing Ethan. She had to agree with the second man's opinion.

Ethan slowly lowered himself onto the bronc's back. Caitlin's stomach constricted into a tight fist of worry. He'd survived two other rides that she knew of, but not unscathed. It could be worse tonight.

Standing on tiptoe, she craned her neck to see over the high wall of the chute. The only thing visible was the crown of Ethan's tan Stetson.

All at once the gate next to Ethan's chute opened and a figure on horseback burst through it. The ride lasted a few harrowing seconds and ended with the cowboy sprawled on his back in the dirt, his chest visibly heaving. So was Caitlin's. The horse, kicking his hind legs, loped in a victory circle until the pickup men were able to safely herd him to the far side of the arena and through the exit gate.

Caitlin, hands on the railing, ready to bolt into the arena if necessary, expelled a sigh of relief when the cowboy rolled over and clambered to his feet. The crowd rewarded him with a round of applause as he walked, then jogged to the gate in order that the next participant—Ethan?—could go. Thankfully, the cowboy didn't appear in need of any medical attention. But another man had earlier in the evening. He'd suffered a nasty gash on his chin when his face collided with his saddle horn.

Caitlin had advised him to take the rest of the week off from bronc riding. He hadn't heeded her advice, but instead had gone right out and put his name in again. Crazy.

Like Ethan.

How did these wives and girlfriends here tonight stand watching the men they loved without constantly breaking down? Caitlin couldn't do it.

The wrangler manning the gates pulled the center one open, scrambling out of the way as he did. All at once a large, dark-colored horse hurtled into the arena, all four feet off the ground and Ethan astride his back.

Caitlin understood very little about bronc riding, despite having watched Ethan a hundred times in years past. There was more, she knew, to a successful ride than just remaining in the saddle for eight seconds. Something to do with how high the horse bucked and how expertly the cowboy rode him.

Both seemed to be happening as she watched Ethan. The horse achieved tremendous height, humping his back into a tight arc while Ethan hung on and rode the tar out of him.

Eight seconds had never lasted so long. Caitlin vaguely registered the sound of a buzzer going off. As the pickup men flanked the horse, one of them grabbed the bucking strap and jerked it loose. The horse immediately stopped kicking and began trotting. The other pickup man extended his arm to Ethan, who reached for it.

Caitlin relaxed, let her shoulders sag. The worst was over.

Suddenly, the horse gave a last mighty buck and unseated Ethan, launching him into the air. Caitlin stifled a cry and clung to the fence railing with such force the coiled wire cable cut into her palms.

By some miracle, Ethan righted himself and landed

on his feet…only to pitch face-first onto the ground. The crowd let out a collective gasp.

Caitlin found herself hurrying along the arena fence, stopping when she was directly across from the spot where he had fallen. The first pickup man rode his horse over to check on Ethan, blocking her view. She was just about to move when Ethan began to rise. The crowd applauded as he stood and hobbled awkwardly away.

Hobbled! Had he hurt his good leg? What would he do? How would he get around? He must be in terrible pain.

She followed him from the other side of the fence, zigzagging between people in an effort to keep up. She lost sight of him when he exited through the gate and had to make a detour around the cattle pens. By now, she was practically running.

Where had he gone?

Finally, thankfully, she located him standing behind the chutes, talking to a group of men. Hands braced on his hips, he leaned forward at the waist. It was a posture Caitlin often observed in people who were injured.

Enough was enough. She'd drag him, kicking and screaming if necessary, to the first-aid station and examine him. Keep him still long enough to listen to her advice to take it easy.

She set out, resolute. At the same moment, one of the men clapped Ethan on the back and laughed loudly. Caitlin was shocked. Did the cowboy have no consideration for someone in pain?

"Ethan," she called.

He turned then. And rather than a grimace, his face wore a wide, exuberant grin.

Sweet heaven, he was handsome. She came to an

abrupt halt, her mind emptying of everyone and everything save him and what they'd once had together. What they could have together now if he would just come to his senses.

He limped toward her. "Did you see?"

"Yes. Are you all right?"

"I couldn't be better."

Realization dawned. Slowly, but it dawned. The men surrounding Ethan were congratulating him. Because he... She recalled hearing the buzzer. He had gone a full eight seconds. He'd said something about that the other night. If he lasted eight seconds, Clay would allow him to compete in the upcoming jackpot.

Dammit!

Fury bubbled up inside her. More at herself than Ethan. What a fool she'd been to think even for a few seconds that they could rekindle their former relationship.

"I just wanted to make sure you were okay."

She expected him to return to his friends. After all, her tone had been anything but inviting.

Only he didn't. He kept coming straight toward her. Before she could object, he hauled her into his arms and swung her in a wide circle.

"Put me down before you hurt yourself again."

"I did it!"

"Ethan, please. Your shoulder."

He released her. The moment her feet touched the ground, he lowered his mouth to hers, stopping a fraction of an inch shy of kissing her.

"I've been wanting to do this for the last three days."

Three days? Was that all?

She'd been waiting the past eight years, eleven months and twenty-one days to kiss him.

Just like that, their years apart melted away. Ethan's lips moved expertly over hers, applying just the right amount of pressure to coax a melting response from her. He'd always been an amazing kisser. That, or they were just amazing together. Their bodies fit perfectly. Her soft curves nestled against his hard planes as his arm circled her waist and drew her against him.

Caitlin was tempted to lose herself in his kiss. Set aside her worries and concerns and embrace the moment. And she did…until sanity returned, giving her a big, solid kick. The hoots and hollers of Ethan's cowboy friends might have had something to do with it, too.

Just how many people were watching them?

Caitlin broke off the kiss and pressed a hand to her flaming cheek. Ethan didn't appear the least bit embarrassed. Of course not.

"That shouldn't have happened," she stammered, and backed away.

Ethan started after her. "But it did happen," he said in a low voice. "And for a minute there, you were liking it every bit as much as I did."

Had they really kissed for more than a minute?

Wilting beneath stares from dozens of eyes, she executed a hasty retreat.

"Caitlin." Ethan appeared beside her.

"I don't want to talk." She couldn't. Her thoughts were in a jumble. She'd wind up saying something she'd regret. "Not now." She brushed past him.

"I need— Wait up, Caitlin!"

Through the haze of fog surrounding her, she heard the note of urgency in Ethan's voice. Still fuming, she almost didn't stop.

Almost.

She spun around just in time to see him crumple, a look of pure agony on his face.

"Ethan! Are you all right?" Instinct took over, and she ran to him. Dropping to her knees, she touched his head and back with gentle fingers. "What happened?"

He pushed himself to a sitting position. "I thought you were mad at me." Labored breathing punctuated each word.

"I am mad at you."

His grimace turned into a lopsided smile. "Then how come you didn't keep walking?"

"I'm a nurse."

"That's not why."

She made a sound of frustration. "Are you hurt or not?"

"It's my leg."

"Did you sprain it?"

"No." He groaned and shifted his weight.

Between their heated kiss and Ethan's fall, they'd drawn a sizable audience. Some of Ethan's friends expressed their concern and offered assistance.

"I'll be all right," he insisted. "My leg came loose in the fall."

His prosthesis. Thank goodness that was all.

Two of his buddies hauled Ethan upright. Still grinning, he slung an arm around their shoulders.

"Where to?" the taller of the pair asked.

"The first-aid station."

Caitlin hurried ahead of them to open the door and flip on the light. The men brought Ethan inside and deposited him in the same metal folding chair he'd sat in that first night.

"You need anything?" one friend asked.

"Naw, I'm fine." He nodded at them both. "Appreciate the lift."

The taller man tipped his hat at Caitlin and followed his buddy outside.

"What can I do?" she asked.

"I've got it." Ethan didn't exactly push her away, but he made it more than clear with his gesture and tone that he didn't want her hovering. Bracing his hands on the chair seat, he managed to stand, though unsteadily. His loose prosthesis hung at an odd angle in front of him.

She rushed forward, stopping short when he snapped, "I've got it!"

"Okay."

Patients often refused help. She had learned to navigate the fine line between respecting their wishes and providing the care they needed. She watched him intently from beside the table, ready to jump in if necessary.

With his free hand, he reached for his belt buckle and unfastened it with a flick of his wrist.

Her breath caught. "What are you doing?"

"Putting my leg back on."

Naturally. How silly of her.

In order to get at his prosthesis, he had to remove his pants. There was no other way.

What had she been thinking?

Once he had his jeans unzipped, he slid them down his hips and sat back in the chair. His shirttails covered him. Only the lower part of his blue—blue?—boxer shorts was visible. Caitlin averted her gaze, concentrating on his feet.

The prosthesis, caught in the pant leg, didn't cooperate. Without thinking, she knelt in front of him and grabbed it by the boot.

"You don't have to." Ethan's hands grappled with hers.

"Let me," she said softly. "Please."

She lifted her face to his. She could read in his eyes how difficult this was for him. He didn't want people seeing him at his most vulnerable.

Gripping the hem, she pushed the prosthesis back up his pant leg.

Ethan didn't move at first. Then, taking hold of the prosthesis around the cup, he fitted it to his stump. There was a quiet whoosh as air escaped. When he was done, he secured the elastic cuff, which had slipped off during his fall.

She said nothing, knowing the more professional she acted, the easier it would be for Ethan. Easier for her, too.

As soon as he was done, they both stood. She placed a hand on his lower back to steady him while he pulled up his jeans and tucked in his shirt.

"Thank you," he said, buckling his belt.

"That's why I'm here, and what Clay pays me for."

"Is that the only reason?" He pinned her in place with those dark brown eyes of his.

If only she could lie. Say that helping him was just her job. Nothing more.

But her mouth refused to listen to her brain's instructions. What they'd just shared had in some ways been more intimate than their earlier kiss. To lie would be dishonoring that moment and the undeniable, yet impossible, connection they shared.

"No, Ethan. It's not the only reason." She straightened, set her mouth in a resolute line. "But we both know it should be."

Chapter 6

Ethan stood outside the round pen. He'd been up since five this morning, working with Prince. His deadline for breaking the mustang, as he'd told Justin the other day, was fast approaching, and he was determined to make some real progress. After two patience-testing hours, ones that aggravated his shoulder considerably, Ethan had the saddle blanket on Prince's back, along with a lightweight pack saddle.

Prince didn't like either, and alternately trotted and loped in circles as if he could outrun them. Each time he stopped, he glared menacingly at Ethan.

"Not yet, pal. A little while longer."

Prince stomped his left foot, then started trotting again.

Gavin came up beside Ethan. "I'm impressed."

"Don't be. The pack saddle may be on his back, but he's far from accepting it."

Prince came to an abrupt halt across from them. Reaching his head around, he took hold of the blanket with his teeth and gave an angry yank. Ethan imagined Prince trying that same move with his pant leg when he finally managed to mount the horse.

"You ready to help me with that wagon before Caitlin gets here?" he asked.

Gavin hitched his chin at Prince. "What are the chances that blanket will be in shreds and the pack saddle in pieces when we get back?"

Prince was now sniffing the cinch holding the saddle in place, and making irritated snuffling sounds.

"I bet he'll quiet down the second we're gone," Ethan said.

"Hmm."

"He always has to put on a show. Let everyone know how tough he is."

"He's not the only one."

"Are you referring to me?" They set out in the direction of the old cattle barn.

"I heard about your fall last night."

"Did you also hear I qualified for the jackpot?"

"I did. And congratulations. So, how badly were you hurt?"

"My leg came loose is all."

"Is that why Caitlin kissed you?"

Now it was Ethan's turn to grin. "It was more the other way around. I kissed her."

"Clay said she didn't act like she objected."

"He was there?" Ethan scratched his head. "Really?" What else had he missed when all his attention was riveted on Caitlin?

"Am I to assume the two of you are back together?"

"No. She's made it pretty clear there's no chance of that."

"Then why the kiss?"

"I'd just finished my ride. And she looked really pretty. I couldn't help myself."

"Be careful you don't hurt her again."

Ethan had been having similar thoughts. But then he'd recall Caitlin's lips, soft and pliant and molding to his. She might be resisting him at every turn, but there was no denying her response.

She still cared, and the knowledge pleased Ethan enormously.

As far as what he'd felt when she'd helped him with his prosthesis, he still wasn't sure. Not since his last visit to the VA hospital had he allowed anyone to view his prosthesis up close, much less touch it. He could argue Caitlin was a nurse, but that wasn't the reason he'd accepted her help.

He trusted her. Simple as that. Unfortunately, she didn't trust him in return.

It was a situation he intended to rectify.

He and his brother spent ten minutes unburying the wagon, and another ten rearranging the surrounding junk, as Gavin called it. They were just rolling the wagon into the open area near the horse-bathing rack when Caitlin's minivan pulled up, an older model sedan following in its wake. Ethan was surprised to see Justin in the passenger seat of her van, considering she didn't want him anywhere near horses.

"Hi." She greeted Ethan and Gavin with a bright

smile that revealed nothing other than her delight at finding the wagon ready for her crew of volunteers to clean, repair and decorate.

Introductions were made. Four helpers beside Justin had accompanied Caitlin—an older man, a middle-aged woman and a couple in their early twenties who were obviously boyfriend and girlfriend. That relationship didn't prevent Justin's gaze from constantly traveling to the young woman.

Poor guy. He looked on the verge of falling head over heels for a woman who was completely unavailable.

Ethan was no different.

"I'm going to check on Prince," Gavin said after a bit. "Nice to meet you all."

Ethan probably didn't need to hang around the volunteers, either, but he couldn't make himself leave.

The older man proved to be quite handy with a hammer, wrench and electric drill. Together, he and Ethan repaired the broken wheel, cracked seat and loose running board. They also replaced a half-dozen missing bolts. The rest of the volunteers cleaned—and cleaned. Ten years of neglect had resulted in a mountain of dust, dirt and grime.

"Would it be all right if we gave the wagon a fresh coat of paint?" Caitlin asked. "We'd buy the paint, of course."

"Sure. As long as you use John Deere green."

She laughed. "I think we can manage that. It'll go perfectly with the wreaths and Christmas lights."

The volunteers were taking a well-deserved break, refueling with doughnuts the older gentleman had brought.

"Justin seems taken with Tamiko," Ethan said. He and Caitlin sat on a pair of old crates, away from the rest of the volunteers.

"I noticed that, too." She cast a worried glance at her brother, who maneuvered his wheelchair in order to be closer to the young woman. "I hope she doesn't break his heart."

"Looks to me like she's more interested in him than she is in her boyfriend."

Justin was holding the hose and filling a bucket with water while Tamiko poured in a capful of liquid soap. There was no mistaking the exchange of smiles and frequent eye contact.

"Tamiko's a sweet, funny girl," Caitlin said. "But to be honest, I don't think Justin stands a chance with her."

"Because she already has a boyfriend?"

"That—" Caitlin turned back to Ethan "—and because he's in a wheelchair."

"Don't underestimate him. Or her."

She said nothing, perhaps because this conversation had started to sound too much like the one they'd had in his bunkhouse earlier in the week.

They finished their doughnuts and spent the next several minutes watching an advanced riding class in the arena. Their break would soon be over, and Ethan didn't think he'd have another chance to speak to Caitlin alone.

"About last night…"

She immediately straightened. "We both agreed kissing was a mistake."

"I didn't agree."

"Ethan." She looked over at her crew of volunteers before continuing. "Can we discuss this later?"

"When later?"

"I brought my table and duffel bag. We can have another PT session today if you're available."

"After what you said, I assumed we weren't continuing."

"I told you, a deal's a deal." She gathered up their trash. "Besides, you need physical therapy if that shoulder's going to heal properly."

He did need it, what with the jackpot only a week away.

And the prospect of Caitlin's hands on him, even if they frequently caused him excruciating pain, was too appealing to resist.

Caitlin waved goodbye to her brother and friends. Had she been wrong, making arrangements for Justin to return home without her? He sat in the backseat next to Tamiko. Her boyfriend, for some reason, occupied the front passenger seat. Given his angry glare, he wasn't too happy about the arrangement.

Tamiko was only being nice, Caitlin told herself. She wouldn't intentionally lead Justin on. But he was following nonetheless.

Work on the wagon had gone well, better than Caitlin had expected. Her emotional state, however, was in turmoil…a continuation from the previous night and this afternoon.

She should avoid Ethan, her common sense urged. The problem was they had an agreement, one that would bring them together often in the coming weeks.

The prospect unsettled her. Made her a little nervous.

It also thrilled her.

Telling herself over and over that she was here for one reason only, she returned to her minivan and drove it to the bunkhouse. Ethan wasn't there. He'd left after bidding Caitlin's friends and brother goodbye. She could see him in the round pen across the way, unsaddling Prince under Gavin's watchful eye. Unless she was mistaken, the horse wasn't making much of a fuss.

A step in the right direction.

Hopefully, Prince would be as gentle when the day came for Ethan to ride him.

He'd been lucky last night at the rodeo arena. Very lucky. His next fall could end differently.

She carried her portable table from the van to the bunkhouse, determined to complete the task before Ethan showed up and did it for her. Again. When he arrived a few minutes later, Caitlin, the table and her duffel bag were all waiting on the porch.

"Sorry I'm late," he said, nudging the door open with his good shoulder.

He kept his left arm tucked close to his chest, as he had all morning. What was wrong with her? She should have insisted he leave all the wagon repairs to her crew. But then she wouldn't have enjoyed his company for over two hours.

It reminded her a little of their senior year in high school, when she'd coerced him into helping her with decorations for the winter formal. He'd hated it, and his football teammates had ridiculed him. Still, he'd done everything she'd asked, and though she hadn't appreciated him as much as she should have, she'd never forgotten.

"Have you been icing your shoulder twice a day and taking ibuprofen?"

"Yes, Nurse Carmichael," he teased.

"How much did it hurt last night?"

"Before or after my ride?"

"Both."

"It hurt before. A lot more after."

"Didn't appear to affect your ride much. You lasted eight seconds."

"The horse was having a slow night." Ethan unbuttoned his long-sleeved work shirt, wincing slightly as he peeled it off. "I won't be nearly so fortunate next time."

After only one PT session, he pretty much knew the drill and completed the exercises with minimal instruction from her. She was glad to see he'd found the old set of weights and was using them. His range of motion, she observed, had improved minimally.

When he finished with the exercises, she patted the table. "Ready?"

He hopped on, then lay on his back. "You going to your parents' house for Thanksgiving?" he asked once she began rotating his arm.

She remembered from their first session that Ethan liked to talk during therapy. Justin did, too. It probably helped them tolerate the pain better. Except she wasn't fooled. The strain in their voices along with clenched jaws and muscle tremors gave them away.

"Actually, they're going to my aunt and uncle's in Green Valley."

"Don't your relatives usually come up here?"

"Not this year. Uncle Lee just had back surgery and

can't handle a long drive. They invited me and Justin. He hasn't decided for sure, but I'm not going."

"Why not?"

"I'm scheduled to work at the clinic Wednesday evening and will be here Friday morning to work on the wagon. Driving to Green Valley and back in one day is too much for me. I'll be wiped out."

"If you want," Ethan said through gritted teeth as she applied more pressure, "come to the house for dinner."

"I couldn't impose."

"Trust me, you won't be. Dad and Sage are doing all the cooking. Can't guarantee you won't get stuck with cleanup duty."

How many times had she done exactly that after dinner with the Powells? Too many to count. "I don't know...."

"This will be our first Thanksgiving dinner in nine years."

She didn't think he was trying to make her feel guilty as much as expressing his pleasure that the family had finally moved on enough after his mother's death to celebrate the holidays.

"Thank you." She lifted his arm high over his head. "But I'd better not."

"Is it because I kissed you last night?"

"Yes." That was only partially true. The bigger reason was that she'd kissed him back. Enthusiastically. "It wouldn't be right encouraging you when there's no hope of us ever...picking up where we left off." She couldn't bring herself to say *falling in love again*.

"My bronc riding," he said flatly.

"I explained already. And now that you've qualified for the jackpot, I'm assuming there's no chance you'll give it up."

"None."

"Turn on your right side," she instructed, hoping the change in position would put an end to their conversation.

It didn't.

"I care about you, Caitlin. And I think you still care about me."

"Of course I do. Just not like I used to."

"Then why are you always putting up your guard whenever we're together?"

"I'm a nurse." Lifting his shoulder off the table with one hand, she pushed down on his elbow with the other. "You're my patient."

"It's also easier to deny your feelings when you distance yourself."

"You're wrong."

"I don't think so."

The wound she'd believed long healed suddenly tore open, catching her unawares and leaving her feeling vulnerable. "I was devastated when you left."

That got a reaction from him—he winced.

Then again, her fingers were digging with excessive force into the soft tissue surrounding his shoulder.

"I don't regret enlisting, only how I handled telling you." His voice seemed to hold genuine regret.

"What about losing your leg?"

"Don't get me wrong, I'd rather that hadn't happened. But I was luckier than a lot of soldiers. At least I came home."

"I'd have gone with you."

"It doesn't work that way."

"Even if we were married?"

"I wanted to ask you."

"Then why didn't you?" Emotion thickened her voice.

"I was afraid something would happen to me. That I'd be killed and you'd be all alone. Like my father was after my mother died."

"Isn't that what you did? Left me alone? Only, instead of dying, you took off."

Neither of them spoke for a moment, and Caitlin relaxed her grip, the tension seeping out of both of them as she massaged his shoulder, upper arm and back.

Lying on his side, his eyes closed, the dim light softening his features, he looked seventeen again. Caitlin's anger faded, and she felt vulnerable all over, but for different reasons.

"I was an idiot," he said, breaking the silence. "I ran away from the very person I needed the most, because I couldn't handle my grief. You have no idea how much I wish I hadn't."

"Thank you for being honest. But it changes nothing." She stepped away from the table.

He sat up so abruptly the table shook. "That's what you're doing, too, Caitlin. You're running away."

"I wouldn't be here right now if that was true."

"Then come to Thanksgiving dinner."

"I told you, I can't."

"Trust me, I have no expectations where we're concerned—despite the kiss last night." He held up his hand when she would have protested. "We were swept up in the moment is all. No big deal."

Maybe not for him. It had been a very big deal for her.

"Come on." He grinned imploringly. "No one

should be alone on Thanksgiving. And Dad would love to see you again."

"Justin may be—"

"Bring him, too. He's more than welcome."

Caitlin couldn't imagine making a bigger mistake, considering her knee-buckling reaction to Ethan's kiss. If only she didn't dread spending Thanksgiving alone in her little condo. And Justin would probably love coming to the ranch....

"All right," she said, relenting. "I accept your invitation. As long as we're clear—*friends only*."

"Yes, ma'am," he answered, his solemn tone in direct contrast to the twinkle lighting his eyes.

Caitlin sighed tiredly.

Had he heard even one thing she said?

Chapter 7

Ethan's father stood in front of the open oven door, fussing over the roasting turkey as if he was competing in a professional cook-off and about to be judged.

"It's not browning right."

"Looks okay to me." Ethan peered around his dad's head. "I'm sure it'll taste fine."

"Humph."

Evidently not the right thing to say to someone who took food preparation seriously.

Wayne Powell shut the oven door with more force than was necessary. Grumbling to himself, he went to the counter and checked on the girls. They'd been assigned the task of peeling potatoes, an entire five-pound sack.

He wasn't annoyed with Ethan, at least not as much as he pretended. He liked being in charge of the kitchen, liked making a fuss. Up until Sage and Isa had entered their lives, cooking was the only chore he regularly performed on the ranch, choosing instead to remain a semirecluse. Even Cassie, his one and only grandchild, coming to live with them hadn't rescued him from the deep depression he'd succumbed to after his wife died. All that had changed when the girls went missing.

Finding them in the box canyon had not only resulted in Prince's capture, it restored Wayne Powell to his former self and his family.

This was truly a day to be thankful.

The reason foremost in Ethan's mind was Caitlin coming to dinner. He hadn't spoken to her about Thanksgiving since inviting her last Saturday, though he'd seen her twice for physical-therapy sessions. He worried that bringing up the topic of dinner might cause her to change her mind. Better to keep cool. Lie low. Feign disinterest.

Yeah, tell that to his gut, which had been churning all morning from nervous tension.

"How's the pico de gallo coming?" Ethan's father asked.

Sage stood at the counter beside the girls, chopping tomatoes, cilantro, green chillies, garlic and onions. "Almost done, and then I'll be out of your way."

Normally Ethan's father would have resisted serving pico de gallo and tortilla chips as an appetizer at Thanksgiving. But he loved Sage and Isa and welcomed their contribution, even if it wasn't a traditional dish.

"Nice day." Gavin appeared at Ethan's side and gave his brother a hand with putting the extra leaf in the dining table. "We haven't had this much commotion in a long time."

"Yeah, real nice." They'd always been a close family. It was just that for the last decade, they'd been a broken one. Like his brother, Ethan was glad to see their family on the mend.

"Too bad Sierra isn't here." Gavin slipped the extra leaf into place, then helped Ethan push the expanded table together.

"I don't know what's wrong with her. She hasn't called yet, and Dad's starting to worry."

"It's still early, and that job of hers keeps her busy."

"On Thanksgiving?"

"It's possible."

Ethan had his doubts. Something was wrong with his sister and had been since her last visit a year and a half ago. Everything had gone well, as far as he knew. Really well. But shortly after she returned to San Francisco, she'd stopped answering her phone, stopped emailing regularly and was always busy when someone did finally get ahold of her.

"Let's wait till dinner's over," Gavin said. "Then we'll call her."

He was always the more reasonable of the two brothers, and Ethan would be wise to listen. Still, he couldn't ignore his instincts, and they warned him to be on the watch where Sierra was concerned.

"I'm going to bring in more wood for the fireplace," he said.

"What about your shoulder?"

"I'm fine." Ethan wasn't exactly fine, though he was considerably improved, thanks to a constant regime of ibuprofen, ice packs and physical therapy. In fact, he was enough better that his confidence was growing. Despite not making eight seconds again since his ride last week, he'd changed his goal from just competing in Saturday's jackpot to placing in the top five positions.

If you want to be a winner, you have to think like one.

His high school coach's advice still rang in Ethan's ears, and he heeded it.

Escaping the bustle of the busy kitchen, he went outside to the woodpile behind the house. On his third trip carrying an armful of cut pine logs, he spied Clay's truck pulling through the main gate. His renewed friendship with his childhood buddy was yet another reason to be thankful today.

"Need a hand?" Clay asked, meeting him on the back porch.

"I think I've got enough for now." Ethan did let Clay open the door for him. "See your dad today?"

"Nope."

"Talk to him?"

No answer.

"Isn't it about time you two buried the hatchet?"

"We will. One day. Just not yet."

Clay and his father had suffered a terrible falling-out when Bud Duvall had refused to honor his agreement with Ethan's dad and had sold the Powell land out from under them. There was likely more to the story, but Clay chose not to elaborate, and Ethan respected his friend's privacy.

Taking his share of money from the family's cattle operation, Clay had struck out on his own, purchasing a large parcel of land a few miles down the road.

He'd used the remaining funds to construct the rodeo arena and bankroll his rodeo stock business. Somewhere in between, he'd married and, after six short months, divorced. But that subject was also off-limits.

While Clay shook hands and dispensed hugs to the other Powell family members, Ethan carried the last load of firewood into the living room, placing it in the log bin along with the rest. He was just glancing at the mantel clock and wondering if Caitlin had changed her mind, after all, when a small commotion rose from the kitchen.

"Nurse Carmichael's here!" Cassie's high-pitched voice echoed throughout the house.

Ethan headed for the kitchen, presenting a welcoming smile that he hoped hid the turmoil in his heart. Caitlin wanted to be friends, and he'd rather have her in his life as a friend than not at all.

It wasn't, however, what *he* wanted.

"Happy Thanksgiving."

He envied the girls, who clung to her with the tenacity of baby possums riding their mother's back.

"Same to you." She smiled brightly. "Sorry we're late."

To his delight, she extracted herself from the girls' clutches and gave him a casual but decidedly warm hug. He resisted the urge to fold her in his arms and bury his face in the soft, fragrant skin of her neck.

Justin appeared in the doorway, having taken a bit longer to cross the porch. He rolled his wheelchair over the threshold and into the kitchen, which was now crowded with nine people.

"Hi, everybody."

Reintroductions were made along with new ones.

When it came to Isa, the little girl hovered behind her mother. She wasn't normally shy, and Ethan suspected Justin's wheelchair had something to do with the change in her behavior.

"Hello, I'm Justin." He tilted his head so he could see her better and winked. "What's your name?"

"Isa," she answered timidly.

"Well, Isa, I was hoping for a tour of the house. Maybe you can show me around."

She crouched even farther behind Sage.

"That's too bad. Because I brought this box of chocolates, and I need someone to help me eat them." He produced a wrapped package from the backpack on his lap. "Possibly two someones."

That was enough encouragement for Cassie. She rushed forward. "Can I touch your chair?"

"Sure." Justin shifted sideways, and Cassie stroked the armrest.

"Wow!" She bent and examined the wheels. "Cool."

Isa slowly emerged from behind her mother to stand next to Cassie. At Justin's smile of encouragement, she also stroked the wheelchair's armrest.

"Come on, you two. Let's get out of here before the grown-ups put us to work."

"Yeah," Cassie agreed. "I hate peeling potatoes."

Including himself with the "kids," even though he was considerably older than them, sealed the deal. Justin and his young tour guides left the kitchen to explore the rest of the house.

Caitlin's smile followed them.

"He's very good with children," Sage observed.

"He's going be a teacher when he graduates."

"A good one, it looks like."

"What can I do to help?" Caitlin held up a container. "I brought a pumpkin pie."

She was instantly recruited to slice the freshly baked bread.

Ethan offered Clay a beer. Gavin joined them, and the three men retreated to the calm of the living room. Taking a seat on the couch, Ethan stared at the fire with its leaping flames and crackling logs. The woodsy scent filled the room, giving it that special holiday feeling.

"Sounds like the girls have coaxed Justin into a game of Uno," Gavin said, craning his neck to see through the archway and into the family room.

"He's a good sport," Ethan answered.

"A real nice guy," Clay concurred, and took a long swallow of his beer. "Shame about the accident."

"Doesn't seem to have slowed him down any."

"You're right about that." He turned to Ethan. "How's the physical therapy going with Caitlin?"

"Great. I have an appointment at the clinic tomorrow. I'm sure the doctor won't find anything."

"I wasn't talking about your shoulder." Clay shot Gavin a conspiratorial look.

Ethan's brother shrugged.

"Caitlin and I are friends," Ethan insisted. "That's all."

Maybe if he said it seven hundred more times, he'd start believing it.

"You weren't acting like friends the other night when you were kissing." Clay looked at Gavin again and received another shrug.

Ethan sipped his beer. He and Caitlin hadn't acted

like friends when they were kissing because it hadn't felt that way.

"What are you going to do?" Clay asked.

"Nothing. She says there's no chance for us as long as I'm riding broncs and breaking horses."

"Then give it up."

"Are you nuts?"

"Isn't she worth it?"

Conner had made a similar comment the other night at the rodeo arena.

"It's not like I wouldn't—won't—give up bronc riding eventually." When he'd erased all doubt from his and everyone else's minds that he was no different than before the car bomb explosion. "Breaking horses, that's another thing. It's my job."

"She's the love of your life."

"*Former* love of my life," he corrected. "And that was years ago."

"She could be again." Clay sent Gavin another look. This one was met with a confident nod.

Ethan was less sure about his feelings for Caitlin and hers for him. Could he ever give up his cowboy ways for her? He'd almost rather lose his other leg.

It was a quandary he continued to ponder all through dinner as he sat across the large table from her. He did his best to keep up with the lively conversations, but was completely distracted by her green eyes and the memory of them drifting shut as his mouth claimed hers.

"I had a wonderful time. Thank you so much for inviting us." Caitlin wrapped her arms around Wayne Powell's generous waist and squeezed.

He returned the hug with great enthusiasm. "It's wonderful to have you back. Just like old times."

She agreed. The only difference was the absence of his late wife, who'd been mentioned often during dinner.

"Give your parents my regards." Wayne released Caitlin. "And don't be a stranger, you hear?" He tapped the tip of her nose with his finger.

"I won't."

If only Caitlin was certain she could return for a social visit. No matter how often she told herself she wasn't interested in Ethan romantically, there was no denying the rush of awareness that stole over her whenever she caught his dark eyes observing her.

"Goodbye, Justin." Isa hung on to his wheelchair, which earlier in the day had intimidated her. "If you come back, I'll let you ride my horse, Chico."

"Deal, kiddo." He bumped fists with her before wheeling himself through the back door.

Caitlin's steps momentarily faltered. Was Isa's invitation spur-of-the-moment or had Justin and the girls been talking about riding? Considering his last visit to the ranch, Caitlin should have seen this coming.

"I'm right behind you," she called to her brother, who beat her out the door.

She'd said her farewells to everyone except Ethan, who'd disappeared at the last second. She tried not to let the obvious slight bother her. They'd see each other again tomorrow when she and her volunteers came by to work on the wagon.

Sound reasoning did nothing to alleviate her disappointment.

"Take your time," Justin called to her.

She scarcely noticed the hint of amusement in his

tone, she was so distracted. Once outside, she almost ran over Ethan.

"I'll walk you to your car."

That would probably be a mistake. It would be much less nerve-racking to say goodbye here, with his family watching from the doorway. Only she didn't, and he fell into step beside her.

Lately, it seemed, the harder she tried to keep him at a distance, the closer he got.

Or was it the closer she allowed him to get?

"Thanks again for coming," he said.

She hoped he wouldn't take her hand, as he had in the bunkhouse. Touching him would break down the last of her defenses.

"I really enjoyed myself. Justin did, too."

"Dad insists I ask you back."

"That was nice of him."

No commitments. Better for both of them in the long run.

"What time will you be here tomorrow? I'll make sure everything's ready."

"Really," she insisted, "I don't want to put you through any more trouble than I already have. It's enough that you're letting us use your wagon during the festival—and will be driving it."

"I like your friends. And I like you."

Here was where she was supposed to say, "I like you, too," but that would be asking for trouble.

"Let's schedule one last physical-therapy session before the jackpot," she said instead. "How about tomorrow after we're done working on the wagon?"

"Yeah, sure. I appreciate all you've done. My shoulder's doing great."

Justin had already hoisted himself into the front passenger seat and collapsed his wheelchair, leaning it against the open door. Ethan went over to him, and, after saying goodbye, grabbed the chair.

Caitlin knew better than to insist he let her get it. Whenever Ethan was around, he carried things. Maybe to show everyone he wasn't an invalid. More likely, that was the way Wayne Powell had raised his sons.

When Ethan had finished loading the chair, he came around to join her at the driver's-side door. For an awkward second or two, Caitlin debated what to do.

"See you tomorrow," he said.

"Ten sharp."

Another second passed. Two. Three.

Oh, what the hell, she thought. Throwing caution to the wind, she looped her arms around his neck for what was supposed to be a brief, casual hug....

Only she was the one to hold on, not Ethan.

The day had been filled with memories. Of the ranch house. Thanksgiving dinner. The Powell family. In truth, the past two weeks had been a constant trip down memory lane. She'd responded to Ethan's kiss the other night out of habit, her body instinctively nestling against his as it had so often in the past.

As it did now.

Emotions, tender and bittersweet, weakened her resolve. She leaned into him and rested her head in the crook of his neck. He stroked her hair, then combed his fingers through it. Another familiar gesture that stirred yet more memories.

She removed her arms, now strangely limp, from around his neck. "I have to go."

"Take care."

Thankfully, Ethan didn't acknowledge the hug.

It would serve her right if he did, after she'd been so adamant that there could never be anything between them again.

Before she quite knew what was happening, she was standing on her tiptoes and pressing her lips to his cheek, her hands resting gently on his chest.

He smelled amazing. Fresh and clean like the outdoors, where he spent most of his time. His flannel shirt was smooth beneath her palms, and the bristles of his five o'clock shadow tickled her lips. She shivered ever so slightly.

I wish you hadn't left.

The thought came from nowhere. No, not nowhere. It came from a tiny corner of her heart where it had remained lodged for nine long years.

Mystified and annoyed at what had come over her, she backed away from Ethan, ready to apologize for her lack of control.

One look at his nonchalant expression and she promptly shut her mouth.

Seriously! Was she the only one whose world was just rocked?

Evidently so.

Muttering something unintelligible, Caitlin dived into the minivan, dreading having to explain her actions to Justin.

How could she expect Ethan to believe all her talk about them being just friends when she'd rushed headlong over the line she'd vehemently insisted he not cross?

Chapter 8

Caitlin stood over a box of Christmas decorations, painstakingly unraveling a knotted mess that promised to be a string of lights. Over in the round pen, Ethan was working with Prince. He hadn't stopped by to help her and her crew, hadn't even waved at them. Considering the way they'd parted yesterday, he was undoubtedly avoiding her. With good reason. One minute she was insisting they couldn't see each other, and the next she was, well, all over him.

The sound of happy laughter distracted her, and she looked over at her brother and Tamiko. They were attempting to twine a string of lights through the spokes of a wagon wheel, and it didn't seem to matter that their efforts weren't producing the desired results. They were having fun.

There was a lesson in there somewhere for Caitlin. She worked too hard. Not just at her various jobs, but at making her and Justin's lives safe. Predictable. Structured. Comfortable.

Thinking back, she hadn't been playing it safe when she'd responded to Ethan's potent kiss at the rodeo arena, or when she'd lost her head yesterday during their hug.

Her glance fell again on Justin and Tamiko. Too bad Tamiko already had a boyfriend. She and Justin were cute together. As she bent close to talk to him, her long black hair fell like a silky curtain, momentarily shielding them from view.

Attraction at its earliest and most innocent.

Perhaps not so innocent, given the yearning in her brother's eyes when Tamiko straightened.

Caitlin's heart broke a little. Her brother was obviously smitten and understandably so. Tamiko was gorgeous, bright and chock-full of personality. But she was also taken. Compared to the strong and towering young man painting the wagon's sidewall, Caitlin doubted her brother stood a snowball's chance. Tamiko was simply being kind to him, not realizing how hard and fast he was falling for her.

Caitlin chuckled mirthlessly to herself. She and her brother were quite the pair. Here he was chasing a girl who wasn't available, while she was trying her hardest to stop Ethan from chasing her.

"You finished with that string of lights?" Howard asked.

"Almost." Caitlin smiled. The older man had turned out to be a big help.

She and her crew of volunteers weren't the only people at the ranch this Friday morning after Thanksgiving. At least a dozen riders were exercising their horses in the main arena. Another group was readying for a trail ride. In a small arena adjacent to the main one, a lone woman riding with an English saddle took her horse over a series of jumps. Clay and four or five of his men were hard at it, hammering, sawing and raising a ruckus as they labored to convert the old cattle barn into a mare motel. Once in a while, one or two of the men wandered over to Ethan's bunkhouse, carrying a toolbox or a ladder or sheets of drywall.

Gavin waved to her as he left the barn and headed to the round pen.

Caitlin did a double take. Ethan had finally gotten a saddle and bridle on the mustang. She stopped working on the lights to watch.

The moment Gavin reached the pen, he and Ethan entered into a heated discussion. Ethan waved off his brother, who in turn demanded to be heard. When Ethan didn't respond, Gavin climbed through the rails and into the pen. The argument continued.

Prince behaved relatively well, all things considered. He was calmer, at least, than when Caitlin and Justin had visited him in his stall. Then again, these were the two people who spent the most time with him, and he was used to them.

The brothers' loud voices eventually drew a crowd of ranch hands. Clay emerged from the barn and, after quickly assessing the situation, hurried over.

Gavin cautioned everyone to stay back. He stood at Prince's head, gripping the lead rope attached to the halter Prince wore beneath his bridle. Ethan positioned himself at the horse's right side, the reins bunched in one hand. With his other, he stroked Prince's neck over and over.

Suddenly, he lifted his good leg and placed his foot in the stirrup.

He was going to ride Prince!

Caitlin dropped the lights and ran toward the round pen to join the others.

"Hey, come back," Howard called after her.

She ignored him.

"Sis!"

She slowed for Justin, who quickly caught up with her.

"Where are you going?"

"Ethan's riding Prince."

"Cool."

That wasn't how she would describe it.

She wormed her way between two ranch hands. As much as watching Ethan terrified her, she had to be there in case something went wrong.

Through the railings, she saw Ethan swing up into the saddle. Prince stood still, a perplexed expression on his face. He slowly craned his head around and sniffed Ethan's leg, his ears twitching. Snorting once, he turned away.

Caitlin expelled a giant sigh of relief. Everything was going to be okay. All that worrying, and Prince was a lamb at heart. Once again she'd overreacted.

"Good boy," Ethan murmured to the horse.

Suddenly, Prince emitted an ear-piercing squeal, his entire body quivering. With no warning whatsoever, he started bucking in place again and again. Ethan was shaken so violently, his hat flew off. Just as quickly, he was flung backward when Prince reared.

By some miracle, he hung on.

The ranch hand beside Caitlin gave a loud whoop and jostled his neighbor's arm. "Did ya see that? Ride 'em, Ethan!"

Caitlin stared, transfixed. She hadn't been this afraid since the day of Justin's accident.

The techniques used for breaking a green horse weren't the same as for riding a bucking bronc.

Ethan transferred all his weight to the lower half of his body. Sitting squarely in the saddle, he pointed his heels toward the ground and squeezed Prince's flanks with his calves. His goal was to hang on until the horse tired, which he hoped would be soon.

He heard his name being called above the whoops and hollers of the people watching him, and thought he caught a glimpse of Caitlin from the corner of his eye. Prince twisted sideways, and from then on, all of Ethan's attention was focused on outlasting the horse on their wild roller-coaster ride. With both hands gripping the reins, he pulled back, keeping Prince's head tucked close to his body, and preventing him from rearing. Gavin stood in the pen, dashing out of harm's way when necessary, but otherwise keeping a close watch on horse and rider.

Clumps of dirt exploded from beneath Prince's hooves as he bucked and bucked, showering nearby spectators. Ethan barely noticed. This was a contest of wills, and he had every intention of winning.

As suddenly as it started, the rocking motion ceased. Prince transitioned into a choppy lope, lungs heaving and nostrils flaring. Ethan took a chance and gave the horse a little more rein. Prince extended his forelegs, and the ride became considerably smoother.

Cheers and applause erupted. Gavin wore a grin the size of a dinner plate. Ethan's chest swelled with satisfaction and accomplishment. This was hardly the first horse he'd broken, but it was definitely the best.

Prince, always eager to be the center of attention, shifted into a high-stepping trot. Head raised, tail arched, he showed off in front of his admirers, understanding on some level that he was equally interesting to them with a human on his back as he was without one.

Ethan let the horse have his fun. Hell, he was having fun, too. The time of his life. One of his first questions to the doctors when he'd woke after losing his leg was whether he would ever ride again.

They'd uttered all the platitudes, that anything was possible with hard work and determination. But Ethan had glimpsed the uncertainty in their earnest expressions.

Too bad those doctors weren't here now. Not only could he ride, he could break green horses and compete in saddle bronc events. He might even win at the jackpot tomorrow. It was less of a long shot today than it had been yesterday.

After a few more circuits of the pen, Ethan brought Prince to a halt and dismounted with Gavin's help. He held out the reins to his brother.

"Your turn."

Gavin took them. "Thanks." He clapped Ethan on the shoulder—his *good* shoulder. "For everything."

Ethan heard what his brother didn't say. There had been a time, after the explosion and during rehab, when Ethan wasn't sure if he wanted to come home and help his family with the failing remains of their once thriving cattle operation. Coping with that loss on a daily basis was more than Ethan could handle. But he had come home, and together he, his brother and father built a new business with the potential to be just as profitable as the old one. Adapt or perish. Wasn't that the saying?

The Powells had adapted and, despite the odds, were succeeding.

Ethan held Prince's lead rope while Gavin swung up into the saddle. The horse's eyes went wide at this sudden change, and he initially balked. Once Gavin was situated, however, he settled down, obediently trotting in a circle.

Ethan moved to the center of the pen, watching Prince and making mental notes for future training sessions.

"See if you can get him to lope," he instructed Gavin.

Prince did, after significant urging. Even then, he refused to lead with his left leg. Training him would take patience and a strong hand. Ethan couldn't wait. And once Prince was fully broke, his intelligence and reliable disposition proved, his value as a stud would increase.

Gavin finished his ride. Ethan once again held Prince's head so his brother could dismount without incident. The horse was doing well for a first day, but he was unpredictable at best, and it was wise to err on the side of caution.

If anything, the crowd had grown in size. Caitlin, Ethan noticed, had yet to move from her spot at the fence.

He went first out the gate, keeping the admirers at a safe distance while Gavin led the horse away. Ethan watched them go, his elation giving way to disappointment.

They had agreed that Ethan would break the horse. In some ways, and on most days, he worked more closely with Prince than his brother did. But there was no doubt Gavin and the horse shared a special bond. It had been Gavin who'd tracked the horse for months and insisted on capturing him. Gavin who'd juggled the family's finances so they could purchase Prince at auction, only to lose him to Clay. Gavin who'd set his differences aside in order to form a partnership with Clay that would benefit them both.

Prince knew who was responsible for his cushy new lifestyle. From the moment they'd brought him to the ranch, he'd tolerated Gavin best, allowing him into his stall when no one else could get within ten feet of him. It had been Gavin's jacket pockets he nuzzled, searching for treats.

Ethan wasn't one to waste time envying others, but his brother did have it all. A beautiful, wonderful fiancée who came with a great kid. A terrific daughter. A job he loved. Loyal employees. Friends. Respect in the community. An incredible horse.

Ethan wouldn't mind having a few of those things for himself.

A voice behind him roused him from his reverie.

"Hell of a ride, pal!" A beaming Clay handed Ethan his hat.

"We still have a long way to—"

"I swear," one of the wranglers interrupted Ethan, "I've never seen anything like that."

Someone else shook his hand. Then another person. His father was there, too. Ethan didn't remember seeing him at the round pen. The next thing he knew, he was pulled into a mighty bear hug.

"I'm proud of you, son."

Ethan swallowed, his throat tightening. "Thanks, Dad."

He recalled a similar celebration when he'd just returned home from rehab. His father had expressed his pride then, too. But there had been an underlying sadness to the gathering of friends and family that dampened the mood.

Ethan had been a wounded man.

Now he was a warrior once again.

And the person he wanted most to share this incredible moment with was Caitlin.

Where had she gone?

He searched for her, spotting her with Justin on the fringes of the now dispersing crowd. He made his way over to her, mindless of the people calling his name and tugging on his jacket sleeves.

Justin's boyish face lit with pleasure at the sight of Ethan. "Dude, that was awesome! I took pictures with my phone. Here, I'll show you." He started fiddling with the device. "Darn it," he grumbled when the photos didn't immediately fill the screen. "Hold on a second."

Ethan gave Caitlin a crooked smile. "Did you see?"

"Yes."

He'd been so caught up with his ride and how great it had gone, he hadn't really looked at her. She wasn't smiling, and her brows were drawn together in a pronounced V.

"Is something wrong?" he asked.

"Not at all."

"She was worried you were going to fall," Justin answered.

"But I didn't fall."

"You could have." Again Justin replied for his sister. She glared at him.

"Hey, don't get mad at me. It's true."

"I break three or four horses a month," Ethan said. "If not one of Clay's rodeo stock, then a client's horse. I'm good at my job."

"She gets scared easily."

"All right!" Caitlin snapped. "I do get scared easily. Who wouldn't? The horse was going crazy."

Ethan liked that she worried about him. It was another sign she cared. What he didn't like was her disapproval, which was tarnishing an otherwise memorable day for him and his family.

"You're upset with me," she said.

"Of course not." Only he was.

"Here we go," Justin announced enthusiastically, and passed Ethan his phone.

There were five photos, two fuzzy and out of focus. In one, Ethan's head and Prince's legs were cut off. The remaining two were quite good for having been taken with a cell phone.

He tried to see his ride through Caitlin's eyes. Prince, his nose to the ground, his back legs straight up in the air, could appear dangerous to a novice. But not once had Ethan lost control or so much as slipped in the saddle. Surely she'd seen that. Everyone else had, and was thrilled and excited for him.

"Thanks, bud." He returned the phone to Justin.

"I can email these to you if you want."

"That'd be great. I'll have Gavin post them on the ranch's website."

"Hey, Caitlin!" Howard hollered though cupped hands. "We have a problem."

"I need to go." She started out at a brisk walk.

"Wait!" Ethan went after her, cursing himself.

She stopped and pivoted slowly.

"Why can't you be happy for me?" he asked.

"I am."

"You have a strange way of showing it. I rode Prince. I'm fine. Not a single scratch."

"You're right."

"I get that you're scared."

"I don't think you do." Her voice shook. "I don't think you have the slightest inkling of how truly terrified I was, watching you ride."

"Caitlin—"

"I admit it, I'm a neurotic mess."

"You're not neurotic. A little obsessive, maybe."

"This isn't a matter of whether my worrying is obsessive or reasonable." She placed a hand over her heart. "It's how I feel, and it won't change or go away because you or I want it to."

"I'm sorry."

"Me, too." She walked away from him then.

Ethan stared after her. Until that instant, he hadn't believed their differences were insurmountable.

No more.

"Go easy on her."

It took Ethan a few seconds to realize Justin had wheeled up beside him. "Yeah?"

"She's crazy about you."

It went both ways. "Could've fooled me."

Ethan wasn't sure where he should go—after Caitlin, back to the stables or to the office. "You want a beer?"

Justin glanced at his watch, shrugged, then grinned. "Sure. I'm not driving. Nothing motorized, anyway."

"Let's go."

Neither said a word on the short walk to Ethan's bunkhouse until they reached the porch.

"Can you—"

"No problem."

Justin reversed his wheelchair and backed it up to the bottom step. Leaning forward, he cranked the wheels and climbed the two short steps inch by grueling inch, the muscles in his arms straining.

"You're pretty good at that."

"I've had a lot of practice." Justin maneuvered the chair through the bunkhouse door, which was just wide enough to accommodate him. "This is nice," he said, and parked himself adjacent to the couch.

Why his sister constantly fretted about him, Ethan didn't understand. Justin was obviously capable of handling himself.

Ethan recalled his own months of rehab, learning how to stand, walk off a curb, climb a ladder, manage stairs. More than once he'd landed face-first on the floor.

"Thanks," Justin said, when he passed him a cold beer from the refrigerator.

Ethan sank onto the couch and propped his feet on the old footlocker that served as a coffee table. The beer tasted good, and for several moments they savored it in silence.

"It's not Caitlin's fault she's the way she is," Justin said finally.

"It's not your fault, either."

"Hell, no, it's not." He took a swig of beer. "She changed after the accident. We all did."

"I can relate." Ethan lifted his bottle in a toast, which Justin returned.

"Don't take this wrong, okay? But when you lost your leg, your family wasn't there. They didn't see you at the hospital afterward."

That was true. Gavin had wanted to fly out to Germany, where Ethan had been transferred for surgery immediately after being stabilized. Unfortunately, the ranch was barely sustaining itself in those days, and they didn't have the money to finance a trip to Tucson, much less halfway around the world.

"Caitlin and my parents spent some pretty harrowing weeks while I was in a medically induced coma. They didn't know if I'd survive, much less walk again."

"I can imagine."

"Caitlin blamed herself, which was ridiculous. I chose to jump off that cliff. She had nothing to do with it. I was bound and determined to show everyone I wasn't the loser they called me behind my back and to my face."

Justin's need to prove himself in front of others was a lot like Ethan's—except his attempt had ended in tragedy. Ethan had a decidedly different outcome in mind for himself.

"Have you told her you don't hold her responsible?"

"Dude, I've practically had it engraved in stone. She doesn't listen."

Ethan pondered Justin's remark while finishing the last of his beer. "Want another one?"

"Sure. Why not? I doubt Caitlin's missing me."

"Caitlin or that girl? What's her name?"

"Tamiko."

"She's cute."

"And has a boyfriend."

"You haven't let anything stop you from doing what you want before now." Ethan retrieved two fresh beers from the refrigerator.

"Her boyfriend, Eric, may be dumber than a bag of hammers, but I think he can take me."

"It's not his decision who she dates. It's hers."

"You're right." Justin copied Ethan and raised his beer in a toast. "And the same could be said for you, my friend."

"About Caitlin?"

"You want her. Don't let anything stop you."

"I'm up against a lot more than a boyfriend. You saw her today. A five-ton steamroller couldn't break through those walls she's erected."

"Chicken."

"Me?" Ethan snorted. "Have you looked in the mirror lately?"

Justin laughed. "Tell you what, let's make a deal. I'll go after Tamiko and you go after my sister. Who knows? Maybe we'll both get lucky."

Ethan stood and hitched up his jeans. "You're on."

Justin's challenge might have been issued in jest, but Ethan took it seriously. If any two people deserved a second chance, he and Caitlin did—and he was determined to see they got it.

Chapter 9

"Is it gonna hurt?" The little girl's eyes brimmed with unshed tears.

"No, I promise, sweetie." Caitlin dabbed antibiotic ointment onto the girl's cut with a cotton swab. "There, see?"

"Ow!" She jerked her knee away, although the ointment couldn't possibly have stung.

The cut wasn't serious. Caitlin had seen far worse this past week alone.

"I don't know how she fell." The mother anxiously smoothed her daughter's disheveled hair. "I swear she wasn't out of my sight more than a minute."

"We were running, and Becky Lynn pushed me."

The girl sat in a folding chair, the same one Ethan had occupied when Caitlin had examined his shoulder, and again when she'd helped him put his prosthesis back on. She hoped to see him today—safe and sound after his ride, not in the first-aid station for a third time.

"You and Becky Lynn have to be careful." The mother hovered, watching every move as Caitlin placed a bandage over the cut and pressed down on the adhesive tabs. "There are a lot of people here today. You shouldn't be running around and not paying attention."

There *were* a lot of people. Caitlin hadn't known how many to expect, considering this was Clay's first jackpot. Someone mentioned fifty-six entrants had registered and by Caitlin's estimation at least two hundred people packed the bleachers.

The little girl was Caitlin's second patient this afternoon, and the event hadn't officially started yet. She'd also treated one of Clay's wranglers after a bull stomped on his foot while they were transferring livestock from the paddocks to the holding pens behind the chutes. Though the cowboy's foot was only bruised and not broken, she'd advised him to take it easy for the rest of the day.

FYI, he hadn't. She'd seen him twice so far, limping as he went about his tasks.

He reminded her of Ethan.

"Can I go now?"

"Sure thing." Caitlin rolled down the little girl's pant leg, covering the bandage.

She hopped off the chair and flexed her knee as if testing the bandage's sticking power.

"What do I owe you?" her mother asked.

"Not a thing. It's part of the service."

"You sure? I really appreciate the help."

"If you'd like, you can make a donation to the Powells' Wild Mustang Sanctuary. There's a collection jar at the chuck wagon."

"I will." The woman's tentative smile bloomed.

Her daughter tugged on her hand. "Hurry, Mommy. We don't want to miss Daddy's ride."

"Oh, honey, don't worry. The bull riders go last, after the bronc riders."

Caitlin thought of Ethan breaking Prince yesterday.

"Isn't it hard watching your husband ride bulls?" she asked the woman, surprised at the boldness of her question. "Aren't you afraid for him?"

"'Course I'm afraid. I start shaking the second that chute opens, and don't stop till he waves at me from the other side of the arena fence."

"Why put yourself through that?"

Why let him do it? was what she really wanted to know.

"My Micky's no champion bull rider and not likely to ever be one. These jackpots, they're his moment to shine, you know? For eight seconds, he's king of the world. I wouldn't dare miss it, and I wouldn't dare take it away from him, either."

"Mommy!" The little girl tugged harder on her hand. "Let's go."

"You be careful," Caitlin told the girl. "I don't want to see you back here."

"And I'll be sure to put a donation in that collection jar," the mother promised as they left.

Caitlin spent the next several minutes cleaning up after her patient and thinking about the woman's remarks. Her support of her husband was admirable. But what if he fell and hurt himself? His loving wife and beautiful daughter depended on him. He put not only himself at risk when he went into the arena, but his family, too.

"Hey." Clay's large frame filled the doorway. "I see you've had a couple visitors already today."

"Your wrangler T.J. was one of them. He should be resting somewhere, elevating and icing that foot," she admonished.

"I told him to take the day off."

"FYI, he didn't listen to you."

"He needs the money, Caitlin. It's a tough economy, and he has bills to pay."

"Right."

"You annoyed at me specifically or the world in general?"

"Sorry." Caitlin was immediately contrite. "That was uncalled for."

"Does your mood have anything to do with Ethan competing?"

"Not at all."

"You sure?" Clay stepped fully into the room. "Because he mentioned you being mad at him. Something to do with breaking Prince yesterday."

Caitlin hadn't been particularly close to Clay when they were younger, even though he was Ethan's best friend. They were always in competition for Ethan's time and attention. Caitlin had wanted him to herself, while Clay was constantly luring Ethan away for football or rodeo or fishing or a night out with the boys.

Working for Clay, however, had changed their relationship. He really was a decent guy, and Caitlin felt bad that his brief marriage had ended disastrously.

"A couple of weeks ago he injured his shoulder,"

she told Clay. "Then his prosthesis came off. Next time could be a lot worse."

"He knows what he's doing."

"He's at a disadvantage. I heard him telling Justin at Thanksgiving dinner he sometimes has trouble keeping weight on his left leg, and it throws him off balance."

"He's learned to compensate."

"How would you feel if something happened to him?"

"Like shit," Clay answered honestly. "But I wouldn't blame myself, if that's what you're asking."

"Not even a little? You did give him permission to enter the jackpot."

"He's a grown man. He makes his own decisions."

Ethan had tried to tell her the same thing about Justin. That he was the one who chose to jump off the cliff.

But there was a difference. While Clay allowed Ethan to ride broncs and enter the jackpot, he hadn't encouraged him. Goaded him. If anything, he'd discouraged Ethan.

"You care, and that's sweet." Clay watched her as she meticulously organized the tray of supplies. "Did you ever think your constant worrying makes him feel like an invalid and not like the normal guy he wants to be?"

Her hand slipped, knocking a box of gauze pads to the floor. She stooped to pick it up. "Did he tell you that?"

"Not in so many words."

"I don't think of him as an invalid."

"You just said he's at a disadvantage because of

his artificial leg. That sounds like you're calling him an invalid."

"I'm not," she argued hotly. "Not on purpose."

"Then go watch him compete. Saddle bronc riding is the first event."

"Leave the first-aid station? What if someone gets injured?"

"This place isn't that big." Clay grinned affably. "We'll find you."

"I…can't."

"Why not?"

"Watching him would be like giving my stamp of approval, and I don't approve. It has nothing to do with his prosthesis. Anyone who climbs on a bull or bronc is an idiot in my opinion."

Clay's response was a loud laugh.

"This isn't funny."

"You're right." He promptly sobered, studying her intently.

"What?"

"I was just thinking how lucky Ethan is to have you."

"He doesn't *have* me."

Clay laughed again. Her steely glare had no effect on silencing him.

The overhead speakers did the trick when they came to life and a man's crackling voice announced the start of the jackpot.

"I'd better get going." Clay hesitated at the door. "Hope you change your mind about watching Ethan."

"I won't."

"This is a big moment for him. He wants you there."

Caitlin was still thinking about what Clay had said

five minutes later as she listened to the announcer call the names of the first three contestants.

How many men were competing in bronc riding today and how soon until Ethan's turn?

What did it matter? She wasn't going to watch him. She managed to stick to her guns until the announcer, during color commentary between participants, mentioned the Powells, their mustang sanctuary and Ethan's military service.

Caitlin dashed out the door and raced toward the area behind the bucking chutes where the cowboys typically gathered to debate the various merits of the bucking stock. He was there, engrossed in conversation with two men.

He noticed her only when one of his companions elbowed him in the ribs and nodded in her direction. If he was surprised to see her, he hid it well.

She slowed, her courage evaporating as quickly as it had come.

He broke away from his friends and met her halfway, ignoring the good-humored jeers they hurled after him.

"Hey."

"I…uh…" She tipped her head back in order to see his face, and promptly lost her train of thought. His dark eyes had a way of doing that to her.

"If you're here to tell me I shouldn't ride, you've wasted a trip."

"I'm not."

His brows rose. "Good."

"I didn't want you getting on that horse thinking I was mad at you. I'm not, and I apologize for my behavior yesterday. I really am happy you broke Prince and proud that you're competing today."

"Thanks." His mouth lifted in a sexy, knee-weakening grin. "Don't suppose I could have a kiss. For luck."

She should have seen that coming. "How 'bout a hug?"

"I'll take what I can get."

Determined not to lose control as she had during their last hug, she looped her arms around his neck, her spine ramrod straight, her cheek averted. She lasted two full seconds before her entire body melted with a gentle sigh and she relaxed into his embrace.

When they parted, he caught her chin between his thumb and forefinger. "I'm going the full eight seconds."

"I just want you to be safe." Her voice quavered.

"I can do both."

She carried that promise with her to the stands, where she perched on the front row of the bleachers, her foot tapping nervously.

Ethan watched Caitlin walk away, her hands stuffed in the pockets of her hoodie, her slim shoulders hunched. It wasn't cold. In fact, the sun shone brightly in a perfect, cloudless sky. But Caitlin looked cold.

Or was she sad?

"Hey, Powell!"

Hearing his name, he sauntered back to his buddies. He couldn't afford to be distracted, by Caitlin or anyone. His upcoming ride was too important. He'd made it this far, paying the price in pain and sweat, and refused to screw up.

"You drew a mean one."

Micky's comment prompted Ethan to reevaluate Batteries Included, the bronc he was about to take for a spin. He'd helped train the big, rangy black, one of Clay's first purchases when he'd started his rodeo stock business, and knew to expect the unexpected. Batteries Included possessed enough bucking power to give a cowboy a championship ride, if he could stay in the saddle. Most who rode the horse ended up in a pile on the arena floor.

Ethan didn't plan on joining their ranks.

"You ready?" Micky asked.

There was a lot that could be read into the question. Was he ready to make a fool of himself in front of a huge crowd? Or was he ready to show everyone he still had what it took to compete professionally, even if he couldn't enter Professional Rodeo Cowboys Association—sanctioned rodeos?

Micky could also be wondering something as simple as whether or not Ethan had his nerves under control.

The answer to that last question was no. He hadn't been this jittery since he was fourteen and competing in his first junior rodeo. He'd fared poorly, getting bucked off in every event. He'd also learned many valuable lessons that stayed with him even today.

"I'm ready," he said, nodding confidently. "Ready to beat the two of you and look damn good doing it."

The three men chuckled.

Letting loose took a little of the edge off his tension and, oddly enough, helped him concentrate.

They moved from the stock pens to the chutes, where they discussed in detail the competitors going before them. Micky straddled the top railing, worming his way between a pair of cousins from Tucson, while Ethan stood beside T.J., his left leg braced on the bottom railing. He could climb the fence, and would have, were he not competing shortly. No point putting unnecessary strain on his prosthesis.

A dozen men were ahead of him, allowing him time to wait. To think. To stress. To envision the worst... and the best.

All day long he'd glimpsed people staring at him, wearing he-must-be-crazy expressions. Who entered rodeo jackpots with a missing leg?

Half a leg, Ethan corrected.

What was the difference? Half or whole, he was still handicapped.

God, he hated that word, and refused to let it define him.

He searched the audience until he found his family. Gavin, their dad, his niece Cassie, Sage and her daughter, Isa. He didn't want to disappoint them. His brother and father especially. He owed them an eight-second ride if for nothing other than the unconditional support they'd given him since his accident.

Not far from his family, Caitlin sat in the front row. So she was going to watch him compete. He hadn't been sure despite the hug. Gladness filled him, and he felt his mouth break in a wide smile. If she was able to conquer her fears enough to sit through his ride, then maybe they stood a chance. Their gazes connected across the distance and held, convincing Ethan she shared his optimism for their future.

Thirty minutes later, another ten contestants had gone. Ethan liked being one of the last, as it gave him the opportunity to analyze the competition and determine what he needed to do in order to beat their scores. Contestants in jackpots were often weekend enthusiasts and not at the same experience level as those competing professionally.

On the other hand, there was always one or two serious contenders. Ethan studied them the closest.

"Powell, on deck!"

Ethan moved into place beside the chute where Batteries Included waited. As he climbed the fence, the horse twisted and snorted, the whites of his inky-black eyes showing. Ethan swung his good leg over the top rung. The horse kicked out with his front hoof. The clang of iron shoe against metal railing rang out like a challenge, one Ethan accepted.

Muscles clenched, nerves strung tight, he lowered himself onto the bronc's back. Placing his feet in the stirrups, he pointed his toes. Next, he checked the reins and tugged the brim of his hat low over his eyes. When he was satisfied, he whispered a silent prayer to his mother.

One last shift in the saddle, and he uttered the word that could possibly give him back the life he'd lost.

"Go!"

The gate opened. Batteries Included charged into the arena, his powerful body rocking forward and backward with enough strength to jar Ethan's teeth loose.

Acting on pure instinct, he marked the horse. Hand raised over his head, he leaned back in the saddle and found his rhythm.

Time slowed. He heard the roar of air rushing into his expanding lungs, the creak of leather stretching and bending, his bones grinding together, someone hollering his name. He slipped once, righted himself and dug his heels into the horse above the shoulders, urging him to buck higher and harder.

From nowhere, the buzzer sounded.

Ethan's heart exploded. He'd done it!

The pickup men materialized beside him. With a strong arm, the nearest one hauled Ethan out of the saddle and deposited him on the ground. The crowd applauded. Ethan readjusted his hat, dusted off his jeans and began striding across the arena to the gate, his glance repeatedly darting to the scoreboard. Finally, the numbers changed and the announcer's voice blared from the speakers.

"That'll be an 83 for Ethan Powell."

Applause followed. Not wild applause. Ethan had done well enough, though he wouldn't place in the top three. Possibly the top six if he was very, very lucky. Still, it was a decent score for a man with a prosthesis.

Stop thinking like that!

"Good ride." Micky sidled up beside him.

"Not bad."

"You've done worse."

He had. In professional rodeos before he'd enlisted. He'd also done better. A lot better.

"You going to try bull riding again?"

"Probably not." Ethan knew his limits.

"Bareback?"

He'd considered it. Without stirrups he might have even more trouble maintaining his balance. Then again, he might have less. "Soon, I'm thinking."

"Glad to hear it." Micky left to join the other bull riders.

Ethan's buddies congratulated him as he made his

way to the pens. Like Micky, they didn't go overboard with their praise. He'd finished, and that was worth acknowledging. Not, he'd finished, and that was an unbelievable accomplishment.

He liked being treated the same as anyone else.

His enjoyment was cut short when the audience gasped loudly. A young man lay prone on the ground. While the pickup men went after the loose horse, wranglers streamed into the arena, surrounding the fallen rider.

The next instant, Caitlin was running pell-mell across the arena, her shoes sinking into the soft dirt. She pushed her way through the wranglers and dropped to the ground, examining the man with expert hands. Not long after, she assisted him to a sitting position, then to his feet. Cheers rose as he limped toward the gate, Caitlin holding his elbow on one side and a wrangler on the other. The announcer wished him well and promised the audience an update on his condition before the jackpot was over.

Returning to work after that was hard for Ethan. He kept thinking about the young man as he supervised the transfer of stock from pens to chutes. News soon spread that the rider had sprained his back. Ethan could easily imagine Caitlin recommending the young man see his regular doctor, and him insisting he was all right. Just as Ethan had done.

He was glad the rider had sprained rather than broken his back. Not only because the injury was less severe. If he'd been driven to the hospital in an ambulance, there would be no convincing Caitlin bronc riding was only moderately dangerous.

Yeah, moderately.

Why was he trying so hard to sway her when she'd insisted there was no chance in hell they'd resume their relationship?

But there had been that hug before he'd competed, and the one at Thanksgiving.

No matter how much she denied it, she liked him. Possibly even loved him, deep down.

He couldn't give up on them.

Two hours later, the Duvall Rodeo Arena's first jackpot came to a close. A brief ceremony followed, and the top three contestants for each event received their belt buckles and winnings. Ethan applauded along with everyone else. He'd rather have been part of the ceremony with Micky and the others.

Soon, he assured himself.

He hung around as long as possible, supervising the wranglers as they returned the remaining livestock to the paddocks and pastures. Every now and then his gaze wandered to the first-aid station. When he saw Caitlin loading up her minivan, he made an excuse to the men and hurried over.

"Need help carrying anything?"

She spun around, nearly dropping the tower of plastic bins in her arms. "Thanks. I've got it."

Not the warm welcome he'd been anticipating after their hug.

"Did you see my ride?" Stupid question. She'd been watching from the bleachers.

"I did." She loaded the plastic bins into her van. "Congratulations. You must be pleased."

"I am."

"Are you celebrating tonight?"

"Hadn't thought of it." He immediately warmed to the idea. "You free? We could have dinner."

She exhaled wearily. "It's been a long day, and I'm exhausted. I'm sure you are, too."

Not really. If anything, he was energized. Had been since his ride.

"Sure. No problem." He hesitated, searching for a reason to stay. "When are you coming out to the ranch next?"

"I'm glad you asked." She brightened, noticeably relieved at the change of topic. "Next Saturday, if that's okay with you."

"Great."

"Any chance we can take the wagon to the park for a test drive? I'd like to experiment with a couple different routes. See which one works best."

"Call me."

No dinner. And a full week before he saw her again. No physical-therapy sessions, either.

So far, this plan he had with Justin to go after his sister was a complete and total bust.

"Good night, Ethan. Congratulations again." She got in her van and left.

As he walked back to the holding pens for a final inspection, he decided he didn't much like being treated the same as every other guy out there.

He much preferred to be special, after all, at least where Caitlin Carmichael was concerned.

Chapter 10

Caitlin waited at the entrance to the park, shielding her eyes from the brilliant morning sun. She could just make out the wagon with its team of two horses plodding along Mustang Valley's main road at a gentle pace. Vehicles going in both directions slowed at the unusual procession, their drivers used to yielding the right-of-way to horses.

The wagon carried two passengers besides Ethan. Cassie and Isa sat with him on the bench seat, their excited chatter reaching Caitlin's ears from a half block away. Musical tones blended with the girls' voices, and it took Caitlin a moment to recognize the source.

Jingle bells hanging from the harnesses! Ethan must have added them after Caitlin and her crew had finished decorating.

How nice of him.

Guilt needled her with pointy barbs. For the past week, ever since the rodeo jackpot, she'd purposefully avoided Ethan, speaking to him only once midweek to firm up their plans to drive the wagon route before the Holly Days Festival. Evidently he'd gotten her message loud and clear, because he hadn't attempted to contact her, either.

Caitlin should be relieved. Happy, even. Instead, she jumped every time her cell phone rang or the clinic buzzer heralded the arrival of a patient.

This morning was no exception. Her insides fluttered annoyingly at the sight of Ethan's broad shoulders and tall physique, and her palms leaked perspiration.

She wiped them on her jeans, then waved. Only the girls returned her greeting. Was Ethan angry with her for turning down his dinner invitation? As the wagon drew nearer, she noticed Gavin sitting in the bed on a bale of hay and holding on to the sidewall.

Good. More passengers. She'd been a wreck for days, uncertain how she would handle being alone with Ethan. As it turned out, her obsessing had been a complete waste of time.

The horses' clip-clopping hooves on the pavement, the girls' lively chatter and the ringing of jingle bells combined to create a merry cacophony. Caitlin stepped out from her spot beneath an ironwood tree as Ethan expertly turned the horses into the park entrance.

"Whoa, there!" He pulled back on the long reins, and the wagon came to a creaky stop.

Caitlin walked over and gasped softly. "The lights are on!" She hadn't noticed their multicolored flickering in the bright sunlight.

"We're testing the electrical system." Gavin climbed

out of the wagon bed, using the rear wheel spokes like a ladder to reach the ground.

Vehicles continued to pass them in a slow procession, the drivers honking or waving. A pickup truck didn't drive past but parked behind the wagon. Caitlin recognized the woman at the wheel. Sage must have followed to prevent potential tailgaters from creeping too close.

The truck door opened and she emerged. "Morning, Caitlin!"

"How are you?"

The two women met up near the wagon. Caitlin liked Gavin's fiancée and their daughters. Another time and place, she and Sage might have become good friends.

Why not now? a voice inside her asked. *Surely not because of Ethan.*

Avoiding Ethan's family on the off chance he might show up did seem ridiculous. What was the worst that could happen?

Plenty. One smoky glance from him, one caress of his lips on her skin, and she'd be all over him.

Not going to happen, and four co-passengers were the perfect deterrent.

"Come on, girls," Gavin said, climbing out of the wagon. "Let's get a move on."

"You're leaving?"

Caitlin wasn't the only one protesting.

"Aw, Dad, please. Can't we stay with Uncle Ethan?"

Yes, can't they stay?

"We have an appointment," Sage reminded them in a motherly voice. She pulled Caitlin to her for a quick hug. "Maybe after the holidays we can meet for coffee or lunch."

"That would be nice," she mumbled, releasing Sage reluctantly.

The girls continued to whine.

"Tomorrow afternoon I'll take the two of you for another ride," Ethan said. "How's that?"

"Really?" Isa clapped her hands.

"Will you teach me to drive?" Cassie asked.

"Yes and yes."

He helped the girls down off the wagon seat into Gavin's outstretched arms, Isa first, then Cassie. They both kissed Ethan's cheek before being lowered, their slim, girlish arms circling his neck.

"Thanks, Uncle Ethan."

"I love you, Uncle Ethan."

"Love you, too, kiddos."

Watching them, Caitlin felt her racing heart slow, then turn to mush. He was incredibly good with the girls, and they seemed to adore him. It had never occurred to her what a terrific father he'd make.

"All aboard!" Gavin beckoned her to the front of the wagon.

"Me?"

"You are riding with Ethan, aren't you?"

She pasted a brave smile on her face. "I am."

"Well, let's do it. Unless you can climb into this wagon by yourself."

Caitlin might be taller than the girls, but she wasn't nearly as nimble. She needed help. Mentally measuring the distance from the ground to the wagon seat, she decided she might need wings.

The footrest was on the same level as her chest. No way could she lift her leg that high.

"Are you kidding me?" She gaped at Gavin.

"Right foot here." He patted one of the wheel spokes. "Left foot here." He tapped the footrest. "Then swing yourself up into the seat."

He made it sound so easy.

The horses chose that moment to shift restlessly, causing the wagon to rock.

Caitlin instinctively drew back. "I can't."

"You'll be fine," Ethan said. "The brake's on."

She wavered, angry at herself. She'd done this before. Granted, that was years ago, when she'd have walked through fire to be with Ethan.

"Okay, okay." She lifted her foot as instructed and placed it on the wheel spoke. Then nothing. Gravity had a hold on her and wouldn't let go.

"Here."

She glanced at Ethan. He'd placed the reins in his left hand and was holding his right one out to her. It was large and strong and appeared more than capable of hauling her safely up into the seat.

"Hang on." Gavin gave her a boost.

She rose up, her left foot automatically seeking purchase. Before she quite knew what was happening, Ethan caught her by the forearm and yanked. Her world tilted crazily. Then she was seated beside him, and everything returned to its proper place.

It had been like that before, when they were young. He had only to touch her, hold her, and all was right once more.

"It's high up here." Higher than she remembered.

Her fingers gripped the thin and unreassuring metal armrest. "No seat belts, huh?" She laughed nervously.

"I don't remember you being so afraid of horses."

She hadn't been, only since Justin's accident. She hadn't been afraid of fast cars, roller coasters, bungee jumping or heights before then, either.

"I haven't ridden for years."

"We should go one day. Get you used to horses again."

"Get me used to the wagon first. Then we'll see about horses."

"One step at a time." Before she could wonder if he was really talking about them, he said, "Molly and Dolly are the two calmest horses on the ranch next to Chico. I wouldn't take you or anyone for a drive if I thought for one second we'd have a runaway."

Runaway! Why had he mentioned that? "How reliable is that brake?"

She immediately imagined the horses galloping hell-bent for election through the park like in those old black-and-white Westerns she used to watch as a kid.

As it turned out, she'd panicked for nothing. The horses, under Ethan's careful guidance, traveled along at a sedate walk. After several minutes, Caitlin started breathing again. Before long, she relaxed enough to appreciate the advantages her elevated position offered. She had a clear view of the workers erecting the miniature Santa's workshop and the obedience trials under way in the dog park across the expansive green. In the far distance, Pinnacle Peak, with its distinctive silhouette, reached skyward as if to capture the sun.

"How beautiful."

Ethan smiled, and they drove for a while in companionable silence.

Eventually, Caitlin pulled a map of the park from her pocket. "I figured we'd have the wagon pickup and drop-off station near the picnic area, next to the Santa's workshop."

He grunted approvingly.

"We could set up a table here—" she tapped the map "—and take donations for the mustang sanctuary. Pass out literature if you have any."

He grunted again.

"Do you think Cassie would be willing to dress in an elf costume and be one of Santa's helpers?"

"Probably."

When he said no more, Caitlin continued examining the map and the routes she'd sketched out. "What do you think about this one?" She angled the map for him to see.

He grumbled instead of grunting.

Fine. He was keeping conversation to a minimum. That suited her, as well. Folding the map, she returned it to her pocket, sat back and kept quiet.

For two full minutes.

"Did I do something to upset you?"

"Not at all."

"I'm sorry about refusing your dinner invitation last Saturday. I figured it was better if we—"

"You're not going to give me the let's-be-friends speech, are you?"

Her cheeks burned. That was exactly what she'd been planning. "No. Don't be ridiculous."

"Because I won't be friends with you."

That stung.

"I want more."

"More?" Her voice sounded small.

"Much more."

Oh, dear.

"Look at me, Caitlin."

She did, tensing as his smoldering gaze raked over her.

"Don't expect me to make small talk with you when what I really want is to make love."

"I'm sorry." Caitlin sucked in air, then released it in a shuddering breath.

"Don't be. I'm not propositioning you, simply stating a fact."

She and Ethan were no strangers to intimacy. They had been each other's firsts, consummating their love shortly after high school graduation. The night had been one of the scariest of her life, and the most memorable. Scary for Ethan, too. Revealing his true feelings had endeared him to her and broken down the last of her defenses. When she gave herself to him, it was without reservation and without regrets.

Magic had happened that night and for many nights afterward. Making love with Ethan had been extraordinary. Fulfilling, satisfying and fun. But physical pleasure—and there had been a lot of it—was never more important than their emotional connection, which only grew stronger the longer they were together.

Yet another reason why his abrupt enlistment in the marines had devastated her. How could he have loved her so completely and so thoroughly and then abandoned her like that?

The horses plodded along the side street circling

the park, the sleigh bells chiming in rhythm to the cadence of their hooves.

Seconds ticked by, then minutes.

"Was there anybody after me?" Caitlin was shocked at her own audacity.

Ethan answered without pause. "I dated some in the marines."

"No one special?"

"No one I fell in love with." He clucked to Molly and Dolly, who had stopped at the sight of an elderly couple walking a shaggy terrier.

"What about since your discharge?"

"Haven't had the time."

Was that true? Or did the loss of his leg have something to do with it?

Justin had been painfully shy around girls as a teenager, frequently becoming tongue-tied. After his accident, he'd refused to even be alone in the same room with someone of the opposite sex.

Not anymore, Caitlin mused, remembering him and Tamiko together.

When had Justin changed? And what had prompted it?

"How about you?" Ethan's sidelong glance gave nothing away. "Date much?"

"Not hardly at all until after college. Caring for Justin took up most of my free time. And then there was homework and work-study programs. I met someone a few years ago."

"Tell me about him."

He wasn't you. The thought came from nowhere and traveled straight to her chest, where it curled around her heart.

Caitlin averted her head to hide the tears that sprang unbidden to her eyes.

"We went out for about two years," she said when she'd composed herself. "Then it just kind of fizzled. No big fight. No drama. We parted friends."

"Too bad."

What she didn't tell Ethan was that her boyfriend had wanted to marry her, and had repeatedly proposed. Caitlin couldn't bring herself to take the next step—because of Ethan or Justin or both, she really wasn't sure. Eventually, her boyfriend grew tired of waiting. There'd been no one since, not even a casual date. Which also meant that Ethan's kiss at the rodeo arena was her first one in years.

"I thought maybe we'd have the wagon rides on Friday and Saturday nights only," she said. "From six to nine." The small talk sounded trite after such a personal conversation. "Is that too long? I don't want to tire the horses."

"I'll have two teams. One for each night."

"Will you take the other team out for a test run, too?"

"Tomorrow. With the girls. Want to come along?" He studied her face intently.

Were there tearstains on her cheeks? She instinctively touched them. Dry, thank goodness.

"I, um, promised Mom I'd go Christmas shopping with her."

If she didn't already have a legitimate excuse, she would have manufactured one. Her resistance to him was at an all-time low. It would be so easy to say she didn't care about his bronc riding, scoot closer and rest her head on his shoulder.

"You having Christmas Day at your place?" he asked.

"Oh, gosh, no!"

"Condo too small?"

"That, and too empty."

"Still moving in?"

"I've been waiting to see if I'm…" *staying in Mustang Valley* "…keeping the condo. I don't have one Christmas decoration up or one card displayed. Mom and Dad are having dinner at their house. My aunt and uncle and cousin are driving up from Green Valley. Some friends from Dad's work will also be there."

"You'll have fun."

"Is Sierra coming home?"

"She hasn't committed one way or the other." Ethan absently clucked to the horses. "I don't know what's with her lately. She's cut herself off from the family almost completely. Dad's pretty upset."

"Is it a man?"

"I hadn't thought of that."

"Getting involved in a relationship is one reason people ignore their families and friends."

"Why wouldn't she tell us?"

"Maybe she's afraid you won't approve of him."

Ethan stared at the road, his jaw working.

"I'm not saying it's a man. Could be anything."

"It makes sense, though."

Caitlin left Ethan to his thoughts, concentrating instead on her own. When they rounded the last bend on the route, the towering Christmas tree the Holly Days committee had erected in the center of the park came into view. Caitlin felt a sentimental tug on her heartstrings. This was her favorite season.

"If you could have just one wish for Christmas," she asked, "what would it be?"

Ethan didn't immediately answer. She assumed he was thinking of Sierra and his bronc riding. Of his desire to compete professionally. His job training horses. Her, and his desire for them to get back together.

"That was a silly question," she blurted when the silence stretched. "You don't have to answer it."

"What I'd want most of all is for things to go back the way they were. Before my mother got sick and we were still raising cattle."

Ten years ago she and Ethan had been planning a wedding in the not-too-distant future. Ten years ago, he had yet to enlist.

"But that isn't possible." He shook the reins. If the horses were supposed to walk faster, they didn't pay attention. "So, I guess I'd wish for the riding stables to do well and Gavin's stud and breeding business to take off. He's trying hard to preserve what little we have left in order to pass it down to his children."

A noble, selfless wish. "What about you, Ethan? What do *you* want?"

He turned his head, the ghost of a smile lighting his lips. "For us, you and me, to be happy. And I don't mean together, necessarily," he added, as if anticipating her objection.

No?

Neither of them had been happy apart.

"I'd like that, too," she said softly, realizing it was her Christmas wish, as well.

Ethan walked the perimeter of the last stall in the nearly completed mare motel. "Looking good."

"I agree." Gavin nodded approvingly.

The crew had finished hanging the twenty-four

stall doors an hour earlier, shortly after Ethan returned home from his ride with Caitlin. While there was a long punch list needing completion, and minor modifications here and there, the mare motel was operational and ready for "guests."

"If I hadn't seen it myself," Clay said, his deep voice resonating with awe and admiration, "I wouldn't have believed this was once a cattle barn."

Indeed, the transformation was nothing short of amazing. Ethan could hardly remember what the barn had looked like in "the old days," as his niece was fond of saying—the remark accompanied by an eye roll.

A wave of nostalgia overcame him, bringing with it memory after memory. He, Gavin and Conner had spent considerable time in this cattle barn while growing up. Working, not playing. Wayne Powell had been a taskmaster, requiring his sons to give one-hundred-and-ten percent. They hadn't really appreciated his strict work ethic until they were adults.

Clay had worked alongside them on occasion, when he wasn't busy with his father's cattle operation. Back then, the future had seemed both certain and endless. Gavin would take over the family business. Ethan would run it with him, after winning a world championship at the National Rodeo Finals. And Sierra would marry a local boy—Conner, possibly—and move to a house just down the road. The three siblings would produce a passel of rascally children to try their parents and entertain their grandparents.

It hadn't turned out that way. All things considered, their lives weren't so bad.

"Mom would be proud," Ethan mused out loud as he, Gavin and Clay strode down the bright and airy aisle.

"She would," Gavin agreed.

Clay smiled fondly. "When is Camelot Farms arriving with their mares?"

The farm's half-Arabian, half-quarter-horse animals would be the first to reside in the mare motel.

"In the morning," Gavin answered.

"How many are they bringing?"

"Just two."

Gavin hoped to keep all twenty-four stalls filled. Unfortunately, a stud and breeding business took months, if not years, to establish. Prince had proved himself capable of impregnating mares, as a recent veterinarian exam had confirmed. But it wasn't enough. His foals had to be born healthy, inherit their sire's best qualities, then grow into fine horses. Only then would customers beat down the Powells' door.

Patience was required, and Gavin's was in short supply.

Even now, as he stared at the cooling fans suspended from the barn ceiling, he seemed distracted. More than once Ethan or Clay had to repeat themselves because Gavin wasn't listening.

"Anything in the bunkhouse the men need to finish before I send them home?" Clay asked.

"Nope." Like the cattle barn, Ethan's bunkhouse barely resembled its former incarnation. During the past two weeks, the workers had pushed hard. "They finished constructing the built-in bookcases yesterday."

"You buy an automatic coffeemaker yet?"

"Very funny." He had bought one, but he wasn't about to tell Clay. The bunkhouse, now an apartment, suited him fine without making accommodations for anyone.

Except for Caitlin.

He'd be willing to change his bachelor ways, and pad, for her. Make concessions. Alter his habits. Compromise.

He wasn't willing to give up bronc riding and breaking green horses.

Until then, there was no point even imagining sharing living quarters with her.

"Gavin," Clay said. "Gavin!"

Ethan jerked. His brother wasn't the only one who was distracted.

"Yeah." Gavin blinked as if orienting himself. "What?"

"I asked where the backup generator is located."

"Nowhere for now. We need to decide, and hook it up."

"You okay?"

"Fine." Gavin grinned stupidly.

"You're not acting fine."

"I'm preoccupied." His stupid grin grew even wider.

Ethan couldn't recall seeing his brother act like that, other than the day he'd proposed to Sage. "Is there something you're not telling us?"

"No." Gavin shook his head, then laughed. "Yes."

"Which is it?"

"I'm not supposed to say anything."

"Sage is bred," Clay uttered bluntly.

Leave it to a cattleman to use animal vernacular when describing a pregnancy.

"Is she?" Ethan felt his own mouth stretch into a smile.

"She took the home pregnancy test this morning. We'd planned on waiting before having a baby. A year at least."

"Congratulations." Ethan pumped his brother's

hand, then captured him in a headlock. "Dad's going to be thrilled."

"Don't say anything," Gavin warned, after enduring a suffocating hug from Clay. "I promised Sage. She wants to wait until she sees the doctor."

"Let's celebrate," Clay suggested. "Lunch at the Rusty Nail. My treat."

The local saloon and grill had been one of their favorite hangouts in years past.

"I'm in."

"Call Conner. Maybe he can cut loose from work and join us."

An hour later, the four friends were seated at a table, having beer with their hamburgers and reminiscing about their high school years and all the trouble they'd managed to get into.

Gavin didn't stop smiling, except when he talked about Sage or Cassie. Then his expression grew soft and his voice low. Ethan was truly happy for his brother. He was also jealous and wouldn't mind having a little happiness for himself.

With Caitlin.

Ethan couldn't see himself loving and living with any other woman but her, which explained why he'd dated only occasionally since they'd broken up.

Caitlin wasn't his better half, she was his *other* half. The piece of him that had been missing for years.

Maybe he should consider quitting busting broncs. After the jackpot last week, everyone knew he could still ride with the big boys.

He toyed with the idea of giving up his lifelong dream, and to his shock and alarm, it no longer frightened the hell out of him.

Chapter 11

Caitlin stood in line behind a dad and his pair of preschoolers. The girl, the older of the two, wriggled excitedly and chattered incessantly. The boy wore a solemn expression and chewed nervously on the tip of his mitten.

"Look at the horses!" The girl grasped her brother by the shoulders and shook him. "Real horses."

Caitlin decided the family must not be from Mustang Valley. Most of the residents owned horses, had neighbors with horses or rented them at the Powells' stables. They wouldn't get that excited over the prospect of seeing "real" ones. As she glanced around, it occurred to her there were quite a number of unfamiliar faces at the Holly Days Festival. Articles in the local newspapers and advertisements on radio stations must have attracted people from all over the Phoenix metropolitan area.

A moment later, the man finished his transaction with Sage. "Come on, kids," he said.

The girl skipped alongside him as they headed to the decorated wagon. The boy lagged behind. Caitlin was convinced he would be as enthused as his sister by the time they returned from their ride. She didn't see how much money the dad had given Sage as a donation, but her cheery, "Thank you so much and Merry Christmas," led Caitlin to believe the amount was generous.

"How's business?" she asked, stepping up to the folding table that was serving as a ticket counter. Tamiko had painted a large poster advertising the wagon rides and the mustang sanctuary, and had taped it to the front of the table.

"Couldn't be better!" Sage gushed. "Most people are giving more than what we're asking for the tickets."

"I'm so glad."

"This was a fantastic idea you had. I can't thank you enough for getting the committee to agree."

"We couldn't have done it without Ethan and his family." Caitlin glanced over at him. Ethan sat in the wagon with his back to her, but they'd exchanged looks often during the evening, each one giving her a small tingle. "The festival is everything we had hoped it would be, and they're a big reason why."

During the past week, the stately pine tree in the center of the park had been decorated with silver and gold ornaments and candy canes. The white lights strung through its boughs flickered merrily. Santa's workshop, complete with artificial snow, a replica North Pole and a life-size Rudolph the Red-nosed Reindeer, had been erected across from the tree. Santa sat on a makeshift throne, his pudgy belly hanging over his belt, his white beard covering his chest. The line of children waiting to have their pictures taken with him extended clear to the back of the workshop.

Cassie and Isa, dressed in elf costumes, complete with fake pointed ears, assisted Mrs. Claus with crowd control.

"I still can't believe how many people are here." Caitlin stepped aside to let another customer purchase tickets from Sage.

"There'll be a lot more tomorrow night, I bet."

The festival was scheduled for a full three days, as long as the weather held, which the forecasts predicted it would. Friday night, all day Saturday, and Sunday till four.

Caitlin couldn't be more pleased with the attendance and the positive feedback she'd been receiving. The hard work of the various committee members and crews of energetic volunteers was paying off.

"Excuse me." A woman leaned around Caitlin. "Four tickets, please."

"This wagon is full," Sage apologized with a bright smile. "You'll have to wait for the next ride, in about half an hour."

"How's Ethan holding up?" Caitlin asked Sage when the woman left, tickets for the next ride clutched in her gloved fist.

"You haven't talked to him tonight?"

"Not yet."

Caitlin didn't admit she'd seen him only once since the previous weekend, when he'd taken her for a drive in the wagon, and that was for a PT session. Nor did she admit how much he'd been on her mind. It seemed for a while there they'd been seeing each other every few days. Lately, hardly at all.

She missed him.

A small part of her wondered if she'd acted too hastily when she'd told him there was no chance for a reconciliation.

"He's fine," Sage said. "Though I bet he'll be exhausted by tomorrow night. Driving a wagon is more tiring than you might think, and it takes hours and hours to get ready. He's been at it since noon. Grooming the horses. Cleaning the harnesses. He even washed and ironed his shirt." She winked at Caitlin. "I like a man who does his own laundry."

"Is his shoulder holding up?"

"He hasn't complained."

"He wouldn't."

"You're right about that. He's still doing his exercises, or so he says."

"That's good."

"Where'd all the customers go?" Sage glanced around. "Oh, well." She used the lull to transfer money from the cash box to a press-and-seal plastic bag. "If I give you my keys, would you mind running this to my truck for me? It's in the parking lot. I don't like sitting here with all this cash."

"Glad to," Caitlin said. The stack of bills Sage stuffed in the bag, mostly small denominations, was three inches thick. "Wow, that is a lot of money."

"I'm hoping by the end of the weekend we'll have enough collected to bring two mustangs down from the Bureau of Land Management facility in Show Low. Our first foster horses for the sanctuary."

"Are they injured?" Caitlin tucked the bag of money inside her jacket and out of sight.

"Only superficial wounds sustained during the roundup."

Caitlin really didn't have a reason to stick around talking to Sage, other than she enjoyed the company. She just couldn't bring herself to leave while the wagon was still parked at the corner.

While Ethan was nearby.

As she watched, he clucked to Molly and Dolly and set out amid whoops and cheers from his passengers, the sleigh bells jingling and the lights blinking.

Caitlin attempted a smile, but her mouth wouldn't cooperate.

What was wrong with her?

Sage paid no attention and continued prattling on about the foster mustangs.

"These two horses are what the BLM considers unadoptable. Even with a reduced price of twenty-five dollars each, no one would purchase them."

"Why? Are they mean?"

"No, just wild and not adapting to confinement. But they're so beautiful and spirited. I'm convinced, with the right training, they can make really nice horses for someone. Ethan's skills will be tested for sure."

"He'll train them?"

Of course he would, Caitlin thought, answering her own question. He broke rodeo stock for Clay and green horses for the Powells' clients.

"He did a fantastic job with Prince," Sage declared.

"You won't believe how well that horse is doing. You should come out to the ranch and see him."

"Prince wasn't unadoptable."

"He was wild," Sage explained. "Living in the mountains. You can't get much more unadoptable than that."

"If these mustangs aren't adapting, are you sure it's safe for Ethan to try and train them?"

"As if I could keep him away."

As if anyone could. Certainly not Caitlin.

...when what I really want to do is make love to you.

How often had she heard him say that in her head this past week?

What would it be like making love with him now? she wondered. Different from when they were younger, certainly. They weren't the same people anymore.

Discovering the changes would be interesting. Exciting. Thrilling.

Enough was enough. She wasn't getting back together with Ethan, and she definitely wasn't going to have sex with him.

She patted the bank bag inside her jacket. "I'll put this in your truck and be right back."

"No hurry."

While Caitlin was crossing the parking lot, she glimpsed the wagon with its multicolored lights and excited passengers. It was a charming sight, one straight off the front of a Christmas card.

Ethan really was working his tail off for the committee.

For *her*.

She should do something for him, she decided. A token of appreciation.

Nothing personal. It wasn't as if she was trying to bridge the distance that had developed between them.

When she returned to the table, Clay was there. Caitlin arrived just as he was pulling Sage out of her chair and into his arms.

"Congratulations," he boomed.

She laughed and pushed him away. "Who told you?"

"Who do you think?"

"What's going on?" Caitlin asked, her interest piqued.

"Nothing." Sage took the keys from Caitlin's outstretched hand, her cheeks flushed a deep crimson and her eyes sparkling.

"Come on. Something's up. Tell me."

"Tell her," Clay coaxed. "You know you want to."

Sage sighed. "I was going to make an appointment at the clinic next week, so I suppose you'd have found out eventually."

"You're pregnant!" Caitlin guessed.

"Not so loud." Sage placed a finger to her lips. "I haven't told Isa yet."

"I'm so happy for you!" Caitlin reached across the table and clasped Sage's hands in hers.

"We were going to wait. It was an accident."

"The best kind of accident."

They didn't have much time to talk because a large group of Red Hat ladies descended upon them. Clay convinced the women to add another ten dollars to their donation.

When they left, Sage asked him, "How's that cowboy who got hurt?"

"Better."

Caitlin stilled. "Who got hurt?"

"Micky Lannon," Clay said.

"Micky?" The father of the little girl with the cut knee. "What happened?" she demanded.

"He got bucked off last night."

"From a horse?"

"A bull." Clay and Caitlin continued their conversation while Sage passed out flyers. "Broke his leg in three places. They had to operate this morning, insert some pins. I just came from the hospital. He's going to be released tomorrow."

"Poor guy." Caitlin pressed her hands to her cheeks. "How's his wife holding up?"

"All right, I think."

"What about his job?"

"He's taking a medical leave of absence. Six to eight weeks."

Caitlin wished she had been there to help. Unfortunately, Clay had hired her only for jackpots and rodeo events, not regular practices. There probably wasn't much she could have done anyway. Not with a break that severe.

"What about health insurance?"

"He has it."

Even with coverage, there would be costs. Hefty costs. And he'd be out of work almost two months, which would put a strain on his family and finances. He should have thought of that before climbing on a bull.

"The men are taking up a collection for him. Didn't Ethan tell you?"

Why did everyone think she and Ethan spoke on a regular basis?

"No. I haven't seen him recently." Even if she had,

she doubted he'd have mentioned Micky's fall, knowing how upset she'd get.

"Can I interest you two lovely ladies in a hot chocolate?" Clay asked.

"Mmm." Sage rubbed her palms together. "Yes, please. It's getting chilly."

Caitlin was so engrossed in her thoughts she barely noticed Clay leaving.

Her mind raced. It could have easily been Ethan in the hospital, recovering from a serious surgery. Her chest constricted at the image of him lying with his leg—his one good leg—elevated in a fiberglass cast.

She couldn't bear it if he was hurt like that.

A moan of distress involuntarily escaped her lips.

"Caitlin? You okay?"

She looked over to discover Sage staring at her, a curious expression on her face.

"You're here!" Caitlin hurried over to Justin and her parents. She'd spotted them in the parking lot while making yet another money run to Sage's truck. "I wasn't sure you'd make it."

"Sorry, I got stuck at the office." Her dad slung his arms around Caitlin and her mother. "How soon till the festival closes?"

"Nine."

He whistled. "Doesn't give us much time."

The lateness of the hour and the dropping temperature had no effect on the crowd. People were still arriving in droves.

"Is Tamiko here?" Justin asked, wheeling along beside Caitlin.

That didn't take long.

"Yes. But so is what's-his-name."

What *was* his name? Eric, right?

The presence of Tamiko's boyfriend didn't appear to deter Justin. "Hook up with you later," he said, and was gone.

"Who is this Tamiko?" Caitlin's mother asked in a concerned tone. "He hasn't mentioned her before."

"One of my volunteers. They met at the ranch when we were decorating the wagon."

Typical father, her dad asked, "Is she pretty?"

Typical mother, her mom asked, "Is she nice?"

"Both." Caitlin laughed. "And she likes Justin."

There was just the matter of that pesky boyfriend.

The three of them strolled to the festival grounds. Caitlin often marveled at how easily her parents had adjusted to her brother's loss of mobility and independent lifestyle. Sure, they had worried when he was first injured. And periodically in the years since, especially when he moved away from home and into his own apartment. But never for long, it seemed.

Caitlin was the one who fretted. The one who couldn't cut the apron strings.

Then again, she was the one consumed with guilt over Justin's paralysis. How could her parents, knowing the part she'd played, love her as they did, forgive her as they had?

Justin, too.

Her mother stopped to take everything in. "Are the wagon rides still going on?"

"There's one more at least, maybe two."

"We'd better hurry and buy our tickets." She was off, leaving Caitlin and her father in the dust.

When they reached the table, Caitlin's dad purchased the last two tickets and gave a very large donation that had Sage practically in tears. "Thank you, Mr. Carmichael. Mrs. Carmichael. Can I add you to our list of newsletter subscribers?"

Caitlin could tell one more foster mustang would be arriving from Show Low.

"Too bad Justin's going to miss out," Caitlin's mother mused. "He'd enjoy the wagon ride."

"He's going," Sage said brightly. "He bought a ticket right before you."

"Wonderful."

No, it wasn't.

Apparently Caitlin was the only one who wondered how he'd get up into the wagon without a lift, and how embarrassing it might be for him with all these strangers watching.

"Doug, let's check out the craft tables while we're waiting." Her mother latched on to her husband's arm.

"Send a search party if we're not back in three days," he called to Caitlin.

"Any chance I can recruit you to help me tomorrow night?" Sage asked as they walked away.

"Sure. I was planning on being here, anyway."

Ten minutes later, the wagon returned from its run, the passengers singing Christmas carols. By the time Ethan reined the horses to a stop at the drop-off point, dozens more people milling nearby had joined in with the carolers.

Cheer spread from person to person, carried by a smile.

Caitlin felt her own mouth curve up at the corners. She had spent considerable effort and energy working on the festival. This was, however, the first moment she'd felt truly touched by the Christmas spirit.

She sought out Ethan. He must have sensed her gaze on him because he turned and looked at her...and kept looking. The warmth within her that had started with the caroling continued to build.

Ethan was responsible for this wondrous night. She'd asked for his help and, as always, he'd given it. Unconditionally. Even during the past couple weeks when she'd been avoiding him as much as possible.

She wanted to give him a gift of appreciation—and affection. And suddenly she knew just what it would be.

"We'd better hurry." Caitlin's mother carried three plastic sacks, last-minute Christmas purchases from the craft tables. "Where on earth is Justin?"

The passengers had stopped singing and were climbing down from the wagon one by one, their faces radiant. They exchanged greetings with people lining up for the next ride.

"Here he comes," Caitlin's dad said.

She saw her brother wheeling toward them. Tamiko walked beside him. They made a striking couple, Justin with his fair complexion, Tamiko with her long black hair and exotic beauty.

Not a couple, Caitlin reminded herself.

Where was her boyfriend, Eric?

"Who's this?" her mother asked when Justin and Tamiko joined them in line, even though Caitlin had already told her.

Tamiko put out her hand. "Hi. I'm Justin's friend Tamiko."

Justin's friend? Not, Caitlin thought, one of the festival volunteers.

"Nice to meet you." Caitlin's mother's eyes were bright with curiosity. "Do you attend ASU, too?"

Justin stared at Tamiko with such raw longing, Caitlin couldn't bring herself to watch them. He'd get hurt if he wasn't careful, and there was nothing she or anyone could do to prevent it.

"You coming, honey?" her father asked.

"I didn't buy a ticket."

"They won't charge you. Not with all the work you've put in."

She could always give Sage a donation tomorrow night.

And the wagon ride would be fun. "Sure, why not?"

Caitlin and her family fell into line. The wagon, with its hay bale seats, could easily accommodate ten people and two or three small children sitting on laps. Another person, usually an older child or teenager, rode shotgun next to Ethan.

While the passengers boarded, he stood, stretched and rolled his bad shoulder. It must have been an arduous day for him.

Justin wheeled to the rear of the wagon and waited for a woman with incredibly inappropriate stilettos to be hoisted up by her husband.

Caitlin had to intervene. "Dad, are you going to help Justin?"

"If he asks me."

"Aren't you concerned how he'll get in the wagon?"

"Not as much as you are."

She grumbled to herself. They could possibly fit the

wheelchair into the bed if a bale of hay was removed. That would require a pair of strong arms.

"You first," Justin told Tamiko.

"Hey, what gives?" Her boyfriend abruptly stepped in front of them. Had he been there all along? "He's not riding with us."

"Yes, he is," Tamiko answered coolly.

"I bought a ticket, dude." Justin held up an orange stub.

"Yeah? Well, news flash, *dude*. No room for your wheels."

"I'm not hooked to this chair by wires," Justin said with a chuckle.

Caitlin willed herself not to say anything. She'd interfered before, only to incur her brother's anger. He insisted on fighting his own battles.

Her parents didn't appear to be concerned. They watched their son closely but made no move in his direction.

"Come on, Tamiko." Her boyfriend snatched her hand.

"What about Justin?"

"You heard him. He's not hooked to that chair."

The other passengers had all boarded and were watching the scene unfolding before them with rabid interest.

"This is better than reality TV," one woman said.

The hell with making Justin mad. Caitlin had reached her limit. "Okay, guys—"

"Stay out of it," her father ordered.

"Dad!"

"I mean it, honey."

"I'm not leaving Justin," Tamiko said stubbornly.

"You'd pick him over me?" Eric demanded.

"We're friends. Why can't you be nice?"

"This is stupid." Caitlin took a step forward.

A large, strong hand on her arm pulled her back. She pivoted, intending to tell her father they should—

It wasn't her dad restraining her. It was Ethan.

"Let me handle this," he said, and brushed past her.

Caitlin started to follow.

"Young lady!" Her father's stern voice stopped her in her tracks. "What did I tell you? Butt out."

"Dammit," she grumbled. Why did she have to butt out and not Ethan?

He walked over to Justin. "You ready?"

"If you are."

A look of understanding passed between them.

Ethan bent down and placed one arm beneath Justin's legs and the other behind his back. He lifted her brother out of the chair and carried him the short distance to the wagon. Another man sitting on a hay bale jumped up. Without being asked, he took Justin from Ethan and gently deposited him on the nearest empty seat. The three of them worked together so smoothly, they might have done this before.

And just like that, it was over.

Caitlin's father helped her mother and then Tamiko into the wagon. Her boyfriend clambered up after her, scowling as he squeezed by Justin.

"You coming, honey?"

"Yeah, Dad."

Ethan appeared next to her. "You can sit with me if you want."

She turned to her father, but he was already halfway in the wagon. "I guess I will."

Conner sat in the seat, holding the reins, while T.J. gripped Dolly's bridle. The two cowboys had been helping Ethan with the horses all night.

Ethan climbed up first. Once he had hold of the reins, Conner jumped down. Molly and Dolly, tired after their long night, didn't so much as twitch an ear.

Ethan held out a hand to Caitlin.

She tried to remember where to place her feet. Wheel spoke left? Footrest right?

"Need help?" Conner didn't wait for an answer, and gave her a boost.

By some miracle, she made it into the seat, clumsily plopping down beside Ethan. Before she was quite settled he clucked to the horses and they were off.

She glanced over her shoulder at her brother. He appeared fine. Not the least bit self-conscious. He seemed to be enjoying himself, talking with the man who'd helped him. Smiling at Tamiko.

Such a change from the shy, geeky kid he'd been.

If Caitlin hadn't encouraged him to go to the river that day, it might have been him sitting next to Tamiko. Taking her to a dance. Walking with her down a church aisle one day.

"He's all right," Ethan said.

"I was checking on my parents."

"Liar."

She sighed. "Am I that transparent?"

"Only to those of us who know you well."

He did know her well, and she him. Which made this game they were playing—drawing toward each other, then stepping back—all the more frustrating.

"Thanks for helping Justin out."

"He's a good kid."

"Yeah, he is. And I'm sure he appreciates what you did for him." She bit her lower lip, worrying it between her teeth. "So do I," she finally admitted.

His reply was a simple, "You're welcome."

"I apologize for the mixed messages I've been sending you."

"Maybe they weren't so mixed."

Maybe they weren't.

A tiny sliver of awareness arrowed through her.

"I'm here for you, Caitlin, and I'm willing to wait. For however long it takes."

That wasn't what he'd said before. He'd left on a whim, broken her heart.

Could she trust him again?

Perhaps the more important question was, did she want to live the rest of her life without him?

Chapter 12

"Isa, come back here!" Sage muttered an expletive in Spanish under her breath. Jumping down from the wagon, she chased her daughter across the green to the Santa's workshop.

"Just think," Ethan ribbed Gavin, who sat on the seat beside him. "Soon you and Sage will have another kid to wear you down and teach you a second language."

"Yeah." His brother grinned, something he'd been doing a lot lately. "I can't wait."

None of the Powells could. Sage's resolve had weakened yet again, and this morning she'd broken the news of her pregnancy to the rest of the family. The girls had squealed with excitement. Ethan's father had cried.

"By the way, you're going to have to buy a new suit," Gavin said. "We're moving up the wedding date from May to February. Sage doesn't want to be fat as a cow in her wedding dress. Her words," he added emphatically, "not mine."

"Can you pull everything together by then?"

"I think so. If we keep it casual and simple."

"Let me know what you need help with."

"Consider yourself on notice." Gavin swung out of the seat, landing easily on the ground.

"Clay can be in charge of the bachelor party."

Gavin moaned. "Whatever you do, don't tell Sage." He headed to the horses to check on them.

Ethan chuckled. He was glad for his brother.

Six months ago, the Powells were barely making ends meet, and their future looked bleak. Gavin had believed it was entirely up to him to put their riding stables in the black. He'd done it, with a little help from the rest of the family and good friends, including Clay. He'd also gained a fiancée and stepdaughter in the process.

Quite an accomplishment for a man who, until recently, considered himself unmarriageable and a poor excuse for a father.

Ethan held a similar opinion of himself. Though lately, with the help of Cassie and Isa, he was learning how to be a good uncle. That was a start.

"Isa forgot her hat." Cassie, in full elf costume, held up a striped stocking cap with an enormous tassel on the end.

She, Isa and Sage had ridden in the bed of the wagon from the ranch, while Ethan's father followed in the truck. He and Gavin had been tapped to help Ethan tonight with the horses.

"Come on, Dad." Cassie scrambled out of the wagon. "I'll show you and Grandpa Santa's workshop."

"You okay alone for a bit?" Gavin asked Ethan.

"Go on. Have fun."

The pair met up with Ethan's dad on his walk over from the parking lot.

All the Powells were together for an outing. Ethan didn't have to search his memory for the last time that had happened. He remembered it clearly—Fourth of July fireworks, right before his mother's body rejected the donor heart, and she succumbed to infection.

He'd taken Caitlin to the fireworks display, naturally, and they'd kissed under the brilliantly lit sky, pledging their love and devotion. No wonder she was still angry at him. If she had up and left him shortly after a night like that, he'd have trouble forgiving her.

She would be here tonight, helping Sage sell tickets and take donations. Ethan intended to get her alone at some point before the evening ended. A small wrapped package was burning a hole in his jacket pocket, and he was eager to give it to her. The gift wouldn't make up for all the grief and misery he'd caused her, but he hoped she would see the meaning behind it and think a little better of him.

One of the horses lowered his head and pawed the pavement, more ready than his buddy to get started.

Ethan had brought a different team tonight. They weren't as nicely matched as Dolly and Molly, but equally dependable. The geldings had been full of energy when they left the ranch. A two-mile walk down the long road had tired them out some, and by their third trip around the park, they'd be beat.

So would Ethan. He hadn't worked this hard since

basic training, but he'd do it again in a heartbeat if Caitlin asked him.

Ethan noticed her then, taking the same route as his father from the parking lot across the green. She carried a large tote bag pressed close to her side, as if the contents were fragile or precious.

Caitlin went straight to the table, waving briefly to him, and seemed perplexed to find no one there. She looked around, set her tote bag down, then picked it up again.

He'd have gone over to talk to her if he could leave the horses. Instead, he imagined her coming to him.

In the next moment she did, wearing a radiant smile.

She aimed it at him, and he swore they were back at the fireworks display, sitting beneath the brilliantly lit sky.

Before she reached him, his father and Gavin met up with her. She gave his dad a hug and a kiss on the cheek. Ethan was jealous. Gavin received the same treatment, and Ethan was even more jealous. He was seriously considering leaping down from the wagon and collecting his kiss and hug when she came to stand by him, her hand resting on the wheel.

"Hey."

"Can I interest you in a ride, ma'am?"

"Maybe later." She laughed softly and transformed once more into the old Caitlin. They were young, flirting outrageously and unable to get enough of each other. "I promised I'd help Sage tonight."

"The supplies are in the truck," Wayne said. "If you're looking for them."

"I'll wait for Sage." She shrugged, causing her tote

bag to slip. She hefted the straps back onto her shoulder, running her fingers tentatively down the side.

"She might be a while. I can fetch them for you."

"Do you mind? I'll go with you."

Ethan saw his opportunity and grabbed it. "I'll do it. Gavin, get over here and watch these horses for me."

"Did you want to leave your stuff here?" Ethan asked. "Dad will watch it."

"No." Caitlin hugged the tote closer. "That's all right."

They walked side by side, though not close and not touching. Small talk came easy.

"Are you ready for Christmas?"

Her question reminded Ethan they'd seen little of each other lately.

"Me? No. I'm a last-minute shopper." He thought of the gift in his pocket. "Usually. But Sage and the girls have transformed the house. There's a tree in the living room, a wreath on the front door and cookies baking in the oven every day. Dad's trying to set some kind of record."

"Sounds wonderful."

"It is." The preparations took him back to when he was a kid and his mother had gone all-out for Christmas with the same gusto as Sage and the rest of his family. "What about you?"

"I've finished my shopping."

"More than I can say."

"Still haven't done anything with the condo or even sent out one card. I'm so bad."

"You're busy."

"Not that busy."

"By the way, Clay's having another jackpot the Saturday after Christmas."

"I'll be there." She hesitated a beat before asking, "Will you?"

"Yes, but not riding. Working the stock."

"Not competing?"

He thought he detected a hint of optimism in her voice, and hated disappointing her. "This jackpot is for high school students. There's a statewide junior rodeo coming up in January. Clay wants to give the kids an opportunity to practice before then."

"High school students? They're so young."

"I was competing at that age."

"I know." Deep creases knitted her brow.

"We don't use the same rodeo stock for them. The bulls and horses tend to be smaller. And Clay will require every participant to wear safety equipment or they don't compete."

He could see the topic distressed her. Too late, he remembered that Justin had been a senior in high school when he'd had his accident.

Fortunately, they reached Gavin's truck, and the discussion came to an end. Digging the keys from his pocket, he unlocked the door and retrieved the box of supplies.

"I'll carry it for you," he said when she held out her hands.

"Wait."

"Just this once, Caitlin, let me carry something for you without giving me a hard time."

"I don't care about the supplies." She hesitated, did that lower-lip biting thing that signaled she was nervous. "I'd planned on giving you this later tonight."

She lowered the tote from her shoulder. "Now might be better, so you can put it in the truck."

His curiosity was piqued. "What is it?"

She removed a wrapped present from the tote bag and held it out to him. "Merry Christmas, Ethan."

He was floored. She'd gotten him a present, too.

Setting the supplies on the hood of the truck, he took the slim, rectangular package from her. "Thank you."

"It's nothing special… I hope you like it."

He tugged at the tape holding the colorful wrapping paper. "I'm sure I will."

The corner of a wooden picture frame peeked out. A moment later, he held a framed photograph in his hands, emotions rioting inside him.

"I noticed you don't have any pictures on the walls in your apartment yet," Caitlin explained. "I thought maybe this could be your first one."

"This is great." He smiled at her and tilted the picture for a closer look in the fading daylight. "I really like it." He also liked the effort she'd gone to and the thoughtfulness behind the gift.

"I hoped you would."

The photo was of him breaking Prince. It was one Justin had taken with his phone, now enlarged to an eight-by-ten. The angle was perfect. Both Ethan and Prince wore determined expressions, Ethan's goal to stay seated and Prince's to throw his rider. At the moment the photo was snapped, no clear victor was evident.

He rewrapped the picture and placed it on the floor in front of the passenger seat.

"Don't take this wrong, but I'm kind of surprised."

"Why?"

"You don't much like me bronc riding and breaking horses."

"Yes." Caitlin tipped her head appealingly to one side. "But it's your life and what you choose to do. I respect that and admire it, too. You've always been true to yourself, Ethan."

That wasn't quite accurate. If he was really true to himself, he'd haul Caitlin into his arms and kiss the socks off her.

"Be careful. I might start thinking you're not as tough as you claim."

"Maybe I'm not."

He was tempted to jump to all sorts of conclusions, and warned himself not to read too much into what she said. Becoming more tolerant of his chosen profession wasn't an open invitation back into her life.

"I have something for you, too." He reached inside his jacket pocket and removed his gift for her.

"Oh." Her eyes lit up. She accepted the present and, unlike him, tore at the paper with careless abandon. "Haverson's?" she asked, reading the name stenciled in gold.

"You've heard of them?"

"Yes." She cradled the box in her hands. "Before I open this, I'm going to say you shouldn't have. Everything in that store costs a small fortune."

Ethan chuckled. "One of the owners is a client of mine. He gave me a discount."

Nestled inside the tissue paper was a handmade Christmas tree ornament. Caitlin lifted it by the silk string and held it up. The wagon, a miniature replica of the one Ethan drove, spun in a circle, the glow from the parking-lot lights glinting off its shiny green paint.

"Ethan," she breathed. "It's charming."

"I know you said you weren't decorating this year because you hadn't decided whether to stay in Mustang Valley or not. I thought you should have something. Blame Sage and the girls. They've corrupted me with their Christmas spirit and—"

Caitlin didn't let him finish. Clutching the front of his jacket, she pulled him to her for a kiss. "I love it," she said, and pressed her lips to his.

Ethan was very glad he'd stowed away the picture she'd given him. Having two free arms enabled him to slip his hands inside her unbuttoned coat and draw her fully against him.

In the span of an instant the kiss went from sweet to sensual to searing. The moment his tongue touched her lips they parted for him. He took full advantage, and she encouraged him, unlike the night they'd kissed at the rodeo arena and she'd held back.

She tasted exactly as he remembered. Her body, firm yet yielding, molded to his. She teased and tortured him by sifting her fingers through the hair at the base of his neck and rocking ever so slightly.

Her soft moan was answered by a low groan from him.

The need to touch her became overwhelming. Too many clothes hampered his efforts, causing him great frustration. He settled for taking hold of her hips and aligning them with his.

"Caitlin?" Sage's call carried from the park.

Ethan cursed his future sister-in-law's lousy timing. He broke off the kiss, gulping air to fill his deprived lungs. He tried to talk. All that came out was Caitlin's name and a ragged breath.

She sighed contentedly, smiled coyly. Standing on tiptoes, she captured his lower lip between her teeth and tugged. It was something she used to do when they were younger, and it always drove him crazy.

Nothing had changed. His body jerked reflexively in response.

He kissed her again, hard, deeply, then pulled away while he still could. "I want to see you. Tonight. After the wagon rides."

"All right."

No objections? No arguments? No insisting he listen to reason?

"I'll get Gavin and Dad to take the wagon and horses home."

Caitlin leaned forward and rested her forehead on his chest. In a quiet voice she said, "We can go to my place."

"You sure?" Ethan lifted her face to his, not wanting there to be any misunderstanding between them.

"I'm sure." She retreated a step, and his hands fell away.

She'd made her decision about them and about tonight. Ethan didn't quite know what that decision was. He could only guess…and hope.

"Thank you, sir." Caitlin put the donation for the mustang sanctuary in the jar. "The last ride will be leaving in about twenty minutes. The line starts over there."

They'd been busier tonight than last night, for which she was glad. The constant stream of customers over the past three hours had enabled her to avoid thinking of Ethan and what might occur later.

She'd invited him to her condo! That hadn't been her original intention. After they'd kissed, her mind shut down and her heart had come up with the idea. She could rescind the invitation, concoct some excuse. Only she didn't want to.

The ornament—Ethan must have had it custom-made for her—wasn't the only reason for the sudden change. He cared for her and showed her as much with his kindness to her brother and his respect for her feelings even when he didn't agree with them.

Hearing jingle bells, she turned her head. From this distance, the wagon looked like a wind-up toy. No, like the ornament. The illusion faded as the wagon drew nearer. Ethan sat in the driver's seat, the collar of his sheepskin jacket pulled up to protect his neck from the cold wind that sailed through the valley, his hat settled low on his brow.

Soon they would be leaving for her place. Her insides tingled with anticipation.

It was then she noticed the teenager sitting next to him was holding the reins, not Ethan. She heard him instruct the boy, "When we get to that tree, pull back and tell 'em 'whoa!'"

The wagon rattled to a stop a minute later, and the passengers, all in high spirits, piled out. Those waiting in line for the last ride of the night eagerly took their places.

Karen Lawler, the chair of the festival committee, stepped into her line of vision.

"Caitlin, my dear, the wagon rides have been an

incredible success. Did you see the picture in today's newspaper?"

"No, but I heard about it."

"You should get a copy." The reindeer antlers Karen wore on her head tipped back and forth as she gestured excitedly.

"I'll check my computer in the morning. See if the picture's in their online edition."

"Do you think the Powells will be willing to give wagon rides again next year?"

"I have no idea. You can always ask."

"I was counting on you to do that, seeing as you're so close to them." There was no mistaking Karen's implication. Like half of Mustang Valley, she'd concluded Caitlin and Ethan were romantically involved.

Caitlin waited for a flood of embarrassment to heat her cheeks and tie her tongue. It didn't happen.

Interesting.

"I'm also counting on you to volunteer again," Karen continued.

A few weeks ago, Caitlin might have hesitated or declined, unsure if she was remaining in Mustang Valley or not.

"Of course I'll volunteer."

"Lovely," Karen trilled, and clasped Caitlin to her. "Merry Christmas, my dear. I must run. I'm meeting up with my grandchildren."

All the passengers had loaded up, and the wagon was ready to depart on its last run of the festival. Caitlin started clearing the table.

"You don't have to do that," Sage admonished, hurrying toward her. "Let me. You were only supposed to relieve me, and you ran the table the entire evening."

"You and the girls were enjoying the festival."

"Go get yourself an ice cream or a cup of coffee before all the vendors close for the night," Sage suggested.

"Okay. If you're sure you don't need me."

Caitlin didn't get ten feet away before discovering she really wasn't interested in food. If no one claimed the seat beside Ethan, maybe she'd go on the last ride with him.

The thought was barely formed when Cassie plunked down beside him and Gavin went over to talk to him.

Well, it had been a good idea while it lasted.

A minute later, the wagon still hadn't pulled out, and the passengers were getting restless. While Caitlin watched, the brothers traded places, with Gavin taking over the reins. He settled next to Cassie, while Ethan climbed carefully down, landing stiffly on the ground.

His leg must be bothering him. Or he was sore. Probably both.

She walked over to him. "Is something the matter?"

He smiled, a not-at-all-tired smile. "Gavin's taking the last ride for me, and then he'll drive the wagon home."

"Did you tell him about our plans?"

"Not a word. He's just giving me a break. It's been a long two nights."

The wagon pulled out at last to a chorus of cheers from its passengers.

"Do you mind if we take your van?" Ethan asked. "Dad's going to follow Gavin home in the truck."

"Of course not."

It wasn't until they were leaving the parking lot that Caitlin realized Ethan had no way home from her condo unless she drove him.

Chapter 13

"You haven't been here before?" Caitlin asked.

"Actually, no."

Ethan didn't intend to gawk at his surroundings, but he couldn't stop himself. They stood at her front door while she fitted the key in the lock. He was quite certain the dirt road that used to cut through the center of Mustang Valley, the one he, Gavin, their father and the ranch hands had driven on a weekly basis, had been right where he was standing.

A surreal feeling came over him, as if he'd walked into someone else's dream.

"Everything's changed. So much."

"Must be hard on you." She twisted the knob and pushed open the door.

"Not as much as when I first came home. I haven't

spent much time in Mustang Village." Hardly any until meeting Caitlin again.

They stepped inside her condo, and he was suddenly struck with a case of cold feet.

He was here at her invitation, which told him she was ready for more. But how much more? He'd hate to jump to the wrong conclusion.

She flipped a switch, and an overhead lighting fixture illuminated the empty entryway. To their right was a staircase. Directly in front of them, a hallway. To their left, an open archway led to the living room.

"Public rooms downstairs. Bedrooms and bathroom upstairs." She laughed. "Though calling the second bedroom a 'room' is a stretch. I've seen bigger closets."

"This is nice."

Caitlin removed her jacket and held an arm out for Ethan's. He gave it to her. "It would be nicer with more furniture."

"Would you rather have a house?"

"Sure, eventually. For right now, this suits me. I don't have the time to take care of a yard or keep up on the maintenance a house would require."

She hung her jacket in the hall closet and draped Ethan's across the banister.

Was she planning on him making a fast exit?

"What about you?" she asked. "Ever think of living anywhere other than the ranch?"

"The bunkhouse is fine for now. Kind of cramped if I were…"

"Married with kids?" she finished for him.

"Something like that."

"You're really good with Cassie and Isa."

"Their parents might disagree. They've learned a

few words from me that aren't, shall we say, appropriate for young ladies."

He followed Caitlin into the living room, which reminded him a little of his bunkhouse. The minimal necessities were there, a couch, a chair, a side table. What was missing were the decorative touches that turned a place into a comfortable home.

They were quite the pair, the two of them, moving through life, staying in different places but never putting down roots. What were they running away from?

What were they running to?

"I didn't even consider having kids for a long time." He sat on one end of the couch. "Not while I was in the marines."

"That's understandable."

Caitlin had brought the wagon ornament inside with her. She removed it from the box and placed it on the table beside an old lamp Ethan was sure had come from her parents' house. The ornament looked out of place sitting there all alone. Had he been wrong to get it for her? Maybe she wasn't ready to stay in one place.

Stay here with him.

"What about you? Want kids?"

"Two for sure. Maybe three," she added with a shy smile.

They'd never discussed having children, that Ethan could remember. In fact, they'd rarely discussed anything of a profoundly personal nature. Having fun had been their priority. Perhaps that was why when his mother died he hadn't turned to Caitlin and confided in her.

"Can I get you something?" she asked, a little too brightly. "Coffee? Beer? Eggnog?"

"Eggnog? I haven't had that for a long time. My mom used to make it."

"I'm afraid the kind I have comes in a carton from the grocery store. I can add a splash of brandy to it if you'd like." A mischievous glint sparked in her eyes.

He hadn't seen that glint since before he'd left for the marines. These days, she was always so serious.

"I'd like to, but you have to drive me home."

"That won't be for a while."

Oh, boy.

She went to the kitchen. Ethan waited on her couch, his heart chugging like a piston. It was just a cup of eggnog, he told himself. Nothing else.

But there had been that glint in her eyes....

She returned shortly and handed him a glass of frothy, creamy eggnog filled to the brim. Sitting on the other end of the couch, she kicked off her shoes, tucked her legs beneath her and sipped at her glass.

Her relaxed pose did nothing to slow the piston inside his chest.

He tasted his eggnog. "Not bad."

They talked after that, about nothing and everything. Gavin and Sage's wedding plans, old friends—who'd moved where and done what—and some of the more memorable shenanigans they'd pulled as teenagers.

More than once Caitlin's eyes misted with sentimental tears. They'd shared so much when they were younger. Ethan couldn't believe he'd walked away from it. From her.

After a particularly good laugh, she stretched out her legs on the couch. Her feet, in colorful Christmas socks, were inches from him.

What would she do if he pulled her feet into his lap?

"Another one?" Caitlin held up her empty glass.

"No, thanks." The eggnog hadn't been particularly strong, but it was probably better that they refrain from having more. "I should be getting home."

The talking had been enjoyable. A good beginning to wherever it was they were heading. Given the choice, he'd move a whole lot faster, but Caitlin was setting the pace, and he was very willing to let her.

"So soon?" She arched a foot toward him.

It was a very small movement, one that could easily be misread. He did nothing at first, then she arched it again. This time her toes brushed his thigh, light as a butterfly's wing.

What the hell.

He rested his hand on her ankle. When she didn't jerk it away, he began kneading her foot, something he'd been aching to do since she'd shed her shoes.

She tipped her head back and closed her eyes. "Mmm...that feels good."

He couldn't take his eyes off her. The smooth expanse of her bare neck cried out for his kisses. Her slightly mussed hair curled sexily around her pink-tinged cheeks.

His hand moved from her foot to her calf. She made a contented sound as he continued massaging her with firm strokes.

In another minute, he wouldn't be responsible for his actions.

"I really need to go. Or not." He'd leave the choice to her.

Caitlin opened her eyes and sat up. Slowly pulling her legs away from him, she set her feet on the floor.

Disappointment cut through him.

Perhaps next time there would be a different ending to the evening.

He braced his hand on the armrest and started to stand.

She slid across the middle cushion separating them. "Or not," she stated.

Ethan sat back down and studied her face, searching for any sign of indecision or distrust. There was none. "Do you know what you're saying?" Honor dictated he give her one last opportunity to change her mind.

She linked her arms around his neck, snuggled against him and whispered, "Stay."

One word, and a whole world of possibilities opened up.

Caitlin might have questioned her actions right up until the moment she and Ethan kissed. They weren't just going to hit rough patches along the way, they were starting out in the middle of a big one.

But being intimate with him felt right and always had. She loved hearing her name on his lips, repeated over and over between heated kisses.

His hand, large and strong and warm, slid down her back and under the hem of her shirt to caress bare skin. Her breasts flattened against his broad chest as she wriggled closer...closer...closer. His low exhalation of breath deepened into a groan as he tore his mouth away, to trail more kisses along the column of her neck.

She'd all but forgotten.

How could she?

Her fingers sought the buttons of his shirt, toyed

with them, finally succeeded in unfastening the top three. A T-shirt impeded her quest for skin-to-skin contact, and she swore impatiently.

Ethan shifted beneath her, almost upending her. In one swift, deliberate move he stripped off his shirt and T-shirt, tugging them over his head and tossing them aside.

"Yes." She skimmed her palms along his hard muscles, felt them constrict as he sucked in air though his teeth. When she would have explored further, seen what other reactions she could arouse in him, he clasped both her hands between his and held them over his heart.

"This is no one-night stand. If it is for you, we stop now."

"No one-night stand." She sealed the promise with a kiss that instantly turned explosive.

The hair-trigger passion they ignited in each other was the same as when they were younger. It was also different. There was a hardness in Ethan she hadn't seen before, an intensity that was almost unbearable at times.

She imagined he noticed changes in her, too. The adventurous teenager had all but disappeared, replaced by an overly cautious woman afraid to take risks.

Except when it came to sex.

Then, and now, Caitlin had no qualms letting Ethan know what she wanted, with actions and quietly murmured demands.

Suddenly, he broke off the kiss and set her away from him.

"What?"

"Not here." He caressed her cheek with his finger-tips. "Upstairs."

She rose from the couch, her body weightless like a bird taking flight, and extended her hand. Ethan took it. She turned, but before she could slip away, he wrapped his arms around her waist and pulled her to him, fitting her back to his front. His erection pressed into her as his lips nibbled the sensitive flesh where her neck joined her shoulder.

"So long," she murmured. "We waited so long."

He groaned in agreement.

She craved more but was loath to leave the warmth of his arms. Her burning need won out, and she led him to the stairs. As they climbed single file, she sensed his gaze on her and purposefully didn't hurry, even when they reached her bedroom. Inside the door sat a dresser with a small lamp. She turned it on. Light bathed the room in a warm yellow glow.

Ethan went to the bed and sat on the edge of the mattress. When she went to sit beside him, he tugged her between his open legs. Resting his hands on her waist, he laid his head on her chest.

"There's been no one for a long time." She couldn't explain her need to reveal such personal information.

"For me, either."

She brushed a fallen lock of black hair from his face. Leaning down, she kissed him again, holding his face in her palms as she ran her lips over his. He sat very still, hardly breathing.

"Touch me," she whispered.

He covered her breasts with his hands, squeezing them through the sweater she wore.

Waves of pleasure cascaded over her, and she tugged frantically at her clothes.

"Let me," he insisted, his voice a husky growl.

Who was she to object? She lifted her arms so he could remove her sweater. Her bra came next.

Filling his hands with her breasts, he ran his thumbs over her nipples until they hardened to tight peaks. It wasn't enough. At her urging, he leaned forward and drew one nipple into his mouth, then the other.

Her eyes drifted shut; her knees buckled slightly.

"Sweet. So sweet," Ethan murmured.

His mouth didn't stop there. It moved to other erogenous zones. The ridge of her collarbone. The valley between her breasts. Her navel.

She was wearing way too many clothes, Caitlin thought, and reached for the clasp on her jeans.

"I have protection," he said.

"Good."

He sat forward, removed his wallet from his pants pocket. "I'm only carrying this because—"

"I don't care why." She stroked his jaw. "I'm just glad you have it."

"Me, too."

She shimmied out of her jeans and panties, liking that he watched her every move with hungry eyes. Naked at last, she stood in front of him.

"You're incredibly beautiful." His gaze traveled from her toes to her face.

"Your turn."

Pushing himself off the bed, he attacked his belt buckle. When the clasp and zipper on his jeans defeated him, she came to his aid. Hooking his thumbs in the waistband, he slid his pants down. This time there were no shirttails to cover him, and Caitlin very much liked what she saw.

He sat back down, extending his left leg.

She knelt in front of him and removed his right boot. Then she grabbed his prosthesis by the ankle.

"Caitlin, sweetheart."

"Let me. I don't want there to be any barriers between us."

After a long moment, he swallowed and nodded. Once he'd loosened the cuff, she pulled gently. The prosthesis came off, sliding out of his pant leg. Giving it only the briefest of glances, she set it on the floor near the dresser.

Ethan removed his jeans, and she rested her hands on his thighs. Tenderly, she ran her fingers over his stump which began a few inches below his knee. He flinched once before relaxing as her gentle caresses continued over skin that was rough and riddled with scars in some places, and surprisingly smooth in others.

Caitlin's throat closed, and she swallowed a sob. In her mind, she could see him lying in some Middle Eastern street, buried in a pile of rubble, broken and bleeding. "This must have hurt."

"It still does some days."

"I'm sorry."

He tucked a finger under her chin and raised her face to his. "Don't be. I'm one of the lucky ones."

She straightened and went into his arms. "You have no idea how glad I am for that."

Ethan pulled her onto the bed and laid her on her back. She didn't stop to think about what he could or couldn't manage when it came to lovemaking. She had every confidence he'd show her.

They spent long minutes reacquainting themselves with each other's bodies. Ethan was still ticklish on his neck. She still broke out in goose bumps when he sucked on her earlobe. She delighted in the reactions her tongue and touch evoked in him. He grinned whenever she sighed softly or shivered with unrestrained pleasure.

She was past ready when Ethan nudged her legs apart and began stroking her intimate places. Her breathing went ragged, then stilled as his mouth moved down her torso to the inside of her thighs.

"I've dreamed of this," he said, placing his mouth on her.

So had she. Often.

Within minutes, seconds maybe, she was arching off the bed and hovering on the brink of climax.

"I want you inside me."

He crawled up her body, his mouth following the same trail up as it had down.

"Hurry!" she urged.

One quick tear and he had the condom open. Levering himself over her, he said, "Look at me."

She did, and he thrust inside her.

A shattering climax seized her almost immediately. She became a piece of driftwood riding a wild, storm-churned sea. He followed soon after, clinging to her as if she alone was responsible for anchoring him to the bed.

Eventually, he loosened his grip. When he started to roll off her, she held him and pleaded, "Not yet."

"For as long as you want, baby doll."

Baby doll. That was the name he'd called her in high school.

Caitlin felt her throat close again. She wasn't usually this weepy, but it had been a long time since she'd let down her guard. A long time since she'd felt so cherished.

"What if I want you with me a really long time?"

"I can do that." He rubbed his cheek along hers.

"I'm serious, Ethan."

He lifted his head to peer at her, his expression filled with—did she dare think it?—love.

"Me, too."

They would talk, needed to talk. Eventually. But not tonight.

"What would your family say if you didn't come home till morning?"

He did roll off her then and lay beside her, his good leg draped over her. "Probably that I finally came to my senses. And that you lost yours."

She punched him lightly in the arm. "Not possible."

"I won't hurt you again, baby doll. I swear."

Caitlin believed he would try his best to keep that vow. She also wasn't naive. Things changed without warning. Shit hit the fan. Worlds fell apart. It had happened to her before and could again.

They needed to proceed cautiously. Lift the lid of this box that was their new relationship one corner at a time.

As Ethan's hands roamed her body once more, inducing tiny tremors in her, she forgot all about erring on the side of caution.

Pushing him onto his back, she straddled his middle, determined to drive every thought from his mind.

* * *

Getting to the ranch early wasn't a problem. Ethan and Caitlin hardly slept all night. When they did doze, it was wrapped in each other's arms. He could still feel her tucked against him, warm and giving. Could taste her lips and skin, smell the light, flowery fragrance of her hair.

He'd brought only one condom with him. That hadn't stopped them from enjoying each other. They'd been careful and innovative, and next time—there would be many, many more next times—Ethan would be better prepared.

"When do you have to be at the festival today?" he asked.

Stifling a yawn, she turned her van into the driveway leading to the ranch.

"Not till ten. I can probably show up at eleven and no one will notice. I just need to be there when we close at four."

"Go home and take a nap," he told her, squeezing her hand.

"I think I will. What about you?"

"We're usually busy on Sundays, but with the festival, I doubt we will be today. If the girls don't pester me to take them on a ride, I might squeeze in a little shut-eye, too."

Any hopes they had of not being caught were dashed the moment Caitlin pulled into the open area in front of the stables. Gavin and Sage, up for an early morning outing, were helping the girls onto their horses.

Sage, Isa and Cassie waved, with big, welcoming smiles on their shining faces. Gavin simply nodded.

"Looks like you caught a break," Caitlin said airily.

"No trail ride duty today." She didn't appear the least bit embarrassed at being spotted sneaking Ethan home.

He decided he shouldn't be, either. What he and Caitlin did in the privacy of her condo wasn't anybody's business, though there would be questions, he was sure, from Sage. His future sister-in-law didn't ascribe to the same to-each-your-own philosophy his father and brother did.

Caitlin continued to the bunkhouse, driving slowly, and parked out front. Their goodbye kiss went on and on.

"Any plans tonight, for after the festival?" he asked, thinking he could never get enough of her lush, ripe mouth.

"Nothing definite. I was considering buying a tree."

He liked the idea. It rang of permanence.

"Why don't I pick you up at four-thirty? We can go for an early dinner and then head to the tree lot."

"A date?"

"Yeah, a date."

"Mexican?"

"Wherever. You pick the place."

She paused for so long he thought she was going to say no. "Mexican it is."

"Good." *Very* good.

"We can talk."

"Ah." He'd been expecting that. "I suppose we have to."

"Yes, we do."

"I wish I could tell you I'll stop riding broncs."

"I wish I could tell you I have no problem with that." She lifted his hand and pressed the knuckles to her cheek. "Be patient with me. I swear I'll try my hardest to cope."

"I don't want you to always be worrying about me."

"It comes with the territory. Because of who I am, my profession, my brother, and because of how I feel about you."

He was tempted to ask her exactly how she felt about him but decided to wait until dinner tonight.

"One day at a time, okay?" she said.

"Sounds good to me."

"See you at four-thirty."

"If not sooner."

Her eyebrows rose.

"I was so busy with the wagon rides, I never got a chance to check out the festival. Is it possible to get a tour?"

"I'll see what I can arrange." Her mouth curved up in a smile that proved irresistible.

They were going to be all right, Ethan thought during another lingering goodbye kiss. This time, their relationship would last. It wouldn't be easy, but unlike when they were young, they knew full well the obstacles facing them, and that would make all the difference.

Chapter 14

Caitlin could hardly believe it was Christmas Day already. The ten days following the Holly Days Festival had flown by in a blur. A happy, exciting, cloud nine kind of blur where she and Ethan were together every possible minute. They didn't run out of things to talk about or places to go. Neither did they tire of making love. Most nights they ended up at her place—no prying eyes and nosy family members, particularly those age twelve and under.

Missing the lower half of his left leg affected Ethan very little. He was an incredible lover. Attentive, considerate and generous. He also brought an emotional intensity to their lovemaking that hadn't been there years ago. She found that aspect more exciting than anything else.

She had wanted to spend today at the ranch with the

Powells, but that wasn't possible because of her family obligations. No way on earth would her mother have tolerated her missing Christmas dinner.

By late afternoon, Caitlin couldn't wait a moment longer to see him, and after calling Ethan, left for the ranch with a promise to return to her parents' by seven. Or seven-thirty. Maybe even eight.

"You made it." He hurried across the back patio to meet her.

"Finally!" Eight o'clock for sure.

Caitlin had attended Christmas Eve service with the Powells, their first time stepping inside a church together since Ethan's mother's funeral. It had been a sentimental and moving experience, for Caitlin, as well.

Afterward, they'd returned to the ranch for coffee and dessert. Isa had hot chocolate. Cassie insisted on drinking coffee like the grown-ups. Her face as she forced down each sip had had everyone in stitches.

"I've missed you." Ethan lifted Caitlin off her feet and held her tight.

"Me, too." She liked being eye level with him, and showed him how much by giving him a smacking kiss on the lips.

He set her down then, but was slow to release her. "Hungry?"

"Are you kidding? Mom made enough food to feed five families."

"Same here. We'll be eating leftovers for a month."

"Everyone inside?"

"Mostly outside. Gavin wants to try riding Prince again today."

"Is he still giving Gavin a hard time?"

"It's funny. Gavin and Prince have always had this special connection. But for some reason, Prince doesn't like him riding him. He hasn't been able to get on the mustang since the day we broke him."

They strolled in the direction of the stables. Caitlin could see Gavin in the round pen with Prince.

"It's Christmas," she said. "Don't you guys ever take a day off work?"

"Riding Prince isn't work."

"Spoken like a true cowboy."

The setting sun gave everyone and everything it fell on long, skinny shadows, and a strong breeze from the east tousled hair and jackets. After the hectic family celebration, Caitlin welcomed the quiet change of pace the ranch afforded.

And she'd missed Ethan.

They hadn't resolved any of their issues. He was still riding broncs at Clay's arena. They didn't talk about it, and Caitlin chose not to think about it. Avoidance, yes. Denial, absolutely. And the day would come when they'd have to deal with both his lifestyle choices and her fears.

Next week, maybe, after New Year's and the high school jackpot. She wasn't about to put a damper on the holidays. Till then, she could almost pretend Ethan didn't court danger on a regular basis. It was easy as long as he didn't show up in her clinic injured, and she didn't have to watch him ride broncs at the rodeo arena.

"Merry Christmas," Caitlin said to Gavin when they reached the pen.

"Same to you," he answered distractedly, without taking his eyes off Prince.

At the sight of Ethan, the horse nickered and bobbed his head.

"He likes me better," he whispered to Caitlin.

"Who could blame him?" she whispered back.

He leaned over and gave her a peck on the cheek, which turned into a brief kiss, then a deep one.

"Ew!"

The comment came from Isa, who rode up on old Chico, the horse's dull clip-clop an excuse for a trot. Cassie was noticeably absent. She'd gone to visit her mother back in Connecticut during the school break between Christmas and New Year's.

"No comments from the peanut gallery," Ethan admonished the little girl, though his voice was hardly stern.

"Caitlin, see my new boots?" Isa stuck out her foot to show off a brand-new pink boot with black trim.

"Very pretty." It had taken some coaxing to get both girls to call her Caitlin away from school and the clinic. "How's Cassie doing?"

"She's coming home next week!" Isa squirmed excitedly. "I can't wait. Mama's going to take us to buy dresses for the wedding."

"Really?" Caitlin looked at Ethan for confirmation. "She's coming home?"

Gavin's custody arrangement with his daughter had been only temporary. There was a chance when he'd put her on the plane to Connecticut that she might not come back until the following summer, if then.

"Cassie called this morning to tell Gavin the news," Ethan said. "She asked to live with him permanently, and her mother agreed."

Caitlin's heart soared. What a truly wonderful

Christmas present for the Powells. "I'm so glad for both of them."

"Gavin's happy. Or he was," Ethan corrected, "until today." He stooped and climbed through the rungs into the pen.

Caitlin watched, leaning her forearms on the second rung. Isa also watched, from her vantage point atop Chico.

Prince was in a mood, for sure. He alternately pawed the ground impatiently and swung his head from side to side. Twice he bared his teeth at Gavin.

Ethan approached the horse with less caution than Caitlin deemed prudent. She bit her tongue to stop from crying out.

"Easy, boy," he crooned.

To her surprise, Prince settled almost immediately. Even pushed his nose into Ethan's hand.

"Try getting on now," he suggested to his brother.

Gavin collected the reins, took hold of the saddle horn and raised his foot to put it in the stirrup.

Huffing loudly and humping his back, Prince danced sideways. He got only as far as Gavin's hold on him allowed.

"Stand!" Gavin commanded.

Prince stared at him, challenge burning in his eyes.

"What's with him?" Caitlin muttered.

"There's some new mares in the motel," Isa answered. "He always acts stupid around mares."

Caitlin didn't want to think about how knowledgeable Isa was on horse breeding.

Ethan reached out to stroke Prince's neck. The stallion permitted it, though he stood stiff and tense.

"That's it…" Ethan murmured.

Caitlin studied the two brothers, alike and yet so different. Both were intense. Ethan, however, was outgoing and gregarious, whereas Gavin tended to be reserved and private. Both loved passionately and both had suffered immeasurably when they'd lost a loved one. While Gavin withdrew, Ethan ran.

What would happen if Ethan was confronted with another devastating loss? Caitlin couldn't bear it if he left again.

"Go on, you ride him." Gavin nodded at Ethan. "One of us ought to."

"I'll warm him up for you."

With the ease of an experienced horse trainer, Ethan swung up into the saddle. Prince's legs trembled violently. But when Gavin released his hold on the bridle, the mustang circled the pen, responding perfectly to Ethan's cues. Walk, trot, lope and walk once more.

Man and horse were so beautiful. Ethan, tall and rugged in the saddle. Prince, strong and athletic, his long black mane and tail flowing in the wind like silky banners.

Caitlin wasn't the only one captivated. She glanced at Gavin and Isa and noted the two of them couldn't stop staring, either.

Ethan nudged Prince into a fast lope, then reined him to a sudden stop that ended with a shower of dirt exploding from beneath his hooves.

Caitlin let out a small gasp.

"Back, boy, back."

Prince lowered his hind quarters and dug his hooves into the ground, each backward step given reluctantly—a hard-won victory for Ethan. Such strength and power in the horse, yet Ethan controlled it with ease. Thrived on it. Reveled in it.

It must be like that when he rode broncs.

Who was Caitlin to take that from him for purely selfish reasons?

After a half-dozen more turns around the pen at a comfortable trot, Ethan brought Prince to a halt beside his brother, an elated grin on his face.

"Your turn."

"What do you think?" Gavin asked the horse.

Prince rubbed his head on Gavin's jacket sleeve and exhaled lustily.

"All right, partner, if you say so." He patted the horse and took hold of the bridle so Ethan could dismount. "Let's give it a go."

Ethan grabbed the saddle horn and removed his left foot from the stirrup. Prince stood quietly, and Caitlin dared to relax. She could do this, she thought—watch Ethan ride and not suffer a panic attack.

One second the air was still, the next a cold gust of wind whipped past them. An empty plastic bag tumbled through the rails and into the round pen.

Prince balked and snorted, disliking the object and the crackling noises it made. That might have been the end of it if the plastic sack hadn't brushed against his underside. The horse went into a frenzy, kicking out with his back legs.

"What's wrong?" Isa asked in a small, scared voice.

Before Caitlin or anyone could answer her, Prince bolted, galloping around the pen. Ethan held on, his prosthesis flapping uselessly.

"Whoa, whoa!" he hollered, sawing on the reins.

Prince came to a stop, only to rear, his front legs

slashing the air. Gavin dodged out of the way, escaping one sharp hoof that came perilously close to his face.

Ethan leaned forward in the saddle, struggling to maintain his balance.

Caitlin pressed her hands to her mouth, willing him to stay seated. He'd ridden a crazed Prince once before, on the day he broke him. He could do it again.

At last Prince came down. Nostrils flaring and flanks heaving, he stood quietly, even hanging his head.

"Is it over?" Isa squeaked.

Caitlin dared to breathe. "I think so."

"Easy there," Ethan murmured, and visibly relaxed.

Without warning, Prince tensed, then bucked again. High.

Ethan flew out of the saddle. Sailing head over heels, he landed in the dirt with a gut-wrenching thud, then lay immobile.

"Uncle Ethan!" Isa screamed.

Blood-chilling fear galvanized Caitlin, and she ran to the gate.

"Stay back!" Gavin shouted.

At the sound of his voice, Prince spun and charged, flinging Gavin against the railing.

Rearing yet again, the horse came down on Ethan's still form, his front hooves striking him repeatedly in the center of his back.

Free at last of both humans and the terrifying plastic sack, Prince loped in circles, stirrups bouncing and reins dangling.

"Are you all right?" Caitlin hollered to both men.

Neither one answered.

Disregarding her own safety, she flung the gate open.

"Look out!"

At Gavin's warning, Caitlin dived to her left, narrowly avoiding being trampled by Prince as he lunged through the opening and thundered toward the stables.

Caitlin raced into the round pen. "Ethan, can you hear me? Ethan!" She dropped down beside him, frantically taking in every detail. The closed eyes. The irregular breathing. The cuts and contusions. "Ethan, sweetie, can you hear me?"

His eyelids fluttered once, then went still.

Gavin stumbled toward them.

She looked up at him. "Do you have a cell phone on you? Call 911."

"Give him a minute. He'll come around."

"A minute? Are you insane?"

She was normally levelheaded in a crisis, one of the qualities that made her a good nurse. With Ethan hurt, being levelheaded flew out the window.

"Call 911 and do it now!"

Removing his phone from his pocket, Gavin placed the call.

Caitlin touched Ethan's bare head, his arm and back with just the tips of her fingers. She didn't dare disturb him, having no idea the seriousness of his injuries. A concussion, no doubt. Fractured bones. Internal injuries. A broken neck. Oh, dear God, he'd landed so hard, and his left arm lay at an unnatural angle. His hat sat upside down on the other side of the pen.

"Ethan, please." Tears blurred her vision, and her voice splintered. "Talk to me."

"He's going to be okay."

She was only dimly aware of Gavin's voice as it penetrated her escalating terror.

"You don't know that."

Her composure crumpled. She was once again in the hospital, pacing the halls, waiting for the doctors to deliver news of Justin's condition. And when it finally came, it had devastated her and her parents.

Sobbing, she barely felt Gavin's hand giving her shoulder a comforting squeeze.

"Go fetch your mother," he told Isa, who scampered off.

"Stay with me, sweetie…" Caitlin would give anything to hold Ethan in her arms, lay his head in her lap and stroke his hair. All she could do was watch helplessly as his chest rose and fell with each shallow breath he drew.

Where was the closest fire station? She couldn't remember.

Ethan groaned softly.

"I'm here. I'm here." She tentatively stroked his cheek with her index finger.

"See, I told you," Gavin said. "He'll be fine."

Only, Gavin was wrong. Ethan didn't rouse, and his face lost even more color.

"Gavin!" Sage came out of nowhere. "What can I do?"

"Keep everyone away. Direct the emergency vehicles here. And tell Javier to find Prince."

How could he care about that damn stupid horse after it had nearly killed his brother?

Finally, mercifully, she heard the distant wail of a siren.

"Help's on the way, sweetie," she told Ethan. "It won't be long now."

Long until what? The doctors came to the hospital waiting area and delivered a hopeless prognosis?

Ethan had been through so much already. He'd lost his mother and his leg. Plus the cattle operation that had been in his family for a hundred years. It wasn't fair. He didn't deserve tragedy heaped upon tragedy.

The paramedic unit pulled up alongside the round pen. Two uniformed men rushed through the gate, lugging equipment. A fire truck came next. As Gavin guided Caitlin out of the way so the paramedics could examine Ethan, more uniformed men arrived. Seven altogether.

They asked questions Caitlin couldn't answer. When she pressed them for details on Ethan's condition, they gave noncommittal responses.

"I'm a nurse."

"Then you know to let us do our jobs," one of the men said, not unkindly.

Within minutes, they had Ethan hooked up to a heart monitor and an IV. They'd checked his respiration, taken his pulse and his blood pressure, and assessed his injuries. He came to, but only fleetingly, and wasn't coherent.

Understanding every move the paramedics made, every medical term they used, just made the situation worse for Caitlin. His vitals weren't good, and his failure to respond was of concern.

The ambulance arrived with its EMTs. Ethan's head and neck were immobilized, and he was carefully lifted onto a stretcher, then transported to the vehicle.

"Can I go with him?" Caitlin beseeched, her gaze going from Gavin to the EMTs.

"It would be better if you met us at the hospital."

The female EMT slammed the ambulance door shut, the sound echoing through the empty corridors of Caitlin's heart.

Another hospital, another waiting room. Caitlin hadn't bitten her nails since she was in middle school, but her right thumbnail was now gnawed to the quick. She was starting on her left one when Justin wheeled into the waiting room.

She jumped up from her chair. Although she was glad to see him, his presence evoked memories of the terrible night she and her parents had spent after his fall from the cliffs.

"Any word?" he asked, throwing his arms wide.

She bent and held him for many seconds. "He regained consciousness in the ambulance. Was able to answer questions, like what's his name and what day it is."

"That's good."

"Yes, but he doesn't remember the accident."

"He may not."

True. Hadn't Ethan told her he still didn't remember the car bomb explosion?

"He's in surgery now."

"What for?"

"Six broken ribs, one close to his lungs. They also want to make sure there are no internal injuries."

The Powells sat huddled together on the couches where they had waited along with Caitlin for the last hour and a half—Gavin, his father, Sage and Isa. Their worried expressions told a silent story. Wayne Powell was a wreck. When he wasn't pacing he was staring out the window. Was he thinking of his late wife, just as Caitlin was thinking of her brother?

"You okay?" Justin asked.

"Fine."

"You sure? Your hands are shaking."

Were they? Caitlin glanced down, startled to see that her brother was right.

"It's nothing." She rubbed her palms on her pants.

"Mom and Dad said to call if you need anything."

Justin took her back to the Powells. They greeted him like one of the family, then everyone fell silent again.

Just when Caitlin was about to crawl out of her skin, the surgeon made an appearance and was instantly mobbed.

"How is he?" Ethan's father asked before anyone else could.

The doctor's eyes were somber, and she didn't mince words. "He's in stable condition, but make no mistake, his injuries are serious. Had the horse landed differently, your son might not be here. He's a very lucky man."

Ethan had said almost the same thing about the explosion when he'd lost his leg. How often could a person escape death?

"What are his injuries?" Gavin asked.

"He sustained a concussion in the fall, and right and left rib fractures when the horse stepped on him—eight in total. One of the fractured ribs missed puncturing his lung by only a few millimeters. His spleen is bruised. Thankfully, it didn't rupture. We need to watch that closely over the next few weeks. And two herniated disks."

The surgeon went on to explain Ethan's treatment, expected hospital stay and rehabilitation.

"When can we see him?" Wayne Powell asked.

"As soon as he's been moved to a regular room. About a half hour to an hour. When you do see him, tell him I said to be more careful next time."

Once the surgeon left, everyone started talking, their relief needing an outlet. Sage broke into racking sobs.

Caitlin wanted to cry, too, but something prevented her. She kept remembering the surgeon's warning.

Had the horse landed differently, your son might not be here.... Tell him I said to be more careful next time....

Next time.

She should never have told him she would try to cope with his bronc riding and breaking horses. Never given him that photo.

Would he have stopped for her?

Maybe, maybe not. She'd basically given him her blanket approval.

This was her fault.

All right, maybe not all her fault. But partially her fault.

Like Justin's injury.

"You okay, sis?"

Caitlin blinked, shook her head to clear it. "Yeah. If you want to leave now, go ahead."

"I'll stay until after you've seen him."

"Thanks." She swallowed.

"Ethan's going to be fine."

"Until the next time."

Gavin turned to stare at her.

She hadn't meant to say that out loud.

Justin didn't seem to notice. "He's tough."

But was she? Caitlin had her doubts.

"You heading back to Mom and Dad's or going home?" she asked.

"Neither. Tamiko's family is having an open house tonight and they invited me. I thought I might drop by for an hour after I leave here."

"What about her boyfriend?"

"He'll be there, too. Unfortunately."

"Oh, Justin."

"Quit worrying about me, sis."

"I can't. I won't. You're my brother." She'd almost said *baby* brother. He wouldn't have liked that.

"Tamiko can do better than him. When she finally wises up, I want to be there, waiting in the wings."

"What if she doesn't wise up? I hate to see you get hurt."

"Life comes with risks."

"We can minimize them."

"We can also live in a bubble." He smiled at her. "What fun is that?"

Not long after, a nurse came by to inform the family that Ethan could receive visitors.

"Don't overwhelm him," she advised. "He's still pretty groggy and needs his rest."

"Isa and I will wait for you," Sage said.

"But I want to see Uncle Ethan," Isa pouted.

"We will, *mija*, tomorrow. You can draw him a picture."

Isa was only slightly mollified.

"I can come back tomorrow, too," Caitlin said. Now that the moment to see Ethan had arrived, she was having reservations.

"No," Gavin said. "He'll be furious with us if we let you leave."

They took the elevator to the fourth floor. Outside Ethan's door, Caitlin hesitated. His brother and father went ahead of her. She watched from the doorway, her feet frozen to the floor.

She was a nurse and knew what every beep and readout on the monitors meant. He was stable; she could see that at a glance. His complexion was pasty, he barely moved and his responses were slow. But his injuries weren't life-threatening, and according to the surgeon, he'd make a full recovery.

Except, at this moment, she wasn't a nurse who thought logically and dispassionately. She was scared and worried and guilty as hell. Seeing Ethan's prosthesis leaned up against the chest of drawers intensified her emotions.

He's a very lucky man.

She gave his brother and father time alone with Ethan. He was considerably more alert than she'd expected. Like Justin had said, Ethan was tough.

He asked about the fall, had Gavin repeat the story twice. He also wanted to know the details of his injuries and what procedure had been performed during the surgery. As they continued talking, he became more and more groggy. Between his injuries and the pain medication, it was to be expected.

"Did the doctor mention how soon until I can ride again?" he asked.

Ride again! How could he even be thinking of that?

"Six weeks at least," Gavin answered. "Depends on how fast you recover. Knowing you, it won't be long."

Gavin was encouraging him. What kind of brother was he? Had he not heard the doctor's warning?

"Maybe you should give it a while," Wayne Powell said, the only sane person in the room as far as Caitlin was concerned.

"Come on, Dad." Ethan smiled crookedly. "Didn't you teach us when we fall to get right back in the saddle?"

And that was exactly what Ethan had done when he'd lost his leg. Why would she think a concussion, a half-dozen broken ribs and a multitude of minor injuries would stop him?

She didn't stand a chance.

"Where's Caitlin?" he asked, slurring her name.

"She's here." Gavin turned and motioned her into the room.

One step was all she could manage before walking into an invisible wall.

"Hey," Ethan said, lifting his head. He peered at her with unfocused eyes, then fell back on the pillow. "Sorry, I'm a little dizzy."

Caitlin, too. Her own head swam and her stomach roiled.

"I'll come back later." She grabbed the doorjamb, desperately needing support. "When you feel better."

"No, don't leave," Ethan croaked.

The invisible wall wouldn't let her through.

"Come on, Dad." Gavin patted him on the back. "Let's give them a minute alone."

They squeezed past her into the hallway, leaving Caitlin alone with Ethan.

She mustered all her courage. For such a small room, it was a very long walk to the bed. She attempted to draw on her nursing experience, use it as a shield.

It didn't work. She wasn't in love with her patients. "How are you?"

It should have been her asking him the question.

"Me? You're the one who got bucked off a horse." And nearly killed. She leaned down and kissed his forehead, a lump rising in her throat.

"I'm sorry," he said.

"For what?"

"Ruining your Christmas."

"You didn't," she said, because that was what he needed to hear. Inside, she was dismayed and distraught. The day had gone from one of the most joyous she'd spent to one of the worst. "I'm just glad you're going to be okay."

"What about us? Will we be okay?"

The lump in her throat burned.

She wanted to reassure him. Tell him that nothing had changed. They were as good as they'd always been. But the past two and a half hours had taken a terrible toll on her, and she had yet to assess the damage.

"Let's talk tomorrow."

"That sounds like a brush-off." He was fighting to stay awake.

She would not have this conversation in the hospital with him lying there in pain and doped up on medication.

"You need to rest," she said.

"That's Nurse Carmichael talking."

"Yes, and she knows best right now." Rest for him, space for her.

"It was an accident."

She hated that word. People used it when they didn't

want to claim any responsibility for a bad decision they'd made.

"I'll see you in the morning."

"You're running away." The medications he was on didn't disguise the reproving tone of his voice.

Why was it okay for him to leave and not her?

His eyes drifted closed and the frown he'd been wearing vanished. Seconds later, he was sound asleep.

She had no trouble crying now. Tears streamed from her eyes as she staggered past the nurse's station to the elevator.

She was in the parking lot before it dawned on her she had no vehicle, having ridden over with the Powells. Were they still in the hospital? She didn't remember seeing them in her hasty exit. Or Justin. Maybe he could drop her off at the ranch to fetch her van, on the way to…where was it he was going? Tamiko's parents' open house.

Thinking was hard, more than Caitlin could deal with at the moment.

Tears continued to fall. Someone asked her if she was all right. Fortunately, sobbing people weren't uncommon at hospitals.

Caitlin found her way to a bench outside the entrance, sat and waited for her composure to return. It did, though her hold on it was fragile and, she feared, temporary.

With quaking hands, she located her cell phone and dialed Justin's number.

"What's wrong?" he asked upon hearing her voice.

He knew what she'd been through after his fall, and would understand her better than anyone else.

"I can't keep doing this," she blurted. "I just can't."

Chapter 15

Ethan hobbled to the pasture behind the barn and the specially designed paddock. Prince greeted him with a friendly whinny and a head toss.

"Don't try and get on my good side. It's too late for that."

He stroked the horse's head and sleek neck. They'd come a long way since his capture, he and this once wild mustang. Had forged a lasting bond against all odds.

Ethan wished he could say the same for him and Caitlin.

While he and Prince still had considerable work ahead of them, they were well on their way. He understood the horse, accepted him for what he was, flaws and all. Tempered his high hopes with reasonable expectations. Prince, Ethan was convinced, felt the same about him.

He wished he had some idea—*any* idea—of how Caitlin felt about him.

She hadn't returned even one of his phone calls in the six days since she'd fled his hospital room. He still wasn't quite sure what had happened. Damn concussion and pain pills had messed with his memory.

What he did remember was that she'd left in tears. Based on what his brother had witnessed in the waiting room, and the previous disagreements Ethan had had with Caitlin, he guessed his cowboy ways were the cause.

How were they supposed to resolve their differences if she didn't take his phone calls?

Justin was no help. He was busy job hunting now that he'd finished college. Ethan had talked to him once, and his advice was to be patient. Caitlin would come around.

Ethan had contemplated jumping in his truck and driving to her condo, surprising her with an unannounced visit, but he'd barely made it to the paddock without stopping four times to rest and let an excruciating spasm recede. Coughing hurt. Yawning, too. Sneezing nearly knocked him to his knees.

Dammit!

Ethan removed his hat and drove his fingers through his hair. He despised this helplessness. He was a doer, a fixer, a problem solver. And he was convinced he could fix whatever had gone wrong with him and Caitlin if he could just talk to her.

"Happy New Year, buddy." Clay came up beside him, his arm raised.

Ethan glared at his best friend. "You clap me on the back, and I swear, I'll deck you."

Clay chuckled. "And I'd deserve it." He gave Prince a lengthy appraisal. "You two make up yet?"

"I was never mad at him to begin with. He's a wild animal. Former one, anyway. I let my guard down when I shouldn't have." Ethan noticed Clay's clothes for the first time. "You going somewhere special?"

"Conner's party. Want to come along?"

Ethan had forgotten all about it. He and Caitlin had planned on going, before he got hurt. Even if he was up to it, which he wasn't, he wouldn't attend without her.

"Maybe next year."

"I noticed the clinic was open tonight. Guess they're having extended hours on account of the holiday."

"And your point?"

"Caitlin's van was in the parking lot." Clay leaned against the stall. "She's on duty and can't leave the clinic. If you were to, say, show up, she'd have no choice but to listen to you."

Ethan grinned. He'd always liked the way Clay thought. "I'd need a ride. I can't drive yet."

"Let's go."

Ethan spent a few minutes cleaning up before leaving with Clay. Caitlin's van was indeed parked in the clinic lot, just as his friend had said, and a handwritten sign on the door advertised extended hours.

"I don't know how long I'll be," he told Clay.

"I don't care, I'm not sticking around."

"You're not?"

"You'll have to find your own way home. I'm counting on Caitlin."

Ethan was, too.

Thanks to his busted ribs, the door to the clinic weighed about three times as much as it had before. Clenching his teeth, he pushed it open and stumbled inside, setting off the buzzer.

"Hi, can I help you?" a pleasant young woman at the counter asked. There was no one else in the waiting room.

"I'm here to see Caitlin Carmichael."

"She's on duty. Is this an emergency?"

He didn't hesitate. "Yes."

"Can I have your name?"

This time, he did hesitate. "Ethan Powell."

The woman picked up the phone and pressed a button. After a moment, she said, "There's an Ethan Powell here to see you. He says it's an emergency."

Seconds ticked by. So many he started having serious doubts.

Finally, the woman hung up the phone. "She'll be out in a minute. Have a seat."

Ethan didn't. Getting up again would be too strenuous. He waited by the window, which gave him an unobstructed view of the door to the exam rooms. The minute the receptionist had promised stretched into five, then eight, then—son of a bitch, what was taking her so long?

A young couple came into the clinic, the man looking like death warmed over and complaining of flu symptoms. While they filled out the paperwork, Ethan debated asking the receptionist to page Caitlin again.

Before he could make his way to the counter, she came through the door.

"Sorry I'm late. I was with a patient." Lines of tension etched her face, and dark circles surrounded her eyes. She hadn't been sleeping well.

"I thought you might be avoiding me."

She didn't acknowledge his joke. "Is everything okay? Are your injuries bothering you?"

"I'm fine."

"You said it was an emergency." She eyed him suspiciously.

"It is. We need to talk."

"I'm at work," she replied in a low, terse voice.

"Take a break."

Her lips thinned.

"Ten minutes. That's all I ask. I wouldn't be here if you'd answered any of my fifteen or twenty phone calls."

"Fine. Let me get my coat and tell Dr. Lovitt."

She returned a few minutes later, slipping her arms into her coat sleeves as she walked to the door.

He beat her there and opened it for her, paying the price as a spear of agonizing pain sliced through him.

"Honestly, Ethan," she snapped. "You don't always have to do things for me, especially when you're hurt."

"My father raised me to be a gentleman."

She squeezed her eyes shut. "I didn't mean to insult you."

"You didn't."

He gestured toward the tables and chairs in front of the coffee shop next door. Caitlin pulled her own chair out when he would have done it for her. She sat gracefully, Ethan with considerable effort.

"How are you doing?" she asked.

"I'll live."

His answer had been intended as another joke, but it

was obvious by her sudden stiffening that he'd struck a chord. He hadn't had long to mentally compose what he wanted to say to her tonight, but talking to her had consumed his thoughts for days. He should've done a better job of breaking the ice.

"It was an accident. Not your fault, not my fault. Not even Prince's fault. The best-trained horses spook sometimes at nothing."

"I know that. I don't blame myself or Prince."

"But you blame me?"

She remained stubbornly silent. When she spoke at last, her words were measured.

"You are who you've always been. You like taking risks. Tempting fate. Pushing your limits. It's what made you a good soldier, good at training horses and a competitive athlete."

"And you don't like taking risks."

"No." Her eyes were full of misery and regret. "And I don't think I can be with someone who does."

A suffocating pressure closed around his chest, worse than when he'd broken his ribs. On some level he'd been expecting this.

"I'll quit riding broncs. Breaking horses, too."

"I wouldn't ask that of you. You were right when you said it isn't fair for one person to force another to give up something that's important to them."

"No, I was wrong." God, he was losing her. He could feel her ebbing away like the ocean at low tide. "People have to make compromises for a relationship to work."

"Giving up your dream isn't a compromise, and I refuse to be the cause of your unhappiness."

A sense of déjà vu came over Ethan, crushing him.

He remembered a similar conversation from nine years ago that had gone much like this one. Except he'd been the one saying, "I refuse to be the cause of your unhappiness."

"The day you were hurt was a nightmare for me," she continued, a tremor in her voice. "The sight of you in that hospital bed—I couldn't deal with it. I nearly broke down. I did later, outside the hospital."

"Why? You're a nurse."

"Not that night I wasn't." She sniffed. "I should have come over to see you after you were released. But telling you when you were laid up…"

"Telling me what?" Ethan braced himself, instinctively knowing that whatever came next was going to change his life irrevocably. Again.

She sat up, determination in her expression. "I'm sorry, I can't see you anymore."

"You're part of me. The missing piece."

"One you can live without." She stood, her chair squeaking as it scraped across the concrete. "You have before."

She left him there, alone in the cold.

Sometime later, a few minutes or an hour, Ethan couldn't be sure, Clay appeared. Had he waited all this time?

"Come on, buddy. I'll take you home."

Ethan went with him, needing help finding the truck.

He thought he might be lost for the rest of his life.

Caitlin sat on the closed toilet lid and stared at the double pink lines on the testing wand she held. Reality, which she'd successfully kept at bay since yesterday morning, hit her full force. The wand dropped to the floor as she caught her falling head in her hands. Home pregnancy tests weren't one hundred percent accurate. Which was why she'd taken a second one this morning. The chance that both tests showed a false positive was astronomical.

She was pregnant.

How had that happened?

Of course she knew how it happened, but...*how?* They'd used protection. Condoms weren't infallible, as she'd heard doctors tell patients many times. And there was that first night she and Ethan had spent together after the Holly Days Festival, when they'd had only one.

She mentally counted backward. Three, no, four weeks along.

What was she going to do? She pressed her fingertips to her throbbing temples and rubbed.

If she told Ethan, he'd go all Ethan on her. Want to get married. Raise the baby together. On top of all the other problems they had, they'd be adding having an instant family to the mix. Not the best way to start out.

She could leave Mustang Valley, maybe even Arizona. Go stay with her college friend in Columbus and have the baby there.

Then what? She couldn't come home, not if she didn't want Ethan to find out. And he would, eventually. Someone would see her and the baby and mention it.

No, she either told him outright and dealt with the consequences, or left Mustang Valley for good.

Not the kind of decisions a new mother should have to make. This was supposed to be a joyous moment she would treasure the rest of her life.

And, suddenly, it was.

She was pregnant! Going to have a baby! Elation bubbled up inside her, then spilled out in a giddy laugh. Tomorrow or next week was soon enough to decide what and if to tell Ethan. She was barely a month along, after all. For now, she would keep her condition a secret, bask in her happiness alone until the right moment to share it.

She no sooner emerged from the bathroom than her cell phone rang. A glance at the caller ID informed her it was Justin. Guilt needled her. She hadn't spoken to her brother much these past two and half weeks. Or her parents. She'd taken the breakup with Ethan hard. Loss of appetite. Insomnia. Churlishness. Depression. You name it, she had it.

After one look her parents would instantly know something was wrong. Caitlin wasn't up to fielding their questions. Justin would be worse. He'd pester her until she spilled her guts.

Briefly, she considered not answering his call, but another prick of guilt compelled her to press the receive button.

"Hey."

"Why didn't you tell me you and Ethan called it quits?"

"We weren't actually going together." A few weeks didn't constitute a relationship.

They were, however, long enough to create a life.

"I knew you were upset with him, but I figured you'd resolved it."

"How did you find out?" Caitlin asked.

"Ethan told me. He's really bummed."

"You saw him?"

"I'm here now. At the ranch."

"You are?" She wanted to ask how Ethan was doing. Instead, she voiced the second question on her mind. "What are you doing there?"

"Tamiko and I signed up for riding lessons."

"Riding lessons!" This conversation couldn't get any weirder. "Since when?"

"I thought you'd be here, considering it's Sunday afternoon, and I'd surprise you."

Wait a minute. Rewind. "Riding lessons? I thought you agreed that wasn't a good idea."

"I never said any such thing. You lectured and I listened."

"Look what happened to Ethan." Fear gripped her and shook her like a rag doll.

"I'm not riding bucking horses."

"I don't care if you're riding a pony. It's too dangerous."

"No more dangerous than white-water rafting on the Colorado River."

She'd been a wreck when he'd taken that hare-brained trip last summer. "At least you were wearing a life jacket."

"And this time I'll be wearing a helmet."

She had to stop him. "I'll be right there."

"Don't come if you're planning on making a scene."

"When have I ever made a scene?" She grimaced. "Okay, I take that back. I have made a scene or two, but only because I care."

"See you when you get here," he said, and disconnected.

Caitlin didn't waste any time. She grabbed her purse and keys and hit the door at a run.

Turning into the Powells' driveway, she reduced her speed to the legal limit and was immediately ashamed of herself. She didn't usually drive like a maniac.

Upon reaching the open area in front of the stables, she started searching for Justin.

And, yes, Ethan.

She'd missed him. And this place. His family, too. How had they become so important to her after only a few weeks?

Maybe because they always were.

She scoured the main arena, where a dozen riders were exercising their horses, none of them Justin.

At last she spotted him in the round pen. The same pen where Ethan had been injured when riding Prince. Justin sat astride a horse, Ethan standing beside him. Tamiko straddled the fence, the empty wheelchair not far from her.

Where was her boyfriend?

Caitlin drove her van right up to the pen, hit the brakes and slammed the vehicle into Park. Shoving the door open, she bailed out, tripping over her own feet in her haste.

"Justin!"

"That didn't take long." An exuberant grin split his face.

"Are you okay?" She was aware of Ethan watching her, studying her.

Her body, always attuned to him, hummed in response.

"Great! This is amazing." Justin shielded his eyes from the afternoon sun and regarded the horizon. "I can't believe how far I can see. Look at the mountains."

The motion unbalanced him and he teetered in the saddle.

Caitlin let out a yelp. "Ethan, help him!"

"Whoa!" Justin grabbed the saddle horn.

Ethan reached up and placed a steadying hand on Justin's leg. "Hang on."

He looked considerably better than the night he'd shown up at the clinic, but not strong enough to catch Justin if he fell. Someone else must have lifted her brother onto the horse. Someone else should be here now.

"No problem." Justin let go of the saddle horn.

Ethan started walking, leading the horse, which Caitlin now recognized as old Chico.

She was going to kill both Ethan and her brother.

"He's doing great, don't you think?" Tamiko said.

Caitlin looked around. "Where's…um…"

"Eric? I really don't know."

She didn't have time to process Tamiko's answer because Justin clucked to Chico, and the horse broke into a run.

All right, not a run. A very, very sedate trot.

Ethan walked beside the horse, letting the lead rope dangle. If Chico reared or bucked, there was no way he could restrain him. Justin would be hurt.

At least he was wearing a helmet and, she noticed upon closer inspection, a safety vest. If Ethan had been wearing a helmet and vest when he fell off Prince, he might not have broken his ribs or sustained a concussion.

Wait! Justin didn't have a harness. Ethan said at Thanksgiving that he had harnesses Justin could use. What if he slipped again?

"Be careful," Caitlin said, sounding like the broken record she was, her white-knuckled hands gripping the railing. Thank God there was no wind today. She scanned the immediate vicinity for stray plastic bags anyway.

"I can't wait for my turn." Tamiko glowed.

Caitlin, on the other hand, couldn't speak. Her heart had lodged in her throat.

Was she the only one terrified?

Yes, she was—the only one. Not Justin or their parents or Tamiko. Certainly not Ethan. And he should be more than anyone, after what had happened to him.

All right, she was a little overprotective. A lot overprotective. But she was hardly unreasonable.

Was she?

She looked at her brother, really looked at him. He was enjoying himself. Now that she thought about it, he always seemed to be enjoying himself. For the past several years, anyway. Ever since he took up wheelchair athletics.

He grinned confidently at Tamiko as he rode past her, a far cry from the insecure, self-conscious geek he'd been in high school.

Caitlin had to stop seeing him as disabled and start seeing him as what he was, a capable, competent young man with endless potential and no need of a hovering older sister.

"Yes, he's doing well," she said, sensing a shift inside her.

After a few more circuits, Ethan led Justin through the gate. They stopped in front of Caitlin and Tamiko.

"What do you think?" Justin preened. "Are we ready for the races?"

Tamiko's smile was radiant and for him alone. "You were awesome."

"I'm impressed," Caitlin admitted, her pride overflowing.

"You're not just saying that?"

"Definitely not."

"Any chance I can ride around the ranch?" he asked Ethan.

"Not by yourself. Not yet."

She sent Ethan a silent thank-you.

He nodded, and the yearning in his eyes reached into her, tugging at her heart and her belly, where she carried their child.

"Can Tamiko take me?"

"How about your sister? And just up and down in front of the stables."

"Me!" she squeaked. "What if Chico starts bucking? I can't hold on to him."

"He won't buck. He has the temperament of a kitten." Ethan thrust the lead rope into Caitlin's hands. "Go on. You can do it."

He was talking about more than her brother riding a horse, she was sure.

"It'll be okay, sis," Justin said, also talking about more than riding.

Yes, it would be okay.

The shift in her was suddenly complete and seamless.

Giving Ethan one last long glance, she took a step, then another. Chico followed like the good, dependable horse he was.

As she and Justin passed the office, he said to her, "Thanks. I know this isn't easy for you."

She didn't respond, afraid she might start crying. Must be hormones.

"You have to stop feeling bad about the accident," Justin said. "I don't. Haven't for a long time."

"But you lost the use of your legs."

"Pretty incidental in the larger scheme of things."

"No, it isn't!"

"It is. I'm better off now than I ever was. I've got my degree. Have two job offers I'm considering. I play sports. White-water raft. I'm learning to ride a horse." He patted Chico's neck. "Have a girlfriend."

"Tamiko? What about Eric?"

"She dumped him. For me. For *me*," he repeated, wearing the goofy grin of a besotted man.

Caitlin wasn't just proud of him, she was impressed. "I'm glad." As long as he didn't get hurt.

She had to stop thinking like that—*would* stop thinking like that.

"I'm happy, sis."

He was. She could see it in his face, hear it in his voice.

The weight she'd been carrying for the last six years didn't lift entirely, but it decreased. Eventually, soon, she'd be free of it.

"You should be happy, too. Ethan loves you."

"I messed up with him." She sniffed and Chico gave her arm a sympathetic nudge.

"Nothing you can't repair."

"I don't know how."

"Talk to him. I guarantee, he'll listen."

"I'm not sure there's a point to it. I can't handle his bronc riding. You saw how I was at the hospital."

"You'd be surprised what you can handle if you have to. Look at me. Look at Mom and Dad."

He made a good argument. And she already felt stronger. Amazing what release from guilt could do for a person.

Chico turned abruptly and started walking in the opposite direction.

"Hey, there!" Caitlin pulled on the lead rope, then gave the horse his head. Chico was going exactly where she wanted to—back to Ethan.

He must have noticed a change in her because his whole countenance lit up at her approach.

"Can we go somewhere to talk?" she said when they were close enough.

His shoulders straightened as if he, too, had had a weight lifted from them. "I'll find Conner and T.J. so we can get Justin down."

"I'm fine," Justin said. "Tamiko will lead me around for a while."

Tamiko jumped off the fence in eager anticipation. Caitlin passed her the lead rope, and the pair took off.

By unspoken agreement, Caitlin and Ethan headed in the direction of the office.

"Do you think they'll be all right?" she asked. Old habits were hard to break.

"They'll be fine."

Caitlin sat on the top porch step, keeping Justin in sight, but not fretting about him. Not like she had, anyway.

Ethan lowered himself down beside her, his movements still stiff.

"How are you doing?"

"Better. The doctor suggested physical therapy. Know a good therapist?"

"I might."

They both laughed and, just like that, the tension between them evaporated.

"You first," she said.

He took a moment before continuing. "Being laid up the last couple of weeks has given me a lot of time to think. About my job. About rodeoing. About us." He cleared his throat. "I've made a decision."

His tone was so serious. Had she misinterpreted his intentions? Good heavens. He was breaking up with her. Now, after she'd finally come to her senses.

"I love you," she blurted.

"Good." He sagged with obvious relief. "That makes what I'm going to tell you a whole lot easier." He fitted his palm to her cheek and rubbed his thumb along her jawline. "After my discharge, I wanted to... needed to ride broncs. To prove to myself and everyone else I was the same man I'd been before I lost my leg."

"I understand. And you don't have to give up rodeoing for me."

"I want to." His dark eyes searched hers. "It isn't important to me anymore. Having you, loving you, is. Nothing I do matters without you in my life. You make me the man I want to be. If Justin hadn't tricked you into coming here today, I would have gone after you myself and begged you to give us a second chance." He chuckled. "Guess that would be a third chance."

"Justin tricked me?" She tried to be mad at her brother, but couldn't. "Remind me to thank him."

Ethan cupped her other cheek and held her face between his hands. "If you'll have me, I'll also give up breaking horses."

"That's your job."

"I'll find another one."

"Not on your life, cowboy, you hear me? You're a Powell."

"Caitlin, baby doll—"

"No. Quitting bronc riding is enough." She remembered Justin's words. "I can handle breaking horses, though. I'll need help. Lots of support and understanding."

"You'll have it."

He kissed her then, and it was the sweetest kiss he'd ever given her.

"Life is full of risks," she said dreamily. "And they're not all bad."

She'd taken a huge one minutes ago when she'd asked to talk to him, and it was already paying off.

"Marry me, Caitlin. I love you, too."

Her eyes went wide. "What did you say?"

"I'd get down on one knee, except between my bum leg and broken ribs, I'm not sure I could get back up."

She drew in a ragged breath, her earlier indecision fleeing. "There's something you need to know first."

"If you're worried about honing in on Gavin and Sage's wedding next month, I can wait. Not long, mind you."

"It's not that."

"We'll buy a ring. Sorry I proposed without one."

"No, no, no. I don't care about a ring. Well, I do, but not this second."

"Then what?"

"Marriage is life changing." She wavered, scared

and yet bursting with excitement. "Having a baby is, too."

He stared at her blankly.

She huffed impatiently. Did she have to spell it out? "I'm pregnant."

His dumbfounded expression transformed into one of unabashed delight.

Ethan struggled to his feet. He barely made it and doubled over, a low sound exploding from him.

"Ethan, are you all right?" She was instantly up and grabbed his arm.

"My ribs." He was laughing, and the sound grew louder as he straightened.

She laughed with him.

Gavin threw open the office door. Caitlin hadn't realized he was in there.

"What's going on?" His glance traveled from Ethan to Caitlin. "I take it you two are back together."

"More than back together." Ethan stopped laughing and pulled Caitlin to him. "You did accept, didn't you?"

"Yes, I'll marry you." She put her arms around him gently, drunk on happiness.

Gavin barreled down the steps and embraced them both, ignoring Ethan's protest to take it easy. "It's about damn time."

Justin and Tamiko came over, her brother still mounted. "What's going on?" he asked.

Ethan let go of Caitlin and shouted through cupped hands, loudly enough for the entire ranch to hear, "We're getting hitched and we're having a baby."

After that, everything was a blur. Caitlin was aware of hugs and kisses and lots of congratulations. Wayne

Powell suddenly appeared. He must have come out of the house to investigate all the commotion. Sage and the girls were with him.

"Ethan's mother would be so happy." Wayne kissed Caitlin on the cheek. "Another grandchild."

Someone had helped Justin down from the horse, for he was suddenly in his wheelchair. He held her fiercely when she leaned down to hug him.

"Thanks," she whispered. "For the advice and for tricking me into coming here. You're the best."

"Anytime, sis."

"Guess I'd better let Mom and Dad know."

Ethan put an arm around her. "We'll drive out there later. Tell them together."

She beamed at him. "Really?" That was exactly the right thing to do.

"You could have a double wedding," Tamiko suggested gleefully, then reddened when everyone stared at her.

Ethan found his voice first. "What do you think? I know it's kind of short notice."

Caitlin could tell by his eager grin that he liked the idea. He'd want to get married as soon as possible, what with the baby coming. "Gavin and Sage may not want—"

"Gavin and Sage *absolutely* want," Sage answered for them both. "All the arrangements are under way. It makes perfect sense."

"Okay." Caitlin shrugged, suddenly warming to the idea, as well. "Let's have a double wedding."

They took their celebrating inside to continue over supper.

Caitlin sat at the kitchen table next to Ethan, across

from her brother, and with the family that had come to mean as much to her as her own.

When the meal was nearing an end, Wayne tapped his water glass with his fork. Everyone fell silent. "Here's to my second future daughter-in-law. Welcome to the Powell family." Wayne smiled at Caitlin affectionately. "I've been waiting nine years to say that."

She'd been waiting nine years to hear it.

The passage of time, the trials and tribulations she and Ethan had confronted and conquered, made the moment all the more meaningful.

Christmas wishes could and did come true.

Beneath the table, Ethan took her hand and linked their fingers. *"Stay with me tonight,"* he mouthed.

As if she would ever leave him or this place again.

* * * * *

She rose from her seat of slab rock. "We'd probably better
be going. We still have one more hiking trail to cover before
we hit another set of campgrounds."

While she gathered up her partially eaten lunch, Sawyer
left his seat and walked over to the edge of the bluff.

"This is an incredible view," he said. "From this distance,
the saguaros look like green needles stuck in a sandpile."

She looked over to see the strong north wind was hitting
him in the face and molding his uniform against his muscled
body. The sight of his imposing figure etched against the
blue sky and desert valley caused her breath to hang in her
throat.

She walked over to where he stood, then took a cautious
step closer to the ledge in order to peer down at the view
directly below.

"I never get tired of it," she admitted. "There are a few
Native American ruins not far from here. We'll hike by
those before we finish our route."

A hard gust of wind suddenly whipped across the ledge and caused Vivian to sway on her feet. Sawyer swiftly caught her by the arm and pulled her back to his side.

"Careful," he warned. "I wouldn't want you to topple over the edge."

With his hand on her arm and his sturdy body shielding her from the wind, she felt very warm and protected. And for one reckless moment, she wondered how it would feel to slip her arms around his lean waist, to rise up on the tips of her toes and press her mouth to his. Would his lips taste as good as she imagined?

Shaken by the direction of her runaway thoughts, she tried to make light of the moment. "That would be awful," she agreed. "Mort would have to find you another partner."

"Yeah, and she might not be as cute as you."

With a little laugh of disbelief, she stepped away from his side. "Cute? I haven't been called that since I was in high school. I'm beginning to think you're nineteen instead of twenty-nine."

He pulled a playful frown at her. "You prefer your men to be old and somber?"

"I prefer them to keep their minds on their jobs," she said staunchly. "And you are not *my* man."

His laugh was more like a sexy promise.

"Not yet."

Don't miss
A Ranger for Christmas *by Stella Bagwell,*
available December 2018 wherever
Harlequin® Special Edition books and ebooks are sold.

www.Harlequin.com

HSEEXP1118

HARLEQUIN®

SPECIAL EDITION

Life, Love and Family

Save **$1.00**
on the purchase of ANY
Harlequin® Special Edition book.

Available whever books are sold,
including most bookstores, supermarkets,
drugstores and discount stores.

✂

Save **$1.00**

on the purchase of any Harlequin® Special Edition book.

Coupon valid until February 28, 2019.
Redeemable at participating outlets in the U.S. and Canada only.
Limit one coupon per customer.

52616105

5 65373 00076 2 (8100)0 12397

® and ™ are trademarks owned and used by the trademark owner and/or its licensee.

© 2018 Harlequin Enterprises Limited

HSECOUP04506

Looking for more satisfying love stories
with community and family at their core?

Check out **Harlequin® Special Edition**
and **Love Inspired®** books!

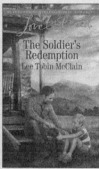

New books available every month!

CONNECT WITH US AT:

Facebook.com/groups/HarlequinConnection

 Facebook.com/HarlequinBooks

 Twitter.com/HarlequinBooks

 Instagram.com/HarlequinBooks

 Pinterest.com/HarlequinBooks

ReaderService.com

**ROMANCE WHEN
YOU NEED IT**

HFGENRE2018

Love Harlequin romance?

DISCOVER.

Be the first to find out about promotions, news and exclusive content!

f Facebook.com/HarlequinBooks

🐦 Twitter.com/HarlequinBooks

📷 Instagram.com/HarlequinBooks

P Pinterest.com/HarlequinBooks

ReaderService.com

EXPLORE.

Sign up for the Harlequin e-newsletter and download a free book from any series at **TryHarlequin.com.**

CONNECT.

Join our Harlequin community to share your thoughts and connect with other romance readers!
Facebook.com/groups/HarlequinConnection

⬙ HARLEQUIN®

ROMANCE WHEN YOU NEED IT

HSOCIAL2018

Jenna hesitated to get out of the car. She didn't want to like the place.

Aww…she didn't know what she wanted.

Dustin opened the car door for her, and she reluctantly got out.

"You must be Mr. Nichols," Dustin said, holding out his hand. "I'm Dustin Morgan, and this is my…uh… friend… Jenna Reed." He nodded at Jenna. "We're interested in looking at your property."

"Call me Nick. And welcome to our ranch," he said, pumping Dustin's hand and then Jenna's.

"Those horses are beautiful. What else do you run here?" Dustin asked.

"Some three dozen horses—Arabians and quarter horses. Prime stock. And thirty bulls." He looked at Dustin. "I think you know a little about bucking bulls." Nick pushed his hat back. "If you're interested in the stock, we can work out a price."

"I'll take a look," Dustin said.

Nick tweaked his hat brim. "I'm rooting for you to win the finals. It'd sure be nice to have an Arizona cowboy win it."

"Thanks, Nick. I'll try my best," Dustin said.

"Why do you want to sell?" Jenna asked.

"My wife and I want to get out of the business. Maybe do some traveling, visit our kids and grandkids. They're scattered all over the place."

"And this ranch ties you down, doesn't it?" Jenna asked, knowing the answer already.

"Sure does. We're busy day and night."

A stately woman with long salt-and-pepper hair and a warm smile walked out onto the porch. She wore faded jeans and a glittery T-shirt. Her cowboy boots were a bright yellow.

"This is my wife, Amber." He turned to Amber with a big smile. "This is Dustin and his friend, Jenna."

Dustin tweaked his hat and Jenna waved, immediately liking Amber's warm smile.

"I'd recognize Dustin Morgan anywhere. I'm a bull riding fan." Amber walked down the porch steps and shook Dustin's hand. "We put a lot of blood, sweat and tears into this place. Call us sentimental, but we both love this ranch and want to place it into good hands."

Jenna nodded. She didn't blame Amber at all for wanting their hard work to go to people who'd appreciate it.

"Shall we go into the house first?" Amber asked.

"Oh, yes. Absolutely," Jenna said immediately.

They all laughed, but Jenna was drawn to the expression on Dustin's face. He really looked happy and at peace at the same time. This was where he belonged—on a ranch.

Suddenly, she didn't want to look at the house, didn't want to like it.

But she followed Amber on the tour and found that she did like it—very much. From the golden knotty pine to the beehive fireplace, and from the chunky log furniture that came with the house to the rustic chandeliers—it was perfect. The kitchen was a dream. The master bedroom on the first floor was in back and its private deck overlooked a built-in pool and hot tub.

She could picture herself in this house—cooking, grading papers, reading. But would she be happy staying put?

Dustin and Nick went outside to check out the barn and stock, fast friends already.

Jenna felt comfortable with Amber. She was warm and friendly and the type of person who was very open and honest.

It was at times like these that she especially missed her mother. She'd like to talk to her mom about Dustin, about whether or not to marry and settle down, about this property.

Amber motioned to the living room. "I'll bring us some coffee."

"Only if it's already made," Jenna said.

"It is. Coming right up. Make yourself comfortable, Jenna."

Jenna picked a chunky log chair with brown leather cushions and sat down. She had a wide-angle view of the downstairs. Looking around, she decided that she wouldn't change a thing. Well, maybe this, maybe that.

What was she doing? She didn't plan on ever living here.

But she could picture raising a family within these walls with its four bedrooms and four bathrooms. She could imagine their children running through the meadow to the right of the ranch house and riding horses under the watchful eye of their father, Dustin.

She'd keep up the little garden in the back for fresh vegetables and herbs. And the flowers would be perfect for cut arrangements on the circular table over there…or maybe even the mantel. She'd put their Christmas tree to the right of the fireplace. No. To the left, so it can be seen outside, too.

She took a deep breath. She was totally getting

ahead of herself, was totally conflicted and wished she'd never came here and seen this fabulous place.

"Here we are," said Amber, returning to the room and handing her a steaming mug of coffee.

"Um… Amber…could I ask you a question?"

Smiling warmly, she crossed her legs and leaned forward. "Ask me anything."

"It's not about the house—it's about…well… I grew up on a ranch, and I know the work involved. I really didn't want to be a rancher. That's why I became a teacher."

Amber nodded. "You're wondering if you'd be happy here."

Tears stung Jenna's eyes, and Amber reached out and patted her hand.

"This was just a cactus patch when we bought it. It was a lot of work—building, making roads, putting up fence, more building, buying stock, breeding. I'm sure you can see that most of the hard work is done, Jenna. Dustin and a couple of hands can do the rest."

"And I can take care of the house," she said, thinking out loud. "Which I'd enjoy. I know I would. And I can still teach. And I can help Dustin in my spare time."

Jenna felt better, but still her mind was racing. Settling on a ranch certainly wasn't in her plan.

But she hadn't counted on falling in love.

When Dustin and Nick returned, they said their goodbyes, and with an invite to return at any time from Nick, they headed west on River Road.

"What do you think, Jenna?" Dustin asked.

"I love it. I love everything about it. I don't think you could find another ranch that had so much care."